For Matt, I miss you every day.

For Chris, thank you for believing in me even when I didn't believe in myself.

Chapter 1

Blackman Smith was having the worst night of his life, which was saying something.

At the age of ten, after his mother's mercifully short battle with cancer, he moved in with his father, and his adolescence had been a series of unfortunate events on the level of Lemony Snicket, except Blackman was, thank God, an only child. His mother had been one of six, but none of her siblings had been interested in taking him. It didn't matter that he was self-sufficient and self-reliant, nor did it matter that he came with a significant amount of insurance money. Something his father would have more than adequately subsidized with hefty monthly child support payments just to be rid of the Blackman problem.

But Blackman's sterling financial benefits didn't seem to outweigh the fact that he was built like a D1 linebacker, towering over his classmates and most of his teachers. Or that he rarely smiled. He didn't quite understand why not smiling much was such an impediment to getting taken in by his actual flesh and blood, but smiling seemed to matter. More importantly, it seemed to matter more than anything else.

A goddamn smile.

Or, in Blackman's case, the lack of.

People, his family in particular, seemed to assume he didn't smile because he was mean spirited and dumb. A kid as big as Blackman probably wasn't going to be a rocket scientist, literally or metaphorically. But Blackman was neither mean spirited nor stupid. In fact, he was the smartest kid in his class, and read voraciously for a ten year old. He was just painfully shy. Thankfully his teachers at the small Catholic school his mother had enrolled him in understood that knowing he was a gentle and sensitive soul. That his mother's sickness and death had been especially hard on him.

Though not as hard as his family's rejection.

They had always been so nice to him at the holidays, and he got along with all his cousins, even the mean ones, or at least he thought he did, but evidently, he was wrong. Never knowing they were all rather intimidated by his size, even the mean ones. Turns out there was a big difference between being nice to a shy boy when his mother was alive and dying and taking in a scared boy whose mother was dead and buried. A Grand Canyon sized difference.

So, Blackman went to live with his father, a well respected and greatly feared defense attorney who catered to a well heeled and typically guilty clientele. His father's specialty: spouse murderers. Evidently, Blackman later learned, those men paid the best. When Blackman arrived at the sprawling estate just outside Philadelphia, his father was going through his second divorce. Divorcing the woman for whom he'd abandoned Blackman's mother, but not before insisting that Blackman be saddled with the ridiculous family name. Blackman was the name all first born sons were given. His father was not the first born son, however, so he escaped the Blackman name. His Uncle Blackman, whom he had never met, abandoned the pirate like moniker for his middle name before he was out of elementary school. However, Blackman's middle name was Emerson, which didn't seem like much of an improvement.

The Emerson name had come from his mother's side of the family, a tradition in its own right. One of the hard lessons Blackman learned young was that nothing really belonged to him, not even his name. A lesson he was reminded of over and over again during the course of his life.

Shortly after Blackman's arrival at his father's house, he was given a sterile bedroom overlooking an expanse of woods and a nanny. The nanny, an old battle ax of a woman who spoke Arabic, English, French, and Italian, wore a hijab that covered all her hair except for her perfectly plucked eyebrows. Evidently, hiring a hijab wearing Muslim nanny was the only way his father could ensure he wouldn't attempt to fuck her.

Thankfully, Fatima was as lonely as Blackman, so she was only a battle ax on the rare occasion his father was around. Over time, Fatimah would become Blackman's second mother and one of the few constant adults in his life.

Before his father abdicated his parental role to Fatimah, he enrolled Blackman in the most prestigious boys' preparatory school in the mid-Atlantic. As much as his old man didn't want Blackman, he also didn't want to send his only son north to a boarding school in New York or New England. Blackman never really understood why, and he never cared enough to ask. His father was a mystery Blackman had no interest in solving.

Blackman was in school less than a week when the hockey coach noticed him walking to class. He took an immediate interest in Blackman's size. And one phone call to Blackman's father, who was boarding a plane for the west coast, changed the trajectory of Blackman's life.

Suddenly, hockey became the center of Blackman's life.

Year round.

Regardless of what Blackman might have wanted.

Because personally, he preferred baseball.

But no baseball team needed a kid his size.

A hockey team, however...

Team coaches, private coaches, and private trainers created a new version of Blackman Smith. One who learned to enjoy the grace and beauty of a game played on a sheet of ice. But it was the gear Blackman liked the most: the uniform of hockey. It was so easy for a shy kid like Blackman to get lost in the layers of clothing: the undergarments, the pads, the uniform itself. He loved a sport in which he could be both visible and invisible at the same time.

A living, breathing paradox.

Out of his gear, in his school uniform, or his street clothes, he was entirely too visible. The jocks loved him because of his size and his scowl, which wasn't really a scowl but the frown of a lonely kid. The academic kids who loved chess over sports shied away from him as if they were afraid of him. As if they thought he wanted to punish them for being small and intellectual. As if it never occurred to them that he might want to play chess with them, that he might want to be small like them. Even the girls who collected jocks like trading cards avoided him because he seemed to be too much.

He scared them.

And they scared him.

By upper school, the frustration of this life started to get to him. His father's absence despite a new wife in the house and his social isolation began manifesting itself in aggression, but because his aggression was limited to the weight room and the ice, no one seemed to care. His grades were exemplary, he was an attentive and polite student, and his teachers seemed to like him; however, he didn't trust that their interest or kindness was genuine.

He'd learned to be wary after his mother died.

On the ice, he started playing a chippier game, but his coaches didn't seem too concerned. In fact, they seemed all too happy about the development. He wasn't the only scorer on the team, and if he went to the penalty box, it was usually for leveling one of the other team's scorers. So, as far as the coaches were concerned, there was no need to worry.

On the rare nights his father and the new wife or girlfriend made an appearance at a game, his father seemed genuinely happy with Blackman's style of play. Happy with his son's aggression and the fear it struck in the opposing players. His father, a tall man but nowhere nearly as tall and strong as Blackman, seemed to derive some sort of pleasure from having produced such an imposing son.

A potentially professionally athletic son.

Only Fatimah seemed concerned with the kind of athlete Blackman was becoming.

***

After one particularly violent game where Blackman scored no goals and spent too much time in the penalty box, Fatimah came to his room holding a tray with a mug of the good hot chocolate and a plate of homemade ginger snaps, Blackman's favorite cookies. When Fatimah knocked on his door that evening, Blackman had been sitting at his desk reading a thick textbook, taking notes in one of his many notebooks. He should have been at a party hanging out with his friends and flirting with pretty girls, but Blackman didn't go to parties, and as far as Fatimah knew, he didn't flirt with pretty girls. Fatimah wasn't entirely sure Blackman was even invited to parties. It made her heart ache to watch this lonely boy do homework or study or read alone in this barren room night after night.

Fatimah hated Blackman's room. The furniture was heavy mahogany and entirely too formal for a teenager. The king size bed with the oversized, ornate headboard fit him but didn't suit him. It was the kind of bed that lovers shared, not a child trapped in a man's body.

The room was painfully neat. No clothes on the floor or hanging over his desk chair. No wayward shoes strewn on the floor, no forgotten dirty dishes. It was utterly devoid of the personal. The sole exception was the threadbare brown teddy bear that sat on his bed. He never talked about the bear. It was entirely possible that bear was his most valuable possession.

Blackman looked up from his work and pulled the expensive headphones from his head. He leaned over and turned off the stereo. His thick chocolate brown hair was still damp from the shower, and his face was covered in dark stubble. He was dressed in a heavy Philadelphia Flyers hoodie and gray running pants. His long feet were bare. He looked so much like a man that Fatimah felt sorry for him because he was still just a boy. At nearly six foot four, she prayed he would stop growing. No child needed to be so tall.

"Habibi, I brought you some hot chocolate. The good kind," Fatimah said with a conspiratorial wink. Blackman's father was partial to the good hot chocolate and tended to bury it in the cupboard where he thought Fatimah wouldn't find it. A smile Blackman reserved only for Fatimah spread across his pale face, lighting up his chestnut brown eyes.

"You only brought one mug, auntie," he said in perfect Arabic as Fatimah walked into the [illegible]om and set the tray on his desk. When Blackman's father was away, Fati[illegible]oke to Blackman in English, and Blackman responde[illegible] Arabi[illegible] the [illegible] way.

"You know this hot chocolate is too rich for me, Habibi, but it is perfect for you." She gave him a warm smile, sat on the edge of his bed, and adjusted her hijab. She watched as Blackman picked up his favorite mug – a big earthenware mug in shades of blue – and sipped the thick chocolate carefully. Blackman didn't have much of a sweet tooth, but he loved hot chocolate. Maybe because he wasn't supposed to drink it, or maybe because Fatimah openly defied his father by giving it to him.

Blackman placed the mug back on the tray and picked up a cookie but didn't eat it right away. Instead, he waited because he knew Fatimah had something to say. Even though he knew what she wanted to say, he wanted her to say it. He needed to hear it.

So, he waited patiently.

"Habibi, I am worried about you." Fatimah sighed.

Blackman met her bright blue eyes for a moment, then dropped his eyes to the cookie in his oversized hand. He didn't say anything, even though he was desperate to tell her he was worried about himself, too.

***

Now, he was drunk.

Blackman avoided going to parties in high school because he knew if he started drinking, he'd have a hard time stopping. It would take a lot of beer or whiskey or tequila to fill up the man-sized hole inside his man-sized body.

But tonight, he wanted to be drunk. Good and drunk. As drunk as he could get without actually dying, or maybe he'd luck out and die on the way home. Maybe he'd fall into traffic or fall and hit his head on a curb. Or maybe get shot during a mugging.

His face burned with shame as the thoughts crossed his mind. Fatimah had already buried two children in her youth. There was no need to subject her to that kind of suffering again.

At least not on his account.

The team had abandoned him after his fourth or fifth drink. They had never seen him drink before, and as eager as they had been to see him throw back a few beers, they didn't expect the booze would make the already reserved winger even more taciturn. So, after a while, they left him to get drunk in peace.

The bar was a typical college joint with sports memorabilia from the local universities adorning the walls, flat screen televisions, a few dartboards, and a pair of pool tables. It kept cheap beer on tap, cheaper liquor on the shelves, and the televisions perpetually tuned to sporting events. Thursday night football played on two of the televisions while West Coast hockey games played on the others.

Blackman tried his best to concentrate on the football game in front of him, but his eyes kept drifting to the mirror behind the bar and the three girls playing pool. Well, to the one girl he'd been watching surreptitiously for over an hour.

She was young, certainly too young to be in here, but she either had a good fake ID or knew the bouncer or bartender. Or all three. She looked like a freshman in her painted-on jeans, showcasing strong legs and an incredibly tight ass. An emerald green shirt showed off strong shoulders and toned arms. Her hair was long and wavy, the kind of red that only came from an Irish mother or grandmother.

He hadn't noticed her eyes since he'd spent so much time staring at her ass, but he imagined they were the same shade of emerald green as her shirt, or maybe an otherworldly green, like a field of ferns after a rainstorm. She was the most beautiful girl he'd ever seen, even if she was too young for him. He thought about going over and talking to her, maybe buying her a beer. Doing all the things that normal guys did. But he didn't. In a fleeting moment of bravado, he tried to catch her eye, but she only had eyes for her two friends.

Probably a dyke.

He immediately regretted the crassness of the thought. Sighing, he realized he'd rather be home sipping hot chocolate with Fatimah than sitting in this shitty bar, drinking alone, and watching a woman he didn't have the balls to talk to.

He signaled the bartender for another beer and added a shot of whiskey.

Fuck my fucking life.

He looked away from the girl and stared at the empty pint glass. The hit he'd delivered earlier that night on the other team's center had been just this side of late and just this side of cheap. Blackman had walked the line without crossing it, so the other team had a right to be pissed, but there was nothing they could do about it. There was no penalty, but Coach called Blackman off the ice when it became clear the freshman wasn't getting up. Blackman watched with everyone else as the trainers called for the stretcher. It wasn't until the kid was being wheeled past Blackman that he noticed the blood. The kid had been the other team's leading scorer, and no one on Blackman's bench was sorry to see him go.

Even on a stretcher.

And if they were, no one was saying anything to Blackman. At six feet six inches tall and 250 pounds, he stood four inches taller than most of his teammates and probably thirty pounds heavier; he was a big son-of-a-bitch.

The kid had been taken to the hospital for X-rays, but Backman didn't know anything more, and he was too ashamed to ask. The kid had barely cracked six feet tall, and Blackman doubted he tipped the scale past 180 with his gear *and* skates.

Blackman's shame sat on his chest like a boulder. This was the line Fatimah had warned him about over hot chocolate and ginger snaps all those years ago.

"Habibi, you must decide what kind of man you want to be. No one can decide that for you. It is between you and Allah."

And now he was drunk in a bar, and Allah was probably not taking his calls right now. And on top of everything else, he had an early class in the morning he couldn't miss. But even that wasn't enough to move him off the goddamn barstool.

He had no idea how long the redhead had been standing beside him, sipping a soda and staring at his profile. But when he realized she was next to him, his stomach dropped so quickly he thought he might actually get sick. Like the time he rode the roller coaster at Six Flags that went forward and backward. The girl carried herself as if she was much older than she appeared. He was surprised but not disappointed to see that her eyes weren't green; they were a peculiar shade of icy hazel that seemed to look both at him and through him.

As drunk as he was, he was surprised to feel a stirring in his pants.

She smelled like jasmine, oatmeal, and expensive shampoo.

She looked at him expectantly with her big almond shaped eyes, and the stirring in his pants threatened to turn into a full blown erection. He felt his face go hot.

"Can I help you?" he asked, pleased he hadn't slurred.

She put her soda back on the bar and gave him a long, appraising look.

"Well," she said in a cultured English accent that wasn't doing anything to help the situation in his pants. "You've been staring at me for so long it only seemed fair I come over and stare at you for a while. Also, I need another soda." Looking up, she waved at the bartender, who nodded and grabbed a fresh pint glass for her.

"How much rum is in that coke?" Blackman asked with something like a sneer. He needed to get rid of her, and rude behavior was the best tactic, at least according to his inebriated brain.

"No rum at all," she said as the bartender handed her the fresh soda.

"What are you, some kind of religious nut or something?" he asked coldly, wincing inside as he thought about Fatimah, and what he'd do if some asshole said that to her.

"Nope, just the designated sober friend. The one who makes sure everyone gets home without making any life altering mistakes."

"What kind of life altering mistakes?" He almost slurred the last little bit but managed not to at the last moment.

"The kind that look like you," she said with a wink.

It took Blackman's drunken brain a second too long to clock the insult.

"Plenty of girls would love to go home with me," he snapped. The girl with the painted-on jeans and the hazel eyes was kind enough not to laugh at him, and he was grateful for the courtesy.

"I'm sure," she said indulgently.

"What about you?" he blurted out just as she turned away. "You wanna go home with me?"

Slowly, she turned back, her eyes shining brightly in the dim light as they took him apart. His heart hammered in his chest, and his cock throbbed. Visions of the two of them in the alley behind the bar flooded his brain. Her strong legs wrapped around his waist, her breath hot against his neck, her voice soft in his ear. The vision was so clear his chest went tight as if someone had checked him into the boards.

"You're drunk." It was a simple observation. A statement of fact, as if she had confirmed that water was wet and the earth was round.

"I am," he admitted, feeling lightheaded.

"You're kind of an asshole," she said with a smile.

"Plenty of assholes get laid," he replied, trying to project a confidence he didn't feel. A confidence he had never actually felt.

"Especially–" she said, leaning toward him "–when they're hockey gods who look like you." She added another wink, and he knew she was mocking him, and he deserved it, but he couldn't back off. God, he wanted her, this strange young woman with the strong legs, amazing ass, unbelievable eyes, and voice that reduced him to nothing more than a caricature.

"Yeah," he retorted almost breathlessly. "Especially then."

She looked at him, her face inscrutable, then leaned so close to him that, for a moment, he thought she was going to kiss him. Blackman wondered if maybe he was supposed to kiss her, and then he was thinking about the alley, and then his apartment and his oversized bed with the soft duvet and the expensive sheets. About what it would be like to hear her whisper his name in the dark. To scream it.

"I'm sorry you're having a bad night. I'm sorry you've decided to crawl into a bottle of cheap whiskey, really, I am." She paused long enough to make sure he was listening to her words. "Because it would have been nice to meet the non-asshole version of you."

They were too close.

His eyes met hers, and for a moment, she seemed to move in closer, almost imperceptibly. Then she turned around and walked away. It took him a while to situate himself, and by the time he looked around for her, she and her friends were gone.

Dejectedly, he pulled his wallet out and dropped a handful of bills on the bar before walking into the bitter night. He walked back to his apartment, where he fell asleep on the couch because he couldn't bear to sleep in a bed where she wasn't beside him.

Chapter 2

Blackman's alarm went off at 5 am, and when he rolled over and then off the sofa, he suspected he was still drunk. He climbed to his feet slowly and walked unsteadily to the bathroom, where he pissed and splashed water on his face.

He felt like shit.

Walking to his empty bedroom, he avoided looking at his neatly made bed, the brown teddy bear sitting alone on top of one of the big pillows. He pulled on clean workout clothes but had to sit on the floor to lace his sneakers because bending over made him nauseous.

Usually, he listened to music when he ran, but this morning, there was nothing he wanted to hear. He locked the apartment door behind him, stretched out his tight muscles on the sidewalk, and ran down the still, dark streets of the city. A half mile into his run, he puked in the gutter, then continued running. At mile five, he puked again, then pushed through another three miles.

On the way home, he stopped at Wawa and bought two coffees, a couple of bagels, and an egg sandwich.

"Morning, Blackman. You look like shit," the gruff tattooed man behind the counter said.

Blackman felt his face go hot.

"Long night," Blackman said, handing over some cash.

"Yeah, but you're still out running. Unbelievable. You should still be home in bed, man. Preferably with someone cute," the man said, handing back Blackman's change.

Blackman pocketed the money and shrugged.

"Too much to do, Bennie. You know how it goes, miles to go before I sleep and all that shit." Blackman smiled and headed toward the door and the cold Philadelphia morning. After looking both ways, he crossed the street and handed everything except one of the black coffees to a homeless woman sitting at the bus stop.

"Morning, Miss Gladys," Blackman said, cradling the hot coffee in his cold hands.

The older African American woman, who could have been anywhere from thirty-five to fifty-five, had dirty dreadlocks, incredibly smooth skin, and a completely mysterious body hidden beneath an oversized winter coat.

"Thank you, baby," she said with a grateful smile as she took the bag of food.

Blackman sipped his coffee as Gladys pulled out the egg sandwich.

"They're calling for snow this weekend," he said as Gladys took a big bite of the steaming sandwich.

"That's silly," she said around a mouthful of food. "It never snows this early; it's not even winter."

"They seemed pretty sure on Action News," Blackman said, leaning against the bus stop shelter and taking a deep breath. The smell of the egg sandwich was making him nauseous again.

"Well, if that Cecily girl says snow, it'll probably snow. That white girl knows what she's talking about when it comes to the weather," Gladys said with a chuckle. Blackman nodded, and Gladys finished the sandwich and wiped her fingers on her dirty coat.

"Maybe you could stop by this weekend, and we could watch the news together," Blackman said casually. "Maybe watch a DVD," he added before he took another tentative sip of his coffee. Gladys cackled like she always did whenever Blackman invited her to stop by his apartment.

"Stop trying to get me into bed, white boy," she teased. "You know you're not ready for all Miss Gladys has going on under this coat."

"Well, you know, Miss Gladys, it *is* a very big bed," Blackman teased back.

"It better be for a boy your size," she said, giving him a long look that was supposed to look lascivious but instead just wound up looking a little motherly. Like she was looking to see if he was taking care of himself, eating enough, getting enough sleep. She looked at him like she worried about him, and it pained him a little. How a woman who lived such a hard life could spare a thought about a guy like him.

Blackman forced himself to chuckle as their pre-arranged dialogue played out the way it had played out dozens of times before. He'd been offering Gladys space on his couch or the use of his shower for the last two years, but she never took him up on his offer. Something about her, about her kind manner, her generosity, her thoughtfulness, made him feel protective of her or as protective as he could be. He knew she always shared some of the food he brought with a younger woman who looked far rougher than Miss Gladys.

The younger woman looked more like a girl than a woman, barely out of high school or, more likely, middle school, and unlike Gladys, she looked like she worked in the sex trade. When he saw her talking to Gladys, he felt overwhelmed by the injustice of it all. The girl should have been in a classroom with kids like him instead of servicing lonely and violent men on the street.

"You best be going, baby," Gladys said, looking around for the girl in question. "You don't wanna be late for that 8 am class."

He didn't know how she did it, but Gladys always seemed to remember his class schedule.

"Okay, but remember my offer," Blackman said, digging into his pocket and pulling out a twenty-dollar bill. He handed it over without meeting Gladys' eyes. Neither one of them minded the sharing of food, but the handing over of money felt different, making them both a little uncomfortable. She patted his hand quickly before waving him off.

Blackman walked back to his apartment, drinking his coffee and concentrating on not throwing up again.

***

After his shower, Blackman tried to eat some food but wasn't up to it. He packed a couple of granola bars into his backpack along with a bottle of orange juice and some extra strength Tylenol, hoping they might improve the state of him before midday practice.

On his way out, he stopped and checked his reflection in the mirror on the wall next to the front door. He was dressed in well worn blue jeans, a pair of brown Doc Marten oxfords, and a dark green sweater beneath a heavy tan barn coat. Running his hand through his wavy hair, he thought about getting a haircut. It was much longer than he usually kept it, and soon Fatimah would be on his case about it. She was always very particular about his appearance. When he went off to college, Fatimah insisted that he always dress neatly.

"Habibi, you will have so many opportunities, and you must take advantage of them. Now, when you go to class, be sure to dress like a serious young man so your professors will know you are worthy."

His father, on the other hand, simply rented him an embarrassingly large apartment, gave him a credit card with an obscene credit limit, and warned him not to knock up a girl.

"I mean, have fun, but for Christ's sake, use a condom. I'm too young to be a grandfather."

Blackman might have felt like a train wreck, but he arrived ten minutes early for class and took his customary seat in the back of the small room. As much as Fatimah wanted him to sit in the front so his teachers could see him and his seriousness of purpose, at six foot six, he was just too tall and was invariably in someone's way. So, he sat in the back corner, making sure his seriousness of purpose was evident from a distance.

In his classes, Blackman did his best to battle his inherent shyness. In group projects, he carried his weight and sometimes the weight of other people. He never made waves, he never complained, and he never missed deadlines. Being perpetually friendly, curious, and hardworking, many students who knew him from class struggled to reconcile Blackman Smith pre-law student with Blackman Smith college hockey enforcer.

Truth be told, he struggled to reconcile it himself. He was a 4.0 student double majoring in history and political science who also might have a shot at the NHL. Something that interested his father more than it interested him. Blackman wasn't sure he wanted to go pro, but he kept those thoughts to himself.

His head was throbbing, and his stomach hurt, but once the professor walked in and sat down on his desk, Blackman did his best to put his distractions in a box.

***

Blackman thought about the nameless girl often. Sometimes, he even dreamt about her. He'd been back to the bar several times, but she was never there. Sometimes, he nursed a beer for hours watching ESPN, hoping she'd show up and put him out of his misery, but she never did. The bartender and the regular bouncer didn't remember her, which he found impossible to believe. He couldn't get her out of his mind, and he couldn't imagine how anyone could look at her and not remember her.

Or forget her.

Because he couldn't do that either.

And God knew he wanted to forget her. He'd had a few dates and some casual hookups in an effort to move on from her, but all he managed to do was to make himself feel guilty. His mother had been a casual Catholic, as had his father, before abandoning the church and their stance on marriage and fidelity for more convenient atheism, but Fatimah had raised him the way she had been raised. She didn't begrudge him bacon with his eggs or pork in his fried rice as long as he remembered to be a good and kind person and help the less fortunate.

"It is our duty, Habibi, to care for our hungry brothers and sisters and to help the less fortunate. No exceptions."

Unless, of course, it was a hungry 16-year old Blackman, and it was between meals.

"Auntie, I'm hungry," Blackman invariably complained in Arabic.

"You just ate, my darling. No more food until dinner. Now you will understand what it is like to go without," Fatimah would reply in English. "Now, out of my kitchen."

"I am not a Muslim, auntie," Blackman grumbled as he walked away.

"I know, Habibi," she said. "But I pray for you anyway."

Whether Blackman woke up alone in his bed or with a woman in hers, the nameless woman was on his mind instead of the woman sometimes lying next to him. Bus rides were the worst. No matter what he brought to listen to or what he brought to read, he'd pass miles staring into space, thinking about her. He wondered who she was, where she went to school, what she studied, what she wanted to do after college, what she liked to eat, how she liked her coffee. He imagined more than once taking her out for coffee, or dinner, or maybe dinner and a movie. Or a long walk along the river near the Art Museum where it was quiet, and he could kiss her.

If she'd let him.

Sometimes, he thought about making her breakfast in his too big for a college kid apartment. He was confident he could impress her. Thanks to Fatimah, he was a fantastic cook.

"Because Habibi," Fatimah said, one day teaching him how to make a proper vegetable omelet. "You are an American, and you will marry an American girl. American girls expect to be taken care of, to be spoiled because their parents spoil them. So, you must know how to cook; otherwise, your children will be too skinny."

"What if I don't want children, auntie?" He wasn't sure he wanted to inflict childhood on another unsuspecting child, especially a child who might look like him. Tall and broad like Frankenstein's monster, but without the awkward facial scars.

"You are a man, Habibi. Men have a wife and children." After a moment, she added, "One wife and at least two children. Maybe three."

"Who makes up these rules, auntie?" Blackman asked as she showed him how to flip the omelet.

"It does not matter who makes up the rules, Habibi. Rules are rules."

And Fatimah's rules were law.

***

By late February, Blackman's obsession with the nameless woman began to fade. Well, a little. The team was making the final push for the collegiate playoffs, and Blackman was thinking more seriously about law school. His father was pushing Columbia and Yale, although he had gone to Stanford, but Blackman wanted to stay closer to home.

He had just started dating a pre-med student a year behind him, and although she wasn't a forever kind of girlfriend, he thought they had some potential. And, of course, there was Fatimah to consider. She wouldn't go to New York or Connecticut with him, and he wasn't ready to be away from her. Not that he'd admit that to his father or her. She was the closest thing he had to a real parent, and there were plenty of local law schools for him to consider, and he liked Philadelphia.

The team had just come home from a grueling road trip, and he was hoping he could talk Fatimah into coming to the game tomorrow night. She only went to a handful of games a season. She didn't enjoy the violence of the game any more than she enjoyed watching the man Blackman became on the ice.

"I promise you, auntie," Blackman said. "If you come, I will be a good man."

Fatimah scoffed. "Silly boy. You cannot make such a promise."

"For you, auntie," he said kindly. "I can."

He meant it; he could be a good man for her.

They were playing to a standing-room-only crowd, with famous alumni from both teams in the stands rubbing elbows with NHL scouts and excited parents. His father was in Paris with his newest wife, touring churches and battlefields or some such. Not that Blackman cared. Whether his father came to a game or not was immaterial. Fatimah was the one he cared about, and knowing she was in the stands made him happy because when she was there all he wanted to do was make her proud.

Knowing that law school was in his future, this game meant no more to Blackman than any other game, but he knew it meant the world to his teammates, and his job tonight was to make them look good. Several of his teammates aspired to go pro in North America or abroad, and a night like this could make or break those dreams. For others, their hockey careers would end with the season and their upcoming graduations. For them, every game counted because an important part of their lives, their identities, was coming to an end. However, Blackman was happy that the end of his hockey career was in sight. He had one more year, and then he could move on from hockey and the man that hockey demanded he be.

As he took the ice for warm-ups, he tried to put the cacophony of the arena out of his mind. For a big man, Blackman moved gracefully, fluidly. As he worked to loosen his body, he concentrated on the feel of the ice beneath his skates and the stick in his hands, the tactile parts of the sport. He flew around his teammates and took shots on the sophomore goalie, who tended to sing to himself while he was in goal. Blackman practiced setting up his teammates.

When he first joined the team, he had the potential to be one of the leading scorers, but because of his size and physicality, he wasn't needed as a scorer. His job was to set up the shooters or clear the way for them. It was far and away from where he started when he fell in love with the sport, but there were expectations for a guy built like Blackman, and ever since he was young, he felt compelled to fulfill others' expectations regardless of his own wants or needs.

Skating around the ice, his eyes wander from his teammates to the fans seated closest to the glass. Many wore the dark blue jerseys of the home team, while others wore Flyers jerseys, the bright orange standing out in contrast to the sea of dark blue.

Blackman was taking another lap around his end of the ice when he saw her standing behind the glass with another woman. They were chatting and laughing while they half watched the warm-up. She was bundled in layers of clothes as if she felt the cold acutely. Her wavy red hair spilled out from beneath a black knit cap, and she wore a heavy blue hoodie beneath an oversized vintage Mark Howe Flyers jersey. She was breathtaking as she laughed animatedly at something her friend said and then quickly slapped a hand over her face as if her laugh might be too loud for the arena.

Blackman wanted to make her laugh like that.

Someone called his name, and he looked back just in time to smack a puck toward the goalie, who was singing "Sweet Home Alabama" while he blocked shots. Shocking himself, Blackman skated over to the nameless woman and her friend. More players called his name, but he ignored them. He spit out his mouth guard and grinned at her as he banged on the glass with a gloved hand.

When she looked at him, those icy hazel eyes looked positively electrifying in the arena's bright lights, and he forgot how to breathe. Her smile was wide and genuine as if she'd been waiting for him to come over and say hello. As if she, too, had been waiting to run into him again.

He'd dream about that smile for years.

Decades.

Until the day he died.

"Hey!" he yelled over the noise of the crowd.

"Hey, yourself!" she yelled back.

"What's your name?"

"Maggie. Maggie Rhymer."

"I'm Blackman Smith."

"I know," she said with a laugh. As if there was anyone in that arena who didn't know his name. He grinned at her like an idiot. All that mattered was the fact that *she* knew *his* name. His teammates yelled for him while people in the stands watched the exchange curiously. Others tried to get his attention as if they were more important than the girl he was talking to, but he ignored all of them. All he cared about was Maggie and that incredible smile of hers.

"I'm going to score a goal for you!" he hollered over the crowd noise and the voices of his teammates. Even the coaches were yelling at him, but he ignored them all.

To him, there was no one in that arena except Maggie Rhymer.

"Just one?" she asked with a gleam in her eyes, and he felt the hot rush of blood to the space buried deep beneath his pads.

"What would two get me?" Blackman asked.

She thought it over for a moment.

"Coffee."

"What would three get me?" he asked, grinning stupidly.

Her laugh was loud and carefree, and he loved it. He wanted to laugh like that with her every day for the rest of his life.

"Well?"

"I'm thinking."

"How about dinner?" he offered.

"Okay, Blackman Smith. You score a hat trick for me, and I'll go to dinner with you."

"Deal!" Blackman yelled as he started to skate backward, away from her. "Think about your favorite restaurant because you'll be making reservations by the end of the second period."

And then he winked at her, and she slapped a hand over her mouth as fresh peals of laughter escaped her. Before he turned back to his bench, he saw her lean into her friend and whisper something in her ear. He swore he could hear more laughter.

Blackman swung his legs over the boards and sat down on the bench. She was almost directly across the rink from him, just in his line of sight.

"Who the hell is that?" Mitchell Czerny, a freshman center, asked. Mitchell had the thickest Downeast accent Blackman had ever heard, and most of the time, he had no idea what Mitchell was saying. After a couple of beers, the kid might as well be speaking in tongues.

"The woman I'm going to marry," Blackman said with a sincerity that shocked him as much as it shocked the kid next to him.

"I thought you had a girlfriend," Mitchell asked surprised.

Blackman didn't reply; he just turned his full attention to the coach as he stepped up and addressed the team in his typical stony manner.

It was time for Blackman Smith to earn himself a dinner date.

Blackman was having the game of his collegiate career. He was on fire. Everything he did was perfect; for once, he wasn't clearing a path so his teammates could score. They were clearing a path so *he* could score. His first goal came five minutes into the first period, and his second goal with two minutes left in the first. Both times, he pointed to her after chest bumping his teammates. During the second period, the other team increased Blackman's coverage, and the game started to get chippy.

When Blackman took a two minute penalty for high sticking, he could feel Maggie's eyes on him as he skated to the penalty box to think on his sins. Blue was ahead by one goal, not his. He knew the other guys needed to look good, to look better, but... but he wanted to have dinner with Maggie Rhymer. He wanted the chance to impress her, a chance to make up for being such an asshole in the bar. And he wanted that more than anything he had ever wanted in his life.

Three minutes into the third period, Noah Caine, a future Hall of Famer, leaned over and asked, "What the fuck is up with you? You're playing like a man possessed."

"See that girl over there," Blackman answered, tilting his head toward Maggie and her friend.

"There are a thousand girls over there."

"The redhead," Blackman said, pointing to Maggie.

"Not helping, man. Did you hit your head or something?"

"If I get a hat trick, she'll let me take her to dinner."

"Is that a euphemism?" Noah asked with arched eyebrows.

"No," Blackman said, staring at Maggie, who was watching the players on the ice.

Morgan Graves, a future Boston Bruin whose career would be cut short by injuries but who would later become a pediatric surgeon, asked. "What's going on?"

"Blackman needs another goal to get a date with some girl over there," Caine said, pointing in the general vicinity of Maggie Rhymer.

"My future wife," Blackman added cheerfully.

"Wife?" Graves asked. "I thought you had a girlfriend."

"It doesn't matter," Caine said. "He needs a goal to get the girl, so let's get Blackman his goal."

"Got it," Graves said. "I'll pass the word."

The final goal of Blackman Smith's career was utterly beautiful and was one of the three things that night memorialized on hockey highlight reels and YouTube. Two beautiful passes and flawless skating put him ahead of the defender who had been plaguing him all night. Then, a blistering slapshot buried the puck in the upper left hand corner of the net before the goalie even had a chance to raise his glove. The red light flashed, and Blackman Smith entered the annals of collegiate hockey history. The arena erupted with wild cheers as Blackman skated over to an open mouthed Maggie Rhymer and shouted, "Make reservations, sweetheart!"

Never in his life had Blackman called a woman sweetheart.

Maggie looked at him with that knee buckling smile he'd dreamed about just as his teammates swarmed him. The crowd noise was deafening, and the air in the arena was charged with unbridled joy and simmering rage.

Blackman skated back to the bench, oblivious to the hateful looks from the other team, none of whom had forgotten the damage he'd inflicted on their teammate earlier in the season. All Blackman could see was Maggie's smiling face and the excitement and pride in her eyes. It was the pride that took his breath away, and he hoped that he had finally redeemed himself from the embarrassing night at the bar.

It would have been nice to meet the non-asshole version of you.

He'd never fallen in love before, but he suspected it felt something like this.

His next shift came with four minutes left in the game. He had earned his dinner with Maggie, so he concentrated on helping his teammates like he should have been doing since the beginning of the game.

As Blackman skated toward the boards to help Francois Babineaux, a man who would forgo pro hockey to teach poor kids in Quebec and coach youth hockey well into his seventies, he didn't see the other player coming up behind him. The one who intended to avenge the freshman Blackman had put in the hospital the night he met Maggie. The hit on Blackman was just this side of late and just this side of cheap.

The same kind of hit Blackman had been doling out for years.

Blackman went down at an odd angle, and his face hit the plexiglass with a crack like a gunshot. His head snapped back sharply. His skates got tangled up Babineaux's, and when Blackman went down, all 250 pounds of him came down awkwardly on his left leg. The snap of his bone echoed in the cold air of the arena.

Blackman crumpled on the ice, and as much as he wanted unconsciousness to sweep over him like warm water in winter, he remained awake. He stared at the roof above him in confusion, as if he wasn't quite sure how it had gotten there. Slowly he became aware of two things: he'd pissed himself, and there was something hot and wet pooling beneath his broken leg. He was vaguely aware of players shoving each other around him and the eerie silence of the crowd.

Soon the trainers were next to him asking him questions, but he couldn't answer them. He was afraid that if he opened his mouth, he would either scream or throw up, and either thing would scare Fatimah. He wasn't really following the conversation going on between the adults above him, but the trainers had been joined by the medical team and the EMTs, who had lowered a stretcher next to him. It was just like the night he leveled the freshmen. He wondered if the freshman had pissed himself, too.

The EMTs asked him some questions, which he answered by either nodding his head or shaking it, which he wasn't supposed to do. They immobilized his head and pulled out a backboard. They looked at one of the trainers, whose face was serious and pale as if what was happening to Blackman was happening to him. Blackman had always gotten along well with the trainers and knew they were great at their jobs. They'd seen their fair share of injuries over the years, but something told Blackman that his injury was different. Somehow worse.

"Blackman, the EMTs are going to move you, and I'm not going to lie, son. This is going to hurt like a motherfucker. You understand?"

Blackman nodded.

They moved him.

He screamed.

Then he finally passed out.

That was definitely going to be on *Sports Center.*

Chapter 3

The hours immediately after the injury were too confusing for Blackman to understand. He remembered Fatimah by his side crying, and he remembered repeating to anyone who would listen that she was his auntie and that she had to be with him, but he was speaking in Arabic, and only Fatimah understood him. He remembered her holding his hand tightly, translating everything he said to the EMTs and the doctors. He vaguely remembered Fatimah imploring him to speak English, but he didn't understand because he thought he was speaking English.

Eventually, he gave up and stopped talking altogether. Then he remembered being rolled toward the surgery suite, and all he could think was that the doctors didn't look much older than he. While he watched the ceiling lights pass above him, he wondered what would happen to Fatimah if he died during surgery because he didn't trust his father to take care of her, but he couldn't tell her any of those things. He couldn't tell her that he was more afraid for her than he was for himself. He could tell her he loved her more than he loved anyone else in his life. Instead, he just repeated to the space she no longer occupied, "Everything will be okay, Auntie. I'll be fine."

He remembered waking up with Fatimah sitting beside him, holding his large hand in both of hers. She was asleep, and her hijab had shifted so he could see her hair. The sight of it embarrassed him because he knew it would embarrass her. He wanted so badly to reach out and adjust it to cover her dark hair, but he didn't have the strength. He worried that she'd be upset that her hair was showing, but he fell asleep before he could do anything about it, before he could protect her from her own humanity. He was sure Allah would forgive her, though. Blackman was her son, after all, so it should be okay for him to see her hair. After all, Fatimah had taught him that Allah was both loving and forgiving.

The pain medication caused hallucinations and fever dreams, and he couldn't tell the difference between fantasy and reality. In those hours after the surgery, Maggie came to him, and Dream Maggie was better than no Maggie at all. In one of his dreams, Maggie was sitting next to him wearing her Mark Howe jersey, her beautiful red hair framing her heart shaped face. She held Blackman's hand, and her hand was soft and warm against his hard, calloused skin. Just feeling her palm pressed against his made him want to cry.

He was in so much pain.

"You'll be okay," Dream Maggie said softly. Her hazel eyes shining with unshed tears.

"It hurts," he admitted.

"I know, but you'll heal," she promised.

He nodded, and she pressed her palm against his cheek, then kissed his knuckles softly.

"It's just not our time right now, but it'll come – our time – you just need to be patient."

"I love you," he said, tears burning his eyes.

"You don't even know me." She smiled a gentle smile.

"I do," he insisted. "I know your smile. That's all I need to know," he said as tears slid down his cheeks.

Dream Maggie reached over, running her thumb beneath his eyes and catching his salty tears.

"I'll wait for you," she promised.

"No, you won't," he answered because he wasn't the kind of man a woman like her waited for.

She leaned over and touched his lips with hers, but before he could deepen the kiss, the dream started to change, to morph into something new and frightening.

Blackman spent almost three weeks in the hospital before being discharged into Fatimah's care. She moved into his apartment, slept on the sofa, and took care of him. His classmates recorded class lectures and delivered the tapes and homework to him daily, and Fatimah edited his papers and homework assignments before submitting them to his professors. Since he did all his work on pain medication, Fatimah might have been responsible for more of his work than he did, but his professors weren't asking any questions. His hockey career was over, and his sports scholarship rescinded. His father complained about the tuition money because his father always complained about money, but his complaints didn't keep him from writing checks. Writing checks was about the only part of parenting his father had mastered.

Despite the gruesome injury, the pain medication, and not being able to attend class, Blackman finished the semester with his customary 4.0, but he was sure he didn't deserve it. Regardless, it was quite an accomplishment considering the extent of his injury. His leg would never be the same again. *He* would never be the same again.

By the summer, he was more mobile, so he took extra classes to graduate early. With all the AP credits he'd earned in high school, he was already more than a semester ahead, so it didn't take much to ensure an early graduation. With hockey out of the equation, there was no reason for him to stick around.

He worked around the clock, prepared for the LSATs, and completed his law school applications with Fatimah's help. As he picked up the pieces of his fractured life, he relegated Maggie to his dreams because all his waking hours were dedicated to his studies and the promise of law school. Law school was one of the few things getting him out of bed every morning.

By late winter, nearly a year after the injury, he'd been accepted into law school in the city, so he didn't have to give up his apartment. By early spring, Fatimah trusted him enough to live alone again and moved back to her apartment a few blocks away. At the same time, Blackman's father divorced his latest wife and took up with an embarrassing young attorney at his law firm.

Not that anything his father did mattered to Blackman. His father paid his rent, bills, law school tuition, Fatimah's rent, Fatimah's bills, and maybe Fatimah herself. So, quite frankly, Blackman didn't care who the old man fucked, married, or divorced as long as the checks cleared. Blackman had set goals for himself in the aftermath of the injury, and his father, who seemed more concerned with Blackman's lost chance at the pros instead of Blackman being in pain for the rest of his life, was nothing more than a checkbook.

Blackman didn't see Maggie again for almost two years.

***

Law school was typically a three year commitment, but Blackman wanted to finish sooner. He had always pushed himself hard; he had been a goal oriented boy, and now he was a goal oriented man, and now law school was his whole life. He'd put his friendships on hold, he stopped dating, and aside from swimming, he had no hobbies. Friends, women, and hobbies were for people with spare time, and Blackman didn't have any of that. He worked, studied, attended classes, and ate dinner twice a week with Fatimah.

The only other person he saw with any regularity was Miss Gladys who had worried about him terribly when he disappeared that winter. The first day he limped up to her on his crutches, she threw her hands up in the air and called out a prayer of thanks.

"Child, what happened to you? I thought you forgot about me."

Blackman felt his eyes sting as the older woman threw her arms around him. Last winter had been particularly rough, and it had aged her.

"I got hurt playing hockey, but I'm better now," he said, giving her a squeeze and trying not to breathe in too deeply. When he stepped away, he looked over at the Wawa and then back at her. "It's too late for an egg sandwich. How about a hoagie?"

Gladys smiled warmly. "Would you mind getting me an Italian, baby?"

"Not at all, Miss Gladys," Blackman said, limping away with a smile.

Unable to run, he'd taken up swimming at the 24-hour gym in the neighborhood five days a week, but it wasn't enough to burn off the excess energy thrumming through his body. Since returning to school full time, he made it a point to stop by and visit with Miss Gladys every morning he went swimming. Many mornings, she was the reason he got out of bed instead of rolling over and going back to sleep for another couple of hours. It would be so easy for him to stay in bed, but if he did that, she might worry, and worse, she might not get breakfast.

It is our duty, Habibi, to care for our hungry brothers and sisters and to help the less fortunate. No exceptions.

That fear and Fatimah's childhood lessons were always enough to get him out of bed, even on the coldest days.

That and he enjoyed swimming.

Blackman's days started early and ended late. Between his classes, study groups, and internships, sometimes, it was all he could do to make it to bed at night. Most mornings, he woke up on the couch, which did nothing for the state of his leg. His doctor suggested an additional surgery to relieve the pain, but the last thing Blackman needed was to be laid up in bed. There was simply no time.

"You make time for what is important, Habibi," Fatimah chided as she made dinner in Blackman's apartment while he pored over a textbook, taking notes.

He pretended not to hear her, and she didn't belabor the point. She knew he was busy, but she worried about him.

He took too little time for himself. He had no life beyond law school, which was no way for a man to live, but Fatimah kept her thoughts to herself. Blackman's life had been changed irrevocably that night, and he was still processing all he had lost, which, she suspected, included the girl from the arena. Fatimah had watched as Blackman skated over to the girl that night, and she'd seen the joy on his face when the girl smiled at him. It was a joy she had never seen before, and her heart ached for him because it was possible that he had lost more than hockey that night.

Fatimah had asked about the girl a few times, but Blackman hadn't wanted to talk about her. Fatimah wanted to see that joy on his face again but knew better than to push him. He'd been through enough, and she knew how to be patient.

Fatimah was an incredibly patient woman.

Since his injury, he'd lost over fifty pounds and looked more like a marathoner than a former hockey player. The weight loss so alarmed Fatimah, she let herself into his apartment several times a week to leave him containers of his favorite foods and fill his refrigerator with fresh fruits and vegetables.

"You are a man, Habibi. You need more in your refrigerator than peanut butter and preserves," she said one evening while she prepared enough moussaka to feed him for a month.

"Don't forget the cheese sticks, Auntie," Blackman reminded.

"La sammah Allah," Fatimah said with a shake of her head. "Lest I forget the cheese sticks or the beer."

Blackman just smiled and continued to write his paper.

***

Like most years, Philadelphia seemed to go from winter to spring overnight. Blackman had been wearing a thick scarf and heavy winter coat over his suit the week before. Today, he was dressed for the office in a charcoal gray suit, a white shirt that had been crisp that morning, and a conservative dark blue tie, and even that felt like too much.

It was midafternoon when Blackman limped into the coffee shop halfway between the District Attorney's office, where he was interning, and his apartment. He was exhausted, and his leg ached. He just needed to rest a few minutes before finishing the long walk home. He was too proud to catch a cab, and he needed the exercise.

He bought a large black coffee and took a table by the window. He loosened his tie and shrugged off his suit coat. He folded it neatly over the chair next to him. He ran a hand through his dark hair and scratched the neat beard he had grown since starting law school and taking the internship at the DA's office. Fatimah approved of the beard.

"It makes you look very distinguished, Habibi. Very gentlemanly," she said one morning as she prepared his breakfast.

He hadn't intended to keep the beard, but he had to keep it after that.

"Is this seat taken?"

Blackman looked up, and it took him a moment to recognize the woman standing in front of him, but he recognized the cultured English accent immediately. As he did, he was surprised by the shock of resentment that lodged itself in his chest. He knew the dream he'd had about her in the hospital was nothing more than a drug induced fantasy, but still he had hoped he'd see her again. He'd hoped she'd make an effort to see him. After all, he'd played the game of his collegiate career just for the chance to have dinner with her, and she hadn't so much as called him. It wasn't like he was hard to track down. There couldn't be that many Blackman Smiths in the phonebook, and he assumed he was in the phonebook. Wasn't everyone in the phonebook?

Maggie didn't wait for an answer. She pulled out the chair opposite him and sat down. She smiled at him, but unlike the night at the bar or arena, her smile was hesitant, almost shy. She was dressed casually in a pair of loose fitting jeans that hung low on her narrow hips and a form fitting concert t-shirt of a female singer he'd never heard of. It hugged her full breasts, which Blackman tried to ignore. When she crossed her legs, he noticed that her heavy black Doc Marten boots needed a polish. Her red hair was loose around her shoulders, her face free of make-up.

She was gorgeous and seeing her broke his heart all over again. He didn't have time for this. For her. For whatever the hell this was going to be.

"You look good," she said, holding his eyes for a moment before looking away.

"Thank you," he said tightly. He worked hard to keep his face inscrutable and his voice toneless. He wanted her to leave, but he couldn't bear the thought of her leaving. So, he watched her, and when she looked back at him, she held him with that gaze of hers that made it hard for him to breathe.

"I wanted to see you after... after you got out of the hospital, but things kept coming up, and it never seemed like a good time," she said weakly. Her smile faltered, and her cheeks turned red with what he hoped was shame. Because he *really* wanted her to feel ashamed that she had abandoned him when he needed her most. He'd *needed* her to be there in the hospital with him. He *needed* her to hold his hand and tell him everything would be okay. He *needed* her to tell him he could still be a whole man even though he was going to limp for the rest of his life, and he'd know every time it was going to fucking rain because, evidently, he no longer needed Cecily Tynan and the channel six weather team to do that for him.

"Yeah, and I couldn't walk," he said coldly, and he was almost pleased to see her flinch.

And I couldn't go back to class, and I couldn't take you to dinner, and I couldn't go pro – not that I was anyway – and I was in pain all the time, and I'm sure your friends wouldn't have found me much fun to be around, and now I have a limp, so there's that, too. His thoughts were coming too quickly, and the sense of being ill used by this beautiful woman was almost too much for him to bear.

"That's not why," she started, but her voice trailed off as she looked at him more closely. Then she nodded more to herself than to him and cleared her throat.

"Anyway," she said, bracing her hands on the table. "It was...I just wanted... it was nice to see you again." She started to get up, and Blackman reached for her hand, his fingers covering hers. The feel of her skin against his shocked him like a live wire.

"Please," he said quickly. "Don't go. I'm sorry, I'm being rude. It's just been a long day," he lied, trying to meet her eyes, but she avoided looking at him, and he could see the hurt and embarrassment on her face. "Please," he repeated, suddenly desperate to keep her from leaving. "Let me buy you a cup of coffee. Maybe a muffin. Are you hungry?"

She seemed uncertain.

"The coffee's amazing, and the coffee cake is the best in the city," he said with his most charming smile.

She looked at him for a long moment. Wary. He had hurt her, and his stomach clenched painfully from the realization. He was back to being the asshole from the bar. He felt cold sweat gather beneath his collar. If she got up to leave, he'd have to limp after her, and wouldn't that be a sight on Broad Street?

Finally, she said slowly, "Coffee would be nice, and I could eat."

Blackman got up and tried not to limp too obviously as he walked to the counter.

They sat in the coffee shop for the rest of the afternoon.

He talked to her about everything. He told her about his dead mother and his emotionally and physically absent father. He told her how Fatimah had buried her own children, a boy and a girl, during the war and how his father had hired her to be his nanny, but now she was more like his mother. He told her how hard it was to be shy and big because people only saw his size, and most of the assumptions they made about him were predicated more on his appearance than anything else, and when it came to hockey, all his coaches ever wanted him to do was clear a path for the smaller, more agile players regardless of his own agility.

"I was always good at working the angles," he said thoughtfully. "But that wasn't what they wanted from me, and I wanted to be liked, to belong, so I didn't push it. I did what I was told because I wanted to play." He shrugged and stared at his coffee, waiting for Maggie to say something, but she didn't.

She just listened attentively, occasionally asking a question or nodding in agreement with something he said. Mainly, she just let him talk. She eventually got them more coffee and a couple more slabs of coffee cake, so they didn't have to give up their table.

Blackman told her about his father's law practice and how he made a fortune by ensuring guilty men went free. Blackman was grateful she didn't point out the hypocrisy of complaining about his father's morality while taking the man's money for college, law school, and the beautiful Center City apartment. He knew she was thinking it, but she did him the courtesy of not saying it, much like the night they first met in the bar.

He told her about his internship in the prosecutor's office and how his boss, an ADA of some repute, had all but guaranteed Blackman an entry level position as soon as he passed the bar.

"Someday," he confided quietly. "I'd like to be across the aisle from my father so I can show him the man I really am."

"And who's that?" She smiled. "The man you really are?"

Blackman met her eyes but didn't answer.

"Tell me about you," he said instead.

Her open expression closed off a little as her eyes shifted away from his to the foot traffic crossing in front of the window alongside them. As someone who spent too much time curating his own life, he recognized the signs of someone who wasn't entirely sure how they wanted to present theirs. He resisted the urge to question her, to put her on the stand of his own private courtroom inside this coffee shop.

"I'm the youngest of five children, all boys but me. I was a..." She paused to consider her words. "A bit of a surprise. My parents were older, and my mother suffered complications during the pregnancy. She died shortly after childbirth." She looked at him and waited for the usual platitudes people offered when she told them the tragic circumstances of her birth, but Blackman said nothing. He just waited.

"But," she continued with a soft smile. "My father and my brothers loved me, so my life isn't some kind of Dickensian novel. My father named me October Margaret and gave me my mother's last name, Rhymer. He wanted me to have her last name instead of his."

"Why October?"

"It was my mother's favorite month."

"Is it yours?"

"No, I prefer winter, but sometimes our names aren't really meant for us; they're meant for other people – to help them remember the past instead of the present."

Blackman knew better than most the truth of that statement.

The weight of a name.

"We're a close family, which is nice, but in a lot of ways, my brothers raised me. I was both their baby sister and their baby brother. I was spoiled, temperamental, and difficult to get along with if you weren't family." Her eyes settled somewhere over Blackman's left shoulder. "When I was fourteen, I got into some trouble, and my dad decided it was time for me to have some structure in my life. He sent me to a boarding school outside of the city, and when it came time for university, I stayed. One of my brothers, Fitz, lives here, and we share a house."

"Why did your dad send you here?" Blackman was curious. He, too, had been sent away, but it was because his mother died. He couldn't imagine what a child could do that would compel a father to put an ocean between her and the rest of her family.

Maggie shifted her eyes back to his, and she waited. Considering him, evaluating him.

"My brother Fitz is gay. Some guys were giving him a hard time, a really hard time. There was a fight." She looked down at her hands. "I hurt one of them. My father had to get involved. The boy recovered, but my father... was... concerned... embarrassed."

"Sending you all the way to the US seems rather extreme. Aren't there boarding schools in England?" He knew he needed to stop asking questions, but he couldn't. He wanted to know everything about her. He'd been dreaming about a version of her for years, but now he wanted to know the real woman.

"Dad felt a fresh start would be good for me. A place where my name wouldn't carry – the same kind of weight it carries back home," she said slowly.

"What kind of weight?" Blackman asked gently.

"Let's just say I don't come from the kind of family an aspiring ADA wants to be associated with." Maggie smiled sadly. Blackman stared at her curiously. *He* didn't come from the kind of family an aspiring ADA wanted to be associated with.

This time, he waited.

"My dad is the kind of guy who needs a lawyer like your dad," Maggie said finally.

"Husbands who murder their wives need a lawyer like my dad," Blackman replied dryly.

"Okay," Maggie said with a small chuckle. "Well, maybe not a lawyer *exactly* like your dad, but I think you understand what I mean."

Blackman considered this, then changed the subject.

"What are you studying?"

She thought about the question for a long time before answering, in part because she knew that wasn't the question he wanted to ask. She searched his face, and he wasn't exactly sure what she was looking for, but if he did know, he would have given it to her. He would have given her whatever she wanted. He didn't give a damn what her father or her brothers did for a living. There was an ocean between them, and she was here in front of him. And he wanted her as much, if not more than he had ever wanted anything in his life.

"Writing. I'm graduating with an MFA in May. Poetry. Then I'm starting a PhD program this summer. I'm going full academia. Publish or perish. I hope to teach at the university level when I'm done."

Blackman asked his next question carefully, hoping he didn't sound as desperate as he felt.

"Are you going home when you're done?"

Jesus, don't let her be going back to England. He had no idea what one had to do to become a lawyer in England, but he'd figure it out. He was an intelligent man. He'd follow her across an ocean, this woman he barely knew. Fuck his dreams of facing off with his father in a courtroom. If he could have this woman, he'd never think about his father again.

A slight smile played on her lips.

"No, I liked it here. There are plenty of opportunities in the city, and I've built a life here. So, I'm planning on staying."

"I like it here, too," he said, trying to slow his racing heart. He thought about reaching across the table and touching her hand again, but he didn't. He just smiled at her, and she returned his smile shyly as she reached for her coffee cake.

It was dark outside when they finally gave up their table at the coffee shop. They didn't talk about where to go next; they just fell into step with one another, heading in the direction of his apartment. They moved away from their personal stories and onto politics, current events, the arts, books, and music. They shared some opinions but not others, and there was just enough disagreement to keep the conversation interesting.

It didn't take long enough to arrive at Blackman's brick fronted brownstone. The streetlamps were on, and the shadows in the small park next to the building were deep. The street was typically quiet, but tonight it was silent and empty.

"This is me," Blackman said, stopping at his front steps.

"Nice neighborhood," Maggie said, looking around.

Blackman tried to meet her eyes, but she wouldn't look at him.

"You hungry? I could make us some dinner," he said softly.

"Not tonight. I have work to do," Maggie said with a small smile. Though there was something sad about her smile.

"Another night then?" Blackman asked.

She turned and looked at him, her eyes so sad it made him ache.

He fought the urge to stroke her face, to replace that sad look with something else, with anything else.

"Blackman," she said gently. "We can't."

"Why?" he asked, stepping closer to her.

She looked at him and shook her head slowly. "I didn't *not* call you because you got hurt, but because you were so – the way you looked at me, the goals you scored for me... no one's ever looked at me... that way. I'm not the girl who winds up with a guy like you." She reached out and touched his cheek. "I'm the girl who makes ..."

"Life altering mistakes?" he half teased.

She smiled, but her eyes were still sad. She ran her fingers over his soft beard and sighed. "No, not really, but someone like me would only hinder your career. It's better that we just leave this at coffee..."

"Is that what you want?" he asked, stepping closer to her.

If she hadn't hesitated, he might have let it go, let her go, but she did, and he couldn't.

He reached out for her hand and pulled her into the shadows of the small park. She didn't resist. Dropping his bag, he slipped his hands under her ass, picked her up like she weighed nothing, and pushed her against the brick wall of his building. Instinctively, she wrapped her legs around his waist as he moved his mouth over hers. She hesitated for a moment, then parted her lips. He slipped his tongue into her mouth as his body came alive. More alive than it had ever been.

In his life.

She wrapped her arms around him and groaned as he pushed his hips against her, his cock pressing thick and hard against her core. She thrust back, and he gasped. Sliding his hands under her t-shirt, he found her breasts encased in delicate lace. He dragged his thumbs over her hard nipples, and she dug her fingers into his shoulders. She moaned helplessly as he ground his body against hers. He slid his tongue over her jawline and down her neck. Her fingers moved to his face and pulled him back to her mouth, kissing him harder. Their tongues tangled as the heat between them built. She broke the kiss and pressed her lips against his ear, whimpering, "Blackman... Blackman, oh God."

He came with a sharp cry. She tightened her legs around him and cried out with him, and he was almost sure she had come, too. Blackman was shocked. He had never gotten off like that. As he gasped for air, he leaned against her, his heart beating so hard in his chest he was sure she could feel it. He'd been out of control. He had never felt need like that, had never felt such an incredible sense of desire. When he kissed her, all he could see was her naked on his bed surrounded by the luxurious white sheets and the heavy duvet that went with them. Maggie was the first woman he had ever brought home, and he hadn't even managed to get her inside his apartment, or even inside the building, for that matter.

Maggie was still gasping for air when he gently lowered her to the ground, setting her on her feet. She was either unsteady or unwilling to step away from him, so he held her tightly against him, grateful she hadn't pushed him away. Instead, she set her long fingered hands on his chest and leaned her forehead against him. She was shaking. They both were.

He bent his head down and kissed her hair; it smelled of lemongrass.

"Please, let me make you dinner," he said against her hair.

"No," she whispered into his chest.

The word was a blow, the worst hit he'd ever taken.

She kissed his chest and slowly stepped back from him.

He didn't move, allowing her to create space between them. He already missed the feel of her against him, the solidity of her soft body against his. He looked at her and waited for her to meet his eyes, which she did. Eventually. Her face was flushed, her lips swollen from his kisses. She smiled at him, and it nearly killed him.

"You," she said unsteadily. "Need to focus on law school, and I need to get ready for my PhD. This isn't our time," she said, touching his cheek.

He stirred in the mess in his pants while his chest constricted painfully.

"We–"

She wasn't wrong.

He barely slept now; how could he start something with her? And what about her? She was beginning a doctoral program in something he'd never heard of. How could they make space and time for each other right now? Intelligence and determination radiated from her; she was a high achiever like him, and she had set a lofty goal for herself. Academia was still very much a boys' club, and he could count on one hand the number of female teachers he'd had in undergraduate and law school. What she wanted to accomplish was going to be challenging enough and throwing in the distraction of a man wasn't a risk she could afford to make, but instead of thinking about herself, she was thinking about him.

Or maybe she was thinking about the two of them.

If she went upstairs with him, he would make her dinner and open that bottle of ridiculously expensive Rioja his father's newest girlfriend had given him on his birthday. Then they'd eat and drink and he'd pull her into the bathroom and into the shower. He'd wash her from head to toe and spend too much time on the parts of her he'd been fantasizing about since they first met. Then he'd make love to her in his bed, and after she fell asleep, he'd get up and work until dawn. He'd crawl back into bed with her, so she'd think that he'd been next to her all night. His work would get done, but hers would not.

She looked at him as if she could read his mind and was grateful that he had reached the same conclusion. She moved toward him again and wrapped her arms around him, pulling him close.

He held her tightly, afraid that when he let her go, he would never see her again.

After a few minutes, she stepped away, put her hands back on his chest, stood on her tiptoes, and kissed him gently. She stroked his cheek one more time as if she was trying to memorize the contours of his face.

He followed her out of the shadows and watched her walk down the street and hail a taxi at the corner. He waited until she climbed in, hoping she'd turn around one more time, but she didn't. Instead, she swiped her face with the back of her hand as the taxi pulled away.

Then she was gone.

Blackman walked inside, and after he locked his apartment door behind him, he walked to the bathroom, stripped out of his clothes, and climbed into a scalding hot shower. Leaning his forehead against the tile, he closed his eyes, letting the water pour over him.

His life had made him no stranger to feeling alone, but he had never felt this alone.

When he finally ran out of hot water, he turned off the shower and pulled on sweatpants and an old college t-shirt. He walked into the kitchen, heated one of Fatimah's many homemade meals, and opened a beer. Spreading his books across the dining room table, he ate, drank, and did his homework, working through the night. It was after three when he finally crawled into bed. His alarm went off at 5:30, and he rode his bike to the pool and started another day.

Chapter 4

Blackman graduated law school at the top of his class and passed the bar exam on his first attempt. Taking the proffered job at the DA's office, he made it clear from his first day that he planned on spending his career there. He wanted to be the best prosecutor in the DA's office and had no interest in the private sector or defense law. He thought Fatimah would die of pride when they met for dinner after his first day at work.

When he emerged from the building in his best charcoal gray suit and the subtle blue tie Fatimah had given him for his birthday, holding the handsome leather messenger bag his father's latest girlfriend had given him on their behalf, Fatimah slapped her hands over her mouth and let the tears roll down her pale face. Blackman pulled her into a hug and kissed the top of her head as she cried into his chest.

"All because of you, Auntie," he whispered in Arabic. "All for you, Auntie."

"All good things happen because of the grace of Allah, Habibi," she answered in English.

"Then I give thanks to Allah *and* you, Auntie," Blackman said in the Arabic she had so lovingly taught him.

Fatimah pulled his face down and kissed his cheek.

"Now," she said, wiping away her tears with a beautiful handkerchief Blackman had given her when he was still a child. "You must take your auntie to a beautiful restaurant because you are now a grown man with an important job."

"Of course, Auntie," Blackman said as he switched back to English and offered her his arm.

"And now I can focus on the task of finding you a wife," she said as she slipped her arm around his and patted it gently.

"Inshallah," Blackman said with a sigh, "but for now, Auntie, let us focus on getting us dinner."

***

Blackman hadn't been on a real date in quite some time. One that included dinner, drinks, or maybe some live music before sex. Then maybe a follow up phone call or, at the very least, a text. The last couple of dates included the drinks and the sex, but that was it. Then he begged off any additional dates because of work. He was growing bored of the late night departures and the excuses about why they shouldn't see each other again. Thankfully, most of the women he was attracted to and who were attracted to him, were just as busy and professionally driven as he and were generally more focused on climbing up the corporate ladder than climbing back into bed with him, so there were never any hard feelings.

The only one who seemed to mind was Fatimah.

"Blackman, why do you never bring these women home to meet me?" she asked one night after she shooed him out of his kitchen so she could cook dinner.

"These are not the women one brings home to meet you, Auntie," Blackman answered in Arabic while he read over emails at the dining room table.

"Then why do you spend time with them if they are not fit to meet me?"

"Because," he said, frowning at something on the screen, "a man needs companionship."

"No," Fatimah corrected sharply, "a boy needs companionship. A man needs a wife."

"I," Blackman said, looking up at Fatimah standing in his kitchen and wearing her favorite hijab, the one he had made for her birthday last year. "Do not need a wife."

Fatimah scoffed as she turned and looked at him. She pointed the heavy chef's knife she had been using to cut herbs at him. "Of course, you need a wife. Did I teach you nothing? Also, I will not be around forever, Habibi. I am old."

This time Blackman scoffed.

"You are timeless, Auntie, and I know that you will not leave me or this world before you hold my firstborn child."

She narrowed her eyes and turned away from him.

"How could Allah burden me with such an ungrateful child?" she muttered.

Blackman grinned as he started to type an email in English and chided Fatimah in Arabic. "Auntie, you have misspoken. You used burden instead of blessed and ungrateful instead of devoted. We will now have to work on your Arabic."

Fatimah muttered something else, and Blackman chuckled and continued to type.

Truth be told, he wasn't entirely sure this was an actual date or a one night stand sort of date, but either way, he had court in the morning and didn't have time to spend half the night rolling around in this woman's bed. Not that she wasn't worth the time or the effort. A former collegiate volleyball player, she was long and lithe, with the kind of long legs that went all the way to heaven. Her hair was thick and blonde, and her breasts seemed to defy gravity. And, of course, she was brilliant. Harvard and Yale or maybe the other way around; he really wasn't sure. She was a corporate lawyer who made three times his salary and drove a sexy little Mercedes coup he didn't quite fit into.

He suspected her interest in him had a little more to do with his father than himself.

They were sitting in one of the trendy new bars in his neighborhood. Close to his new loft, but she didn't know that, so he wasn't worried. She'd suggested it because it had been featured in *Philadelphia Magazine* as a place where all the hot new lawyers were spending their money. Blackman had been in a few times to watch a West Coast hockey game or Thursday night football when he didn't want to sit alone in his apartment.

Now he and the former collegiate volleyball player turned corporate lawyer sat at a high top sipping overpriced cocktails and picking at an egregiously priced charcuterie board. She was talking about work, some big client he wasn't familiar with, and he found himself staring past her at the college hockey game playing on one of the televisions above the bar. He had played both teams in college and was impressed with the improved style of play under their new coaches, at least one of whom he had played against himself.

"I'm sure your father remembers Martin from his Stanford days," she said as she reached for her drink.

There it is.

Blackman smiled, looking back at her. It was a shame his father had given up dating age inappropriate women after his last heart attack. Blackman wondered if his father would make an exception for this particular age inappropriate woman as he was between women at the moment.

"I'm sure he does. I'll see if he's available for brunch one Sunday. I'm sure he'd love to meet you," Blackman lied with a smile. It was a dick move, but he was feeling like a dick. He had no intention of introducing this woman to his father any more than he had any intention of having brunch with either one of them.

"That would be fantastic," she crooned. "I know just the place."

Her wide, genuine smile should have made him feel guilty, but he wasn't the type. He reached for his cocktail, wishing it was a beer, and surreptitiously checked his watch. 8:10. He'd been there for thirty minutes.

The front door opened, and he instinctively looked over as his boss, Jon Pierce, walked in.

Thank Christ.

If anyone could take his date off his hands, it was Jon Pierce.

In his mid-40s, John Pierce was a ruggedly handsome man who stood just over six feet tall with short salt and pepper hair and the strong, stocky build of a man who spent a fair amount of time in the gym. A former Marine and JAG lawyer, he was the most connected guy at the DA's office and had the worldliness a man like Blackman lacked. Never married, he went through women like M&M's, always on the prowl for the next woman to take up space in his bed.

"Blackman Smith, as I live and breathe," Jon said, walking over to the high top. "Shouldn't you be home getting ready for court?" His expensively tailored suit came from the kind of wardrobe that reminded everyone John Pierce came from old money because only old money could afford Jon Pierce's social conscience. Only old money could keep his dance card so full.

"Hi, Jon," Blackman said with a smile.

Jon leaned against the table and took an olive from the platter.

"I'm Jon Pierce. Blackman's boss," Jon said, extending a hand, and Blackman's date gripped it firmly.

"Wendy Jennings of Bailey, McNamara, and Williamson. Corporate Division."

"Really?" Jon said with a rakish grin. "Let me get a martini, and you can tell me all about that."

He walked to the bar, leaving Blackman with Wendy, who now seemed more interested in Jon Pierce than him. *Thank Christ.*

Blackman continued to make conversation with Wendy about the complexities of corporate law, as more friends from the office appeared. His date shifted from a one-on-one sort of thing to more of a group affair, and Blackman finally relaxed. Maybe he'd switch to beer, have one more drink, then slip out while Jon worked his magic on Wendy. Suddenly, the comfort and quiet of his apartment held an appeal it hadn't held earlier in the day.

When Jon returned with his martini and pulled up an extra chair, Wendy lost herself in conversation with him, and Blackman once again let his eyes drift over to the hockey game.

He watched the game, sipped his drink, and munched on the charcuterie board, never letting his eyes drift around the crowded bar until the commercial breaks. One commercial break, his eyes were drawn to a redhead with long wavy hair, leaning against the bar, talking with another woman. She wore tight blue jeans, heavy motorcycle boots, and a loose fitting green blouse that was unbuttoned so that the top of her black lace bra was visible.

Maggie.

He looked in the mirror behind the bar and caught her eye. She smiled at him.

His stomach flipped, and for a moment, he felt lightheaded. Then he gathered himself, took a deep breath, and turned back to – he blanked on her name for a moment – *Wendy* and Jon. He listened to their conversation for a little while and drained his drink. Then picked up a square of cheese and popped it into his mouth as he stood up casually. Neither Wendy nor Jon seemed to notice him leaving.

He walked to the bar with the casual gait of a long limbed man comfortable in his body and waited for the bartender to walk down to get his order. He was so close to Maggie he could smell her lemongrass shampoo. Her full attention was on her friends, but she took a half step back and intentionally or unintentionally brushed against him. For a moment, all he could think about was her body pressed against his, her legs wrapped around his waist, his hands cupping her breasts through her lace bra.

She slowly turned to him, those hazel eyes icy and electric.

"Hey," she said, her accented voice the sexiest thing he would ever hear.

"Hey yourself," he said as the bartender finally came over and asked him what he wanted. He ordered a beer, never once taking his eyes off Maggie.

"Congratulations on the job at the DA's office," Maggie said after a moment. "I hear you're making quite the name for yourself."

"How do you know that?" he asked.

"I'm a remarkably well informed woman," she said, and he knew her smile would be the end of him; it would wreck him for all other women for the rest of his life.

It already had.

"I passed the bar, and you didn't call," he said with faux disappointment. A smile playing at the corner of his mouth.

"I'm still in school," she said before taking a sip of wine.

"You're an academic. You'll always be in school," he observed. She chuckled, and he smiled. She looked past him to Wendy, who was clearly hanging on Jon's every word. Blackman didn't move his eyes from Maggie's face.

"Your date seems distracted," Maggie said as she shifted her gaze back to Blackman.

"She's not my date."

"She was."

"She isn't now."

Blackman was desperate to reach out and touch Maggie, to trace a finger along her cheek, over her jaw, down her neck, over the swell of her perfect breasts. He stirred in his pants just like he did whenever he saw her. Maggie seemed to read his mind and blushed.

"It's not polite to show up at a bar with one woman and then try to pick up another," she said, looking at his mouth. He suspected she was having similar thoughts because that night in the park next to his apartment building hadn't been one sided.

"Is that what I'm doing?" His voice was low, his eyes on her mouth. That beautiful mouth.

"I certainly hope so," she said, looking up at his eyes. Waiting.

"Well, in that case," he said in his best prosecutorial voice. "You are correct. I did indeed arrive with Ms. Wendy Jennings of Bailey, McNamara, and Williamson, corporate division, but—"

"Please tell me that is *not* how she introduces herself." Maggie laughed.

The bartender put a beer in front of Blackman, who picked it up and took a sip.

"Who's she talking to?" Maggie asked as she turned her head and looked at Wendy.

"My boss."

"She seems *really* interested in him."

"Half an hour ago, she was interested in my father," Blackman deadpanned.

Maggie snorted and reached for her wine. When she returned her glass to the bar, she gave Blackman an appraising look. He could tell she liked what she saw, and that knowledge buoyed his confidence. As a kid, he'd made a fool out of himself in front of her in a bar, and then won a hockey game for her. As a law student, he couldn't get her to give him a chance, but as a grown man, he was more than capable of picking her up in a bar.

And that was exactly what he was going to do.

"It's my friend's birthday," she said, her voice light and flirty.

"Happy birthday to your friend," he said, matching her tone.

"I'll pass on your birthday wishes. She just got out of a messy relationship, so she's planning on getting really drunk."

Just then, the friend in question yelled out, "Shots!!!"

Maggie winced.

"What about you," Blackman said leaning in closer. "Are you planning on getting sloppy drunk?"

Maggie shook her head solemnly. "No, I'm the designated sober friend. Two drinks, and then it's club soda for me. In any case, I have to teach tomorrow morning. Intro to 17th Century American Women Writers."

"Sounds fascinating. Maybe I'll sit in one day," Blackman said before he took another sip of his beer.

Maggie laughed that laugh he still dreamed about.

"It *is* fascinating, and maybe you should do that."

She finished her wine and Blackman ordered her another. She looked at him and cocked her head as if she was wrestling with some decision she seemed disappointed she'd have to make.

"You need to get back to your former date," she said after a moment.

"What if I don't want to?"

"It's the right thing to do," she said softly.

"What if I'm tired of doing the right thing?" he asked, picking up his beer.

"I have responsibilities. I can't leave these two on their own. They've been drinking since six," Maggie said sincerely.

"Maggie Rhymer: responsible adult friend," Blackman teased.

"We all have our burdens to bear." Maggie reached for her wine.

"Okay," Blackman said with his best lawyer's smile. "I'll make you a deal. I'll leave, but only if you agree to have dinner with me Friday night."

"Blackman," she sighed with a sly smile, and the sound of his name coming out of her mouth made him do more than just stir in his pants. If he wasn't careful, he'd have a full blown erection that his dress pants wouldn't be able to hide.

"That's blackmail."

"Not at all," he said with his own sly smile. "You can have dinner with me Friday night, *or* I can stay here all night and do shots with the birthday girl," he said, straightening up to his full height so he could look over Maggie's head to the birthday girl in question. He hit her with his sexiest come-fuck-me-smile and a wink, and the birthday girl turned bright red and looked away and laughed.

"Isn't that your friend from the bar? And the game? God, you're a loyal one, aren't you?" He smirked.

"Jesus, Blackman," Maggie laughed, pulling on his tie so hard he had to lean forward, and for a quick moment, he thought about kissing her. Just sweeping her into his arms and kissing her until she agreed to go home with him.

"Just say yes, and I'll get out of your hair," he said in a low, sexy voice. "Otherwise, it's tequila time."

"Fine," Maggie said, letting go of his tie.

"Pardon?" he asked, wanting her to say yes one more time.

"Yes, fine. I'll have dinner with you. Now go away," Maggie said more loudly.

Blackman gave her a megawatt grin as he pulled his wallet out of his back pocket, flipped it open, and withdrew a business card from it.

"Now, the question is, can I trust you?" he asked, putting on his most serious face. He reached over the bar and plucked a pen from a shot glass full of them. He stared at Maggie so intently that she blushed.

Again.

He didn't wait for her answer, just wrote his home address neatly on the back of the card, then added his cell phone number and held it out to her.

"Really. Can I trust you? I don't give my home address out to just anyone."

He didn't give out his home address, period.

She narrowed her eyes. "What about Wendy Jennings, corporate lawyer?"

"She thinks I live at the office," he said, his voice pitched low, as if he were sharing confidence. Maggie bit her bottom lip as she reached out and took the card from his hand. Her fingers brushed his, and she said in a gentle, private voice, "Yes, you can trust me."

He held onto the card for a moment longer, then let it go.

"Enjoy your night, and I'll see you Friday at seven. Don't be late, and bring red wine," he said with a grin. He wanted to make sure she understood he was no longer the awkward law student she'd left with a mess in his pants after they dry humped against a wall. This time, he wasn't letting her walk away without a fight.

She tapped the card against her lips before she slipped it into her back pocket. Resisting the urge to kiss her, he walked back to his table. He could feel her eyes on him the entire way, and this time, he didn't limp.

***

He had switched from beer to seltzer water. He had court in the morning, and he really needed to go home, but Maggie was here and not in his apartment, and he wasn't ready to walk away from her yet.

He knew she would call him and come to dinner on Friday night. They weren't kids anymore; it was time to see where this thing was going. He knew she was interested in him, but he also knew whatever made her walk away in the past, whatever made her unsure about him, whatever was holding her back, was still there. He might get one dinner out of her, but it was entirely possible he wouldn't get two. Unless he could make her believe whatever she was worried about wasn't worth worrying about.

Could it just be her family? Her father? Okay, maybe the guy was a nefarious type back in England, but England was three thousand miles away from Philadelphia. Maybe, Blackman thought as he sipped his seltzer water, it was him. Perhaps she didn't think her family would approve of him, of his job at the DA's office.

That was ridiculous, he told himself.

But is it?

Instead of staring at her all night like some sort of stalker, he talked with his colleagues and law school friends, who seemed to fill up the place.

Clearly, *Philadelphia Magazine* hadn't been exaggerating. This was definitely the place for lawyers to be seen.

Wendy and Jon had moved to a private table where they shared a bottle of expensive wine and the lobster risotto.

Occasionally—well more than occasionally – Blackman watched men walk over to the bar and chat up Maggie and her friends, but each time they were rebuffed gently but firmly, and each time they went on their way, except now.

Three guys in expensive suits, who had been sitting on Blackman's side of the room for the last hour or so, had made their way over to the three women. Rage swelled in Blackman's chest as he watched the biggest of the trio move closer to Maggie. There was something about him Blackman didn't like. He'd watched the man go to the bathroom more times than was probably necessary, and from where Blackman was sitting, the man's frenetic energy didn't seem to be coming from the beer he'd been drinking. More likely the coke he'd been snorting. The guy was probably about five foot ten, with the stocky build and broad shoulders of a guy who might have once played D2 college football but wasn't good enough for anything else. He probably wasn't good enough for D2. As the man talked to Maggie, he leaned in too close for Blackman's comfort but evidently not for Maggie's. She spoke to him quietly and patiently. If she knew Blackman was watching, she didn't let on. She was clearly a woman who could handle herself.

While the stocky one-time-football player ran interference, his friend, who was about the same size with dark hair and a pronounced widow's peak, focused on the birthday girl, who seemed uncomfortable with his attention. The smile she'd had on her face all night had been replaced by concern verging on outright fear, and Blackman didn't like it. Maggie tried to excuse herself and step around the stocky blond to get closer to her friend, but he blocked her, then leaned in and whispered something into her ear as he ran his fingers along the slope of one breast.

Blackman stood up so fast he knocked over his chair, but before he could take a step toward Maggie, she punched the blond in the throat, then took the side of his head and bounced it off the bar.

The man crumpled to the floor in a heap.

She stepped over him and pulled the dark haired man with the widow's peak roughly away from her friend. He turned around and caught Maggie across the face with the back of his hand. The blow didn't have enough force behind it to knock her off her feet, but it snapped her head back. Recovering quickly, she hit him with a quick three punch combination, breaking his nose with a resounding snap.

He hit the ground hard and awkwardly, staring up at her dazed. She lifted her foot as if she intended to stomp his head with her heavy motorcycle boot or maybe kick him, but before she could do anything, Blackman wrapped his arms around her waist, spun her away from the two men, and carried her toward the hallway leading to the bathrooms and the kitchen.

Considering the heft of her boots, it was entirely possible she could have fractured the guy's skull. A broken nose could be taken care of with a bag of ice, but a fractured skull required an ambulance and the police.

And he couldn't make that go away. Well, not easily.

He moved with Maggie pressed close to him. She seethed against him, shaking with fury.

"Put me the fuck down," she hissed.

He dropped her unceremoniously, and she stumbled. When she took a step toward the bleeding men and her crying friend, Blackman blocked her way.

"Get the fuck out of my way," she said sharply, loudly.

"No," he said with a calm voice that belied his pounding heart. He'd never actually witnessed a bar fight, let alone one that left two grown men bleeding on the floor. Two grown men he had fully intended to put on the floor himself.

Maggie tried to brush past him, and although he wasn't as broad as he'd been during his playing days, he was still a solid man. Blackman gently put his hands on her shoulders and pushed her back a step.

"Maggie, you need to take a breath. Your friend is fine," he said calmly, as soothingly as possible.

"She's scared," Maggie shot back defiantly.

Blackman turned back and saw Wendy comforting the crying woman while Jon and another friend from the office, Anthony Cortez, pulled the two bleeding men to their feet and pushed them toward the door. Raised voices carried a litany of swear words from the two dazed and humiliated men.

Seeing that Blackman was distracted, Maggie tried to get around him again, but he was too quick. He threw his arm out, blocked her way, then turned back to her and walked her backward until she was against the wall. He pulled an empty chair from a nearby table and gently pushed her into it.

She sat down, and her breathing began to slow. The adrenaline seemed to be wearing off, and a look of exhaustion and the beginnings of embarrassment settled over her face. Blackman knelt in front of her, swallowing back the pain in his bad leg, and pushed her hair away from her cheek. A dark bruise was starting to form, and he willed back the overwhelming desire to go outside and take apart the dark haired man.

"She needs some ice," Blackman called back to the bartender, who nodded and turned away.

Blackman pulled a handkerchief out of his pocket and wiped the blood from Maggie's bruised and bleeding knuckles.

"It's okay. Everything's okay," he said quietly. Her hands shook in his, and he resisted the urge to tenderly lean forward and kiss her forehead to gather her in his arms and hold her.

One of the waitresses came up behind him and handed him the ice. He took it, then gently placed it against Maggie's cheek. She inhaled sharply, and tears shone in her eyes.

"You're going to have to keep ice on that. It's going to bruise," he said.

Maggie nodded. She lifted a trembling hand and took the ice and pressed it against her face like she'd done it before. She lowered her eyes and stared at her bleeding knuckles.

"Hey," Blackman said softly.

She kept her eyes on her shaking hands.

"Maggie, sweetheart," he said gently, tilting her face up to look at him.

When she finally met his eyes, he could see the fury that had been there moments before dissolve into shame. Her eyes shone with tears.

"I need you to stay here, okay? I'm going to go outside and talk to those guys."

"Please don't," Maggie whispered.

"It's okay. Just stay here. Promise me," he said firmly.

After a moment, she nodded. Blackman stood up slowly, his bad leg aching with the effort. As he turned to walk outside, Maggie's two friends hurried over to her and knelt beside her, wrapping their arms around her.

Jon Pierce was standing in front of the dazed men, the third of whom was uninjured and holding an expensive Blackberry. He looked at Blackman with nervous eyes when Blackman stepped into the cold, still night. Blackman had straightened his tie, tucked in his shirt, and arranged his face into the cold scowl he wore during his hockey days. He stood at his full height and crossed his arms across his broad chest.

He looked dangerous.

And he knew it.

"That cunt hit me," the blond growled, seemingly unaware of Blackman's presence.

Blackberry guy blanched.

"Yes," Jon said patiently. "My office will be happy to file charges."

"Good. Fucking bitch had it coming." The blond smiled smugly.

"Yes, and first thing in the morning, Mr. Smith over there will be filing charges against you." Jon smiled a shark's smile.

"What the fuck are you talking about?" the blond sputtered. "That fucking bitch punched me in the face and broke my friend's nose. What do you mean you're pressing charges against me? Do you know who I am?"

"A guy who just got his ass handed to him by a girl?" Jon asked with raised eyebrows.

The blond seethed and turned to look at Blackberry guy.

Jon turned his attention to the dark haired man with the widow's peak and the badly broken nose.

"And as far as you go, there are fifty lawyers in that bar who will sign affidavits stating that you struck Ms. Rhymer *before* she handed you your ass. Those bruises are being documented as we speak, so if you would like to pursue legal action against Ms. Rhymer, I can promise you that *my* office will be happy to press charges against you for assault."

"This is bullshit," the blond yelled angrily at Jon, completely ignoring Blackman.

The dark haired man with the widow's peak and the broken nose looked uncertain, and unlike his blond friend, he was very much aware of Blackman's presence on the sidewalk, and he looked adequately afraid. From the size of his pupils, Blackman thought he had more than one thing to fear.

"Do you know who my father is?" the blond added, trying to look intimidating but failing.

"A man whose son is such a pussy he picked a fight with a girl and lost?" Jon smiled beatifically.

Blackman and the blond both stiffened.

"I'm sorry, son. Was that not the answer you were looking for? I mean, if you still have a little fight left in you, I'm sure my colleague here would be happy to take you back into that alley and show you what it's like to fight a man," Jon offered.

The blond finally turned and looked at Blackman. He didn't move.

"Now," Jon said. "I'm going to go back inside and check on Ms. Rhymer. Mr. Smith, here, will let me know what you decide." Jon turned for the door.

Before Jon had taken more than a step, Blackberry guy, who was clearly more sober or less stoned than his friends, said quickly, "I think it would be best if we just put this unfortunate incident behind us. Chalk it up to high spiritedness on everyone's part." He turned to his friends and made it a point *not* to use either of their names. "We'll be on our way. Come on."

Jon turned back before the two injured men could argue further. "Sounds good to me. Have a good evening, gentleman."

The three men exchanged looks, then walked away without another word.

Blackman watched them walk down the street, probably headed to another bar even though a trip to the ER wouldn't go amiss, especially for widow peak's nose. Blackman knew from experience that a break like that rarely healed well, having doled out enough of them during his hockey career.

After the three men disappeared around the corner, a taxi pulled up and idled. A minute later, Maggie and her friends emerged from the bar. Her friends climbed into the taxi, but Maggie lingered at the door for a moment.

"I'm sorry," she said, looking up at Blackman. Shame radiated off her in waves, and her hazel eyes were dull and red rimmed. The sight of her tugged at his heart, and it made him want to take her home, wrap her up in a warm blanket, and watch television with her until she fell asleep in his arms. He wanted to make her feel safe.

Blackman looked down at her, then wrapped his arms around her and pulled her into a loose hug. He kissed the top of her head. "Friday, seven o'clock. Don't be late."

She looked at him and shook her head sadly. "Blackman –"

"We had a deal," Blackman said sternly. "Seven sharp, and remember, bring *red* wine." He smiled and closed the door behind her after she climbed into the taxi. Then he thumped the roof twice and stepped away like a man who was used to putting women into taxis.

Standing there, he put his hands in his pants pockets and watched the taxi make a left at the corner. He heard Jon light a cigarette and inhale deeply.

"You think that's a good idea?" he said after he blew out a lungful of smoke into the still night air.

"What?" Blackman said, feigning ignorance, but his voice was cold and his mouth tight. He stood up a little straighter and waited patiently. He knew what was coming.

"You and October Rhymer?"

Blackman watched his boss closely as the older man leaned against the brick façade of the building and inhaled deeply on his cigarette.

"*Maggie* Rhymer," Blackman corrected. "How do you know her?"

Jon blew out a stream of smoke.

"I know her father. Actually, I know *of* her father and her family. She didn't tell you?"

"All she said was her family – that she came from a family that an up and coming prosecutor might not want to be associated with," Blackman said carefully.

Jon took another drag off his cigarette and blew out another stream of smoke.

"She's not wrong," he said with a shrug.

"Is *she* up to something illegal?" Blackman asked. The care he had put into his early comment abandoned.

"Nope," Jon replied casually. He watched Blackman closely through the smoke of his cigarette.

"The brother she lives with?" Blackman asked cooly.

She'd been gone less than five minutes, and he missed her so much he ached. He hadn't even thought to get her number so he could call her and make sure she got home okay. He wanted to remind her to ice her knuckles and her face and to take a hot bath because there was nothing better for coming down off an adrenaline high than a hot bath with some Epsom Salts. He wondered if she had any back at her house. Maybe he should pick some up for her or some of those nice bath bombs that Fatimah was always talking about. Maybe he could figure out her address and *not* look like a serial killer.

"We thought so a few years ago, but, no, he's not," Jon said, bringing Blackman back to the present. "Those two are far, far removed from the family business. Her brother owns a gallery and fancies himself a sort of patron of the arts. He's as gay as the day is long."

"And she's a student," Blackman added. "Her dad sent her away when she was a teenager. Boarding school."

"I heard. How do you know her?" Jon asked looking at Blackman closely, curiously.

"We met in college," Blackman answered, holding his boss' eyes.

Jon looked at him, then huffed a laugh.

"Don't tell me that's the girl you won that hockey game for?"

Blackman ignored the question.

"Is this going to be a problem? Her and me?" Blackman asked.

Jon pitched his cigarette into the gutter and blew out one last stream of smoke. He seemed to consider the question before answering. It might not be an easy answer, and Blackman knew if he didn't like it, he'd have to make some hard choices. Choices, he realized suddenly, he was all too willing to make. He'd waited too long for tonight to do anything else.

"Not for me," Jon said, then popped a piece of gum into his mouth and chewed thoughtfully. "Mind if I take your date home?"

Blackman shook his head.

"No. Not at all."

"Good." Jon turned around and walked back into the bar.

Blackman waited a moment, then followed him back inside. Everything was back to normal, the fight forgotten. He found one of the waitresses and settled up for himself, Wendy, and Jon. Figuring, as he signed the credit card slip and left a hefty tip, it was the least he could do.

Chapter 5

When Blackman let himself into his apartment a little after 5:30 on Friday evening, the first thing he noticed was how clean the place smelled. He was a neat man; he knew how to clean his apartment, but this smelled like *Fatimah* clean. He had no idea how she did it, how she made a room smell so good, but she did. And no matter how often he tried to emulate her cleaning routine over the years, he'd never managed it. Pulling his phone out of his pocket, he dialed her number.

"Auntie –"

"Hush, Habibi, and listen carefully. There is lamb marinating in the refrigerator, and the rice cooker will finish at 7:30. I made fresh flatbread this morning. It's on the counter. And there are the good olives next to the lamb. I went to your favorite market this afternoon."

"Auntie, I only asked you to pick up a few things. I can cook. Really," Blackman said a little impatiently. "*You* taught me how to cook."

"Yes, my dear, but you are a busy man, and you cannot put together a wonderful meal in sixty minutes. It is simply not long enough, and you still need to shower."

"Auntie," Blackman sighed, looking at the vase full of wildflowers on the dining room table.

"Please, Habibi, promise me one thing," Fatimah implored.

Blackman groaned, but Fatimah ignored him.

"Please do not overcook the lamb."

"Of course, I won't overcook the lamb. *I know how to cook*," he repeated loudly.

"Yes, yes, good boy. Now, when will I meet this girl?" Fatimah continued as if he hadn't said just reminded her that he knew how to cook a little too loudly.

"I'm going now, Auntie."

"I will call tomorrow, and we will have tea, and you will tell me all about her."

"Of course, Auntie," Blackman sighed. "I love you."

"Yes, yes, I love you, too, but just be careful not..."

"Goodbye, Auntie."

Ending the call, he walked to the bathroom to take a long shower. Like everything else in the apartment, his bathroom was spotless.

***

At seven o'clock exactly, the buzzer sounded.

Blackman hit the button, then propped open the apartment door, and went back to the kitchen, where he was putting the finishing touches on a colorful platter of cut vegetables, olives, and ramekins full of Fatimah's homemade hummus.

I'll never ask that woman to go to the Lebanese market for me again.

As he set the platter on the dining room table, a sharp knock came from the front door.

"Come in," he called.

Maggie stepped through the door and closed it behind her. The sight of her took his breath away. She was dressed in wide leg black wool pants and a dark red silk blouse that cinched at her side, showing off her narrow waist and full breasts. Her long hair was piled high on her head in some kind of complicated looking bun. Her make-up was a little dark for his taste, but it did wonderful things for her hazel eyes. She stood tall in expensive black stilettos and a black great coat hung from her strong shoulders, completing the look. In the crook of her left arm, she held a large, expensive leather bag where two bottles of wine protruded. Diamond studs shone in her ears, and a heavy silver knot hung around her neck.

She was gorgeous beyond words, and he felt ridiculously underdressed in faded blue jeans, a dark blue button-down shirt, and his old brown Oxford shoes. She must have read his face because she laughed.

"My brother's gallery is having an event this evening. I usually work them, but obviously, I had plans. But I needed to stop by to make sure everything was sorted. The wait staff are always more attentive when they think I'm writing the checks at the end of the night. Fitz never pays attention to the wait staff," she said, extracting two bottles of expensive red wine from her bag. "I didn't have time to stop by a wine shop, but I did manage to lift these before I left."

She held the bottles out to Blackman, who took them and set them on the dining room table. He helped Maggie out of her coat and hung it on the old fashioned coat rack he had found in one of the many antique shops in the neighborhood. Then he took the bottles and carried them into the kitchen.

"Please, make yourself at home," he said from the kitchen, putting one of the bottles into the wine fridge and uncorking the other. He poured the wine into two glasses and brought one to Maggie as she looked around the spacious, open concept apartment.

She loved the exposed brick walls and wood beams that ran across the ceiling. Her stilettos clicked on the hardwood floor until she reached one of the beautiful Persian rugs. She took in the black and white nature landscapes hanging from the walls and the neatly organized bookshelves that contained a wide array of books, all of which had broken spines. His sofa and chairs were custom made for a man his size, and the rest of the furniture was a pale wood that set off the deep red of the brick.

The surfaces were almost entirely bare except for the framed pictures of him and who she assumed was Fatimah. Even in his youth, he towered over her veiled, petite form. In every picture, her face shone with uncontainable pride. Maggie took her time with the pictures, looking at them closely as if they told the story of his life. He had always been a handsome young man, and she wondered whom he favored: his dead mother or absent father.

Heavy brass lamps stood over one end of the sofa and a reading chair, but most of the light in the space came from the floor to ceiling windows.

Blackman's bedroom was set up in the far corner of the apartment. His king sized mattress sat on a wooden frame, and another bookcase was built into the headboard. Another brass lamp stood over the left side of the bed. A worn brown teddy bear leaned against the big pillows.

Maggie turned away from the bedroom. Her eyes were drawn back to the photographs, which seemed to be the only personal things in the beautiful space—well, and the teddy bear. Blackman followed Maggie's gaze back to the photographs, pointing to a picture that looked like it had been taken in Paris.

"Fatimah single handedly got me through high school French. Dad sent us to Paris one summer upon her insistence, and she wouldn't let me speak a word of English. If I couldn't say it in French, I couldn't have it, or I couldn't do it. It was torture," Blackman said with a smile that conveyed the summer had been anything but torture. In fact, it was one of the best summers of his life.

"Did you learn French?" Maggie asked, looking up at Blackman. Even in the stilettos, he was still much taller than she.

"I'm fluent." He grinned. "She was merciless. I'm also fluent in Arabic, and I can get by in Spanish, but it's not always pretty."

"Anything else?" Maggie asked with a smile.

"I can order bar food in Portuguese, Italian, and Czech."

Maggie laughed and followed him back to the dining room table, where she kicked off her shoes and sat in one of the large wooden chairs. Leaning back, she put her bare feet on the chair in front of her, watching Blackman as he worked in the kitchen.

"And in addition to teaching you French and Arabic, she taught you how to cook?" Maggie asked, dragging a piece of purple cauliflower through the hummus. She moaned with pleasure; it was the best hummus she had ever tasted.

"Oh my God, did you make this?" she asked as soon as she swallowed.

"No," Blackman admitted. "But I make hummus, and it's just as good." That was a lie. His was good, but it was not as good as Fatimah's.

Maggie chuckled and picked up another vegetable, scooping more hummus. "I'm sure," she said with a knowing smile.

Dinner was much easier than Blackman had imagined. They ate his perfectly cooked lamb, which he would be sure to tell Fatimah about when he got the chance. The fact that she even thought he would burn the lamb annoyed him. He knew how to cook lamb. He was grateful that Maggie preferred it on the rare side because there was nothing worse than overcooked lamb.

Maggie talked at length about her research and her poetry, and he loved how her face lit up when she talked about her studies. They talked about their time in undergrad, some of the professors they knew, and some of the friends they'd had in common without even realizing it.

Blackman talked about work, and the case he was working on with Jon Pierce, and how much he enjoyed working for the DA's office. Maggie talked about her brother and his gallery. Admitting how little she knew about art despite her AP Art History class from boarding school and the art history classes she took in college at her brother's insistence.

"He's a hopeless artist," she confided as Blackman refilled her wineglass. "But he's a wonderful businessman. He knows how to manage an artist's money, so they don't starve, or worse, give up. Honestly, there are worse things for a failed artist to do."

She tried to help Blackman with the dishes, but he shooed her out of the kitchen the same way Fatimah shooed him away on the nights she cooked. He sent Maggie off with a mug of tea and a plate of Baklava.

"Tell me," she said, folding her legs beneath her as she settled into a corner of the oversized sofa. "How much of that dinner was you, and how much was Fatimah?"

Blackman groaned as he carried his mug of tea and sat down on the other end of the sofa.

"I cooked the lamb," he admitted after a long moment.

Maggie's laugh was rich and alive, echoing around an apartment that was typically too quiet. She filled up the space in ways he only dreamed of.

"But in my defense," he said quickly. "I only asked her to pick up olives at the Lebanese market. I swear to God. Next thing I know, I come home, and the apartment smells Fatimah clean..."

"Fatimah clean?" Maggie asked with an arched eyebrow.

Blackman nodded solemnly.

"Look, I'm a neat person, and I clean my apartment, but no matter what I do, I can never get it to smell the way Fatimah makes it smell. It's impossible." He shook his head. "I mean literally impossible. I've tried. So many times."

His seriousness made Maggie laugh.

"Oh my God, she's still your nanny!"

"No," Blackman said, thinking Fatimah had never really been his nanny, but he didn't want to spoil the light mood of the evening. "I do my laundry."

"But," Maggie said with a mischievous twinkle in her eye. "She..."

Blackman blushed.

Maggie waited.

"She buys all my bed linens," he admitted as a blush crept over his cheeks.

Maggie howled with laughter, setting her tea mug on a coaster on the coffee table, afraid she'd spill tea on the beautiful carpet.

"Oh my God, that's priceless!" She clapped a hand over her mouth in a failed attempt to stifle her laughter. Blackman adored the way her eyes narrowed when she laughed, the way her whole body shook with the force of her delight. He wanted to kiss her so badly he didn't know what to do with himself. Leaning forward, he set his mug on the table, then leaned back and did his best Fatimah impression.

"Habibi, you are an American man, and although I disapprove, I know someday you will bring a woman home, and you cannot expect such a woman to sleep on the terrible sheets you buy. An American woman expects something better."

"Oh no!" Maggie exclaimed, wiping away the tears gathered in the corners of her eyes. "She sounds lovely. So doting. Does she have children of her own, or are you it?"

Blackman reached for his tea and took a sip before answering.

"She had two children, but she lost them in a bombing in Lebanon years ago."

Maggie's face turned serious, which was exactly what he didn't want.

"I'm sorry," she said softly,

Blackman set the mug down again.

"She was young, and they were toddlers. She never talks about a husband, so I'm not sure if he left after the bombing or before, but either way, she left Lebanon. She spent some time teaching in Egypt before she came here. I really don't know how my dad found her, but I guess we were both lucky he did." Blackman paused for a moment. "I suppose we were each other's second chance at a family."

Maggie leaned over and touched his hand gently. Her skin was warm and soft, everything he'd ever wanted.

"For the record, counselor, I'm not planning on seeing your sheets," she said with a serious face.

"Faitmah," Blackman deadpanned, "will be so disappointed."

Maggie snorted.

The evening passed as they sat quietly on the sofa, watching the flames dance in the gas fireplace, listening to soft acoustic music playing on the stereo. It wasn't cold enough for a fire, but Blackman liked the idea of one, and it turned out that so did Maggie. It was late, and he knew she was thinking about going home, but so far, she hadn't said anything.

The tea was gone, as was the Baklava, and the conversation had petered out maybe twenty minutes ago. He was desperate for her to stay, for her to fall asleep in his bed, but he didn't want her to think that was the reason he had invited her over instead of taking her out, that having her over and cooking her dinner was just a prelude to sex. He reached out and twirled a strand of her vibrant red hair in his long fingers. She had taken her bun down some time ago, and her hair hung loose around her shoulders. It was soft and smelled of vanilla and honey. She leaned her head back on the sofa and looked at him. He could see the bruise faint beneath her make-up.

"I wanted to kill him. The man from the bar the other night. When he touched you," Blackman admitted, his voice soft.

"I'm glad you didn't," she murmured. Her eyes were bright in the firelight. He moved his thumb to her cheek, then to her jawline, to the shell of her ear. She shivered beneath his touch.

"I didn't invite you here for this," he said.

"No, you invited me here for dinner," she said with a sigh as he moved his hand down to her nape and massaged it gently. She closed her eyes.

"Do you want me to stop?"

She didn't say anything for a minute, maybe two. Then she opened her eyes and pinned him with the icy stare that had been driving him crazy for years.

"My father is an arms dealer," Maggie said, her voice holding no hint of shame. Blackman nodded his head, continuing to massage her neck.

"I know." He was grateful she trusted him enough to tell him.

"On paper, he runs a security firm, but that isn't what he does," she continued. "He's been to jail, but only when he was young." She held his eyes, and he could tell she was gauging his reaction. Waiting for his judgment.

"I know that, too," he replied. Maggie nodded more to herself than to him.

"My other brothers, they work for him. Fitz isn't involved. He doesn't want to be. Nick, my oldest brother, will take over one day. He'll run the business, keep it in the family."

Blackman stayed silent, not wanting to push for more. He waited for her to tell her story the way she wanted to tell it.

"I love my father and my brothers. I spend the holidays with them. We have a villa in Greece, a home in France, and this old stone monstrosity in the Scottish Highlands, which is a bitch to heat in the winter. I love my family, and I'm not ashamed of them or what they do." There was a defiance in her eyes Blackman loved. She *loved* her family, and she wanted him to know that because if he couldn't handle that, then he couldn't handle her. She waited, and Blackman felt like, this time, she was waiting to judge him. Waiting to see what he was made of.

Blackman looked at her for a long moment, her face glowing in the firelight. Then took a deep, centering breath.

"My father's been married five times, and he's cheated on all his wives. He'll fuck any woman with a pulse. He only hired Fatimah because he was sure *she* wouldn't fuck *him*. He made his fortune making sure wife murderers and pedophiles from good families didn't go to jail. He has no moral compass, and I'm ashamed he would defend such people, even when he knows they're guilty."

He paused, and she waited. Her eyes never wavered from his.

"I don't love my father; I don't even like him, and if not for Fatimah, I'd never talk to him. But I took his money for college and law school, and I didn't complain when he rented me an embarrassingly big apartment in college, or when he bought me this place. Honestly, I think it's the least he can do because he never wanted me. He doesn't love me."

He watched Maggie consider his words.

"No, Blackman," she said softly. "I don't want you to stop."

Blackman leaned forward, brushing his lips against hers. The kiss was soft, tentative. A world away from the desperation he felt outside his apartment on that warm spring night. This time, he was going to be patient. This time, he was going to kiss her and touch her the way she deserved.

She leaned into the kiss, set one trembling hand against his face, and opened her mouth slowly, slipping her tongue into his mouth. He breathed her in, pulling her against him. Their kiss grew in heat and intensity as he ran his hands over her strong back and down her legs. Finally, she put her hands on his chest and slowly broke the kiss.

He searched her eyes, wondering if he had done something wrong. Her breathing was ragged, and her face was flushed, and her eyes shone in the firelight.

"Blackman."

He covered her hands with his own. "Maggie," he breathed her name like he was praying.

She took a deep breath.

"I –uhhh – my whole life has been school – studying – writing – there has never been time for boys," she paused and held his eyes. "For men."

Blackman looked at her for a moment before her words finally clicked into place. He took her hands in his, brought them gently to his lips, and kissed them. Her knuckles were still bruised, and they looked painful.

"Do you want to stop?" he asked, and he meant it. If she wanted him to stop, he would. If she wanted him to hold her until dawn or put her in a cab home, he would do that, too. He would do whatever she wanted.

He'd waited this long for her; he could wait longer. He could be patient. He could be a good man.

"No, I don't want to stop ... I just wanted you... to know," she said shyly.

At that moment, Blackman was sure he finally understood what love felt like. He stood up slowly and pulled Maggie to her feet. He led her to his bed and laid her down gently. Then stretched out alongside her and ran his fingers over her face.

"You are the most beautiful woman I've ever known."

He leaned forward and kissed her, and she wrapped her arms around him, pulling him close. She was lean and soft against him, and he ached for her. He moved his lips over her jawline, then down her neck as he slid his hand gently over the swell of her breast. She gasped as he painted kisses on her chest. He unfastened her shirt and pulled it open, exposing a black lace bra. She helped him take off the shirt, and he dropped it to the floor.

"God, you're incredible," he whispered as he ran his hands over her full breasts. He brought his lips to one nipple, teasing it through the lace. She writhed beneath him, panting, and a thrill shot through him. He was the first man to do this to her, to touch her this way, to drive her wild, to please her.

And God, I want to please her.

Unhooking her bra, he dropped it on top of the silk shirt. Then cupped her breasts gently, running his thumbs over her hard nipples. Swirling his tongue around one breast, then the other, until her cries became desperate.

I need to slow down. Take my time.

He moved to her stomach and kissed her gently, dipping his tongue into her navel. She ran her hands through his hair and arched into him. He slowly pulled off her wool pants, exposing long, strong legs. His long fingers ran up and down her legs, reveling in the softness of her skin and the scent of vanilla.

He looked up at her and watched as he ran his fingers gently over the hot, wet lace of her panties. Her eyes opened wide as she gasped.

He kissed her stomach, pulling off her panties.

She was gloriously naked, and he took in the indescribable beauty of her body. Every dream he had of her over the years didn't do her justice. She was beyond his imagination.

He kissed the base of her belly gently, then got off the bed to kneel in front of her. He pulled her close, kissing the inside of her thighs, moving his way slowly toward the center of her.

"Blackman," she moaned helplessly as he slid his tongue over her, into her.

Her cry was loud and desperate, and she let go of his hair and fisted the duvet, panting. She moved with him as he slipped one finger and then another into her, shocked by the unbearable tightness of her. His tongue deep within her, then over her clit.

"Please," she begged. "Don't stop. Oh, God, Blackman..." Her voice cracked, and a sob escaped her. He suckled her clit as he stroked her. Deeply. She arched her back, yelling out, trembling beneath him. Her orgasm seemed to take her by surprise with its speed and intensity. When he was sure she was finished, he laid his cheek against her belly and held her tightly.

Slowly, he moved back onto the bed and gathered her in his arms. She was still trembling, and when he ran a thumb over her cheeks, he could feel wetness.

"Did I hurt you?" he asked, suddenly afraid, searching her shining eyes.

"No," she whispered. "It was beautiful."

After a few minutes, her breathing steadied, and she turned to him. With trembling fingers, she unbuttoned his shirt, and he helped her take it off. She ran her fingers over his strong chest and the dusting of fine, black hair. She kissed his chest gently, running her tongue over his nipples. He breathed in sharply as she ran her fingers down his stomach and over the line of fine black hair, pointing toward his aching erection. She unbuttoned his jeans, and he lifted his hips so she could pull them and his boxers off. He felt her looking at him as she slid her hands over his aching cock. He gasped as she stroked him, but he took her hand and moved it away.

If she continued, it would result in a repeat of the night outside of his apartment.

Instead, he pulled her up to him and pushed down the duvet so they could slip beneath the covers. He kissed her breathless as he ran his hands down her back and over the swell of her backside. She opened her thighs, and he slipped his fingers into her hot center stroking her as she moaned into his mouth.

Stilling his hand, she broke the kiss, looking at him, searching his eyes.

"Please," she whispered.

He turned over and reached into his bedside table, but she stopped him. "I'm on the pill," she murmured. "I'm safe."

Blackman met her eyes and nodded. "I've been tested. I'm safe, too. I've never... I always use a condom."

Maggie touched his face with trembling hands, and he leaned down to kiss her gently, slowly. Then the heat between them built, and their kisses became hungry, desperate. He moved over her and settled himself between her legs.

"I don't want to hurt you," he said against her lips.

"I know." She looked at him with so much trust and affection that it was hard for him to breathe.

"I'll go slow," he promised. "I'll do whatever you need."

She held his gaze and wrapped her legs around his hips.

He moved more slowly than he ever had. Up until now, sex had always been sex, an itch that needed to be scratched. Not to say he hadn't enjoyed it or that he didn't like the women he fucked, but he'd never been in love with them, even on the rare occasions they seemed to think they were in love with him.

And he'd never had a woman in his bed.

And at that moment, he understood why. He'd never brought a woman home because the only woman he had ever wanted to bring home was finally here with him.

He entered Maggie slowly as she gasped and tensed beneath him. He waited for her to adjust to him, for her to let him know that she was ready, and when she did, he pushed deeper. She was wet and tight and felt like nothing he'd ever experienced. She was perfection. She moved slowly, moving with him, until she had taken all of him. She ran her hands over his back and buried her face in his neck, her breath hot against him as they moved together.

He listened to her breathe, and then to her moan as they found their rhythm. Dipping his face down, he kissed her. He reached for her breast, ran his thumb over her hard nipple, and she moved her hands down to his backside, pulling him deeper.

He kissed her neck and then her ear. Sliding his tongue over the shell, he whispered, "My beautiful Maggie. You feel so good. So good..."

"Don't stop... God...I'm so close..." Maggie said breathlessly.

"Come for me, Maggie... just for me..." He desperately wanted her to say his name the way she had that night in the park, her body hot against him.

"Please," he begged, begging her to say his name. If he could hear her say it, he'd be alive for the first time in his entire life. Truly alive. Truly worthy.

Truly loved.

"Blackman," she cried, finding his eyes, holding them. Unflinching. Bare and vulnerable, and in that moment, he was entirely hers. There was nothing he wouldn't do for her.

Nothing.

"Blackman... please... God... I'm..."

He felt her tighten around him and watched her face as she came undone.

"Blackman," she cried out sharply, gripping him.

And with a roar, he let himself go. He imagined pouring himself into her, giving her everything he had. His orgasm lasted so long that lights flashed at the corners of his vision. He had never come like that, and when he finished, he struggled to hold his weight on his arms so he didn't crush her. Sensing his struggle, she moved to his side and pulled him against her. Wrapping her arms around him, kissing him gently.

This time, he was shaking.

Until this moment, Blackman had thought he had never been in love, but the fact of the matter was he had been in love with this woman since he was barely twenty-one, and when he looked at her sleepy, satisfied face, he knew he would love her for the rest of his life.

Chapter 6

Blackman had the best night's sleep of his life. He woke up Saturday morning and stared at Maggie sleeping beside him with a sense of awe. She was on her stomach, her red hair tangled on the pillow. She snored softly, and during the night, she had pushed the covers down so they were settled around her waist. He looked at the strong expanse of her back. She had the muscles of a woman who worked out regularly. Across the top of her spine was a long tattoo of a mountain range in shades of blue and purple. Fine script beneath it read: *Miles to go before I sleep...*

He rolled onto his side, kissed her shoulder softly, and settled his hand on her back. Closing his eyes, he fell back asleep.

The next time he woke, the bed was empty. He sat up, inhaling the smell of brewing coffee. Slipping out of bed, he pulled on a pair of warm-up pants and a t-shirt from a drawer built into the bed frame. Barefoot, he walked into the kitchen, where Maggie stood in one of his old hockey jerseys, sipping a mug of coffee. It was so big on her that it hung down to her knees. Her hair was pulled into a loose knot. He walked over to her, wrapped his arms around her, and kissed the top of her head.

"Good morning," she murmured, setting down her coffee mug and turning around so she could wrap her arms around him.

"Good morning, you look good in that," he said as he leaned down and kissed her neck. How many nights had he fantasized about her wearing nothing but his hockey jersey, and now she was standing in his kitchen like a fantasy incarnate. He stirred in his pants, and he wanted nothing more than to take her back to bed.

"I made coffee, and I found some muffins in the fridge. I hope you don't mind. They're in the toaster oven," she said, leaning her cheek against his chest.

"Not at all. The coffee smells good, and you look amazing," he said, looking down at her.

"I bet I never told you 42 is my favorite number." She smiled shyly.

"Well," Blackman said, tilting his head. "It *is* the meaning of life."

"All roads lead to the *Hitchhiker's Guide to the Galaxy*. I always wondered if you were that geeky or if 42 meant something else to you."

"I prefer *well read*," he said with a grin.

"I bet you do," she said with a laugh. She pulled him close and hugged him again, then gently stepped away and walked to the toaster oven, pulling out the warm muffins. She put them on a plate and cut them in half. She set them on the counter as Blackman poured himself a cup of coffee. She watched him closely, and when he looked at her, there was something a little closed off about her expression, like a woman who was concerned about something but trying not to appear concerned.

He, in turn, was not concerned about anything.

She turned her attention to the plate of muffins, tore off a piece, and popped it into her mouth. She chewed thoughtfully, and unlike last night, this morning, she seemed unsure of herself.

"I have a study group today. At noon. And I can't be late," she said, avoiding his eyes.

He smiled and picked up half a muffin and ate it. He watched her as he chewed.

"Okay, that's good because I have work to do. Why don't we get together for dinner around six? I'll pick you up at your place. Do you like Cuban?"

She looked up at him, and he could see the gears in her head turning.

"You don't have to... I mean, I'm sure you already have plans..."

If Blackman had been a different man, a younger man, he would have been hurt by her comment. He would have construed it as an admission that she herself had plans. But he wasn't the ten year old boy who'd been rejected by his mother's family anymore. He was the man who had been loved unconditionally by Fatimah. He knew he was good enough for Maggie, and more importantly, he knew she wanted him. No woman went to bed with a man, lost her virginity to a man at this age, only to reject him in the morning. No, this was the posturing of a woman who was preparing herself for rejection. She was giving him an out because she was unsure he really wanted her, or at the very least wanted something more than last night with her.

But he definitely wanted more.

Much more.

And he'd wanted more for years.

For fucking lifetimes.

He picked her up in one fluid motion and set her on the counter. Stepping between her legs, all swagger and confidence.

"I do have plans," he said as he kissed her neck gently. "I'm having Cuban with you."

"Blackman, is this really what you want?" she asked biting her lip to stifle a moan as he moved his lips to the sensitive skin just below her ear.

But he knew that wasn't what she was asking. She was asking, *Am I really what you want?*

"Yes." He didn't hesitate.

"I'm an academic," she said, pushing him away so she could see his face, meet his eyes. "My studies are everything to me."

"That's fine. We're both ambitious, and it's not like we're the only ambitious couple out there. In general, we don't have much time for people, but we can make time for each other. Can you do that? Can you make time for me, Maggie?" He hoped the answer he wanted to hear was the answer she was willing to give.

She searched his eyes, and after finding whatever she'd been looking for, nodded.

"Yes."

"Good. Because I can make time for you. I *want* to make time for you."

She opened her mouth to say something, but then decided against it.

Blackman leaned into her, pressing his forehead to hers. "Tell me you don't want this, tell me you don't want me, that last night meant nothing to you, and you can walk out of here, and I'll never bother you again. No harm, no foul. Tell me that, and I'll call you a cab." He stepped closer to her. He ached for her, and he knew he was taking a chance.

"No – I... I just... wanted to make sure ..." she said slowly.

"Cuban, six o'clock. Your place. Maybe some live music after. And bring a change of clothes because you'll be staying here tonight." He leaned in, kissed her, and slipped his hands under his jersey to find her wearing nothing beneath it.

"Jesus, you're in my kitchen wearing nothing but my jersey," he said breathlessly. "When do you have to meet your study group?"

"Noon, but I have to stop by my house to pick up my books."

"Plenty of time," he breathed as he kissed her neck. "I'll be fast."

She laughed. "What every woman wants to hear."

"I promise I'll go more slowly tonight, but right now – this moment – I've fantasized about this more times than is strictly decent," he said, cupping her breasts gently.

She moaned, and he pulled her closer. He found her mouth as she pushed his running pants down and took his thick erection in her hand. She guided him inside of her and wrapped her legs around him.

She did manage to make it to her study group on time.

But just barely.

***

Blackman met her at the Rittenhouse Square townhouse Maggie shared with her brother Fitz, and they caught a cab to a casual Cuban place owned by the parents of a friend from college. They were dressed in jeans and sweaters and shared everything the chef brought to the table while drinking mojitos and laughing at each other's ridiculous childhood stories. Afterward, they walked to a small concert venue near the river, where they watched an up and coming singer/songwriter from Austin, Texas. They danced slowly in a dark corner, swaying to the music, sharing tender kisses.

When they got back to Blackman's apartment, they made love in the shower, and then on the floor in front of the fireplace. Then they slept soundly in his bed.

On Sunday morning, they made love again before they even found time to brush their teeth.

They spent Sunday working on their own projects. Blackman claimed the dining room table, and Maggie spread her books on the living room floor. As he watched her laying on the floor, dressed in baggy jeans and one of his hoodies, he promised himself he'd order a desk for her so she could work more comfortably. After dinner, they went to bed early, made love, and slept.

On Monday morning, his alarm went off at 5:30 am, and he left her asleep while he went to the gym for his morning swim. The note he left, with a heart drawn next to his name, was next to the spare key.

Within six weeks, they were practically living together. Her clothes were in his closet, her toiletries and cosmetics in his bathroom, and her favorite foods in his kitchen.

Fatimah took the news better than he anticipated.

"I only want you to be happy, Habibi," she said gently.

"I know, Auntie."

And after a long silence, she asked, "When can I meet her?"

"Very soon, Auntie. I promise."

Some weeks, Blackman and Maggie didn't see much of each other despite their living arrangements. Blackman was preparing for a trial, and Maggie was busy with her studies and teaching duties. Some nights, he would come home, and she was already asleep in the bed, which he had already started to think of as *theirs*. Her red hair splashed over *her* pillow like lava. Other nights he'd come home exhausted, and her work would be spread across the living room floor despite the desk he bought for her, Spanish guitar playing softly on the stereo.

And some nights he'd come home, and the apartment would be empty because she was doing something with her brother or her friends. Those nights he'd lay in their bed and stare at the ceiling, longing for the feel of her body against his. It amazed him how quickly he'd gone from a man who wanted nothing more than to sleep alone in his own bed to a man who couldn't sleep if he was alone in his own bed, but he never complained to her. It would make him sound needy, and he preferred to keep his neediness to himself.

When they had the time, they went out to dinner alone or with friends, sometimes hers, sometimes his. Sometimes they went to see live music in one of the many hole in the wall venues in the neighborhood. Some nights, they went to places where they could jump around and dance, and other nights, they went to places where they could cuddle together in a shadowy corner. Some nights, they came home and couldn't get each other's clothes off fast enough, making love on the dining room table or the kitchen counter. But other nights, they'd take their time in the shower or bed. Still other nights, it was enough to sleep next to one another.

Blackman had never been so happy.

And he hoped Maggie was happy, too. He hoped he made her as happy as she made him, but sometimes, she was difficult to read. Sometimes, he sat at the dining room table doing work and watched her sitting on the sofa reading a book, wearing one of his old t-shirts over her leggings. He loved how she got lost in books, the faraway look that settled on her face, the smiles that played across her lips. The frown lines that creased her face when she had to puzzle through something complex. At those times, she seemed both present and absent, both near and far, and sometimes, he feared he loved her so much more than she loved him.

On his worst nights, the nights when the old insecurities plagued him, he wondered if she loved him at all.

Of course, those were the early days, and he wondered if what he was feeling wasn't actually love, per se. Maybe it was something else? Since he'd never been in love, how could he be sure what he was feeling was actually love? And on those nights when he struggled to understand what was happening or what she was and was not feeling, he'd look away from her. Lose himself in his work until she'd come up behind him, rest her hands on his strong shoulders, and whisper into his ear in her beautiful, lyrical voice, "Time for bed, darling."

***

It was a cold evening in mid-winter when Blackman emerged from his office building. It was already dark, and he wasn't quite done for the night, but he wanted to get something to eat before he headed home to finish working. Maggie had been in Austin, Texas all week for a conference, and he missed her terribly. He found that he was filled with a restless energy no amount of swimming or lifting at the gym alleviated. He turned in the general direction of home and thought about calling Fatimah to see if she wanted to have dinner when a man fell into step with him.

"Mr. Smith?"

Blackman stopped and looked down at a short, slight man with a delicate face, expensively cut blond hair, and dark blue eyes. The man was well dressed in a black suit tailored for his slight build, a rich red tie, and a handsome wool overcoat. He was maybe five years older than Blackman. Blackman didn't recognize him and wondered if the man was a friend of his father's, or God forbid, one of his father's clients. His father wasn't doing much work nowadays, but if the money was right, he'd do it. That man was never one to turn down a paycheck.

"Yes?" Blackman asked warily. The last thing he needed was some weird wife killer/pedophile client of his father's asking him for a favor.

Christ, that would totally be something his father would orchestrate.

"Hello, I'm so sorry to bother you like this, but I'm Fitzwilliam Harrington."

Blackman looked at the man blankly.

"October Rhymer's brother. *Maggie's* brother. I'm Fitz," the man said, extending his hand with a warm smile, and for the first time, Blackman registered the rich English accent.

Blackman, more out of habit than genuine courtesy, extended his hand. "Blackman Smith. Pleased to meet you."

They shook hands, and Blackman was acutely aware of how Fitz's small hand disappeared inside his own, making Blackman feel oversized and awkward, something he hadn't felt in a long time.

"Forgive me for showing up unannounced, but I was hoping I could buy you a drink. Maybe dinner?" Fitz asked with what looked like a genuine smile. The man's face was delicate, reminding Blackman of something fragile, like porcelain. Blackman searched Fitz's clean shaven face for a hint of menace, but all he could see was an open sort of cheeriness as he waited for Blackman's answer.

"Umm... sure. A drink would be fine," Blackman said, his wariness evident in his voice.

"Splendid!" Fitz exclaimed, clapping his hands together; actually, clapping them together like a pleasant but eager child.

"How do you feel about martinis?"

***

"First of all, my sister would kill me if she knew I was here talking with you. Possibly literally. She has a frightful temper, but I've barely seen her for nearly two months, and I just had to meet you," Fitz said, leaning back against the bar in an Asian fusion place two blocks from work that Blackman had never heard of, but Fitz seemed to be a regular.

"And," he added with a wink. "Since she's out of town, there would be less of a chance of her finding out. Of course, unless you tell her, but I suppose I'll have to take the chance that you're discreet. You seem like a discreet sort of man since you work at the DA's office. That seems like the kind of job that requires tact and discretion."

Blackman raised his eyebrows. *Tact and discretion?* The man had clearly never been arrested, or visited the DA's office, or watched an episode of *Law and Order.*

Fitz had shed his overcoat and suit jacket and loosened his tie, sipping a dirty martini, watching Blackman with keen and inquisitive eyes. Blackman still wasn't sure what was happening, so he didn't do anything beyond take off his overcoat. He sipped a beer and let Fitz talk, which was easy because Fitz liked to talk.

Fitz liked to talk *a lot.*

"So, you must imagine my delight when I found out she was finally having dinner with you. I mean, I was absolutely over the moon," the small man exclaimed happily.

"Finally?" Blackman raised an eyebrow.

Fitz picked up his martini glass, then tilted it toward Blackman.

"She's been talking about you for years. For *years*. Ever since that night in the bar back in college. I don't know what you said to her, but you certainly intrigued her. I mean, my sister is hardly loquacious under the best of circumstances, unlike me, of course. But suddenly, she's talking about you over dinner, and I was just floored."

Blackman just stared at him.

Incredulously.

Nope, just the designated sober friend. The one who makes sure that everyone gets home without making any life altering mistakes.

What kind of life altering mistakes?

The kind of life altering mistakes that look like you.

"And then she used to see you around campus all the time, and I always told her to just go up and talk to you. I mean, what could it hurt? So, what if you were this big time hockey player guy? I mean, my sister's hardly Quasimodo," Fitz said with a chuckle.

Blackman almost knocked over his beer.

"Wait? What? What do you mean she used to see me around campus?" Blackman was painfully aware his voice had risen an octave like he was an over eager teenager who had just heard the head cheerleader harbored a secret crush on him. Not that a head cheerleader had ever harbored a crush on him, secret or otherwise.

Fitz nodded, picked up his martini glass, and finished it before motioning for another.

"Yes, I think you two had some classes in the same building or something like that. I mean, it wasn't a big campus, right? And I think she used to see you in the library all the time. My sister spent more time in the library than anywhere else. I mean, we share a five bedroom townhouse; you'd think she'd find a spot fit to write poetry, but she's an odd duck, my sister." Fitz nodded, accepting another martini from the bartender, who took a long look at Blackman before he walked away.

Blackman felt like he'd been punched. He'd looked all over for Maggie, but he'd never seen her, and she'd been right there in front of him all along, and she'd been watching him, thinking about going up and talking to him. And he'd missed it. He'd missed her. How hadn't he noticed her?

"Why," Blackman asked, trying to sound casual, "didn't she talk to me?"

He didn't think he sounded at all casual.

Fitz turned those sharp blue eyes to him, and a smile played at the corner of his lips.

"That's a good question. This is going to stay between us, correct?" Fitz said playfully, conspiratorially. A younger brother with a secret, even though he was actually the older brother with a secret. Jesus, Blackman loved this guy.

"Of course, just between us," Blackman said with his most charming smile, the one he brought out when the defense started to float the idea of a plea bargain for a defendant Blackman had taken a personal interest in putting in jail. The smile Blackman used when he wanted to convey that *he* was a trustworthy man when he had no intention of being a trustworthy man. The smile he used on Wendy Jennings when he told her she could have brunch with him and his father twenty minutes before hitting on Maggie. *Okay,* he admitted to himself, *I'm an asshole*. But at this point, he would have promised Fitzwilliam Harrington whatever he wanted as long as the man kept talking.

Fitz smiled slyly.

"Maggie has lived like a nun since our father sent her here. She was a bit of a wild one when she was young, and that's probably our fault – my brothers and me – but then she got in trouble, and Dad decided she needed *more structure*." Fitz rolled his eyes at the world structure, then paused to sip his martini. "And no matter how much we begged Dad to change his mind, he was intractable. My father is a decisive man, and once he's made up his mind, he rarely changes it. Maggie, of course, was devastated. Family is everything to her; *we* are everything to her. I was able to convince him to send her here so she wouldn't be completely alone, but it didn't matter.

Once she arrived, she just shut the world out," Fitz said, and Blackman could hear the sadness in the older man's voice, regret for a decision he didn't make.

Blackman sipped his beer patiently. Listening. His heart aching for Maggie; he knew what it was like to be discarded, but then he'd found Fatimah.

Alhamdulillah. Thank God.

"Once she started boarding school, it was all about earning top marks, as if she could leverage her way back to England with good grades," Fitz said as he turned his martini glass in lazy circles on the bar. Blackman wondered what level of guilt Fitz carried with him because he was the reason his little sister was sent abroad. She'd been punished for defending him, and after seeing what she'd done in that bar a couple of months ago, Blackman knew she'd do it again. She'd nearly stomped a man's head for upsetting her friend. Blackman could only imagine what she'd do to someone who hurt her brother.

"She spent all her free time writing and studying, and her breaks and summers were spent attending enrichment programs all over the east coast. She didn't go home for years. Not even for the holidays. Our brothers... well, her choices were hard on all of us." Fitz's voice trailed off. He picked up his martini and took a sip before he continued.

"I've never met an artist as emotionally detached as Maggie," Fitz paused as if trying to decide what exactly he wanted to say, and how best he could say it. "Once she decided to pursue academia, it was her sole focus. She has a few friends, of course, but boys, however, have always been off the table. *Verboten* as it were," Fitz said quietly. His body language told Blackman the man knew he was overstepping, sharing such intimate details about his sister's life, but he didn't seem to want to stop.

"I suppose," he said with a sigh. "She justifies it by saying she must stay focused on school, but I think it's about not wanting to get hurt. Again," Fitz said, his voice tinged with sadness.

Please come inside.

No... this isn't our time.

Blackman picked up his beer. He wanted to say something, but he wasn't sure what he should say. He got it, what Maggie had gone through. He understood what it was like to lose everything at a young age and then have to find a way to put your life back together before you even really knew who you were.

As if understanding that he had taken them both down a darker road than he intended, Fitz's mood changed again.

"But then she met *you*," he said with a rakish grin. "And you are temptation incarnate. Sometimes I'd see her watching one of the games on telly, but I could tell she was really watching you. Number 42." Fitz's easy smile returned. "And then that night at the game. She was convinced you'd forgotten about her, and she was sure you'd never recognize her."

"I'd recognize your sister anywhere," Blackman said.

Except right under my fucking nose, apparently.

"That final goal, when you skated up to her and yelled something. It was right out of a romance novel," Fitz said wistfully.

"Make reservations, sweetheart," Blackman said softly. "She said if I scored a hat trick, I could take her to dinner."

"Well," Fitz said, picking up his drink. "It was all over ESPN. You could even see her expression; it was the sweetest thing. I hadn't seen my sister glow like that in years, if ever, truth be told. She was radiant. Jesus, our brothers even called from England to find out what was going on."

"Then I got hurt," Blackman said thoughtfully.

Fitz nodded, and Blackman drained his beer and signaled for another.

"Maggie was devastated. She was convinced she'd been the cause. That you were showing off for her, and that was why the player targeted you."

Blackman didn't say anything.

The bartender brought him another beer, and Blackman thanked him. Turning the beer glass in lazy circles, he thought about what he wanted to say next. He took a long pull and then set the glass on the bar.

"It was just bad luck," he said finally. "Hockey's a tough sport, and I was an aggressive player. And honestly, I was a dick. Injuries happen. Christ knows I caused enough over the years," Blackman added quietly.

He met Fitz's eyes and waited, but if Fitz cared about the admission, he didn't show it. "That's exactly what I told her, but she has a poet's gentle heart, no matter how much she tries to hide it. I know she wanted to see you, but she was afraid." Fitz finished his martini and signaled for another. "My sister has an overdeveloped sense of responsibility, something else to thank our father for, and once she decided she played some role in your injury, there was no talking her around. She can be quite stubborn, so she just buried herself in work again. Deciding it was a sign from the universe you weren't meant to be."

Blackman didn't say anything; he hadn't been distracted that night. If anything, he'd been more focused than he'd ever been. He'd played the best game of his life, but things happen, people get hurt. Careers get cut short.

It was the nature of the sport. All sports really.

"But," Fitz said, interrupting Blackman's thoughts. "It seems like the universe keeps bringing you two back together."

Blackman thought about how much of an asshole he'd been at the coffee shop, and how lucky he'd been that she hadn't just walked out on him.

"And now her toothbrush is in your bathroom, and half her wardrobe's hanging in your closet, so I figured this would be the best time to meet you. God knows I wasn't about to wait for her to get around to introducing us."

"To see if I'm good enough for her?" Blackman asked. It was a fair question. This was her brother, after all. Her older brother. It seemed only appropriate he'd want to meet the man fucking his sister, and, of course, there were the other brothers who would naturally be wary of him. This was a dangerous family, and they would have every reason to want to know Blackman was sincere in his pursuit of their little sister. Blackman knew dangerous people attracted other dangerous people. Perhaps Fitz Harrington was concerned that Blackman had some ulterior motive, that Blackman might intentionally or unintentionally hurt Maggie, and Maggie had been hurt enough.

Fitz laughed. Loudly. And it was so much like Maggie's that Blackman's chest tightened painfully. He hadn't understood just how much he missed her laugh until now.

"Oh God, no. You're lovely! Everyone I've spoken to about you all say the same thing. You're a good, upstanding man with an amazing work ethic and no skeletons in his closet." Fitz paused and wiggled an eyebrow. "And God knows you're as lovely as sin. No, my sister is lucky to have caught your eye."

Blackman blinked. "Then I'm not sure what's going on here. Is this just about you buying me a drink?" Blackman asked, ignoring the fact that Fitz Harrington had been checking up on him, which really seemed only fair considering Blackman had been doing the same thing since Jon Pierce had made his comments about the family outside the bar. Because if he was going down this road, and he damn well was going down this road, the more he knew, the better off he'd be. It was one of the few things his father taught him: always be prepared because if things go to shit, you don't want to be the one asshole standing there who didn't see it coming.

"Well, maybe my being here isn't entirely selfish," Fitz admitted. "I'm here because, yes, in part, I wanted to meet you, but also because I wanted to..." Fitz paused and considered his words carefully. "Okay, look, I'm just going to be honest here. I'm here on behalf of my emotionally stunted sister, but before I get into all of that, I think we should get some dinner. Are you hungry?"

"I could eat."

"Michael." Fitz waved to the bartender. "We're going to head over to my usual booth."

"Of course, Fitz. I'll send Diane over."

"Thank you, dearest," Fitz said with a flirty smile as he climbed to his feet, turning his attention to Blackman. "Come now, let's get some food in us."

***

When Blackman said goodnight to Fitz Harrington, he was a little drunk, and much *more* in love with Maggie Rhymer. He walked down the shop lined street toward his apartment, *their* apartment, but stopped in front of a boutique jewelry store getting ready to close. He pushed open the door and looked at the carefully dressed woman standing behind the counter.

Blackman returned her smile, withdrew his wallet, and put it on the counter. And with the same shocking confidence he'd had the night of the hockey game, when he scored a hat trick just for the chance to take his future wife out to dinner, he said, "I would like to buy an engagement ring. A big one."

Okay, maybe I'm more than a little drunk.

Chapter 7

Maggie was miserable. The week away at UT Austin was interminable. Sure, the weather was great, and she was catching up with people she hadn't seen in ages, but she was so lonely she ached. She had a beautiful suite with a lovely view of downtown Austin and a king sized bed that was too big and too empty.

She had to end things with Blackman.

During the course of the week, she had delivered two papers, both of which were well received. One paper focused on the poet Phyllis Wheatley, and the other focused on the function of creative writing in helping rape survivors process trauma. She'd had coffee with former teachers who were eager to hear about her writing, drinks with former classmates eager to hear about campus gossip, and dined alone so she could finish her final draft of an essay that would be in a book about the unique experiences of the next generation of female academics.

Hands down, she was doing her best writing.

Ever.

She had even workshopped two new poems she'd been working on the last several weeks, and two literary journals had already shown interest.

And of course, all of this was fantastic; it proved that academia was where she belonged. If her time in Austin proved nothing else, it proved she had the talent and the drive to be successful, to leave her mark. To finally be found worthy. And as long as she was working, and as long as her mind was occupied, she was fine. But the minute she stopped writing, the moment there was a pause in the hectic schedule that defined these kinds of conferences, she was no longer fine.

She was a mess.

Well, not really a mess, per se.

She was definitely distracted, and she didn't want to be distracted because she hated being distracted. She had designed her entire existence around not being distracted. But all she could think about was Blackman and all the ways that this thing she had started that she had been foolish enough to let begin was going to destroy her. She was no more prepared for the intensity of the emotions she felt for Blackman than she was built for any functional relationship. She had been alone for years, and she had fully expected to be alone for the rest of her life.

With dogs.

Because she really didn't care for cats.

She could surround herself with dogs, and her writing and teaching, and all the things that would ensure her safety, and everything would be okay. Because as long as she was alone with dogs, she couldn't get hurt. One didn't have to worry about letting down one's defenses when there was no one with whom to let down one's defenses. Or something like that.

But Blackman wouldn't give up.

Yes, she had wanted to go to bed with him that night, but in the morning, she had fully expected him to let her down easy. Sure, he'd been interested in her for years, but she was convinced his interest was rooted more in curiosity than anything else. So, she'd gone to bed with him. *Why wasn't his curiosity sated?*

Then she'd given him an out in the kitchen that morning, and she fully expected him to take it. Yeah, sure, he'd wanted her the night before, *really wanted her*, if she was completely honest with herself, but what had her brothers drilled into her? All men wanted a woman when the lights were out; it was the cold light of day that brought them back to their senses.

And it was definitely the cold light of day in his kitchen that morning, but instead of taking her up on her offer with dignity, he'd doubled down and had sex with her in the kitchen.

On the counter.

What the hell was she supposed to do with that?

So instead of ending things where they should have ended, they had Cuban, and then went to see a band, and then spent another night together. Then she'd gone to a work happy hour with him, and then she'd taken him to a poetry reading at the university. The next thing she knew, she was doing her homework at the desk that had suddenly appeared in front of one of the floor to ceiling windows. Then her toiletries were in the bathroom, and her clothes were in the closet. Her favorite foods were in the cupboards, her favorite wines in the wine fridge, and it seemed she'd completely and rather accidentally moved in with him.

And now she was in Austin, Texas, and she was coming apart at the seams because she had made a terrible mistake that would invariably end in disaster. And that inevitability was growing more obvious with every passing hour. When she'd arrived in Austin on Sunday afternoon, she'd been content with exchanging a few breezy text messages with him, so he knew she'd arrived safely, and the weather was fine, but before she knew it, they were texting all the time. The breezy texts turning into something more serious.

More intimate.

And soon she found she was aching to hear his voice, but she wouldn't let herself call him. She was a strong, independent woman, a future academic, a future prize-winning poet, and she didn't need to hear a man's voice to feel complete, to feel whole.

Then one morning after a terrible night's sleep, she called him.

"Blackman Smith," he said, his voice deep and official.

She imagined him sitting at his desk in her favorite charcoal gray suit with one of the red striped ties he favored. And honestly, how many red striped ties could one man own? It was why she'd started slipping more colorful but tasteful ties into his wardrobe.

"Hey, it's me," she said, hating herself for the neediness she heard in her voice.

"Maggie, honey, it's so good to hear your voice," he said warmly, switching to the easy, cheerful voice that greeted her every night when she walked through

the front door. Her eyes started stinging, and she wanted the earth to swallow her whole.

"Everything okay?"

"Yes," she said too quickly. "I just wanted to say hello; my first panel isn't for another hour."

"I'm so glad you called, and I wish I could talk, but I have to be in Jon's office in two minutes."

"Of course, I understand," she said with false cheerfulness.

"Are you still coming home on Saturday?"

"Yes, I land at noon."

"Great, I'll be there. Also, don't forget we're having brunch with Fatimah on Sunday. I know you'll probably be jet lagged, so I'm sorry about the timing."

"No, it's fine. It'll be fine."

Nothing was fine. Nothing was ever going to be fine again if she didn't get out of this mess she'd landed herself in.

"Great. Well, I have to go. I miss you, honey."

"I miss you, too." She disconnected the phone before she could blurt, "I love you."

Fuck my life.

Fitz, who fell in and out of love with shocking frequency, believed Maggie was emotionally stunted, which was both unkind and untrue. She wasn't emotionally stunted at all. If anything, she felt too much all the time. Love, anger, frustration, loneliness, unworthiness. Guilt, desperation, a pathetic and pathological need to be loved.

Fear.

She was afraid of everything, especially love.

She'd loved her brothers and father wholeheartedly, and she'd been everything they wanted her to be. Then, she made one mistake, and her father sent her away. Of course, the adult Maggie understood why those decisions had been made, but the child Maggie still felt abandoned. Mind you, her abandonment had hardly been Dickensian. She'd been sent to a posh boarding school, Fitz less than an hour away, but damned if she didn't want her dad, her brothers, her friends all the time. She wanted her home.

And yes, she'd been too indulged, and she'd been difficult, and she'd had a breathtakingly horrible temper, but she could have changed if her dad had just let her stay.

But he wouldn't.

It's better this way, love.

I don't want to go, daddy.

She had cried so badly, begging him to change his mind, and even then, she hated the sound of the weakness in her voice.

I know, love. But I need you to be strong.

But being strong was what had gotten her there. Fitz had taken her, still crying, onto the jet her father had chartered, and Maggie cried until she fell asleep with her head in Fitz's lap.

She hadn't cried again until the night outside of Blackman's apartment. The night he had kissed her so desperately, the night he had picked her up and pushed up against her, touched her like he *needed* her. Like she was the only woman he had ever *wanted*, and the feeling had been otherworldly. Her desire for him had been primal, and she had never wanted a man more than she wanted him that night, and those foreign feelings had terrified her. And Blackman was so far out of her league that it was almost comical. He was tall and handsome and brilliant, and when they were in school, he was always surrounded by beautiful women. Brilliant women. Future lawyers or doctors. Not English major poets who were more comfortable in old jeans and concert t-shirts than pretty dresses and fancy shoes.

But now she was practically living with him, and she felt like everything was spinning out of control. He looked at her like he'd been waiting for her his entire life. He touched her like he was afraid she was going to disappear if he wasn't paying attention, and she loved it. She loved how he touched her when they walked down the street. The gentle brush of his fingers against hers before he took her hand, or the way he touched the small of her back when he wanted her to walk ahead of him. The way he smiled at her when they were out with his friends from the office, the pride he showed when she talked about her studies or the classes she taught.

It was unbearable.

She didn't deserve such attention.

Any more than she deserved the promise of that kind of devotion.

What would happen when the novelty of fucking a poet wore off? When he found a more worthy woman. The kind of woman a man his stunning good looks deserved? The kind of woman who belonged on a District Attorney's arm or maybe a judge's arm? God, he could run for public office. What if he wanted to be a Senator or something?

She had to end this.

She caught the first flight out of Austin Friday afternoon. Everything had wrapped up, and the only thing left was one last drinks event, but she'd had enough to drink. The flight was supposed to land in Philadelphia at seven o'clock East Coast time, but she got stuck in Denver because of bad weather and didn't land in Philadelphia until half past eleven. By the time she claimed her bags and caught a taxi back to the apartment, it was nearly one in the morning.

She was exhausted, emotionally wrung out from all the hours she'd spent writing and rewriting dozens of iterations of her breakup speech. She'd even written it in verse at one point while sitting at a bar in the Denver airport, drowning her sorrows in overpriced Merlot. That particular version of their breakup included an itemized list of all the reasons she wasn't good enough for him, all the ways he could do better, and all the reasons this thing between them needed to end before she was too invested. That last part was clearly bullshit, though, because she was already invested and more than half drunk when she finally boarded her flight.

She was sober now.

As sober as the judge Blackman Smith would probably be one day.

She set her keys in the blown glass bowl Blackman had bought for her at a small artists' market they found one afternoon walking through the neighborhood. She loved the cobalt blue bowl so much it hurt to look at it.

She loved Blackman.

And that was why this had to end, no matter how much it hurt.

She set her bags down next to the dining room table so they would be easy to retrieve when she walked back out in twenty minutes and caught yet another cab back to Fitz's place. She figured their break-up couldn't take more than twenty minutes.

Clearly, he'd understand.

He would probably even agree.

Maybe he'd been planning his own exit while she'd been away. A week apart tended to give one clarity.

She unlaced her boots and set them by her bag so she could step back into them on her way out the door. Then she dropped her coat on her bags and drew in a deep, cleansing breath.

She could do this.

She could do hard things; she was, after all, her father's daughter.

She walked slowly into the living area where Blackman, still wearing his work clothes, was asleep on the sofa. He was leaning back awkwardly in the corner where she usually sat, his feet propped on the coffee table, work papers on his lap. The soft glow of one of the brass floor lamps illuminated his face. He was so beautiful she thought her chest was going to crack open. She looked at the purple tie loose around his neck.

Why couldn't she be enough for a man like this?

Blackman opened his beautiful brown eyes and looked at her.

"Did I oversleep? Did I miss picking you up?" His sleepy voice was thick and gravelly, and it cut her to the bone like a rusty knife.

"No," she said quietly. "I caught an earlier flight. Why are you sleeping on the couch? That can't be good for your back."

His back? Really? She was trying to break up with him, and she was talking about his fucking back? Jesus Christ.

Blackman yawned, pushed himself into a seated position, and gathered his papers together before they could fall to the floor.

"Bed's too empty without you; I can't sleep in it," he said, yawning.

"So, you sleep on the sofa?" She stared at him. He was still half asleep as he tried to drop the papers on the coffee table but missed. They fluttered to the ground making a sound that reminded Maggie of birds taking flight.

"Sometimes. Sometimes I just lay in bed and stare at the ceiling thinking about you," he said guilelessly. And right then, she understood she couldn't do it.

She couldn't leave this man.

He'd most likely break her heart, and honestly the pain would probably kill her, or more likely she'd probably kill herself. Maybe she'd pile rocks in her pockets and walk into the river like Virginia Woolf or put her head in an oven like Sylvia Plath. That would have to be okay, though, because she couldn't hurt him.

She loved him too much.

"Come here," he said, and he opened his arms to her. "You should have called me. I would have met you at the airport. Did you at least get Fitz to send a car?"

Maggie walked over to him and straddled his lap.

"No, I took a taxi," she said softly.

"At this hour?" he asked, alarmed.

Evidently, the thought of her taking a late night taxi was finally enough to wake him up. Before he could say anything else, she pressed her lips to his. He tasted faintly of beer and pepperoni pizza. He slipped his arms around her and pulled her against him. Nudging his lips apart with her tongue, she finally let herself go. Finally willing to take the chance with him that he'd been so willing to take with her time and time again over the years. She took off his tie and dropped it to the floor, then unbuttoned his shirt and pushed it open and off his shoulders. Her hands slid down his body and pulled his undershirt out of his pants. He trailed his hands down her back and cupped her backside possessively.

He leaned forward and let go of her long enough to help her pull off his undershirt. Then she pushed him back against the sofa and put her hands against his chest. Running her fingers over his hard muscles and through his fine hair. He reached for her shirt, but she whispered against his lips, "Not yet."

He groaned as she moved her lips away and kissed her way over his jawline, tasting him with her tongue. She shifted her body to kneel on the floor between his knees so she could trace the hard planes of his chest with her lips. He moaned as she teased his nipples with the hot tip of her tongue.

He whispered her name as he tunneled his fingers through the thick waves of her red hair. She kissed her way down his taut stomach, pausing at his belt buckle. He held his breath as she unbuckled it and unbuttoned his pants.

"Maggie," he breathed as he lifted his hips so she could pull down his pants and his boxers. She left them in a puddle on the floor behind her, leaving him gloriously naked and beautiful in front of her. In the dim light, she turned her attention to his long legs. She found the horrific scar where his bone broke through his skin the night of the hockey game.

The night she first fell in love with him.

She kissed it, running her tongue over it slowly, sensuously.

Blackman's breathing grew shallow as he leaned his head back against the sofa cushion.

She traced the myriad surgical scars from the half dozen surgeries he'd had to repair the irreparable damage to his leg. Then she found the scar where his knee had been surgically repaired between his junior and senior years of high school. Again, she traced the scars with her tongue and her lips. Finally, she traced the long scar along his right calf where a skate caught him during a mid-ice collision when he was 12; it had taken more than fifty stitches to close him up.

He had passed out before they put in the first stitch.

Maybe her scars were internal, the kinds of scars that an attentive lover couldn't gently kiss away, but that didn't mean he didn't have his share, too. His life hadn't been easy. He had known rejection and loss as well as physical pain. At least she had been spared some of that, at least her father hadn't outsourced familial love to the nanny.

Maggie kissed every scar, running her tongue over them slowly before moving back to his thighs. He was trembling beneath her touch, thrumming with pent up energy. When she looked up at him, his head was tilted back, and he was flushed, gasping for air. She watched his hooded eyes as she took him in her hand.

"Maggie, you don't..."

She slid her tongue up the length of him, and he cried out and thrust his hips instinctually toward her. She had never done this to him before.

She had never done this to anyone before.

Slowly, she took him into her mouth.

"Maggie, oh my God, Maggie," he moaned helplessly. She felt him reach for her, groping around until he found her hand. He laced his fingers through hers and held tightly. She moved the way she imagined she was supposed to, and his reactions had her assuming she was doing everything correctly. He whispered her name over and over again like a prayer, as he thrust his hips desperately, quickly losing control.

"Maggie – you don't – I'm so close – you need..."

He tried to move away from her, to stop her, but she didn't want to stop. How many times had he done this to her? How many times had he buried his face between her thighs and stayed with her until she was spent? She squeezed his hand as she moved her other hand to find the sensitive spot at the base of his balls that always sent him over the edge.

He came with a shout. She held him, drawing out his orgasm until she was sure he was spent. Then gently released him from her mouth, and rested her cheek against his thigh, watching him come back to his senses. When he looked at her, his eyes were so full of love she found it difficult to breathe. He was still trying to catch his breath when he reached for her and pulled her into his lap, holding her tightly against his sweat slicked body. He pressed his face into her hair, and she could feel his heart pounding.

When his breathing slowed, she looked up at him and stroked his face with a steady hand.

"I love you, Blackman," she whispered so softly she wasn't sure he had even heard her, but he had.

He had heard her very clearly.

His long fingers roamed her body, finding the hem of her sweater. He pulled it over her head and dropped it on the floor. He unbuttoned her jeans and pushed them down so she could shimmy out of them on her own. He ran his fingers along her strong thighs and over the wet lace of her panties.

Gently he pushed her off his lap, so she was standing, then stood up alongside her. She thought he was going to lead her to bed, but he reached around and unhooked her black lace bra, then slid his hands underneath her panties and pushed them down until they puddled around her feet. He leaned over and turned off the brass lamp, plunging the apartment into darkness. The only light came from the city outside their window.

He picked her up like he had in the park outside his apartment years ago. Then he walked them over to the floor to ceiling windows and set her back against the winter cooled glass, soothing her hot skin. He kissed her deeply, twining his tongue with hers until he was hard again. Then he looked at her, waiting for her to meet his eyes. When she did, he whispered, "My sweet, sweet, Maggie. I love you so much."

She reached for him, guiding him to her entrance.

"You are my one and only," he whispered as he pushed himself inside of her.

She gasped, closing her eyes instinctively, overwhelmed by the feel of him inside of her, overwhelmed by how raw she felt, how vulnerable.

"Look at me, sweetheart," he commanded gently. She opened her eyes and tried to hold his, but the intimacy he demanded of her was difficult. It was too much, but she tried. She tried so hard.

He stroked her slowly, so slowly it was agonizing.

He stroked her like they had forever.

And maybe they did.

She lost track of time as she got lost in those dark brown eyes. The feel of his hands on her bare bottom, the painful pleasure of his cock filling the tight space of her, leading her slowly toward the edge of everything.

She started to chant his name louder and louder as she felt the heat and desire burning her from the inside out.

"Blackman, my love – my love..."

When she came it was with a ferocity she had never known. She cried out so loudly her voice echoed off the hard brick walls of the apartment. Her fingers dug into his back. He looked at her, watching her come undone in his arms with incredible tenderness. Stroking her slowly throughout her climax, continuing to move inside her.

"Give me another, Maggie."

Her eyes widened as he kissed her neck and rubbed his fingers over her sensitive nipples. He slipped his tongue over her earlobes and slid his fingers into the valley of her bottom, playing with her most secret places.

"One more time, Maggie, just for me. Only for me," he whispered.

"Just for you," she panted.

"Just for me," he gasped as he moved faster. He found her mouth and kissed her hard, his hand finding her swollen clit, touching her the way she liked. She moaned into his mouth, and she felt him thicken inside of her. His fingers were everywhere at once.

"Blackman, God..." she howled as she came again.

He slammed his hips into her, going as deep as he could. Crying out painfully as he let himself go, as he gave her everything he had to give. When they were done and spent, they slid to the floor slowly. He pulled her tightly against him and held her until they were able to get to their feet and walk to the bed. Then they slipped beneath the covers and fell asleep tangled up in one another.

***

They spent that Saturday quietly getting used to the changes in their relationship. Their declarations of love and the intimacy of the night before left them feeling vulnerable and a little afraid. Thankfully, it was a cold rainy day, and they spent it in front of the fireplace. They couldn't stop touching one another, so Blackman spread most of his work out on the coffee table and sat on the floor working on his laptop while Maggie curled up behind him on the sofa, reading a book, absently running her fingers through his hair.

They ate a quiet dinner at the dining room table, where they chatted about nothing, and then returned to the sofa, where they curled up together and watched a hockey game. Maggie, jet-lagged from the Texas trip, spent most of the evening curled up in Blackman's arms, dozing contently, while Blackman watched the game and gently rubbed Maggie's back. When they went to bed that night, their lovemaking was gentle and slow, and they slept soundly afterward.

That Sunday, they met Fatimah at her favorite brunch place, a small restaurant near the Art Museum, where she was a regular. Maggie expected to be the only one nervous, but Blackman seemed equally nervous about the meeting, and that, in turn, made Maggie feel worse. Unwilling to meet Blackman's de facto mother in blue jeans and a t-shirt, Maggie dressed neatly in black tights, calf height black leather boots, and a soft cream colored wool sweater. Blackman settled on a pair of khaki pants and a button-down white shirt beneath a dark green sweater. They didn't say much on the cab ride to the restaurant. Both lost in their thoughts.

When they arrived at the restaurant, Blackman paid the driver, then took Maggie's hand and led her inside. The restaurant was small and cozy, overlooking a tree-lined street. The owners, a Lebanese couple who had known Blackman since he was a child, greeted him warmly.

Maggie watched curiously as Blackman spoke to the couple in rapid Arabic. The couple looked from Blackman to Maggie, and then the wife, Salma, stepped forward and wrapped her arms around Maggie warmly.

"It's such a pleasure to meet you, Maggie," Salma said in accented English. She turned to Blackman. "Fatimah is at her usual table, dearest. Go in. I will be with you in a moment."

"Thank you," Blackman said in English.

Placing his hand on the small of Maggie's back, he gently pushed her forward. She walked slowly, taking in the warm space with the beautiful photographs of the Lebanese coast. Then she saw a petite woman with porcelain skin and bright blue eyes stand up slowly. She wore loose fitting gray pants and a pale blue tunic with a matching hijab. Her smile was wide and bright and welcoming, and her eyes were filled with a mother's love. Before Maggie could say anything, Fatimah reached out and took Maggie in her arms, squeezing her tightly. Then she stepped back and cupped Maggie's face in her warm, soft hands.

"You are even more beautiful than Blackman said. I cannot tell you how pleased I am to finally meet you, dearest," Fatimah said in a soft voice as she let go of Maggie's face.

"Thank you, ma'am," Maggie said, meeting Fatimah's lively blue eyes.

Fatimah shook her head. "Please, dearest, I am Fatimah or Auntie if you would prefer. We are not a formal family."

Family.

"Thank you... Auntie," Maggie said slowly.

Fatimah's face positively glowed as she looked from Maggie to Blackman who said something in Arabic as he leaned over and kissed Fatimah's cheek.

"In English, Habibi," Fatimah chided as she motioned for Maggie to sit in one of the comfortable chairs.

"Sorry," Blackman apologized as he pulled out Maggie's chair for her. "Force of habit. I always speak to Fatimah in Arabic. That's the only way I can be sure she won't forget," Blackman said with a smile as he took the chair next to Maggie.

Maggie looked from Blackman to Fatimah and smiled.

She was definitely meeting Blackman's mother. The only family that mattered.

Taking a deep breath, she tried to calm her pounding heart. She folded her hands on her lap so neither Blackman nor Fatimah would see them tremble. Since she had never had a boyfriend, she had never had a meet-the parents-moment, and she had no idea what she was supposed to do. God, she wanted a drink, but it was ten o'clock in the morning, so that was probably not appropriate, and Fatimah was clearly a devout Muslim. So, Maggie was sure ordering a drink would not make a good impression.

"So, Maggie. Tell me all about your paper on Phillis Wheatley," Fatimah said leaning forward in her chair, pinning Maggie with her bright blue eyes.

"Are you familiar with Phillis Wheatley?" Maggie asked, surprised.

"I wasn't, but as soon as Blackman told me about your paper, I purchased one of her collections, and I was enthralled. I don't know if Blackman told you, but I studied literature at university."

"No, he didn't," Maggie said, looking at Blackman, who was looking intently at the menu. A small smile played at the corner of his mouth.

"Yes, French and Italian literature mostly, and then I went through a Russian phase. I made Blackman read *Crime and Punishment* in the summer between 8th and 9th grade. We had the most wonderful conversations," Fatimah said with a nostalgic smile.

Blackman muttered something in Arabic, then looked at Maggie sheepishly.

"That's not how I remember it," he repeated in English.

Fatimah sighed. "Blackman has a very selective memory."

Maggie laughed. "I must admit I prefer *Crime and Punishment* to *War and Peace*. Although I did enjoy *The Brothers Karamazov*. Unfortunately, the Russians are not my favorite."

"Whom do you prefer?" Fatimah asked.

"Since my mother is French, I'm supposed to say the French, but no one knows how to break a heart like the British."

"Ahh, yes, but have you read the Palestinians?" Fatimah smiled.

"I have not," Maggie admitted.

"You will come back to my apartment, and I will give you poems that will break your heart like no other," Fatimah said, leaning over and taking Maggie's hand in her own. Then she turned to Blackman. "Finally, you have found a literary woman, Habibi. It took you long enough."

"Yes, Auntie, I have," Blackman said, looking up as a waiter stopped at the table. "Two mimosas. Please."

Blackman Smith had never been so nervous in his life.

Ever.

It wasn't helping that he was having a terrible day at work. In fact, it might have been the worst day of his relatively short career. For the first time, he lost in court, and he didn't just lose in court, but he lost *spectacularly* in court. Case studies would be written about this loss. He would become a cautionary tale for law students everywhere: *Whatever you do, don't do what Blackman Smith did!*

A case he'd been working on for months fell apart in the eleventh hour, and he wasn't entirely sure how it had happened. The case had seemed airtight until it wasn't, and in the minutes leading up to the judge's dismissal of the case with prejudice, meaning Blackman was good a truly fucked, she wasn't shy about handing Blackman his ass in open court. Blackman wasn't entirely sure he had ever been taken to task as readily as he'd been taken to task that afternoon. Much like Saint Paul, Judge Althea Gibson-Johnson didn't suffer fools gladly or lightly or whatever the saying was, and she made it abundantly clear to Blackman Smith that she thought him not just a fool but a fucking idiot. Even the defense attorney, an old friend of Blackman's father, looked sympathetic, making the entire experience more humiliating.

Then upon returning to the office, Jon Pierce handed him his ass again, and even though his office door had been closed, everyone in the office could hear it. Because when Jon lost his temper, his voice carried.

Throughout the office.

To other floors.

Possible to other buildings.

While Jon took Blackman to task, Blackman stood tall and silent, his face impassive, his hands loose by his sides, his eyes focused on the bookshelves behind his boss' desk, and his mouth shut. He was a man who knew how to take a hit. This was not his first rodeo.

"Now get the fuck out of my office," Jon finished as he sat down and reached for his reading glasses. Blackman nodded and walked away. When he closed the door behind him, he noted that no one looked at him. Dozens of eyes were glued to computers, Blackberries, or case files until Blackman walked past. Then he could feel all those eyes on him as he walked out of the office.

And it's only Tuesday.

When Blackman reached the lobby, he looked at his watch and realized he was going to be late for Maggie's poetry reading. More importantly, he was going to be late for his marriage proposal because tonight was the night he was finally doing it.

He was finally proposing to Maggie.

He'd bought the ring months ago and had been trying to find the perfect way to pop the question ever since. However, nothing he'd thought of seemed romantic enough. *Memorable* enough. The holidays had come and gone, and he'd considered asking her over Thanksgiving, but she'd been drowning in work. Then he thought about asking her before her flight to London on Christmas morning, but he'd decided against it. A Christmas morning proposal seemed too cliché, and then she'd be gone for a week, and he'd still be home because as low man down in the office, he was the one who had to work during the holidays.

Then he thought about doing it on New Year's Eve, also cliché, but her flight had been delayed because of bad weather, and he'd celebrated the New Year miserable, alone, and drunk. He considered proposing on New Year's Day while they watched the Mummer's Parade pass beneath their window, but proposing while hungover didn't hold quite the same allure.

He almost asked her on Valentine's Day because now he was feeling desperate, but a nasty stomach flu that hit Maggie like a freight train nixed that plan. Then, of course, the stomach flu hit him next. Because why the hell not?

"Jesus Christ, Blackman, take the woman to dinner and ask her already," Fitz chided him one night over drinks.

"I want it to be special," Blackman said defensively. "I want it to be memorable."

"Honestly, I would just prefer that it happen. Nick is not thrilled with his little sister living with a bloke out of wedlock. At least not for this long."

"You can't be serious," Blackman replied. Although he knew Fitz was serious. It wasn't like Fatimah loved the living arrangements either, although she kept her displeasure to herself, probably because she knew he had a ring.

"Of course, I'm serious. Nick is very protective and old-fashioned." Fitz replied.

"What about your dad?" Blackman asked. He was sure he already knew the answer. If Nick was unhappy with the arrangements, Mr. Harrington couldn't be thrilled.

"We haven't told Dad about Maggie's new living arrangement."

"Fuck me," Blackman groaned. Apparently, he hadn't known the answer, and now people were lying to Mr. Harrington, and that was not the way Blackman wanted to join this family. He didn't want to be the guy other people had to lie about.

"Did you at least tell your brother I have a ring?"

"Blackman, darling," Fitz said sternly. "A ring sitting in your sock drawer is much different from one sitting on our sister's finger. Even I'm starting to think you're having second thoughts."

Blackman gave Fitz a wounded look.

"I am not having second thoughts," Blackman said quietly.

"Well, then, make a decision so my brother can breathe easier."

As Blackman walked through the lobby, he typed a text message to Fitz.

Blackman Smith:

Running late. Be there ASAP.

Fitz Harrington:

Are you fucking serious?

Blackman pushed through the lobby doors and into the cold afternoon. Dark, gray clouds hung low in the sky, promising rain. He wondered for a moment if rain was a good or bad omen for a wedding proposal. Fatimah would know. Maybe he should call her and ask. Of course, if she said *bad omen*, then he would have to put this off another day, and he wasn't about to do that. As a lawyer, he knew better than to ask a question he didn't already know the answer to. He was already doing that once tonight because Blackman was 95 percent sure Maggie would say yes. If he was being totally honest with himself, which he usually was at three in the morning when he was lying in bed watching Maggie sleeping beside him, wondering how he had gotten so lucky, he wasn't entirely sure she would say yes.

And that fear made him afraid to rock the boat of their relationship.

He knew he loved her, knew he wanted to spend the rest of his life with her, but Maggie... even after all these months living together, was still difficult to read. It scared him that he wasn't a hundred percent sure she loved him as much as he loved her, which wouldn't be a problem if she agreed to marry him. He could be the one who was more in love as long as she loved him enough to choose him, to stay with him. However, if she didn't love him enough to stay... well, yes, Blackman was a man who knew how to take a hit, but he wasn't entirely sure he was man enough to take that kind of hit from Maggie.

He sighed and typed out another text.

Blackman Smith:

Court was a shit show. Had a judge and my boss hand me my ass.

Will be there soon.

Fitz Harrington:

Your future wife looks positively stunning. If you're not here in an hour, I will introduce her to the cardio-vascular surgeon who came into the gallery yesterday. He makes three times your salary and has impeccable taste in art.

Blackman collided with someone as he read the text. He looked up and apologized quickly to the high school girl who was already telling him to go fuck himself. Blackman pocketed his phone and walked faster.

Blackman was well over an hour late. More like an hour and a half late. He'd gotten home as quickly as he could and showered, but then he wasn't sure what he was supposed to wear to a poetry reading. He'd been to a dozen poetry readings over the last six months, but this was *Maggie's* poetry reading. She was reading *her* poetry, and then he was proposing to her. What the hell was he supposed to wear for that? A suit? Like his best court suit? Or something less formal? Jeans? Maybe a button down shirt? Or that sweater that Maggie got him for Christmas, which she liked, but he didn't. He wasn't a turtleneck kind of guy. It was like wearing a tie, yet somehow worse. Finally, he settled on jeans, a white button down shirt, and a tie he could rethink in the cab ride to the bookstore. When he was finally dressed, he couldn't find the ring, which he had not only buried in his sock drawer but actually hid inside a pair of socks. As if Maggie routinely went through his sock drawer. As far as he knew, Maggie didn't even know he had a sock drawer. Half the time, she didn't put away her own laundry, let alone his.

Then he had to wait twenty minutes for a cab because the weather was shit, and everyone in downtown Philadelphia had decided to cab it to their Tuesday night destinations instead of walking in the rain. *Honestly,* he thought while he stood in the lobby waiting for the cab, *how many people go out on a Tuesday night?*

Fitz texted Blackman no fewer than a dozen times, but Maggie hadn't texted him once, which meant she was either incredibly forgiving or incredibly pissed. Fitz's last text was the worst of them all.

Fitz Harrington:

Did I mention that the cardiovascular surgeon has a house in Belize?

BELIZE, Blackman.

Blackman wanted to throw up.

When Blackman finally arrived at the small bookstore a few blocks from campus, he was relieved to see Maggie still seated at the long table of poets waiting for her turn to read. Blackman said a quick prayer of thanks to God, Allah, and the universe because he'd finally caught a break.

Blackman sat in the last row of chairs set up in the small area that had been set aside for the reading. Maggie, who had been staring intently at the poet speaking at the podium, a short, curvy woman with dark brown skin and a Nigerian accent, didn't notice Blackman take a seat. Or, if she noticed, she didn't acknowledge him, which could mean a variety of things. Either she was intently focused on the poet, or she was angry at Blackman for being an hour and a half late. Or worse, maybe she'd simply accepted that he would miss the poetry reading because Maggie took Blackman's job at the DA's office seriously. In some ways, she took it more seriously than he.

As Blackman settled into the uncomfortable wooden chair that was not quite big enough to accommodate him, he watched the poet with the Nigerian accent. She was a beautiful woman who recited her poetry from memory despite having a notebook open before her. Her work was lyrical and lovely, and it reminded Blackman of music. Although Blackman had read Maggie's published work, he had never heard her read any of it, and he was excited to watch her stand before this small crowd and read her words in her own beautiful voice.

His Blackberry vibrated in his coat pocket.

Blackman pulled it out and read the message.

Fitz Harrington:

About fucking time.

Blackman rolled his eyes and pocketed the Blackberry. Five minutes later, it vibrated again, so Blackman pulled it out again. The Nigerian poet was taking her seat when another poet, a man this time, stood up and walked to the podium. Blackman read the text.

Jon Pierce:

Call me.

Blackman watched the poet and typed a response without looking down.

Blackman:

Busy. Will call later.

Jon Pierce:

Fucking call now.

Blackman closed his eyes. There were times in his life when Blackman wished he was a smaller man. Smaller men could discreetly get up and leave a room. Smaller men could slip out of a chair without everyone noticing what they were doing. Smaller men could disappear into a crowd. Blackman would bet good money that he was taller than every person in this room, so if he got up to call his boss, everyone would notice. More importantly, Maggie would notice, and he didn't want her to think he was bailing on her on this night of all nights. He also didn't want to embarrass her by being the boyfriend who not only showed up late but left early. His phone vibrated again.

Jon Pierce:

NOW

Blackman flexed his jaw. He slipped out of his chair slowly and stepped behind some tall bookshelves that weren't quite tall enough to shield him. Instead of walking out of the store, which would mean walking in front of the poets, again, he walked deeper into the space. He found a set of doors that led into a small storage room cum office. When he dialed Jon's number, he noticed his hands were shaking. It had been a long time since he'd been this angry.

Jon answered on the first ring. He barked, "Where are you?"

"A poetry reading," Blackman answered through clenched teeth.

"Well, I need you back at the office now."

Blackman counted to five.

"No."

"No? What the fuck do you mean no?" Jon asked sharply. Blackman could hear his boss moving around and imagined him stalking around his office looking for his cigarettes. Tired and furious and fully prepared to fire

Blackman Smith, fuck-up of the day. Blackman closed his eyes and searched for his composure.

"I'm in the middle of something," Blackman said slowly. Precisely.

"You're in the middle of a fucking poetry reading," Jon snapped.

"It's *Maggie's* poetry reading," Blackman replied calmly. "And I'm going to propose to her afterward. Tonight. I am proposing to my girlfriend *tonight*."

"No. You're not. You're making your excuses, and you're coming back to the office. You can propose to your girlfriend tomorrow. *This* is important." He said *this* as if proposing to Maggie wasn't important. As if Blackman wasn't about to ask the single most important question of his life. Blackman, a man who asked questions for a living, understood on a primal level that no question he would ever ask would be as important as this one.

His entire life hinged on the answer to *this* question.

His very existence.

Blackman took a deep breath.

"I'm off the clock, Jon, and I'm busy. If this is so fucking important, call Donovan or Tony. Laura's back from New York, and you know she'll come in if you need her. If you need *me* specifically, you'll have to wait until tomorrow."

Blackman swore he could hear Jon grinding his teeth. It sounded like he was about to crack a molar. Blackman knew this because he was making the same sound. Probably cracking the same molar.

"Or you can fucking fire me. It's your call." Because Blackman was a man with options, that might have been one of the few things he learned from his old man: have options. Men with options were difficult to corner. Men with options were hard to bully. Men with options could tell you to go fuck yourself, and depending on *your* options, you might have to do just that: go fuck yourself. And if Jon fired him, well, fuck it. There was more money in defense law anyway. Then maybe he could afford Fitz's overpriced art and the doctor's house in fucking Belize.

"I expect your ass in here first thing tomorrow morning. *First thing*. Before the motherfucking sun is up, do you understand me?" Jon growled.

Blackman was sure that Jon had spent the last few seconds doing the mental calculus to determine whether it would be easier to let this go or give Blackman his walking papers.

"Yes, sir," Blackman said, dialing down the *fuck you* tone of voice he'd been using. Jon said nothing more and ended the call. Blackman took a deep breath and pocketed his phone. When he turned around, Fitz stood behind him, looking... shocked and maybe a little guilty.

Blackman shot his future brother-in-law – if he was fucking lucky – a hard look. Fitz could go fuck himself, too.

"Don't ever doubt how much I love your sister," Blackman snapped, his voice sharp like broken glass.

Fitz nodded. Speechless.

"And fuck Belize. No one likes Belize other than goddamn tax cheats," Blackman added as he stepped around Fitz and walked out of the room.

When Blackman took his seat in the back row again, Fitz sat beside him. The older man looked contrite, and Blackman assumed he had heard the entire conversation with Jon, which was fine. Perhaps it was time Fitz understood Blackman better, understood what kind of man Blackman was.

The poet, who had followed the Nigerian woman, was finishing his reading, and there was a polite round of applause as he returned to his seat. Then Maggie stood up. As Blackman watched her walk the short distance to the podium, he forgot all about how shitty his day had been. Maggie was beautiful. A goddamn vision. Her hair was up in a messy bun, and she was dressed entirely in black: heavy black boots, black tights, a tiny black skirt that barely covered her perfect ass, and a black sweater that dipped low in the front. An antique silver locket Blackman had bought for her was the only piece of jewelry she wore.

As he watched her open her notebook, he marveled at how a woman as breathtaking as she could love him. She was everything to him, and if Jon had fired him, Blackman wouldn't have cared. Because this was where he had to be, this was where he belonged. With her.

And only her.

For the rest of his life.

Maggie cleared her throat, looked up from her notebook, and found Blackman in the back of the room. She met his eyes and started to speak.

After all the poets finished, there was a brief question and answer session followed by a wine and cheese reception. Fitz, who hadn't said much to Blackman since overhearing the phone call with Jon Pierce, chatted with the other poets as he sipped a glass of cheap Merlot. A proud Blackman stood beside Maggie as she talked with the other poets and audience members. Each time she said, "This is my boyfriend, Blackman Smith," Blackman imagined what it would be like to hear her say, "This is my fiancé Blackman Smith. We're getting married this summer."

Or Fall.

Fall weddings were nice, too.

He wondered how long it would take to plan a wedding. He only knew a few people he'd invite to a wedding, and one of them might still fire him in the morning. Or maybe he and Maggie could elope. Go down the shore and get married, or maybe fly to Vegas?

Yeah, no. Fatimah would kill him, and God knew what Maggie's family would do to him. Evidently, it was bad enough that they were living in sin together – because it was still 1962 somewhere – but then, if he whisked her off to get married in front of an Elvis impersonator, they would definitely hate him. Or murder him.

And he wanted Maggie's family to like him.

And not murder him.

It was just after ten when the wine and cheese ended, and the dozen or so people lingering in the bookstore were finally asked to leave. *You don't have to go home, but you can't stay here.* The worst of the rain had finally stopped, and Maggie, Fitz, and Blackman walked into the cold night together. The bookstore was across the street from a small park where someone had strung up fairy lights. The lights cast soft shadows over the trees and benches. A soft mist hung in the air.

"Do you want to share a cab, Fitz?" Maggie asked as she leaned into Blackman, who had an arm slung over her shoulder. Fitz looked at Blackman, whose face still held some residual anger, and then back to Maggie.

"Actually, I was thinking about stopping in over there and having one more drink before calling it a night," Fitz said, tipping his head toward a bar on the far side of the square.

"That sounds lovely," Maggie said, looking up at Blackman. "Do we have time for one more drink, or do you need to get home?" Maggie's eyes were bright in the light, and her face flushed with the excitement of a woman who didn't want her special night to end yet.

"Sure, that sounds great. Fitz," Blackman said, looking at Fitz. "Save us a couple of seats at the bar. We'll catch up with you."

"Of course. See you in a mo," Fitz said with a smile. Then he walked away, and Blackman wrapped his hand around Maggie's and pulled her gently toward the little square across the street. Maggie walked next to Blackman, her arm around his waist.

"I'm so glad you could make it. I was worried that you might have gotten pulled into something last minute at work," she said, leaning her head against his chest and looking up at him with those beautiful hazel eyes.

"I... work was a little hectic today. That's why I was late. But I promised you I'd be here," Blackman said. He kissed the top of her head as he maneuvered them around a puddle.

"I know, but I know things happen, especially in *your* office," she said. "What you do is so important, love," she added with a note of pride in her voice that made his chest go tight.

"Your poems were beautiful," Blackman said, changing the subject. Maggie stood a little straighter, and Blackman could imagine her face blushing. She always blushed when he paid her a compliment. She wasn't good at taking them. He hoped that was something he could work on with her because Maggie deserved every kind word people said to her and about her. She was extraordinary, and he wanted her to know that. To accept it.

"I loved hearing you recite them," Blackman said softly. He kissed her hair again.

"I'm so glad you liked them. I've been working on them for a while. I'm about to submit two of them to a magazine. I'm hoping..." Maggie's voice trailed off as Blackman stopped walking. He stepped in front of her and took her hands in his. Maggie looked up at him, surprised. A little confused.

"Is everything –" She didn't get the chance to finish the sentence. Blackman looked away from her as he lowered himself to one knee. He didn't want her to see the pain that flashed across his face as he knelt in front of her.

"Maggie," he started softly. "I love you. I love you more than anyone or anything in this world. You bring me such joy, you..." He paused as tears flooded his eyes. "You make me whole. You make me happy—happier than I've ever been. And I want to spend the rest of my life making you as happy as you make me."

"Blackman," Maggie breathed. Blackman could feel her hands shaking, or maybe he was the one shaking. Maybe they were both shaking. He let go of her hand, reached into his pocket, and pulled out the ring box he had been hiding in a pair of sweat socks for too long.

"October Margaret Rhymer, will you do me the honor of being my wife?" Blackman opened the ring box, and Maggie pressed a trembling hand to her chest. She looked from the ring to Blackman back to the ring. It was beautiful. A diamond solitaire set in platinum. Maggie looked at Blackman and watched the tears trail down his face as he looked up at her.

She nodded several times before she found her voice.

"Yes, Blackman Emerson Smith. I would be honored to be your wife," she whispered as her eyes flooded with tears.

Blackman took her hand and slipped the ring onto her finger. She looked at the ring in awe. Then she stepped forward and wrapped her arms around Blackman. He held her tightly, and she could feel his tears through her sweater, could feel him trembling in her arms. She had never loved him more than in that moment.

"I love you so much, Blackman. So much, so very much," she said, kissing his hair. Blackman stood up slowly, cupped her cheeks, and kissed her deeply. Slowly. Like they were the only two people in this park. Like they were the only two people on Earth.

When they turned around, Fitz stood behind them, a handkerchief pushed against his face. His eyes shone with tears.

"That is the most beautiful thing I've ever seen," he said, his voice wet. Maggie laughed and launched herself at her brother. He wrapped her up in a tight hug, and when she let go, Fitz looked up at Blackman with a wide smile.

"Welcome to the family, brother," Fitz said tremulously. Blackman stepped forward and wrapped Fitz up in a tight hug. As he clutched his soon-to-be brother-in-law, he could hear Maggie shouting into her phone, "Nicky, I'm getting married."

Chapter 8

When Blackman first met Lennie Harrington, a man whose online bio Blackman knew frontward and backward, he'd expected an intimidating man. A dangerous man who would be concerned about his daughter's well being as well as Blackman's suitability as a husband. He expected the man would threaten to do terrible things to him if he hurt his little girl, but instead, he found an older, kind faced man with a thick head of graying hair, a working class accent, and the same brilliant blue eyes as Fitz. When Lennie Harrington took Blackman's hand in his, he grinned like a man who was already naming his grandchildren.

"Blackman, it's a pleasure to finally meet you, son!" The older man's smile was shocking in its sincerity. Blackman's own father had never been so happy to see him. They were standing in the library of an old, refurbished London townhouse that Blackman was convinced he'd seen in a BBC adaptation of an Austen novel. Maggie's brothers were standing behind their father with neutral looks, all watching Blackman curiously, wondering what kind of man could thaw their sister's frigid heart. Joseph once openly admitted he expected his sister would die alone in a houseful of cats who would consume her before anyone realized she was dead. He didn't know she was a dog person.

"It's a pleasure to meet you, Mr. Harrington," Blackman said, his voice steady. He did his best to adopt his best courtroom demeanor in an effort to avoid conveying his bone deep nervousness. He was wearing a new charcoal gray suit, with a white shirt, and a pale blue tie, even though Maggie had expressly told him not to wear a suit.

He had never met a girlfriend's parents, and now he was meeting Maggie's father *after* he proposed to her, which he didn't think was a problem until Fatimah pointed out that it was a problem. That it was a big, mountain-sized problem.

"Habibi, you must wear a suit. Your best suit, and your best tie, and you must get a haircut. You must look your absolute best."

"But, Auntie," Blackman replied in Arabic as he and Fatimah sat in her favorite cafe drinking Turkish coffee. "Maggie said not to worry about formalities."

"Don't be a fool, Blackman," Fatimah said sternly, and Blackman was momentarily taken aback by the use of his Christian name as well as her harsh tone.

"No daughter understands her father, let alone a father like this man. This is a dangerous man, Blackman, and you are not used to men like him. He is a man that even your father would have avoided. Now, when you meet him, you need to make sure he understands that you *understand he is your better, and that he knows how much you love his daughter. His only daughter," Fatimah stressed. And then she added darkly, "His only daughter with whom you are living out of wedlock."*

Blackman looked at Fatimah and said deferentially, "Of course, Auntie."

So there Blackman stood in front of Lennie Harrington and three of his four sons in a new suit, a fresh haircut, and a cleanly shaven face because Maggie preferred him clean shaven.

"We don't stand on ceremony in this house, son. Lennie is just fine, and these are my sons. Nicky, Joey, and Oliver."

Handshakes were exchanged, and the five of them stood around looking at one another. Finally, Lennie, who was dressed casually in a pair of jeans and a polo shirt, leaned against a wingback chair. He met Blackman's eyes and held them.

"Now that we've all been introduced let's get the awkward bit out of the way. So, you're a prosecutor back in the States?" Lennie Harrington was asking questions he already knew the answers to. His blue eyes shone with a keen, ruthless intelligence.

"Yes, sir," Blackman answered.

"You like putting villains in jail?"

"Yes, sir." There was no way Blackman was lying to this man. Not now. Not ever.

"You know what I am, yeah? What I do? What *we* do?" Lennie asked.

"Yes, sir," Blackman said, his brown eyes never moving from Lennie Harrington's piercing blue ones.

Lennie nodded thoughtfully. "We never involve October in the family business."

"Doesn't matter, sir. Family is family," Blackman said.

Fatimah had taught him that.

Lennie looked at Blackman and tilted his head, clearly taking the measure of the man in front of him to see if what he'd said was bullshit or not. Blackman stood at his full height, his shoulders back, his back straight, unmoving.

After what felt like an eternity, Lennie Harrington pushed himself off the wingback chair and walked over to Blackman, putting his arms on Blackman's biceps. It would have been too awkward to clasp Blackman's broad shoulders because Blackman was nearly a foot taller.

"Oliver," Lennie said, still looking at Blackman.

"Yeah, da?"

"Get your brother here a beer."

"Yeah, da."

Lennie gave Blackman a fatherly smile that nearly broke Blackman's heart. Never in his life had his own father looked at him with such love.

***

Blackman hadn't been on a vacation in years. Not since high school when his father would send Blackman and Fatimah away for Spring Break and summer vacation as if his father, who was rarely home, needed a vacation from his son and his son's nanny. Sometimes he and Fatimah went to Europe, where Fatimah would take Blackman to museums and libraries and World Heritage sights to imbue him with culture, and Blackman would dutifully follow and listen attentively while surreptitiously looking at girls. Sometimes, for Spring Break, they went skiing in Vail, where his father kept a condo. Sometimes, they went to Miami, where his father kept *another* condo, to eat good Cuban and thaw out from a long, cold Philadelphia winter.

However, as soon as Blackman went to college, there was no longer time for vacations. Occasionally, he and Fatimah would go to New York City or DC to see a show or a museum exhibit, but he hadn't been further than that in years. The long weekend in London notwithstanding.

Now, Maggie was standing in his office doorway scowling at him, and he was sitting behind his desk, looking for one more excuse not to get out of his chair. His administrative assistant Julia had warned him an hour ago that he needed to get his ass in gear. She didn't deliver her warning quite like that, but it was close enough. Before Blackman started dating Maggie, Julia had been more than a little enamored with him.

He didn't think she actually had a crush on him, but she was loyal and devoted, and every once in a while, he caught her checking him out when he wore his best court suit. Because his dad had always been a douche to every woman who had ever worked for him, Blackman went out of his way to be a good boss. If he stopped for coffee on the way back from court, he'd pick her up an iced coffee or the blueberry coffee cake she liked. He always remembered her birthday, her favorite restaurants, and her parents' names because she still lived with them.

Now, he was pretty sure Julia was in love with Maggie, and more than half of her loyalty had been transferred to Blackman's fiancé. He wasn't going to lie, because he'd put his lying days behind him, he was a little jealous.

"We're going to be late," Maggie grumbled. Blackman typed something on his computer and avoided his fiancée's eyes.

"We're not going to be late. Your father chartered a flight. It *can't* leave without *us*." As soon as the words were out of his mouth, he knew he'd made a mistake. He not only heard Maggie's deep sigh, but he was fairly sure he heard her growl. Like actually growl. Like a bear or something else that might kill him in his sleep or his office.

"Darling," Maggie said with exaggerated patience she clearly wasn't feeling.

"Sweetheart," Blackman responded hitting send on an email before proofreading it. Clearly, he was living dangerously on multiple fronts today. When he finally looked up, Maggie's arms were crossed over her chest, and her face was thunderous. She had been leaning against the doorframe, but now she was standing straight. She uncrossed her arms, reached for her backpack, and slung it over her shoulder. Then she reached for *her* duffle bag and picked it up. Without a word, she turned around and walked away.

Fuck.

Blackman pushed his chair back and got to his feet just as Julia appeared in the doorway with a disappointed look on her face.

"Really? I warned you an *hour* ago," she said exasperatedly.

Blackman groaned. He was not bringing her back a present from Greece. Not even a little one. He quickly turned off his computer, grabbed his suit coat from the coat stand in the corner of his office, and his backpack from the floor. He shrugged on the suit jacket as he crossed the small office in two long strides. He grabbed his duffle bag just as Julia stepped out of his way.

"Safe travels, boss," she said. Was that smugness in her voice? Honestly, she was *his* employee. Well, she was the DA's office's employee, but he was her boss for Christ's sake.

"Let Jon Pierce know I'm leaving," Blackman said with a sharpness Julia ignored. "And email me the brief for the Quinlan case when it comes in, and if Detective Semple calls, let him know I'll be back... ummm...," Blackman tried to remember when he was supposed to be back.

Instead of acknowledging anything he had said to her, Julia said cheerfully, "Enjoy Greece."

Maggie was just getting into the black town car Fitz had invariably sent for her because he was always sending cars to pick up his sister as Blackman crossed the lobby. She didn't bother to look back to see if he was coming; she just slammed the car door—hard.

"Fuck," Blackman said, increasing his pace. He bumped into a few people and quickly apologized. As he passed the two lobby guards, the young one with the bare left hand snickered at him, and Blackman could imagine the subtext. *Pussy whipped bastard.* The older man, the one with the thick wedding band on his left hand, shook his head sympathetically. Blackman gave him a small smile and fought the urge to flip off the other one.

Blackman burst through the lobby doors, almost knocking over a jogger with remarkably bad timing. He said he was sorry as the jogger flipped him off. When he reached the car, the trunk popped open. He threw his duffle bag in, and for the first time, he wondered why Maggie had brought both their bags to the office. He wondered if she had walked from their apartment with their bags because she didn't quite trust him to keep his promise to go on vacation with her family. The thought made him wince. Yes, he wasn't excited about a week in Greece, but it wasn't because he didn't like her family or that he didn't want to go away with her. It was just...

Blackman took a deep, centering breath and slammed the trunk shut. The driver had stepped out and was holding the door open expectantly. Blackman nodded at the woman and climbed into the car.

Maggie, her arms once again crossed over her chest, stared straight ahead. Blackman, knowing his fiancée's temper, said nothing. He buckled his seatbelt and settled his hands on his lap. He thought about pulling out his Blackberry and checking his email, but he didn't want to make things worse. Instead, he stared forward and kept his face neutral. After a little while, Maggie uncrossed her arms and settled her hands on her lap. Blackman waited another few minutes before he reached over and took her hand. He threaded his long fingers through hers, but she didn't react. Then Blackman gently brought her hand to his lips and kissed it softly.

"I'm sorry," he murmured.

She ignored him, but after another minute or so, she closed her fingers around his, and they drove in silence to the airport. When they boarded the Gulfstream, Fitz was already sitting in one of the luxurious seats sipping a martini. He took one look at his sister, then looked at a sheepish looking Blackman.

"Perfect timing!" Fitz announced with a grin. "The martinis are heavenly!"

Maggie ignored her brother, walked to the rear of the cabin, dropped into a seat, and within seconds had a book in her hands and headphones over her ears. Blackman didn't even consider taking a seat next to her. Instead, he looked at his future brother-in-law and sighed.

"How long did you make her wait?" Fitz asked knowingly.

Blackman shrugged guiltily as he sat on the sofa across the aisle from Fitz's chair. Like Blackman, Fitz was dressed in a suit because Fitz was always dressed in a suit. Blackman wasn't entirely sure how Fitz spent his days, but however he spent them, he was always dressed to the nines. Because of Blackman's size, he had all his suits custom made, and they were nice, but they weren't *Fitz* nice. Fitz had his own Saville Row tailor, and Blackman was sure Fitz's wardrobe cost more than Blackman's apartment.

"Five minutes," Blackman said a little tightly.

Fitz raised a perfectly sculpted eyebrow.

"Okay, ten. But no more than ten minutes," Blackman said as one of the flight attendants walked over to him.

"What can I get you, Mr. Smith?"

Blackman eyed Fitz's martini.

What the hell.

"I'll take a martini, please." Blackman hadn't drunk martinis before meeting Fitz, but he had also never paid more than $20 for a haircut nor heard the term manscaping either. People said it was a new lover who changed a man. In Blackman's case, it was his fiancée's brother.

"Of course. And Ms. Rhymer?" The flight attendant could clearly see Maggie's *do not disturb* sign from across the cabin.

"Cabernet Sauvignon, and if you have some cheese and crackers, can you bring her some, too? Thank you," Blackman said, taking a quick look at his watch. Considering how busy Maggie's morning had been, he doubted she'd eaten much. Probably just some toast with her morning coffee and maybe some fruit for lunch. Blackman was probably lucky she hadn't murdered him in his office. Or at least tried.

The flight attendant, a pretty brunette with straight black hair, pale skin, and a slight Korean accent, smiled.

"Of course," she said. When she walked away, Blackman hazarded a look in Maggie's direction, but she was engrossed in her book. Her face and shoulders had relaxed, and Blackman felt slightly better. The flight attendant arrived with his martini, and he thanked her politely. He watched the flight attendant bring Maggie a large glass of wine and a platter of cheese and crackers. Blackman loved the way Maggie's face lit up. As he watched, she put her book down as the flight attendant arranged the wine and the platter on a small table. When the flight attendant walked away, Maggie looked at Blackman and gave him a small smile. He returned the smile and mouthed: *I love you.*

Maggie rolled her eyes, but her smile brightened a little more.

Okay, not completely forgiven, but a little forgiven.

He could live with that.

She'd forgiven him by the time the flight attendant brought out dinner. By then, she was on her second glass of wine and decided to join Blackman and Fitz at the front of the cabin. They ate a lovely meal of sea bass steaks, fresh asparagus, and roasted fingerling potatoes. By the time they finished dessert, angel food cake with a mixed berry compote, Maggie was curled up next to Blackman on the sofa. The plane had one bedroom, and it was decided quickly that Blackman and Maggie would take the bed. The seats were big and comfortable but not nearly big enough to accommodate Blackman.

"No, funny business back there," Fitz said as Maggie stood up to follow Blackman to the rear of the plane. She looked at her brother and said, "Just for that comment, I'll be sure to make him scream because I know how."

Fitz grinned.

"I'm sure you do, Maggie. I'm sure you do," he said with a wink. Maggie chuckled as she leaned over, gave her brother a quick peck on the cheek, and whispered goodnight.

By the time they arrived at the villa in Lefkada, Greece, it was nearly eight in the morning, and it appeared that nobody was up yet. While Fitz thanked the driver, Blackman pulled the bags out of the trunk.

Maggie, who had pushed her sunglasses up on her head, took in the villa with an enormous grin. Her father had been renting this villa out for family vacations for years, and this was one of Maggie's favorite places. When she turned to Blackman with that electric smile, his heart skipped a beat. In the early morning sunlight, she was breathtaking. Before they landed, she had changed into linen shorts and a tank top. The boots she had been wearing on the flight were in her hands, and she was wearing a pair of Teva sandals, her toes painted a cheerful shade of purple. She was the most beautiful woman in the world. He watched as she walked over to him and wrapped her arms around his waist. She rested her head against his chest and inhaled deeply.

***

Blackman stood at the window staring at the teal blue sea stretched before him. Their bedroom was spacious, with a king sized bed and a comfortable sofa beneath one of the windows. The sun was high in the sky, and it was already hot outside, but the villa was cool. The bedroom windows let in a sea breeze rich with the scent of salt water and flowering trees. It was entirely possible this was the most beautiful place Blackman had ever been. He thought about Fatimah. He wondered if he could bring her next year. It was a family vacation, after all, and she was *his* family. She would love it here. He could imagine her sitting on the patio, a book in her hand and a teapot filled with her favorite black tea steeping on the table beside her.

"I thought you were going to change." Maggie said from behind him. Blackman turned around and looked at Maggie, who looked beautiful in a two piece purple bathing suit that brought out that blue in her hazel eyes. She pulled a white linen cover over herself while she waited for Blackman to answer. As soon as she was covered, Blackman missed the sight of her firm body in that two piece that didn't leave enough to the imagination. If Blackman were a jealous man, the suit might have bothered him, but he wasn't a jealous man. He was a lucky man, and Maggie was his.

And he was hers.

"Yeah, I'm going to," Blackman stalled. He was standing at the window bare chested wearing running pants that hung low on his hips. He met Maggie's eyes and then let his drift away. Maggie watched him for a moment, then walked over to him and stood in front of him, her palms on his chest, waiting. When he finally looked down at her, she gave him a tender, understanding smile.

"You swim almost every day," she said evenly.

He didn't say anything.

"People see those scars every day," she reminded him gently. A slight blush crept over his face, and he started to look away, but Maggie reached up and touched his chin gently. He hadn't shaved, and his face was rough and dark with stubble.

"I... ummm... I don't know those people," Blackman said, not quite meeting her eyes.

Maggie moved her hand and cupped his face. He closed his eyes and leaned into her touch. She knew plenty of men whose scars were worse than Blackman's, but she knew the scars didn't matter to him. What mattered to him was his limp, and even though they had flown in a chartered jet, Blackman had still been in transit for well over twelve hours, and his bad leg was stiff, and his limp was more pronounced than usual. He should have swum in the pool earlier to loosen up his body, but he hadn't. Instead, he'd stretched in the privacy of their bedroom, but the stretching didn't do much to alleviate the pain or the limp.

"Love," Maggie said softly. "Love, look at me." Maggie waited until Blackman opened his eyes and looked at her. The pain and uncertainty in his brown eyes broke her heart a little.

"No one is going to judge you," she said. She ran a thumb over his rough cheek. "No one will think less of you because your leg hurts you."

I suppose this means you won't be able to go pro.

That was what his father had said to him when he returned from his trip to find Blackman still in the hospital. Blackman never forgot that his father hadn't cut his trip short after Fatimah told him about the injury, even after she explained the extent of the damage to Blackman's leg and the additional surgeries he was going to need.

It sounds like you have it under control, Fatimah. You don't need me there. Write a check for whatever he needs. We'll be back next week.

And that was his relationship with his father in a nutshell.

God, he fucking hated that man.

But he didn't hate Lennie Harrington, and he didn't hate the Harrington brothers, although, aside from Fitz, Blackman didn't know how the others felt about him. Not really. Joe seemed pleasant enough, and Oliver had been more than happy to talk sports with him, but Nick was more reserved. Maybe because he was the oldest. Maybe because he was the heir apparent, and, sure, heavy was the head that wears the crown, but heavier was the head that would *inherit* the crown.

Or maybe Nick just didn't think Blackman was all that impressive.

Sure, Blackman had size going for him, and he'd been a fighter once, a good one, but now he was a lawyer whose leg hurt so badly some days it brought tears to his eyes. Blackman hated how much he *wanted* these people to like him. How much he *needed* these people to like him because he loved Maggie more than he loved life itself.

Blackman met Maggie's eyes, and he wanted to say something, but everything that ran through his head sounded insecure and pathetic, and he didn't want to give voice to those thoughts. He knew Maggie liked the confident Blackman, the Blackman who didn't back down from a fight, the Blackman who projected fearlessness and strength. He'd done his best to shield her from the rest of him. As if reading his mind, she said with a voice that brooked no argument, "Put your swimsuit on. We're already late."

When Blackman and Maggie arrived on the beach, the lounge chairs and umbrellas had already been set up. A long table beneath a white tent was filled with covered dishes, plates, and utensils. Coolers filled with water and beer were set up at the far end of the table, and a large bucket filled with ice and bottles of wine sweated on the table.

Fitz reclined on a chaise lounge in the sun, wearing a swimsuit that left little to the imagination. Blackman had to admire the courage of such a pale man. Lennie Harrington, dressed in white linen pants and a pale pink linen shirt, sat beneath a large beach umbrella reading a paperback novel. An attractive woman, younger than Lennie but not egregiously so, with thick black hair and a face that reminded Blackman of a Flamenco dancer, sat on a chair close to his. She, too, had a book in her hands, but it was thick, and from the cover, it looked like something deep and complex. The kind of literature Maggie favored.

In the surf, Joe and Oliver splashed around with two topless women. Blackman tried not to gape. Maggie leaned into him and whispered, "Welcome to Greece, darling."

Blackman looked down at Maggie. "Why –"

"Hello, da," Maggie said brightly, giving Blackman a *you're an idiot* look. Lennie looked up from his paperback and grinned at his daughter.

"Maggie, love, it's about time you two got out here," he said as he got to his feet and wrapped his arms around his daughter. Then he stepped back and opened his arms to Blackman. "It's so good to see you again, son."

The emotion that welled up in Blackman as Lennie hugged him took him by surprise. He hugged the older man, then stepped back and cleared his throat, hoping Maggie's father couldn't sense his reaction to the fatherly hug. Blackman was a man unaccustomed to fatherly hugs.

"Thank you for having me. This place is incredible," Blackman said, knowing full well that incredible didn't begin to describe the ocean-side villa.

Lennie, who didn't do false modesty, nodded. "It is." Then he turned back to the woman in the chair beside him. "Marta, love, meet Blackman Smith. Maggie's fiancé. Blackman, this is my friend Marta."

Marta rose to her feet and took a long look at Blackman.

"Blackman, darling, I've heard so much about you. It's a pleasure to finally meet you," she said in a thick Spanish accent. Then she reached up, cupped his cheeks with beautifully manicured fingers, and brought him down so she could kiss his cheeks in the European way. Marta was so tiny Blackman nearly had to bend in half so her lips could find his cheeks.

"It's a pleasure to meet you, too," Blackman said with a smile as he straightened up to his full height, feeling awkward. Before he could think of something to say, Lennie turned to Maggie.

"Joey and Oliver were here for less than an hour when those two birds sauntered up. Why don't you go down there and remind your brothers this is a *family* vacation. And let them know they should keep their *extracurriculars* to a minimum. The last thing Nicky needs is to hear his brothers going at it like rabbits with those girls," Lennie said. Then he looked at Blackman. "Nicky's girlfriend dumped him last week. No one's supposed to know, but *everyone* knows." Lennie gave Fitz a meaningful look. Fitz didn't so much as move. Blackman nodded, unsurprised Fitz was the family gossip.

"I have to admit," Lennie began as Maggie stripped out of her cover and tossed it on an empty chair. Blackman tried not to look away from Lennie, no matter how much he wanted to check out his fiancée's ass in that bathing suit. Lennie continued, seemingly oblivious. "Honestly, we never cared much for the girl. Marta and I, but Nicky's a stubborn one. They all are, I suppose."

Lennie turned and watched Maggie jog down the beach toward her brothers, who both started yelling when they saw her. Soon the topless girls in the water were forgotten as Maggie's brothers took turns hugging her.

"Maggie says you're self-conscious about your leg," Lennie said apropos of nothing.

Blackman blinked, unsure of how to handle Lennie's directness. As Blackman searched for something to say, Lennie smiled kindly.

"I know you haven't spent much time with us, and I'm hoping that changes with time. But I want you to know from the beginning that you've got nothing to worry about. You're safe with us, son."

Lennie looked at Blackman, but Blackman kept his eyes on the water in front of him. Joey had just thrown Maggie into deeper water, and Blackman could hear her screams of delight from where he stood. Swallowing down a lump of emotion in his throat, Blackman said quietly, "I understand. Thank you."

"Good!" Lennie said, clapping his hands together. "Now get down there before Joseph drowns his sister. She's a terrible swimmer."

Blackman nodded, peeling off his t-shirt and dropping it on the chair next to Maggie's wrap. He limped down to the water. Once he greeted Joseph and Oliver, he wrapped his arms around Maggie's waist and pulled her into deeper water.

"I hear you can't swim very well," Blackman purred into her ear.

"I swim just fine," she said with a giggle. "But if you're looking to play naughty lifeguard, I'm more than willing to play naughty drowning victim."

Blackman laughed and held her closer.

They'd returned to the house in the late afternoon, and everyone disappeared into their bedrooms for a late afternoon nap after agreeing to meet for dinner at seven. Blackman couldn't remember the last time he'd spent a day at the beach, but he'd enjoyed it more than he imagined he could. Once Maggie grew tired of the water, she returned to the beach and laid out in the hot sun. Blackman then spent the next hour swimming laps in the warm ocean water. By the time he emerged from the water, his leg had loosened considerably, and his limp had eased.

While Blackman and Maggie had snuggled together in bed, Maggie explained that Marta and her father had started spending time together years ago.

"I'm not sure how they met," Maggie said with a yawn. "But she's good for him. I don't know why they keep up the friend charade. Mom's been gone for years, but that's what he likes, so who am I to argue?"

Dinner was held on the expansive patio while the sun set over the water. Maggie and Marta had changed into sun dresses, but the men had settled on jeans and t-shirts, except for Lennie, who wore another pair of white linen pants and a blue linen shirt that matched Marta's dress, and Fitz, who wore a summer weight suit.

Lennie sat at one end of the table, and Nick, looking sullen and distracted, sat at the other. Marta sat to Lennie's right, and Maggie and Blackman sat beside her. On the other side of the table, Fitz sat to his father's left, and Oliver and Joseph sat alongside him. Blackman found himself sitting next to Nick and across from Joseph. He wondered if that was by design. The day at the beach had been pleasant, and Nick had eventually shown up only to take a lounge chair beneath a beach umbrella and immediately go to sleep.

As they ate a fantastic dinner of freshly caught fish served over greens, Blackman let his attention slide from one conversation to another. Maggie sat close to him, and as was his way, Blackman kept an arm around her. He wasn't a possessive man, but Blackman had waited so long for Maggie that he found that his need to touch her was almost visceral. As she talked to her father or Marta or her brothers, Blackman sat with one arm draped over her chair, his fingers playing with the ends of her long red hair. Eating dinner, one handed for the most part, he half listened to Maggie's conversations while holding his own conversation with Joseph and Oliver. As dinner continued and more wine was poured, people became more relaxed and animated, but Blackman noted that Nick remained remote and quiet. Nick listened intently to the conversations around him, but he didn't seem interested in participating in them. He sipped his whiskey and ate his dinner as if he couldn't quite taste what was on his plate. Blackman felt for Maggie's brother. Any guy would.

After dinner, the local staff Lennie hired cleared the table. Once the sun had set fully, another table was laid out with traditional Greek desserts, coffee, and teas. The temperature dropped as the sun went down, and Maggie went back into the house to get a sweater. Blackman took a clean plate and piled it high with triangles of Baklava, a slice of Karidopita, and a slice of Sfakianopita. He would definitely have to swim extra laps in the morning.

He poured himself a small cup of Greek coffee and walked to the far end of the patio so he could look out over the dark water. It was a beautiful night, and stars blanketed the sky. As he ate the best Baklava he'd ever tasted, he felt more than heard Nick come up behind him. Blackman continued to eat as Nick stepped up alongside him, holding his own plate of Greek desserts, but instead of a cup of coffee, he had another tumbler of whiskey.

Blackman had nearly eight inches on Nick, and he considered putting some distance between himself and the other man if for no other reason than to appear not so tall. He didn't move, though. He didn't imagine Nick would appreciate the gesture. Whether Blackman was standing next to Nick or a foot away, he was still significantly taller. Nothing was going to change that.

"You hurt her, and I'll gut you like a fucking fish," Nick said softly. He sounded a little drunk and more than a little sad.

"I understand," Blackman said easily. He'd rather cut out his own heart than hurt Maggie, so Nick had nothing to worry about. Not that Nick needed to know that.

"Sorry about what happened between you and your girlfriend," Blackman said after a while.

Nick scoffed.

"Fitz is such a fucking gossip," Nick said on a sigh. He watched the water stretched out in front of him for a long moment. "I guess it was for the best. She wasn't the type of girl to be okay with..." His voice trailed off, and he took a sip of his whiskey. Blackman didn't say anything. What was there to say?

"Why are *you* okay with this? You're a fucking... whatever they call it in the States. How can *you* be okay with this?" Nick asked, his voice sharp with incredulity. A man itching for a fight with someone bigger than he because that was how much he was hurting. Sometimes the only thing that made a man feel better was when a bigger man handed him his ass. Blackman had never had the experience, but he'd had smaller men pick fights with him enough times for him to understand the dynamic.

Blackman took a bite of the Sfakianopita and promised himself he'd look up a recipe as soon as he got home. Or maybe he'd find a cookbook in the small village up the road. He took his time chewing so he could collect his thoughts.

"I love your sister more than I like my job," Blackman said simply. He could feel Nick's eyes on his face, but he didn't move. He just stared at the ocean.

After what felt like forever, Nick turned and followed Blackman's gaze out over the water. He seemed to weigh his words.

"That break must have hurt like a motherfucker," he said.

"Yeah. I pissed myself," Blackman said easily because it was the truth.

"Fuck," Nick said with a low whistle. "The bone went right through the skin?"

"Left blood and piss all over the ice," Blackman said as he picked up another Baklava and popped it into his mouth. He chewed thoughtfully. "I walked with a cane for six months. Fucking twenty-one years old, and I was walking with a cane. It was fucking unreal," Blackman admitted thinking back to days he preferred not to remember. The looks people gave him when they didn't think he was looking. The sympathy. The pity. The *thank God it wasn't worse* platitudes people felt compelled to say to him whenever the subject of his injury came up. Yeah, it could have been worse. He could have lost his leg; however, that didn't change how bad things were right then because when he was standing on a college campus leaning on a cane, things seemed pretty fucking bad.

"Yeah, well, you don't worry about a fucking limp with us. You got that?" Nick said sharply. "You're fucking one of us. You don't forget that."

Blackman looked down at Nick for a second and then said, "Fuck that girl. You deserve better."

Nick looked up at him and blinked slowly. "Fucking right I do."

Blackman smiled before he went back to looking at the ocean.

***

Years later, Blackman and Maggie were having dinner at an Old City restaurant with Fitz and his boyfriend James when Nick called to tell Blackman that Lennie Harrington was about to die.

Blackman's phone had been buzzing in his pocket for nearly ten minutes, and he finally apologized and pulled it out to check it. Maggie had a strict no cell phone policy at the table, and although Blackman was loathe to break it, the persistence of the person at the other end of the line proved impossible to resist.

He looked at the screen.

Brother Nick:

Call me NOW.

After saying something about work, Blackman excused himself from the table and stepped out into the cold fall night.

Nick picked up on the first ring.

"Thanks for calling back," Nick said. His voice was strained. Emotional.

"Everything okay?" Blackman asked, knowing it was not.

"Da's had a massive stroke. He's on life support, but only until everyone gets here."

"Jesus," Blackman said, turning around quickly and looking up the street as if he had expected to see Nick standing there. He took a few steps away from the restaurant so Maggie couldn't see him through the plate glass window. Tears stung his eyes.

"Yeah, I know, fucking awful. He was watching football with the grandkids. It's a fucking mess," Nick said, and Blackman could hear his brother moving around on the other end of the phone and the occasional tapping of computer keys.

Blackman took a deep, steadying breath that was neither deep nor steadying.

"He loved you so much, Blackman. You were as much his son as any of us," Nick said in that same strained voice.

I know you haven't spent much time with us, and I'm hoping that changes with time. But I want you to know from the beginning that you've got nothing to worry about. You're safe with us, son.

And Blackman had always felt safe with the Harringtons. Safe and loved.

Tears slid down Blackman's face, and he wiped them away with the heel of his hand. He hadn't cried when his father died, but his father hadn't loved him like Lennie Harrington had loved him, and Blackman hadn't loved his father the way he loved Lennie Harrington.

"I loved him, too, Nick," Blackman said quietly.

Blackman waited as Nick took a deep breath.

"Oliver's going to call Fitz and Maggie in a minute, but I needed to talk with you first. You know I love you, Blackman. You're my brother. You know that, right?" The Harrington's didn't do in-laws. Once you married into the family, you were blood.

"Nick," Blackman said unsteadily.

"Blackman, you need to listen to me. Da's funeral will be a who's who of nefarious types. People you don't want to be in the same room with, let alone have your picture snapped with. For the sake of your professional life, brother, you need to consider staying home. Maggie's going to tell you the same thing," Nick said. He paused, then added, "Da would tell you the same thing. He'd want you protected. Safe."

Blackman wiped away more tears with the back of his hand. When Fatimah died three years ago after a bout of pneumonia, the entire Harrington family came into town en masse. Lennie and Marta, and Nick, Joey, and Oliver along with their wives, children, and nannies. Even cousins Blackman had grown close to over the years made the flight to Philadelphia. Dozens of Catholic and Protestant men, women, and children joined Blackman to help him bury his mother. The Harringtons followed all the Muslim traditions without question or comment. Lennie and Nick stood on either side of Blackman while the Imam led the service in the garden outside of Fatimah's apartment building.

Blackman recited all the prayers in the Arabic Fatimah had so lovingly taught him as a boy. His family did what he did as best they could, and when Fatimah was transported to the beautiful cemetery at the edge of the city, each of the men threw three handfuls of dirt into her grave as tradition dictated.

If the women resented being relegated to the back of the group or being required to cover their heads, they never complained. Once the burial was over, they ate lunch with Fatimah's friends at the same Lebanese restaurant where Fatimah had first met Maggie. That day the Harringtons drank tea with Fatimah's friends and celebrated her life. That night the Harringtons took Blackman to a bar, got him well and properly drunk, and listened to his endless stories of the woman who loved him like a son and whom he loved like a mother.

"Nick, I need to call Jamie's nanny so she can get him packed. He doesn't have a suit that fits. If I text Sherry his measurements, can she pick something up for him?"

"Blackman –"

"And I'm going to have to check flights. There should be a red-eye leaving in a couple –"

Nick sighed.

"I've charted a flight. Fitz will know the details."

"Okay, we should be able to make it to the airport in maybe 90 minutes. If Oliver is going to call, have him do it now. I don't want Maggie to know about this conversation."

"Okay, Blackman. I love you, brother."

"I love you, too, Nick."

Blackman ended the call, wiped his eyes, and took a deep breath before he walked back into the restaurant.

Maggie hadn't put up as much of a fuss as Blackman expected. Of course, he assumed the real battle would come the day of the funeral, but for now Maggie didn't have the energy to argue with her husband about his life decisions.

Three hours after Blackman hung up with Nick, they were flying east on a chartered jet to London. Jamie was asleep on a sofa, buried beneath his favorite blanket, clutching the well worn teddy bear everyone pretended he didn't sleep with. Fitz was dozing in a captain's chair with a Jonathon Franzen book open across his lap. Blackman and Maggie were sharing another sofa opposite their son.

Maggie was asleep with her head on Blackman's lap, her face red and swollen from crying. Blackman absently stroked her hair and listened to her breathe. Her relationship with her father was complicated, which made her relationship with everyone else in her life complicated, but she loved the old man fiercely, and she would feel his absence acutely.

They all would.

On the day of the funeral Maggie tried to pick an argument with Blackman, but her heart wasn't in it.

"This is a terrible idea," she said, sitting on the edge of her bed worrying her wedding ring as Blackman fixed his tie. He was dressed entirely in black like the other Harrington men. He looked at Maggie's reflection in the mirror. She was gorgeous in a high neck black dress and black opaque tights that did wonderful things for her legs. Blackman stopped adjusting his tie and turned to look at his wife.

"It'll be fine."

"He would understand if you stayed away. In fact, he'd probably prefer it." She met her husband's eyes with exhausted and pained eyes that shone in the soft light of the bedroom.

"He," Maggie said quietly. "He would want you to think about your career."

"You worry too much about my career," Blackman said dismissively.

"Maybe you should worry more," Maggie chided, but Blackman wouldn't take the bait. Instead, he walked over to the bed and sat beside her. Putting his arm around her, he pulled her close. She leaned her head against his suit coat, and he kissed her hair.

"Honey, my career isn't more important than my family. What lesson would I be teaching Jamie if I stayed away? If I didn't stand beside my family on this of all days?" Maggie knew the question was rhetorical.

"I loved your father, and I love your family, our family. I'm where I belong," he whispered. Maggie turned and wrapped her arms around him.

"I couldn't do this without you," she admitted weakly.

Before Blackman could respond, there was a sharp knock at the door.

"Come in," Blackman said, still holding Maggie.

Jamie, dressed in black like all the Harrington men, pushed the door open.

"Uncle Nick says it's time," Jamie said solemnly.

Blackman looked at his son, who, at barely ten years old, was long and lean like Blackman had been at that age. His red hair, which always seemed to need a cut, was combed back from his forehead, and it looked like one of the older cousins had gelled it into place.

Blackman got to his feet and walked over to his son, pulling him into a tight hug. Jamie wrapped his arms around his father and hugged him back. When Blackman released him, he stepped back and placed his hands on Jamie's shoulders, waiting for the boy to meet his eyes.

"Today is going to be a hard day, Habibi," Blackman said softly.

Jamie nodded.

"It's okay to cry if you want to, just like when Jedda died. I cried. Crying is fine."

Fatimah had been the only grandmother Jamie had ever known.

"What about the other boys? They'll think I'm a baby." Jamie looked down at his feet.

Blackman shook his head and took his son's chin in his hands and tilted it, so Jamie was looking at him.

"No, they won't, Habibi. We're all family here, and you can always be yourself in front of family. Did any one of your uncles call me a baby when I cried at Jedda's funeral?" Blackman asked. Unlike the other children, Jamie had stood with the men on the day of Fatimah's funeral, and had watched everything closely, doing as his father did, trying his best with the Arabic Fatimah had been teaching him.

"No," Jamie said quietly.

"That's because we're family, and your cousins love you, Habibi, so you must trust them to keep you safe today."

Jamie nodded. Maggie came up beside them and opened her arms, and Jamie stepped into his mother's embrace without hesitation.

"You look so handsome, my love. Your grandfather would be so proud of you." Maggie kissed her son's cheek.

"Thanks, Mom," Jamie said, then kissed her cheek in return.

"Okay." Blackman set his hand on the small of his wife's back and pushed her gently toward the door. "It's time."

The funeral mass was held at Westminster Cathedral, the largest Catholic church in London. The Harrington family took up the first several rows of pews at the front of the church, and hundreds of mourners took up much of the rest. There was a media presence that surprised Blackman and a police presence that did not.

The priest, an elderly gentleman who had Baptized all the Harrington children as well as buried their mother in their younger days, said mass and delivered a thoughtful and beautiful eulogy that focused on Lennie the doting father, the loving husband, and the devoted longtime partner to Marta, who sat flanked by her sisters Helena and Rosa. Fitz delivered the eulogy for his siblings, and Lennie's brother Martin delivered the final eulogy that waxed quixotic about their humble beginnings and youthful indiscretions, earning a few laughs amidst the tears.

Then Fitz, Oliver, Joseph, Nick, Blackman, and longtime family friend Hugh Sutter, who was almost as tall as Blackman, carried Lennie's coffin to a waiting limo that took him to his final resting place. Lennie was buried in the family plot alongside his beloved wife.

By the end of the day, dozens of photos of Lennie Harrington's sons and his American son-in-law, Blackman Emerson Smith, were published in the online editions of British and European newspapers. On the way back to the family townhouse, Jon Pierce texted Blackman.

Jon Pierce:

Saw you on BBC. Did you have to carry the coffin?

Blackman looked at the text for a long time before he answered it.

Blackman Smith:

Yes. He was more of a father to me than my own.

Then he slipped his phone back into his pocket. Considering that his new boss spent most of his day watching Fox News, Blackman wasn't too concerned about blowback, and if there was any, he'd deal with it.

Back at the townhouse, Jamie disappeared with his cousins, and Maggie started to make the rounds visiting relatives whom she hadn't seen in years. Blackman made himself a plate of food, grabbed a beer, and sat down in his favorite chair in the library—the one that overlooked the back garden where the cousins, still dressed in their mourning clothes, played a pick-up game of football.

Blackman loved watching Jamie play with his cousins, many of whom were older than him but who always included him. All the cousins doted on Jamie in a way that made Blackman's heart ache with love. When the family was together, Jamie was never alone. Whether they were in London or Greece, his cousins took him everywhere. Even when Jamie was little. Blackman was grateful that Jamie's childhood was so antithetical to his own. Yes, Blackman had had some friends, and he'd had Fatimah, but it was nothing like what Jamie had with his cousins. Jamie could be himself with the family, and he'd always be loved and accepted.

Unlike a young Blackman.

Blackman took a long drink of his beer and fought the melancholia that threatened to slip over him. When his phone buzzed with a text from Nick, he was grateful for the distraction.

Brother Nick:

Can you come up to Da's office?

Blackman texted back a thumbs up emoji.

On his way to the stairs, he set his empty plate on the counter, picked up two more beers from the refrigerator, and took the back stairs to Lennie Harrington's attic office. When Blackman knocked on the door, he waited patiently for Nick to invite him in. When Nick called for him to enter, Blackman pushed open the door and took in Nick sitting in his funeral clothes behind Lennie Harrington's massive oak desk.

The King is dead.

Long live the King.

Blackman had never been in Lennie's office, but its understated beauty didn't surprise him. It was an airy space with cream colored walls and skylights that flooded the room in late afternoon sunlight. Aside from the desk, there was little furniture. Two wingback chairs sat on the business side of the desk, and an overstuffed sofa sat against one wall. Modern art canvases hung on the walls, and pale wood floors gleamed beneath expensive silk Persian rugs.

Nick looked at Blackman and waited.

"You look good sitting there," Blackman said with a smile as he stepped into the office and shut the door behind him. He walked over to the desk, handed Nick a beer, and waited to see where Nick wanted him to sit. Nick nodded to one of the wingback chairs, and Blackman sat down. Nick walked around the desk and settled into the chair opposite Blackman. He looked at his beer for a moment and then held it out to Blackman.

"To Da," Nick said.

"To Dad," Blackman repeated as he clicked bottles with Nick. They drank their beer, and Blackman waited.

"This is what Da wanted," Nick said, looking Blackman in the eye.

"Joey and Oliver good with it?" Blackman asked, although he already knew the answer.

Nick nodded. "Joey's not a numbers guy, and Oliver doesn't want to be tied down to a desk. And," Nick said with a smile. "Sherry wants me around more. The boys are a handful, the way boys are meant to be."

"And Maggie?" Again, Blackman knew the answer, but he asked the question anyway.

"Maggie's okay with it. She's never had an interest in the business. She has her own professional life, and Fitz is Fitz. He prefers the art world."

Blackman nodded.

"What about you?" Nick asked.

Blackman's beer stalled halfway to his mouth. He lowered it without drinking and looked at Nick, whose eyes were so much like Maggie's they were unsettling.

"What about me?" he asked, lowering the beer to his thigh. The bottle was cold through the material of his dress pants.

"I'm asking you if you're good with this," Nick said, holding Blackman's eyes.

"Nick, this is a family decision about the family business," Blackman answered.

"And you're family," Nick reminded him.

Blackman swallowed a lump in his throat, then cleared it for good measure before he spoke, unsure of what to say. Nick leaned back in the chair and crossed his legs. This time Nick looked like his father.

"Nick," Blackman started, his voice slightly unsteady.

"Blackman," Nick said, one side of his mouth quirking up.

"The family business is out of my purview," Blackman said slowly.

Nick opened his mouth to say something, but Blackman interrupted him. "*But* if you're asking me if you have my support, the answer is yes. Unequivocally. I fully support you taking your father's place at the head of the table."

Nick's face grew serious.

"I appreciate that, brother. Really, I do."

The men fell into silence and drank their beers.

"Blackman, can I ask you something?" Nick asked, putting his empty beer on the desk.

Blackman nodded.

"Does Maggie ever talk about coming back to London?"

That was not the question Blackman had been anticipating, and he was grateful for the surprise.

"No."

Nick nodded. Thoughtful. "What about you? Would you ever consider moving to England?"

Blackman considered the question in earnest. Maggie had always made it sound like returning to England wasn't an option, and he'd always assumed it wasn't an option because Lennie wanted some distance between her and the family business. Blackman wondered if maybe Maggie's remaining in Philadelphia had nothing to do with the family or what the family wanted. Maybe it had been about Maggie, and Maggie's willingness to return.

"Depends, I suppose," Blackman said after a moment.

"On what?"

"Honestly, on what Maggie wants."

"What do you want?" Nick asked.

"My wife to be happy," Blackman answered without hesitation.

Nick chuckled. "Good man. What about your job?"

Blackman looked at Nick thoughtfully. He knew where Nick was going and what Nick was asking as much as he knew what he was supposed to say, and what he *wanted* to say.

"I'm a lawyer, Nick, and a damn good lawyer," Blackman said carefully. "And I can be a good lawyer anywhere."

"Even here?"

"If *here* is where Maggie wants to be, sure."

Nick looked at him as if he had more to say, but he remained quiet. They sat in companionable silence.

Chapter 9

The day before the shooting had been lovely, unseasonably warm for that time of year. A brief respite in a week that had been book-ended by wintery cold days. Jamie's class was on a field trip to the Franklin Institute, and Fitz was chaperoning. Afterward, he was keeping Jamie for a rare school night sleepover so he could take Jamie to the opera.

"Opera, Fitz? Really? He's 11." Maggie shook her head as she stood in line for coffee at the student union. She had ten minutes before she had to get to the class she had been covering all week.

"Just because you have the artistic sensibility of a goat—"

"I'm a published poet, Fitz," Maggie said as she put her phone between her chin and shoulder and tried to fish her wallet out of her backpack. "Literally. You own my books. I've won awards," she reminded her brother as she finally found her wallet and moved up in line. She tried to look around the big kid standing in front of her to see if there was any coffee cake left.

"Oh, I'm aware of your *published poetry*," Fitz sighed, clearly unimpressed by her contributions to the arts.

"If he doesn't enjoy it, I don't want any complaints from you. What are you taking him to see?" she asked as she finally got to the counter. She looked at the bored looking kid standing in front of her. "Large drip coffee, and a piece of blueberry coffee cake. Thanks." She handed over her debit card and waited.

"*Carmen*," she heard Fitz say.

"Pardon?"

"I'm taking him to see *Carmen*. Honestly, can you focus for five minutes?" Fitz said sharply.

Maggie took back her debit card and slid it into her back pocket, knowing that in five minutes, she would forget it was there, and then she'd probably wind up putting it through the wash again. She probably had the cleanest debit card anywhere. Then she took her coffee and coffee cake and mumbled a thank you as she stepped out of line. Maggie tried to remember the last time she'd seen a production of *Carmen*. Maybe ten years ago? Fifteen? Either way, she remembered a lot of low cut dresses and heaving breasts.

"I'm sure he'll love it," she said as she hit the glass door with her hip a little harder than she meant to, just as Fitz said something pithy and ended the phone call.

Maggie sighed. At least Jamie's trip to the opera with his uncle left her and Blackman with a rare night alone.

Although Blackman had court in the morning, he had cleared his afternoon schedule. Maggie was on a reduced teaching schedule that semester to finish a book she was writing on female veteran poets and the unique stories they had to tell. She'd been traveling extensively, and for a while, she seemed to be away more than she was home.

Blackman could count how many good night's sleep he'd had since September, but he wouldn't tell Maggie. He didn't want her to feel guilty about the traveling. It was important to her, and they were making the best of their time together. They were happy; they were a team. They still held hands, shared inside jokes, and were still in love. Not every couple they knew could say that.

The afternoon before everything changed, Maggie met Blackman outside his office and stood on tiptoe to kiss him hello. They walked, hand in hand, through the crowded city streets. Blackman told Maggie about his morning in court and the defendant who didn't show up. Maggie told Blackman about her morning covering her friend's class and the writing she'd squeezed in. It seemed that her morning had been far more productive than his. They stopped at their favorite sandwich shop and got lunch to go. They walked to the park, where they ate and laughed at each other's funny stories. When they were done, Maggie stretched out on the grass, resting her head on Blackman's thigh.

They sat there for hours, wasting the day as they talked and people watched. Blackman absently ran his fingers through her thick red hair, picking locks of it to twirl around his fingers. It had been months since they'd had a few hours to themselves, let alone an entire day, and although they felt like they should be doing something more productive, they were incredibly content to be outside, alone and together on this shockingly warm day.

"We should go away together. Just us," Maggie said, taking Blackman's hand. She kissed his knuckles gently, then opened his hand and traced lazy circles on his palm.

"Where do you want to go?" he asked, smiling at her.

"I don't know. How about New York or maybe Boston?" she asked.

"We could go somewhere warm. How about Miami?" he countered.

"Oh, we could go down to the Keys. That would be brilliant," she exclaimed. They hadn't been to the Keys in years. Blackman closed his hand around hers and brought her hand to his lips. He kissed her soft skin, and then rubbed his cheek against his hand.

"That sounds great," he said. "I'll check my schedule tomorrow."

Maggie closed her eyes, "I'm going to need a new bikini."

Blackman chuckled. She wouldn't need much more than that.

Later in the afternoon, they shared a cab to a new bar down by the river, where they got drinks and played a few rounds of pool, each taking turns hustling the other. Blackman poured money into the jukebox and enjoyed watching Maggie swing her hips to the music between shots. More than once, he found himself leaning over her, pretending to show her how to make a complicated shot, but all he wanted was to be closer to her, to brush his lips over her neck, to smell the lavender scent of her hair.

And let every man in the bar know that *she* was with *him*.

Him.

After they were good and buzzed, well, she more than he, they walked to the river and watched the sky grow dark. Blackman stood behind Maggie, his arms wrapped around her. They were quiet as they watched the boats move along the still, dark water. Leaning his cheek against her hair, he thought, not for the first time, that he was a lucky man.

On their way home, they stopped at their favorite Thai place and picked up takeaway. It was well past dark when Blackman finally let them into the row house they bought after they found out Maggie was pregnant.

It was a beautiful house on a spacious corner of a wide, tree lined street. The house had been renovated right before they bought it. It was an open concept space with hardwood floors and buttery yellow walls. They'd kept their furniture from their old apartment but added more eclectic pieces over the years. The walls were filled with a mixture of modern art from some of Fitz's favorite artists as well as family pictures featuring the Rhymer-Smith trio and the extended Harrington family at various family homes and functions.

Blackman flicked on the lights as he led Maggie through to the kitchen. They were chatting about nothing, as he gathered the plates, and he thought she was setting out the food, but when he turned around, he saw Maggie leaning against the counter, a mischievous look on her face.

"We're alone," she said, meeting his eyes.

"We are," he agreed.

Maggie pushed herself up on the counter, and Blackman walked over to her, stepping between her legs. She reached for his face and ran her fingers over his lips. Her big hazel eyes looked at his mouth.

"Here?" he asked.

She reached for him, sliding her hand over the hardness of him. He placed his hands on either side of her hips and leaned into her hand as she stroked him.

"Maggie," he whispered. "I can't."

His leg was hurting. In fact, it had been hurting him more and more lately, and she wondered if surgery was in his future. She leaned forward, kissed him gently on the mouth, and then pushed him back so she could slide off the counter. She took his hand and led him upstairs.

In the soft glow of the fairy lights she had strung around their room, Maggie undressed her husband and thought about how he always seemed to wear so many clothes at one time. It was like he traded in the layers of protective gear he needed for his hockey life for layers of protective clothing he needed for his professional life. The layers made him look formidable, unapproachable, and unforgiving when he stood in a courtroom trying to give the hurt and the grieving the justice they deserved. Yet there was so much more to him than that, so much more to her husband, whom she loved so dearly. A man who was as much a part of her as her heart and lungs. She couldn't imagine what she'd be without him.

If she could even *be* without him.

She took off his suit jacket and dropped it on the bench at the foot of the bed, then slipped off his tie and unbuttoned his dress shirt. After she pushed it off his shoulders, she pulled off the white undershirt beneath. She kissed his bare chest, where the first hints of gray were starting to show. His breath caught as she ran her tongue gently over one nipple.

"Maggie," he murmured, cupping her neck with one hand, and massaging the strong muscles. She unbuckled his belt and pushed his pants down, then pushed him gently so he sat back on the bed. Kneeling in front of him, she took off his pants and socks.

So many clothes.

"Lay back," she whispered.

Blackman pushed himself back on the bed, settling against the soft pillows, staring at his beautiful wife. Unlike his job, Maggie's job didn't require her to wear a metaphorical suit of armor to get through her day. She pulled off her favorite purple sweater and let it drop to the floor. Beneath it was one of the many lace bras Blackman liked so much. She braced one foot against the other, stepped out of her heavy black boots, and shimmied out of her blue jeans. Leaving her in only her bra and a pair of lacey boy cut panties that drove Blackman crazy.

"God," he whispered. "You are so fucking beautiful."

Maggie grinned a vandal's smile and sat down on the bed next to him, her back to him. He closed his eyes as she reached for his damaged leg. Then groaned as she kneaded his sore muscles the same way she had been doing for almost twenty years. She knew exactly how to touch him to ease the pain that never went away but only seemed to get worse with time.

The first time she'd done this, he'd been embarrassed. He had taken her ice skating for the first time, and he had been a patient teacher, but she'd struggled. She'd fallen more times than either of them could count. And more often than not, she'd taken him down with her.

"Love, you can't keep falling like this. You need to let go of me," she said, exasperated, as he struggled to his feet again and put on a brave face.

"You'll get better," he promised, and she did.

By the time the session ended, she was skating more and falling less, but the damage had been done. That night, he'd been barely able to take off his shoes, let alone his pants, because he'd been in so much pain.

"Show me where it hurts," she'd said quietly as she stood beside him.

"I'm fine," he said through gritted teeth as he limped toward their bed. Maggie followed him. He tried to bend down but couldn't, and he sank down on the bed, defeated and humiliated. His face was red with shame as Maggie knelt in front of him and waited until he met her eyes.

"If I were hurt, wouldn't you want to help me?" She looked at him, love shining in her eyes. "Wouldn't you want to make me feel better? Try to ease the pain?"

Blackman didn't answer, and he didn't move.

Maggie persisted. "Would you want me to feel embarrassed? Would you want me to feel like I'm less because I hurt?"

Blackman shook his head slowly. He didn't trust his voice.

Maggie bent over and unlaced his shoes, and pulled off those old, brown Doc Martens he loved so much. Then she took off his socks. She straightened up and reached for his belt, and she felt his whole body go rigid. Looking up, she glared at him, and he glared right back, but he couldn't hold her eyes for long. She unbuckled his belt and pulled down his jeans. He groaned as he lifted his hips so she could get them off. She moved his jeans carefully over his legs and left them in a pile behind her.

She put her hands on his bad leg.

"Please, Maggie, don't," he pleaded softly.

She ignored him and started to massage the tense muscles. Her hands were everything: strong, gentle, soft, warm, and loving. So incredibly loving. He moaned in pleasure as her hands moved over his thigh, easing the pain. He leaned back on the bed. It felt so good, so intimate, that he felt tears sting his eyes. He blinked them away. There was only so much humiliation a man could stand, not that her touch or acknowledgment of his pain was meant to humiliate him because she was right. He'd do the same for her. More importantly, though, she understood the depth of his pain and loved him anyway. She understood this was going to be with him for the rest of his life and would limit some of the things he could do with her, but she didn't care.

She loved him anyway.

When she finished, she crawled into bed next to him, and he pulled her close. They didn't make love that night; they just fell asleep together. His body wrapped around hers, his hand resting on her hip, her body soft and warm against his.

So lost in his nostalgia, Blackman didn't notice when Maggie stopped massaging his leg, but groaned when her lips touched his hot skin, her tongue sliding along the hard length of him, her lips soft and wet as she took him in her mouth. He found her hand, laced his fingers through hers, and lost himself in her love for him, his love for her.

The next day, Blackman was distracted. They had stayed up too late, and he had nearly slept through his alarm. He got up and moved around the dark room with the practiced grace of a long married man who kept earlier hours than his wife. He dressed for the gym, packed his clothes for work, and kissed Maggie's still sleeping form before he left.

At the gym, he swam enough laps to loosen his back and hips, then swam some more. He spent a little more time than was strictly necessary in the sauna before hitting the showers and getting dressed for work. He was supposed to be in court by nine, but the defense attorney asked for a continuance as her client finally decided to consider the plea deal on the table.

So, Blackman caught up on a mountain of paperwork and finally met with two detectives who had been avoiding him for the better part of a week. That meeting had gone better than he anticipated, but by noon, he needed some air. He was restless, and a walk would do him good.

It was a bitterly cold day, and an unforgiving wind stirred up fallen leaves and trash as it blew through the city streets. Leaving his office building,

Blackman walked west toward Broad Street. Even though Thanksgiving was still a week away, many stores were already decorated for Christmas.

He stopped in front of Tiffany's window and looked at an emerald and diamond necklace and matching earrings that would look beautiful on Maggie. Fitz was hosting a holiday themed fundraiser in a few weeks, and the set would look perfect with the black dress Maggie always looked stunning in. He filed the jewelry away in his mind and continued walking. He would come back later and pick up the set. Maggie always loved an early Christmas present.

A few stores down, he stopped at the window of a small boutique lingerie shop and looked at a mannequin wearing barely there panties and a matching lace bra in a bold shade of green. He imagined Maggie in nothing but the lingerie, the jewelry, and those Christian Louboutin shoes he loved so much, then reached for the door.

"Counselor."

Blackman turned around.

From that point forward, his memory of the event was hazy at best. Sometimes, he felt like his memories of what happened were accurate, but other times, he knew they were not. In his dreams, he could see it all so clearly, but those weren't memories per se, just his brain playing the movie of what had happened according to the police reports he'd read a hundred times. A thousand times.

As a prosecutor, he knew eyewitnesses made the worst witnesses – only slightly worse were the victims themselves. Because when you didn't expect the Spanish Inquisition, you didn't look for the Spanish Inquisition. When you didn't expect to be a victim of a crime, you tended not to pay attention to all the details that would later prove to be so important.

And who expects to get shot on a city street in the middle of the lunch rush? Who expects to get shot walking into a lingerie shop so they can buy their wife something expensive and slutty?

In fact, who expects to get shot, period?

Not Blackman Smith.

Blackman turned toward the voice that sounded like any other voice and looked down at a man who was shorter than he, but most men were shorter than Blackman Smith. The man was wearing a black knit hat, just like the one Blackman was wearing, and a dark colored winter coat, maybe a Patagonia or a North Face. It was cold, and the guy was dressed for the cold like everyone else on the street.

Then there was a loud bang, and the door Blackman had reached for shattered.

Blackman didn't remember moving or falling to the ground. He would learn later the first bullet went through his side, shattering the door behind him before it buried itself in the far wall of the store, narrowly missing the head of a part time college student. The second bullet entered Blackman just to the left of the first bullet and exited his back, burying itself in the doorframe, but not before taking a golf ball size chunk of Blackman's skin with it. The third bullet buried itself deep in his gut.

Then Blackman was on his back on the winter cold concrete, and for a moment, he thought he was back on the ice in that final hockey game. He looked up at the gray sky and the bare tree limbs above him, but he was having trouble focusing his eyes. He felt blood pooling around him, and for the second time in his life, Blackman Smith pissed himself. Then he became aware of the screams around him, but he couldn't scream himself because he was having trouble drawing in enough air to breathe.

"Can you hear me?" a heavily accented voice asked. "Come on, mister, look at me." The voice was sharp, and dark fingers snapped in front of his eyes. Blackman slowly moved his eyes and looked at a young woman's face, or at least she looked young. Young and terrified. She had a tight black hijab covering her head and neck. Blackman wondered for a moment if it was Fatimah, but he couldn't find his voice. He couldn't ask his auntie what had happened, why he was bleeding. If he was going to die.

He nodded slowly at the woman as he tried to focus his eyes.

The woman yelled at someone behind her as she shrugged off her coat, balled it up, and pushed it against Blackman's stomach. The pain was excruciating, and he felt hot tears slide down his cold face.

He could hear sirens, but this was Philadelphia; he could always hear sirens.

"Stay with me, honey. Keep those eyes open. You hear me?" The woman looked over her shoulder at someone Blackman couldn't see. "Where the fuck are the cops?"

"Maggie," Blackman said weakly. He could taste blood in his mouth.

The woman with the hijab and the coat pressed to his stomach turned back to him and said as calmly as she could, "What honey, what did you say?"

"Maggie," Blackman repeated. "Tell Maggie I love her."

"You're going to tell Maggie that yourself, honey. You just stay with me," the woman said as she pushed the coat harder against his belly.

The sirens grew louder, and Blackman's heart stopped for the first time.

Chapter 10

Maggie was so caught up in what she was saying she wasn't aware of the police detective standing in the doorway. She was mid-sentence when she followed the gazes of her students toward the door. She tried to finish what she was saying, but her mouth no longer worked.

She had met the young detective at a happy hour over the summer and remembered thinking he seemed too gentle to be a big city cop. The youngest of seven children born to Haitian immigrants, he spent his time with Maggie talking about his mother's cooking, his sisters' children, and his love of French poetry. He had the most beautiful smile, and the moment she found out he was gay, she promised herself she'd find a way to introduce him to Fitz, but she hadn't gotten around to it. Now he looked at her, and there was no softness in those deep brown eyes, no smile on that full, beautiful mouth. He was all business, standing tall in a dark suit and pale blue tie.

A young woman sitting toward the front of the class looked from the detective to the professor she only knew in passing and slowly got to her feet. Her mother was Atlanta PD, and her father was Atlanta FD, and she knew when a cop showed up at your place of work the news was never good. And *everything* about this guy screamed cop. She turned to the other students in the class whose eyes were moving between the cop in the doorway and the professor.

"Everyone out now," she said in an imitation of her mother's *don't fuck with me* voice.

No one moved.

"NOW!" she yelled in a tone that dared defiance. Finally, the other students gathered their things and headed for the door. The detective stepped into the room and watched Maggie as the students filed out of the room. The young woman walked over to Maggie and took her hand, then looked at the detective. She said, "My mom's on the job. Atlanta."

The detective ignored her.

"He's alive," he said in a slight Haitian accent. "But it's bad."

Maggie didn't move.

"Maggie, we have to go. Now," he said. His voice was stern. Urgent.

Maggie still didn't move. She just looked at those brown eyes as she tried to take in the words. *He's alive... it's bad.* Never in her life had she imagined she'd ever hear those words in reference to her husband. Blackman was a lawyer. He wasn't a cop. He wasn't a soldier. He wasn't one of her goddamn brothers.

The woman holding Maggie's hand squeezed it gently. "Dr. Rhymer, don't make the detective wait," she said as kindly as she could. Maggie looked at the woman and nodded, then walked toward the detective and a life that would never be the same again.

Blackman was already in surgery when Maggie and Detective Gabriel Marcellus arrived at the hospital. The ER waiting room was filled with cops and people Maggie recognized from the DA's office. They were quiet and solemn, a few crying quietly. Jon Pierce, retired and dressed casually in blue jeans and a green fleece pullover, leaned against a wall drinking shitty hospital coffee. Maggie walked in and the people who had been talking quietly fell silent. Scanning the crowd, she found the face she was looking for. She strode forward with long purposeful steps toward Detective Terrence Semple, who stepped forward to meet her.

"Dr. Rhymer –"

The first punch she threw broke his nose and cracked two of her knuckles; the second blow, a vicious left hook, loosened two of his molars and cracked a tooth. She was about to throw another punch when Jon ran forward and grabbed her around the waist. He pressed his head against her back so he didn't take an elbow to the face as he spun Maggie away from

Detective Semple just like Blackman had done the night she beat the shit out of the two yuppies in the bar.

"You fucking piece of shit," she screamed. "You said he had nothing to worry about. You said he'd be safe!"

Semple, a third generation cop from south Philly, had never been hit by a woman, not even his mother. His father used to beat the shit out of him, and if his father was still alive, he'd never let his son live down this moment. Not for the first time, Semple was grateful the old man was in the ground.

"Bitch," he breathed as he spat blood on the floor.

Jon set Maggie on the floor, where she immediately turned back to Semple. She started back toward him, clearly looking for round two. Uniformed police moved forward, and Jon pushed her back roughly making her stumble.

"Calm down, Maggie," he said sharply.

"Get the fuck out of my way," she yelled. Hysteria creeping around the edges of her voice. When Jon didn't move, she threw a punch he dodged, then shoved her again until she slammed into the wall behind her. Maggie's face was wild with fury, and terror poured off her in waves. She shook with every breath. Jon moved closer until he was all she could see. His face was inches from hers.

"If you don't get a hold of yourself, one of those dipshits is going to put you in cuffs. Do you hear me?" Jon hissed into her ear.

"He said..."

"There's nothing to worry about." Maggie heard him say the day she went to Blackman's office because they were going to see Jamie's football game, and it was easier to leave from Blackman's office than the house. His office door had been ajar, and she had nudged it open with the toe of her boot.

Blackman was sitting behind his big desk, and Semple was facing him. She'd met Semple before, and she didn't like him. He reminded her of the kind of sycophants who were always trying to get into her brothers' good graces. Semple was the kind of guy who wanted to look more dangerous than he was. A bully with a badge and a gun because guys like him always needed a gun. She figured he saw himself as the kind of guy who could hold his own in a fight, but Maggie knew he was wrong. She knew how to fight; her brothers back home knew how to fight; Blackman knew how to fight. This guy knew how to shoot a gun and call it in so other men and women who knew how to fight could come around and clean up his mess.

"We're running this down, but there's nothing to worry about, counselor," Semple said with a cocksure attitude Maggie didn't like either.

Fucking wanker.

Maggie was staring at the back of Semple's head when Blackman looked up and caught her standing in the doorway. He looked more than a little annoyed to see her standing there, but she just smiled. The picture of innocence.

"Sorry, sweetheart, the door was open. I thought you were alone," Maggie said with a wide smile. She ignored Semple because she could, holding her husband's eyes until he looked back to the detective and nodded.

"Thank you for coming by, Detective," Blackman said, getting to his feet. Semple did the same, and the two men shook hands over Blackman's desk. Then Semple turned around and looked at Maggie, and as usual, his eyes lingered on her tits a beat too long.

Christ, this guy.

"Nice to see you again, Dr. Rhymer," Semple said in a voice that reminded Maggie of an oil slick. Not the kind found in the ocean, but the small kind poorly maintained cars left behind. A reminder that they had been somewhere and that no one cared about them.

"Detective," Maggie said as she stepped into the office so Semple could walk by her without getting too close.

As Semple crossed the threshold, Maggie looked to Blackman cheerfully. "We better get going, or we'll miss kickoff."

"Fuck what he said. You need to listen to me. Beating up a cop and getting yourself thrown in jail will not help Blackman. You understand me?" Jon asked, his breath hot against her face. He smelled like coffee and gum.

Maggie glared at Semple, who refused to look at her.

"Do you fucking understand me, *October*?" Jon hissed.

Maggie took a deep breath and nodded.

"Words, October."

"Yes," she said through gritted teeth.

"Okay," Jon said more calmly. "I'm going to step away, but if you take a step toward Stemple, I will put you on your ass. You understand me?"

"Yes," Maggie said, meeting his eyes. Except for the gray in his short hair, Jon hadn't changed at all over the years, and unlike Blackman, Maggie knew Jon would have no compunction putting her in her place or on her ass if it was for her own good. That was why she liked him so much. Jon stepped back, and Maggie straightened up, pushed her shoulders back, and stood tall.

Semple glared at her, and she glared back, but neither of them moved. Jon turned and looked at the detective, who was bloody and seething because a girl had broken his nose. Which, Jon thought, was fitting considering how the cop's old man had knocked around more than his fair share of women when he was on the force.

"Get your nose looked at, Detective," Jon said coolly.

Semple didn't move. He pointed at Maggie.

"You keep that cunt away from me." He spit more blood onto the floor.

Several of the patrol officers looked away, and a few winced. Jon felt Maggie move behind him, and he shifted his body so he was blocking her again. Finally, Semple walked away, his partner Gabriel behind him.

"I'll –" Maggie started.

Jon rounded on her.

"You'll keep your fucking mouth shut is what you'll do," he barked.

Maggie's mouth snapped shut.

"You can pick a fight with every cop in here, but that won't change what happened." Jon paused and took a steadying breath. "You need to start making phone calls."

Maggie blinked rapidly. Panic rising in her chest, tears burning her eyes.

"Is he going to die?" she asked terrified she already knew the answer.

Jon looked her in the eyes.

"Probably."

He wrapped his arms around Maggie, and pulled her close, so she didn't fall to the floor when her legs gave out.

An hour later, Fitz, who had been at the gym when Maggie called, ran into the ER dressed in black joggers and a hoodie, his blond hair unusually messy, a terrified Jamie standing by his side. Jamie, who at thirteen years old stood well over six feet tall. He was a little boy trapped in a man's body, just like his father had been at that age. Jamie saw his mother and pushed past the uniformed police officers to get to her.

"Mommy!" Jamie called. When he reached her, he practically threw himself into her arms. Maggie had to take a step back because he was not only taller than her but outweighed her as well. She took a deep breath and wrapped her arms around her not so little boy. As soon as she pulled him against her, he started to cry in earnest.

"I want daddy," he said through his tears. Over and over again.

I want daddy...

I want daddy...

I want daddy...

He hadn't referred to her or Blackman as mommy or daddy in so long that the word felt foreign and weirdly painful. She pulled him down into a chair so they'd be closer in height and tried to calm him as best she could. She whispered what she hoped were soothing words into his ear. Fitz stood next to them, looking pale and sick.

Jon touched Fitz's arm, then motioned to a corner of the waiting room away from Maggie and Jamie. Fitz followed without comment. The two men had met several times over the years, at Blackman and Maggie's wedding, a few dinner parties, and the occasional gallery event or fundraiser. Fitz always knew Blackman's mentor as a calm, unflappable man. So, when Fitz looked into his face and saw fear, his stomach clenched, and he fought the urge to vomit.

"What happened?" Fitz asked quietly. "Maggie wasn't making any sense on the phone, which is to be expected, I suppose," he babbled. He always babbled when he was nervous, and Maggie had been barely coherent on the phone.

"Details are sketchy," Jon said. "It sounds like Blackman might have been doing some early Christmas shopping. He was going into a store when someone shot him. The first two bullets were through and through." Jon

Pierce looked at Fitz, who seemed perplexed. Where the hell had Blackman been shopping? Kensington?

"That means that the bullets went through him. In and out."

"I know what it means," Fitz said coldly.

"The third bullet lodged in his gut, and that's the problem. His heart stopped on the scene, but the EMTs got it going again."

"Christ," Fitz breathed, his hand pressed absently against his chest.

"The woman who stopped to help him was an ER nurse coming off shift, thank God, otherwise..."

"Is he—will he?" Fitz couldn't finish the sentence; his voice was too thick with emotion. Tears filled his bright blue eyes. Jon looked back at Maggie and Jamie and cleared his throat.

"You need to call your family."

Fitz nodded and wiped his eyes as he dug his phone out of his pocket, but before Fitz stepped away, Jon touched his shoulder. Fitz turned and met the other man's eyes.

"Fitz, they need to come here to be with Maggie and Jamie. They can't get involved with this," Jon said softly but sternly.

Fitz face hardened, a world away from his usual affability.

"Blackman is family," Fitz said. He stopped and cleared his throat. "And the family will do whatever they think is appropriate."

Jon sighed and nodded as he looked away. "Detective Terry Semple will probably be lead on the investigation. He's an asshole, but he's not an idiot, and your sister just broke his nose in front of twenty cops."

Fitz groaned.

"Make your calls," Jon said with a parting nod, then walked back to Maggie and Jamie, who had curled up against his mother like the terrified child he was.

Blackman was in surgery for fifteen hours and needed so much blood he practically exhausted the blood bank. His heart stopped two more times on the table before the surgical team was able to stabilize him; he survived the surgery, but the surgeons weren't hopeful.

By the time they wheeled him into post-op, the only people left in the waiting room were Jon and Maggie, who sat on one side of the room, two uniformed police officers who stood against the far wall staring at their phones, and two men who had arrived around hour two, and took seats close to Jon and Maggie.

They were big men, broad, with short dark hair and sharp eyes. Dressed casually in blue jeans and hoodies, they watched the room with cold, intent eyes. Jon was sure they had been sent on behalf of the Harrington family, who were undoubtedly getting regular updates on the state of things at the hospital. Jon also suspected the Harringtons were preparing for their descent on Philadelphia, and God knew what kind of hell they would rain down on whoever had been dumb enough to shoot their brother-in-law.

It was early morning when Blackman was wheeled into a private room. He was hooked up to a dozen machines that looked like they were not so much keeping him alive but waiting for the moment they could alert the staff to his inevitable passing.

Maggie, beyond exhausted, curled up in a chair next to her husband's bed, took his hand in hers, and closed her eyes. Less than an hour later, machines started screaming, and nurses and doctors flooded the room. Maggie was pushed out of the way, and her chair kicked to the far corner of the room while men and women worked on Blackman, whose heart had stopped again.

They shocked him several times as Maggie watched in horror before his heart started doing what it was supposed to. Then, they wheeled him back to surgery. Maggie was still in the corner crying when Fitz walked in and found her curled up in a ball on the floor.

Blackman survived the second round of surgery and was wheeled back into his room just after dark on the second day. Maggie resumed her vigil, holding his cold hand in hers as she rested her head on the bed next to him.

The Harringtons arrived in waves. First Nick and his wife Sherry, then Joseph and his wife Jemma, then Oliver. His wife Pippa had stayed behind to monitor the half dozen children they shared between them. If things didn't improve, Pippa planned on flying over with the children so they could say their goodbyes in person and be there for Jamie and Maggie.

While Maggie sat by her husband's side, Sherry and Jemma ensured Jamie was taken care of, shuttling him back and forth to school with two other men who spent their days sitting in a car outside the boy's school and their nights sitting outside Maggie and Blackman's house.

On the fifth day of Blackman's hospitalization, Nick insisted Maggie leave the hospital and go home for a shower and some sleep. She hadn't eaten much since she'd arrived at the hospital, and her face was thin and drawn, and she looked on the edge of collapse. Nick drove Maggie home, and after some tense moments, Sherry and Jemma were able to get an overwrought Maggie into the bath before getting some sleeping pills in her. Maggie slept for almost thirty hours.

On the same day, the police responded to the report of a burning car in a rundown neighborhood in South Philadelphia. The man in the car was burned beyond recognition, and when the police ran the car's VIN number, they discovered it belonged to a low level drug dealer who had a side hustle selling guns to unsavory people. Assuming the burning corpse in the car was the same man, the police determined no further investigation was warranted. Bad things tended to happen to bad people in bad neighborhoods.

The day the burning car was discovered, a kindergarten teacher in Baltimore reported her husband of ten years missing. He was a truck driver for a local company that transported small electronics between Baltimore and Providence, Rhode Island. The police took her report and said they'd look into it, but as the officers left, they figured the man had probably done a Bruce Springsteen and gone out for cigarettes and never came back. Six months later, the body of a male was found at a rest stop off 1-90 in Massachusetts. His hands, feet, and head were missing, and it looked like an industrial sander had been taken to any identifying tattoos or scars. What was left of the body was eventually cremated and buried in a potter's field.

Hours after the kindergarten teacher filed her missing person's report, an accident snarled traffic north of the Philadelphia International Airport. A truck moving old tires lost its load after swerving to miss a car changing lanes without signaling. Several tires slammed into a new Lexus, two going through the windshield and killing the driver and passenger instantly. The two young children in the back seat suffered only cuts and bruises in the ensuing crash. All vehicles involved in the accident stopped and waited for the police. The truck driver, a young man who had recently turned twenty-one and had a pregnant girlfriend at home, was devastated and wept at the scene as if his heart would break.

No citations were issued.

A day later, a prisoner at Graterford Prison hanged himself in his cell. He left behind a note explaining that he could not live in a world without the brother who had been killed in the car accident the day before.

Two days later, the father of the two dead men stepped into traffic on a busy Center City street without checking for cars. He was struck by a ride-share driver, a middle-aged man working extra hours to help cover his daughters' college tuition costs. The impact didn't kill the old man, but he suffered a heart attack in the ambulance and was dead by the time he arrived at the hospital. An autopsy was performed as a matter of course, but nothing out of the ordinary was found. He was simply an old man who had been looking at his phone when she should have been paying attention to the world around him.

The old man and his sons were buried in the family plot alongside the old man's first wife, who had died thirty years before. She had allegedly fallen down the stairs after a night of drinking or so went the story. At the time, the police and the DA's office suspected the death was not accidental, and charges were filed against the old man; however, Blackman Smith's father took the case, and the trial was a quick affair, the acquittal a foregone conclusion. Blackman Smith would have been lying if he said he didn't feel more than a little smug when he secured the conviction against the old man's son thirty years later for a similar crime.

So many tragedies befalling one family in the days after Blackman Smith's shooting made an already angry Detective Terry Semple curious. Very curious. And Detective Terry Semple might be an asshole, but he was stupid. In fact, he was a very smart man, and once he got something in his head, he wasn't a man to walk away. He could be a dog with a bone, and that tenacity made him a damn good detective.

A day or two after the old man died, Semple arrived at the hospital with his partner, Gabriel Marcellus, in tow in order to ask Maggie Rhymer Smith some questions. Much like Jon Pierce, Terry Semple knew the kind of family Maggie Rhymer Smith came from, and he didn't like the idea of a bunch of mobbed-up Brits causing problems in his city, but instead of speaking with Maggie, Semple and Marcellus spoke with an intractable Fitz, while a curious Jon Pierce leaned against a wall, taking in the exchange.

Watching.

Waiting.

Fitz, wearing a dark gray three piece suit with a blue button down shirt and paisley tie, stood in front of Semple as if Fitz was a man without a care in the world. Semple, who stood a few inches taller than Fitz and weighed significantly more, glared menacingly at the smaller man, a look of disgust in his dishwater gray eyes. Semple clearly intended to intimidate Fitz, but Fitz was not about to be intimidated. He was Lennie Harrington's son, after all, and his father would roll over in his grave if he knew Fitz had ever allowed himself to be intimidated by a copper, especially a copper dressed in an ill fitting off the rack suit that looked as if it had been slept in. Fitz knew quite well that just because one had to buy off the rack, one did not have to look cheap.

Case in point, Fitz thought as he let his eyes slide away from Semple to Gabriel Marcellus, whom he took in one delicious inch at a time. Gabriel, who probably made less than Semple, looked handsome in a dark blue wool suit with a cream colored shirt and a dark blue tie. Fitz's sharp blue eyes made it clear to Detective Marcellus that Fitz thought the detective's suit would look perfect hanging in Fitz's closet or puddled on the floor next to Fitz's bed.

"I'm here to talk to your sister. Can you get her for me?" Semple asked gruffly, trying to ignore the way Fitz was looking at his partner. Fitz slid his eyes slowly from Gabriel's perfect cheekbones to Semple's crooked nose.

"No," Fitz said breezily as he eventually met Semple's eyes.

"No?" Semple asked. The request to see Maggie Rhymer Smith was simply a point of courtesy. He intended to see the woman, whether her brother liked it or not.

"No, Detective," Fitz said with a small smile. "I will not fetch my sister for you as she is sitting with her critically injured husband. If you –"

"Get your fucking sister, now, Mr. Harrington," Semple snapped. Semple straightened to his full and unimpressive height, his face hard, his eyes cold.

Jon Pierce pushed off the wall, but Fitz held up a hand. Then he gave Semple a disappointed look.

"There's no need for such language, Detective," Fitz said as he reached into the inside pocket of his suit coat and pulled out a business card.

He handed it to Semple, who asked through gritted teeth, "What the fuck is this?"

"Our lawyer's contact information. If you have any questions, please direct them to Ms. Wendy Jennings-Pierce of Bailey, McNamara, Williamson, and Jennings. I'll be sure to let her know to expect your call."

Semple glared.

"Is your brother in town?" Semple asked after a moment. The card still clutched in his beefy hand.

"*All* my brothers are in town, along with their wives. Well, two of three of the wives. Here–" Fitz handed over another card. "–is the contact information for our family's London solicitor, but if you need to speak to my brothers while they're in town, you can go through Ms. Jennings-Pierce."

Semple's face went red with rage. "You're a real piece of work, Mr. Harrington."

Fitz could feel the unspoken homophobic slur as clearly as he felt water in the shower, but he said nothing. He simply smiled.

"Detective," Fitz said in a voice that sounded more like he was indulging a recalcitrant child than addressing a police officer. "My sister is an esteemed academic, an award winning poet, and a pillar of the community who has dedicated her life to teaching and writing. I will not have her bullied by you or anyone else. You were tasked with ensuring the safety of my brother-in-law, another esteemed member of the community, and you failed. Miserably. You'll be lucky if *I* don't start making phone calls to people who can make *your* life difficult. Honestly, my brothers should be the least of your concerns," Fitz said with an easy smile.

Semple glared at Fitz who held his eyes. Semple looked away first.

Bullies always did.

Semple turned and walked away, but before Gabriel could join him, Fitz withdrew another card from the inside pocket of his coat and extended it to him.

"What this?" Gabriel asked with a raised eyebrow.

"A dinner invitation," Fitz said with a rakish smile.

Gabriel waited a moment, then took the card. He slipped it into his coat pocket, nodded at Jon, then walked after his partner.

"Christ, you've got a set of balls on you," Jon said, clearly impressed.

"Regardless of what Maggie thinks, I *am* my father's son," Fitz said.

Jon nodded. "Is there anything I need to know?"

"Nothing at all," Fitz said airily. "Can you take Maggie back to the house so she can take a shower and maybe get some sleep? I'll sit with Blackman."

Jon held Fitz's blue eyes and waited to see if Fitz would say anything else, but Fitz did not. Finally, Jon nodded, and walked into Blackman's room to get Maggie. Fitz pulled out his phone, considered it for a moment, and then put it back in his pocket as Maggie and Jon emerged from Blackman's room. Fitz hugged his exhausted sister tightly, and then watched her walk away with Jon.

Semple, Fitz reasoned, was just angry because Maggie had broken his nose. Fitz couldn't fault the man his anger. Maggie defaulted to violence too quickly, and it always cost her in the end. Fitz couldn't help but wonder what it would cost her this time.

What it might cost all of them.

Fitz walked into Blackman's room.

Blackman was no longer on a ventilator, and the number of machines required to monitor him had been reduced. His survival was no longer in question. He had weathered the worst of his wounds, and now it was just a matter of time before he opened his eyes and started his recovery. As opposed to his early days in the hospital, Blackman looked more like a man sleeping deeply than a man on the cusp of death.

Fitz looked at his brother-in-law for a long time. His dark hair needed a cut, and his sunken cheeks accentuated his now too sharp cheekbones. When Blackman was better, Fitz was going to take him out for a proper steak dinner because Blackman was now a man who needed some meat on his bones. Fitz had liked Blackman from the first time he met him. He liked his easy smile, his deep voice, his loud booming laughter. He liked the way Blackman was with Maggie.

One of the first times they spent an evening together as a threesome, they went to see a concert at the Theatre of Living Arts on South Street. The venue was a big, open space that only sold general admission tickets. Everyone gathered in the big space in front of the stage where they could do whatever they wanted: stand, dance, or crowd surf. Fitz remembered how happy his sister looked with this too big man with the neat beard and the prep school haircut. Fitz couldn't remember the band, but he could vividly remember how Blackman's big hands looked on Maggie's slim hips as they swayed to the music.

Blackman was the touchy type when it came to Maggie. His hands were always on her: her hips, her shoulders, the small of her back, but there was nothing aggressive or possessive in his touch. Instead, it seemed Blackman touched Maggie the same way someone absently touched a necklace handed down from one generation to the next. He touched her not because he wanted other men to know she was with him but because she was precious, and he was genuinely pleased she had chosen him.

Fitz knew Blackman had won Maggie the night he scored the hat trick. The night he skated over to her before he even celebrated with his teammates and yelled at her to make dinner reservations. That moment lived immemorial on YouTube, his deep rooted love for her available for public consumption or private remembrance.

Now Fitz sat beside his beloved brother and dear friend and pulled out his phone.

"Well," Fitz said cheerfully. "Let us pick up where we left off, shall we, brother?"

Fitz started chapter seven of Amor Towles' *A Gentleman in Moscow.*

Blackman had been thinking about his wedding day, or maybe he had been remembering it. Or maybe he was dreaming about it because it seemed, to him, both real and imaginary. First, the setting was wrong. He and Maggie had done a church wedding because her father had insisted that his only daughter get married properly, and proper weddings took place in churches. Blackman and Maggie had discussed getting married in London, but Blackman's father hadn't been well enough to travel.

"Why don't we just go? I don't care if he's there, and Fatimah doesn't mind the trip."

"Darling, your father must be there."

"Why?"

"Because you're his only son. It's only proper."

"I seriously doubt I'm the old man's only son."

"Well, you're the only son on paper, so we'll get married here. My family doesn't mind traveling."

And the Harrington's didn't mind traveling. In fact, Blackman suspected Lennie Harrington quite enjoyed traveling with the extended family. He liked the attention it garnered him because Lennie liked being a family man more than he liked being a dangerous man. Maggie's brothers flew over with their wives, nannies, and children in tow. Family friends flew in from the UK and Europe, and the church skewed more Harrington and Rhymer than Smith.

Blackman's side was made up primarily of his father, college friends, hockey friends, and colleagues from work. He chose not to invite any of his mother's family because he sure as shit wasn't feeding any of those people.

Fatimah was positively radiant on that day in her aubergine gown, with its high neck and intricate lace wrap that covered her shoulders and hung down to her waist. She wore an elegant silver hijab and clutched a handkerchief Blackman had given her when he was just a boy, which she used to wipe away tears from her bright blue eyes.

Blackman remembered how she kept trying to get away from him so she could take a seat in the back of the church, but Blackman worked hard to keep her at his side.

"Habibi," she insisted quietly, "I must go and find a seat."

"Not yet," Blackman replied in Arabic, as always.

Fatimah sighed as she turned to Blackman and picked invisible pieces of lint from his shoulders, and smoothed the lapels of his tuxedo. She reached up and touched his smooth cheek.

"I am glad you got rid of your beard. It did not suit you," she said in Arabic.

Blackman scoffed. "You loved that beard."

"Yes," she said with a smile. "But you are now becoming a husband, and you must make your bride happy. Maggie prefers a smooth face."

Blackman smiled as he reached up and took Fatimah's hands in his own. He steadied them and brought them to his lips. Then he let them go, reached into his pocket, and withdrew a black velvet box. He handed it to Fatimah, who clucked her tongue.

"Silly boy," she said gently. "You do not give your auntie a gift on your wedding day."

"No, of course not," Blackman said carefully. "But a son is permitted to give his mother a gift on his wedding day."

Fatimah did not take her eyes from the box.

"Open it, please, mother."

Fatimah opened it with trembling fingers. Inside was a silver chain with a heavy silver locket on which was etched a blooming tree. Fatimah's hands trembled as she opened the locket and saw a small picture of Blackman on his 11th birthday as well as a picture of Fatimah from the same year. Her eyes filled with tears.

"It is beautiful, my son," she whispered. "I will treasure it always."

Blackman pulled Fatimah into a tight hug.

That day, Blackman barely spoke to his father or acknowledged him, but he took great pride in introducing Fatimah, his mother, to a family who never once asked why a man with the name Blackman Emerson Smith had a mother named Fatimah Hammadi. Instead, they simply congratulated her on her son's wedding.

Years later, Blackman buried Fatimah with the locket wrapped around her gentle, loving hands.

When Blackman saw Maggie in the dream, he didn't see her in the church. Instead, he saw her in a field filled with thousands, millions of sunflowers. She was wearing her wedding dress: the high neck, the low back, and the veil that was longer than the dress itself. There had been a wide purple sash that matched Fatimah's dress wrapped around Maggie's waist, the only bright color in a sea of ivory. Maggie's long hair was gathered at the nape of her neck, and her mother's diamonds were everywhere: her ears, her neck, her wrists. When Blackman looked at her, his chest ached as if it would break open. In the dream or memory or combination of both, he stood a few feet from her. Both close and too far away.

"Am I dead?" he asked.

"No, my love, you're not dead," Dream Maggie said, still and tall and unmoving, and all he wanted was for her to reach out and touch him.

"I'm scared," he admitted.

Dream Maggie smiled. "You were scared the day we got married."

"Because I thought you would change your mind."

"You're such a silly man, Blackman Smith," she chided.

"Not silly," Blackman said quietly, "just in love."

"So am I."

"Are you?" he asked. "Still? Even now?"

"Of course, my love. You're not going to die."

"I want to touch you," Blackman said as he tried to move toward her but couldn't

"Then wake up, darling. Wake up, and I'll be there next to you, waiting for you."

"Will you?"

"Yes, my love. Trust me."

Then she held out her hand to him, and he reached for it.

***

When Blackman opened his eyes, his room was bathed in late morning sunlight. He turned his head instinctively toward the window, drawn to the wintery light coming through the glass. He blinked against the light as he looked at Maggie asleep in a chair next to his bed.

Her face was pale and thin as if she wasn't eating enough. There were smudges beneath her eyes, so dark it looked as if she'd been struck. Her feet were propped up on the bed, and the position looked painful. Her bare feet poked from beneath a thin hospital blanket.

Blackman tried to say her name, but he was too weak, and his mouth didn't want to work. He stretched the fingers of the hand that was closest to her feet and, after a tremendous effort, brushed the side of her foot.

Maggie's eyes snapped open, and she drank in the sight of Blackman's open eyes like cold water on a hot day. A variety of emotions moved over her beautiful face one after another: shock, relief, gratitude, love – so much love – and shame. He'd seen that look of shame before, in the bar, after she came to her senses and recognized she had done something wrong when she beat those men. He had no idea how long he'd been unconscious, but he knew in no uncertain terms Maggie had been left to her own devices for entirely too long, and something had happened. She had done something. For years, he had been her voice of reason, but this time, he hadn't been there when she needed him most.

He had failed her, and there were going to be repercussions.

Maggie pulled her feet off the bed and winced as she sat up and reached for his hand with both of hers. Tears filled her eyes as she pressed her lips to his cool skin. Then she climbed to her feet and touched his face, her fingers warm against his ragged beard.

"My love," she wept softly, "Thank God." Tears slid down her face as she looked into his dark brown eyes. "Thank God you came back to me, my love. My love."

Blackman tried to smile, but he didn't have the energy. The feel of her lips against his dry skin was almost more than he could bear, and he started to close his eyes and slip back into sleep when he looked past Maggie and saw the Harrington brothers standing in his room, smiling gratefully at him. Blackman let his eyes fall shut as he clutched his wife's hand tightly as if she alone was his anchor to this world.

Chapter 11

Blackman spent more than a month in the hospital, including Christmas day, which he celebrated with a joyous family and a rather shy Gabe who came along with Fitz. After he was finally discharged, he spent another three weeks in rehab, getting his legs back in shape. It was nearly February by the time he was able to come home and another month before he returned to work. The Harringtons decamped for London once they were sure Maggie could handle everything, including Jamie, who struggled in the aftermath of his father's shooting.

Although Blackman missed all of Jamie's basketball season, he didn't miss baseball. Once baseball started, their small family spent most Saturdays and some Sundays sitting in the warm sun watching their son strike out one player after another.

Blackman seemed to put his brush with death into perspective, and although his office required him to see a trauma counselor, which he did without complaint, he seemed to be spared the worst of the PTSD that most shooting victims experienced. Jamie, however, was a different story. He had taken his father's shooting badly, and he struggled in school for most of Blackman's hospitalization. Thankfully, an attentive therapist and a supportive school helped him through the worst of his trauma. However, Jamie became a more reserved child, and as soon as Blackman came home, Jamie was near constant presence at his father's side. They spent most evenings or weekend afternoons together watching basketball, hockey, or baseball on television. And as Jamie grew closer to his father, he grew more distant from his mother, as if the boy could only love one parent at a time.

Fitz, however, thought the change had more to do with Jamie transitioning from middle school to high school, from the in between years to the full blown teenage years.

"He has to break someone's balls," Fitz said one night as he and Maggie sat at a neighborhood restaurant. "And considering his father nearly died, you must appear to be the more reasonable choice."

Maggie sipped wine while she watched Jamie, Blackman, and Gabe play pool.

"I know you're right, but it's exhausting," Maggie said. Being the bad guy all the time was fucking exhausting.

"Well, you were the same way at that age, always with the smart-ass comments. This is just your payback," Fitz said as he sipped a martini. Maggie didn't reply. She had been paying for her teenage transgressions her entire adult life, and she'd like to think the debt had been paid. But as she watched her not so little boy with his father, she couldn't help but feel that all too familiar pang of jealousy. A reminder that she was all too often the one standing on the other side of the window watching happy people sitting together by the fire. She was fucking J. Alfred Prufrock. A woman playing the attendant lord in her own life. A well-spoken but obtuse fool making the same mistakes again and again. A fool who puts themselves out there only to be left disappointed when others find them wanting.

Okay, it was possible she was being dramatic.

"How are things with Blackman?" Fitz asked after a few minutes.

"Fine," Maggie responded, motioning for another glass of wine.

"You sure?" he asked a little too kindly. The kindness pained her.

"Of course, I'm sure," she answered breezily. Fitz let the lie hang between them. Maggie waited for him to say something more, but he didn't get the chance. His cell phone rang, and when he read the caller ID, he excused himself.

"I have to take this, love. It's the gallery."

Maggie didn't say anything as Fitz walked away, and when the bartender brought her a second glass of wine, she nodded at him politely. She knew Fitz was worried about her, and about her and Blackman, and he had a right to be worried because things were *not* okay.

Maggie was *not* okay.

She had no idea how Blackman had done it, but he had managed to deal with his near death experience so much better than she. He had no trouble sleeping, that she could tell, no nightmares, no lingering sense of dread or fear or anxiety about what happened.

But she did.

In fucking spades.

She hadn't had a decent night's sleep since Gabriel had walked into that classroom, and sometimes, she felt like she would never have a decent night's sleep again. Most nights, she just stared at the ceiling, listening to Blackman's breathing. In the first few weeks after he came home, she was so grateful he was alive, that she could actually hear him breathing, she didn't mind not sleeping. Then, after a while, she resented him and his ability to sleep, and she hated herself for it.

On the rare nights she slept, she dreamed about the shooting or, better, the events leading up to the shooting in graphic detail. She would follow him on that busy street and watch him stop at the jewelry store and look in the window at something she couldn't see. She would try to catch up with him to tell him to go back to work where he'd be safe, but she was always too slow, or too far away, or there were too many people between them. Then she'd watch him open the door to the lingerie shop she liked so much, and again she'd try to call out to him.

But it never worked.

He never heard her, and the crack of the gunshot was a sound that followed her into her waking hours. Blackman had been shot while he was out shopping for her instead of staying at work where he was safe on the other side of the metal detectors and armed guards. His shooting was both her fault and not her fault, and she was having a difficult time living with that.

And she wasn't writing.

At all.

She had the most crippling writer's block of her life. She had to shelve the book she had been writing when Blackman was shot and return the advance the publishing house gave her, and she hadn't written a poem in months. The way her mind had seized up, she wondered if she would ever write again. Intellectually, she knew that even the best writers struggled with writer's block: Coleridge, Toni Morrison, Virginia Woolf, and Ralph Ellison. Writer's block was a universal experience, and like most universal experiences, the internet was filled with strategies to overcome it.

First, Maggie tried Maya Angelou's "Just Write" strategy to no avail.

Then there was Mark Twain's outlining strategy, but she had nothing to outline because *she couldn't fucking write*, and if she spent any more time away from her desk like Hillary Mantel recommended, she'd forget where her desk was.

Nothing worked.

Not to say that she was in the same league as any of those writers, but she'd won some impressive awards over the years, and she'd once been long-listed for the National Book Award for a collection she'd published while pregnant with Jamie.

So, she *could* write. She was an *actual* writer. She had physical proof on her bookshelves.

At the moment, though, she didn't seem to be much of a writer.

Or a writer at all.

Then there was her sexual relationship with Blackman.

Up until the night before the shooting, their sex life had been fantastic, toe curling, in fact. Worthy of being immortalized in dirty limericks, which she would gladly write if she could fucking write. After the shooting was a different matter altogether. For months, Blackman hadn't been healthy enough for sex, and she had longed for him, ached for him, and then once the doctor cleared him, she just... couldn't. She couldn't relax enough to get into the mood, couldn't quiet her exhausted, overwrought mind enough to enjoy herself, which made her self-conscious, something she had never been with Blackman.

On top of that, she found herself uncomfortable and afraid. Afraid she'd hurt him, afraid she'd disappoint him, afraid he wouldn't find her attractive anymore. Afraid he wouldn't want her the same way she wanted him.

She'd been afraid of so many things.

Of course, Blackman had his own fears. He, too, was self-conscious about the terrible scars. The exit wound on his back was a large knot of scarred flesh, and the wound on his side was a train track of *Frankenstein*-esque proportion. The scars on his stomach were long and unforgiving.

When she touched them, she went cold inside because she felt responsible.

He had looked at the jewelry.

For her

He had looked at the bra and panty set.

For her.

He had been shot.

Because he was out looking at things *for her.*

She stopped wearing jewelry: her only concession being her wedding set. She wouldn't wear cute underwear anymore. Everything she wore was utilitarian, plain, and simply ugly.

When they finally made love for the first time, it was awkward and quiet and uncomfortable. No words were spoken, no loving entreaties, no whispered obscenities or requests, no panted names.

Nothing.

Just the sound of their breathing.

He'd come quickly because of how long it had been.

She'd faked her orgasm.

And he knew it.

They showered immediately after, which they had never done before as if they wanted to wash away any evidence of what had just, and not just, transpired between them.

They showered separately, of course.

After they kissed each other goodnight, they slept as far away from one another as the Blackman sized bed allowed, and then they didn't talk about it the next day, or any other day for that matter.

Maggie assumed things would get better with time.

They did not.

The cracks were starting to show, and she didn't know how to make things better, and she couldn't bear to talk to Blackman about it. Or anyone else.

That fall, Jamie started high school and earned the backup position on the varsity football team, which quickly turned into the starting position when the quarterback was benched for bad grades and a worse attitude. Blackman and Maggie spent every Friday night watching high school football with all the other football parents. As much as it galled Blackman to root for the purple and gold, his high school rivals, he fulfilled his fatherly duties without hesitation.

In the bleachers, Blackman and Maggie sat close enough to one another so no one would think they weren't a happy couple, but still far enough away from one another so they didn't have to touch any more than necessary. When they stood around talking to the other parents, and Blackman touched her out of habit, Maggie tried not to flinch. No one noticed except Jamie. He'd always been a sharp kid, a perceptive and observant kid, and he could feel it: the cracks. He blamed Maggie for something he didn't really understand, and he let her know he blamed her with every biting, sarcastic remark he made, and she took it. She didn't have the energy to fight her son while watching her marriage fall apart.

***

The night Maggie accompanied Blackman to a work happy hour for one of their friends who was leaving the DA's office to marry her longtime partner, Maggie hadn't wanted to go. However, Maggie had known the woman for years, and it would have felt unkind not to say goodbye.

The happy hour was held on a Thursday night of a particularly trying week, and Maggie felt lonely and defeated. She wanted her old life back. She wanted to sleep, to write, and to wrap her arms around her husband so he could wrap his arms around her and make everything better. She wanted to tell him about everything: the sleepless nights, the guilt, the shame of what she had let her brothers do. She wanted to go home and make love to Blackman like they were young again.

She wanted *that* more than anything.

Blackman, of course, wanted the same things. When they walked into the bar with the exposed brick interior and the hardwood floors, Blackman expected Maggie to move away and find someone else to talk to because that was what she'd been doing for months. Finding anyone else to talk to, but instead of leaving, she stayed close to him, and for the first time in months, he tasted hope. More than once, he felt Maggie brush up against him, felt her tentatively touch his fingers with her own, and when he put his hand on the small of her back, she didn't flinch or stiffen. For a moment, she even leaned into him.

Blackman took advantage of every opportunity to touch her, and he reveled in the fact that she didn't move away. He wondered if they could go home and, instead of retreating to their sides of the bed, finally meet in the middle.

Maybe they could finally talk.

Finally make love.

Maybe he could finally make her come. Because knowing she was faking her orgasms was killing him. He felt like he was failing her in such an intimate and fundamental way, and every time it happened, he promised himself he would ask her about it. Ask her how he was disappointing her, ask her what he could do better, ask her why she felt she had to pretend with him, but he was too afraid to ask, too afraid of the answer. Too afraid that it was him.

He was so fucking tired, and he suspected, for the first time, Maggie might be tired, too.

When Maggie finished her first glass of wine, she walked over to the bar and ordered another. While standing there, she was pulled into a conversation with a group of women from the office and settled onto a barstool. Blackman watched her as she leaned in and talked, occasionally laughed and sipped her wine. Every so often, she'd look into the mirror behind the bar and see Blackman looking at her. Smiling.

And she smiled back.

A tentative smile, but a genuine smile. The first real smile he'd seen in months.

Blackman's heart soared with hope.

When Maggie finished her second glass of wine, she excused herself from the group of women at the bar and walked to the steps that led to the second floor, where the bathrooms were located. As she neared the stairs, Detective Terrence Semple stepped out of the crowd and blocked her way. She hadn't seen the detective since the day Blackman was discharged, and the intervening months hadn't been kind to him. His nose hadn't healed well, and Maggie felt a pang of regret when she looked at him. She really shouldn't have hit him. His face was pale and drawn, but his eyes were bright and sharp with hatred.

And disgust.

"Dr. Rhymer," he said, looking down at her. He wasn't much taller than Maggie, but he was tall enough and not hiding the fact he was taking a nice long look down her shirt. He wanted her to know he was staring at the swell of her breasts and that she couldn't do a damn thing about it.

"Detective Semple," Maggie said. She tried to keep her voice level. Neutral.

"It's been a while," the detective said as he leaned against the wall, blocking Maggie's way. He held a half empty pint glass, and Maggie suspected it wasn't his first or last drink of the evening.

"It has been a while. How have you been, Detective?" Maggie said, trying to sound sincere and friendly. She failed at both.

"Peachy," he said with a belligerence that rivaled her son's.

"Glad to hear it," Maggie said with a forced smile. "Well, if you'll excuse me. It was nice to see you."

He didn't move.

"Do you know who Emilio Hernandez is? Or was?" Detective Semple asked, not moving.

Maggie had the distinct feeling he wanted her to touch him, to push him, to swing at him again because he had enough Dutch courage in him to beat the shit out of her in front of half the DA's office and then hide behind his badge, which seemed fair because she'd beaten the shit out of him and hidden behind Jon Pierce. Well, not hidden per se, but she was protected, which was probably more shameful.

And honestly, if he beat the shit out of her, she'd almost welcome it. Christ knew she had it coming. She'd had it coming for years.

Fucking decades.

"No," Maggie said evenly. "I don't."

Semple smiled and took a swig of his beer, and Maggie waited patiently because she had to. He probably didn't have the balls to hit her, not really, but there were other ways he could hurt her, and they both knew it.

Guys like Semple always knew how to leave a mark.

"Emilio Hernandez was an import, export guy. Made a fortune after 9-11. Middle Eastern and North Asian antiquities. The war was good for him, but he had a temper, though, and when his first wife took a convenient tumble down the stairs, the DA's office got involved. DA thought it was murder," Semple said with a leer, then nodded to Blackman, who was deep in conversation with someone Maggie didn't know. "But Smith's old man got him off. Man, that son of a bitch was fucking brilliant." Semple took another sip of beer. "Hernandez's son – he had twins with the old bitch he killed– had daddy's temper. Years later, his son killed his wife, and the yoga instructor dyke she was fucking. But this time Smith's old man was unavailable to run the defense because he was long dead, and although the defense attorney daddy hired was good, he wasn't *Blackman Smith's father* good. Christ, your husband could be making a shit ton of money in the private sector if he wasn't such a fucking saint," Semple said, shaking his head.

Maggie said nothing. For once, she kept her mouth and her temper in check.

"So, sonny boy is doing a long stretch at Graterford, and he's not getting anywhere on appeal because Smith's case is air-fucking-tight. And dad's nursing one huge motherfucker of a grudge, and then one day, boom!" Semple said, holding up his hands dramatically. "The counselor takes three to the body."

Maggie's mouth went dry.

"So, there's nothing tying Hernandez and his money to Smith because Smith puts a lot of bad guys away. Probably doing penance for his douche bag old man." Semple's grin was more like a leer, as if he was thrilled that Blackman had been shot on a city street during the fucking lunch rush. Maggie said nothing; she just balled her fists because she was starting to shake. The room had gone cold around her.

"So anyway, while your husband's in a coma, Hernandez's son, the one who's *not* in prison, is in a freak accident on 95. Yeah, a kid hauling a load of tires loses them in front of Hernandez's Lexus. Kills Hernandez and the wife instantly, and let me tell you, everything points to 'accident.' The driver, he's just a kid, stops at the scene, and he's a hot fucking mess. Crying his eyes out and shit. And he checks out, except–" Semple leans forward "–when I try to follow up with him, the kid's gone. Poof. Nowhere to be found."

Pause.

Drink.

"Then the brother in Graterford hangs himself. According to a note, he couldn't live in a world without his brother." Semple paused to sip his beer. "Fucking pussy," he added as an afterthought.

"Then Daddy Hernandez isn't paying attention and walks in front of a ride share. Dies of a heart attack on the way to the ER, which is strange because he's in great shape for a man his age, better shape than me, that's for sure," Semple said with a cruel smile.

Maggie remained silent and still.

"But it turns out he was a party guy, so maybe the heart attack wasn't so surprising because he was with some whore the night before who might have brought some particularly potent treats to their party, but we can't find her either."

Semple took another drink.

"Seems like the same world that swallowed up the truck driver swallowed up that bitch, too. I mean, I'm not smart like you, with your Ph fucking D, or your husband with his law degree or private school pedigree, or Main Line money, but I'm *sharp*," he said, tapping his temple.

"And all this smells pretty fucking weird. Like something strange is going on, but I can't prove it, and I hate when I can't prove things," Semple said, stepping so close to Maggie she wanted to gag from the stench of him, the mixture of beer and hatred and something already in the process of dying.

"I'm sure, as a teacher, you can relate," he said. "You know some fucking kid is up to no good, but no matter how many times you Google that shit, you just can't prove it. Doesn't shit like that just stick in your fucking craw? Drive you fucking crazy?"

Maggie met Semple's eyes with as much defiance as she could muster, which was a little more than she anticipated because she was her father's daughter, after all.

"You know, though, the Hernandez family is really all pieces of shit." Semple took another sip of his beer. "So, maybe the world is a better place with all those assholes six feet under, but you know who I think about?"

Semple fucking grinned like a clown in a Stephen King novel.

"The kids in the car. I mean, they survived all right, which is good, but you know they were old enough to know their parents were dead. They were stuck in that car for over an hour crying for their mommy and daddy, but mommy and daddy were dead. Right there in front of them." He took another step toward Maggie. "I can't imagine how hard that must have been. I mean, I don't have kids, but *you* do. That boy Jamie of yours. Could you imagine him trapped in a car calling for his mommy and daddy, looking for comfort from two people who were already rotting in front of him?"

That was the shot that landed, and they both knew it.

"That's quite the story, Detective. Can you prove that anything other than a series of awful coincidences resulted in the deaths of those people?" Maggie said after a long moment. Her heart wasn't in the comment, and they both knew it. Semple had won.

"Nope. Not at all. As far as everyone is concerned, it's just a Lemony Snicket book." He sneered. "Just a series of unfortunate events that happened *after* the Harrington clan arrived in town."

Maggie swallowed. She could hear it, and she was sure he could hear it, too.

"Detective, if you think my family or I had anything to do with what happened, you should talk to Blackman," Maggie said with a confidence she didn't feel. This time, Semple leaned in so close to her he could have kissed her, brushed his lips against hers, slipped his tongue out, and tasted her lips like a snake.

"You know I can't prove shit, but *you* know, and *I* know what really happened, and you're going to have to live with that. They say getting away with murder is a great thing, but you're an English teacher, so you know the truth. This is your Raskolnikov moment, Rhymer, and I hope you fucking choke on it," he said with a lazy smile, and then he flicked his eyes over to Blackman. "You know, the one thing that I could never understand was how a guy like that married a piece of shit like you," Semple said quietly. Almost intimately.

That shot landed, too.

"You have a nice evening now, professor. I'm sure I'll be seeing you around." Semple stepped back. Maggie didn't look at him, just slowly walked past him and climbed the stairs. She didn't look back.

Blackman, nursing a beer, was talking hockey with another lawyer who had played D2 in Minnesota and then semi-pro before going to law school. He'd been so involved in the conversation he had forgotten to check on Maggie, and when he finally looked at the bar, she was gone. For a moment, he was afraid she had decided to leave and go home without telling him, that maybe the signs he had interpreted as a thawing between them had been wrong, that this Thursday night would be like every other Thursday night. Either he'd go to bed horny and frustrated, or he'd go to bed unsatisfied and disappointed. As he scanned the room, he found Maggie standing at the bottom of the stairs with Detective Semple. Semple was not only blocking her way, but by the embarrassed look on Maggie's face, he'd also taken a long look down her shirt. Semple was making it difficult for her to move, to get past him, without touching him. It was as if he wanted her to touch him so that maybe he could touch her.

Blackman seethed.

As he watched, Semple leaned forward and said something into Maggie's ear, something quiet and menacing because Maggie stiffened and then looked down wounded.

Hurt.

Blackman set his pint glass on the table next to him, excused himself, and walked over to Semple, who had finally stepped back so Maggie could walk by him.

As if he *let* Maggie walk by him.

As if he *let* Blackman Smith's wife do anything.

Semple turned around just as Blackman reached him. Surprised, Semple took an automatic step back, which put him closer to the wall he had just had Maggie pinned against. Blackman had several inches on the detective, whose florid face and red nose made him look like he was one cheap steak dinner away from a coronary. *Inshallah.*

Blackman hummed with suppressed rage like high tension wires on the side of a dark back road, and Blackman knew Semple could hear those vibrations, could feel them in his motherfucking bones.

"Counselor," Semple said, straightening to his full and unimpressive height.

They were so close to one another that Blackman could have reached out and slammed the detective's head into the wall a half dozen times before anyone would have known what was happening. He could have beaten the man to death before anyone would have had the chance to pull him away, and God knew he wanted to.

He *wanted* to kill this man.

"Detective," Blackman said coldly.

"You're looking good," Semple said with an awkward approximation of a smile.

Blackman took another step toward Semple, which forced the older man to take another step back, putting him not quite against the wall but close enough to it that he felt uncomfortable, crowded. Discomfort shone on his face. Blackman wondered if he was flirting with getting shot for the second time in a year. Except this time, he'd take this bullet with a smile because he was defending his wife against this sack of shit.

For a long time, Blackman said nothing; he and Semple just stared at one another. Blackman's eyes were hard, but Semple's eyes seemed oddly soft, almost pitying as if he couldn't help but feel badly for a man who had clearly married so far beneath himself.

"Detective," Blackman said, his voice low and menacing. "If I ever see you talking to my wife again, I'll bury you so deep in shit, the only way you'll be able to get out will be to eat your gun. Do you understand me?"

Semple blinked, his florid face going pale.

"Are you threatening me, counselor?" Semple asked.

Blackman took a half step forward, which forced Semple to bend his neck awkwardly to look up at Blackman's face. Blackman's brown eyes were black with fury. The hum of his rage was loud, a persistent buzzing in his ears.

"Unlike you, Semple, people *like* me. They *respect* me. They want *me* to owe *them* a favor because it's great when the ADA owes you one. Then there are the people who remember my father, who *owe* my father – powerful men, Semple. *Dangerous* men, and since my dad's dead, I'm more than willing to call in his markers," Blackman said quietly. "So, if I ever see you so much as look at my wife, I'll spend the rest of my life ruining yours."

Semple said nothing for a long moment because, at the end of the day, all bullies were pussies.

"That sounds like a threat counselor," Semple said, but the intimidating voice he was trying for fell flat.

Blackman gave him a dangerous smile and lowered his voice.

"No, Detective. That's a fact."

The two men looked at one another, and then Blackman patted the detective's shoulder as he stepped back and let the detective walk away like Semple had let Maggie walk away. Then Blackman walked up the stairs. He could feel the detective's eyes on his back, but he didn't care. Blackman had made his point. Blackman may have been Fatimah's son, but he was also his father's son, and his father had been a ruthless son-of-a-bitch, and as Blackman looked at his wife framed in a window overlooking the busy city street below, he knew he could be, too. He could be so much worse than his father. Because his father had never loved anyone the way Blackman loved Maggie.

When they got home that night, Jamie was watching a hockey game in the living room with two friends from school, pretending to work on math homework. All three boys acknowledged the two adults who walked through the room and then returned to their poorly executed subterfuge. Blackman followed Maggie into the kitchen and watched as she made tea.

"What did Semple want?" Blackman asked, waiting to see if Maggie would like to him.

Again.

"Just checking up on your recovery," Maggie lied because Maggie always lied anymore. They both did because lying was easy. Honesty was what was so motherfucking hard.

Blackman nodded as if he believed her when she turned and looked at him with unnaturally distant eyes. In fact, everything about her seemed even more distant and more closed off than it had been earlier in the evening. She reminded him of an abandoned lighthouse they had once visited, full of promise and heartbreaking disappointment. Blackman searched for something meaningful to say but failed.

In hindsight, he should have crossed the room and hugged her, kissed her. Told her he loved her more than anything in the world, told her he didn't care what Semple thought or knew or did. He should have held her close and told her she had nothing to fear because Blackman could ruin Semple's life with a few well placed phone calls. He should have told her that after almost twenty years together, he was not the saint she made him out to be in her head.

He was just a man like every other man.

And if someone had done to Maggie what they had done to Blackman, Blackman would have let Nick burn down the city if he wanted to. He would have let him fill up the morgues. He would have let Nick do whatever he wanted, and Blackman wouldn't have cared at all.

Not even a little bit.

But instead of saying any of those things to Maggie, instead of holding her close and finally being honest, he sighed. “Do you want to go upstairs and watch a movie?”

Maggie shook her head, turned away, and poured hot water into a travel tea mug.

“No,” she said lightly. “I have work to do.” Then she gathered up her things and walked past him. It would have been so easy for Blackman to reach out to touch her, to brush his fingers against her arm, to force her to talk to him. To stop this silence before it did any more damage to them.

To tell her that he knew her secret.

But he didn’t do any of those things.

Instead, he let her walk away and go to her office where she drank tea and stared into space while Blackman sat in their room staring at a paperback book he couldn’t see.

Chapter 12

"I want a divorce."

Blackman had suspected the demand was coming for months. In some ways, it had probably been coming since the day he was shot. Today was December 7th, Pearl Harbor Day, the day that would live in infamy, so it seemed fitting that it was also the day his marriage would finally collapse under the weight of everything he and his wife no longer said to one another. And like every other day he spent with his wife in the time after the shooting, there were a dozen things he should have said to her, but instead of opening his mouth and saying anything, even the wrong thing, he just stood there. A man caught in the middle of a busy highway, his wife's anger bearing down on him like a tractor-trailer that had lost its breaks. He thought that he'd be better prepared when she finally said those words, the words he feared more than anything in this world. In fact, he could not have been less prepared, and that was saying something.

So many nights when he came home from work, sometimes later than necessary, he'd expected to find an empty house and an empty bed, but every night, Maggie was there, in their home, sad and quiet. Every time he saw his wife, he thanked God and Fatimah that there was still some mercy left in the world, but whatever grace he had been extended had finally run out. The other proverbial shoe had dropped, and there his wife stood, facing him in all her glorious anger with their wedding dishes stacked neatly in front of her on the kitchen island.

However, if she still cared enough to be standing there, he could reason with her; he could save his marriage.

Their marriage.

If she was still there, he knew he could convince her to stay if only he could open his goddamn mouth.

But there he stood, mutely watching her. He had no idea why she was so angry tonight or why she was even angry at all. He had not only come home early, but he had come home holding two sacks of food from her favorite kabob place and two bottles of her favorite wine. More importantly, he had come home ready to talk, prepared to lay bare his soul to her. Ready to say everything he hadn't said to her for months.

Ready to finally figure out what had gone wrong.

It seemed, however, that he was too late.

Blackman stood staring into the kitchen dressed in his best suit, the one Fitz's favorite Saville Row tailor made for Blackman one Christmas. He wore it especially for Maggie, for tonight. He even wore the purple tie she had slipped into his tie rack shortly after she moved in with him because she liked that, too.

Maggie's anger radiated off her like waves in a North Sea storm as she stood on the other side of the kitchen, the island between them, the wedding dishes her father had given to them piled high in front of her. Her hazel eyes were unflinching, shining with the kind of anger that made her look dangerous, the kind of anger which, in fact, actually made her dangerous.

She was positively radiant.

The most beautiful woman in the world.

Her wavy hair hung loosely around her strong shoulders, her face scrubbed clean of make-up. She was a powerfully built woman who had discovered rock climbing and martial arts in her twenties instead of spin class and Pilates, like many of their friends' wives.

She wore her favorite blue jeans, the ones with the tear in the left knee that showed off her amazing legs and perfect ass, and the purple sweater that brought out the blue in her eyes. The sweater dipped low in the back, showing off her muscular shoulders and the mountain range tattoo she'd had done before they met.

Miles to go before I sleep...

And even though he couldn't see her feet, he knew she was wearing her favorite motorcycle boots. He loved those boots so much, especially when they were the only thing she was wearing.

Not that *that* had happened in quite a long time.

"I. Want. A. Divorce." She enunciated every word as if he were deaf, or slow, or both.

Blackman had no idea how long they had been standing there in silence, but it had not been nearly long enough for him to formulate a good response. An adequate response.

Or any response.

At all.

Maggie held his eyes and dared him to speak. He had seen her angry before, but he had never been on the receiving end of this kind of Maggie's anger. He could have gone the rest of his life having not had the experience and counted himself a lucky man.

Still he said nothing.

His mind was completely blank, except for the part trying to convince him to throw caution to the wind. To drag her onto the kitchen table, where they would have angry sex and then make-up sex. The kind of sex that would make her scream when she came, the kind of sex that would make her draw blood as she scratched her short nails down his back or bit his shoulder in ecstasy. Then they could have the kind of sex that might remind her that she loved him too much to leave him.

Maggie picked up one of the plates stacked in front of her and frisbeed it as hard as she could into the wall just to the left of Blackman. It hit the wall and exploded like a shot.

Like a gunshot.

Blackman was so shocked he didn't move. He didn't even flinch. He simply stood in horrified silence.

"I–"

Another plate shattered.

"Want –"

Another plate.

"A –"

This time, a serving bowl.

"Divorce!"

She picked up a stack of plates and slammed it on the floor. A shard of porcelain ricocheted off the floor, nicking her cheek and drawing blood.

Maggie didn't notice, but Blackman had gone pale. Slowly, he set down the sacks and held up his hand in an awkward attempt at a calming gesture he assumed wasn't the least bit calming. Enraged by his protracted silence, she reached for the crystal champagne flutes they used to celebrate all their milestones: their marriage, her PhD, his promotions, the birth of their son, her tenure, their house.

"Maggie, NO!" Blackman yelled loudly, finally finding his voice.

Maggie's face went crimson, and her eyes flashed brilliantly, and for a second, he thought she'd come across the room and punch him, which would at least spare the rest of the dishes. Instead, she swept the remaining dishes off the counter. They shattered on the floor with a deafening crash.

The champagne flutes were spared.

Maggie took a long look at Blackman, her cheeks flushed, chest heaving, hands balled into fists. Then she walked across the kitchen, her boots crunching on the shattered porcelain, and brushed past Blackman, daring him to reach out and touch her, but he didn't. He didn't move until he heard a door slam and the garage door open.

When he finally moved, he stepped further into the kitchen and saw a bottle of expensive bourbon and a handwritten note on the kitchen table. He walked carefully over the broken pieces of his eighteen year marriage.

He picked up the note and read it.

Heard through the grapevine you scored the Dixon case. This could put you on the bench. Don't fuck it up. JP

Blackman closed his eyes for a moment, and when he opened them again, he picked up the bottle and inspected it. Then he threw it as hard as he could against the wall, where it exploded, raining glass and bourbon over the already desecrated kitchen.

Maggie wasn't the only one who could break shit.

***

When Maggie walked into the garage, her biggest hiking backpack was already packed and sitting on the hood of her black Jeep Wrangler, which was parked next to Blackman's Volvo SUV. She stared at her Jeep, remembering she was supposed to take it into the shop tomorrow because the check engine light had been on for over a week. She didn't want to take Blackman's Volvo. She hated that thing, and she didn't even know why. Maybe because it was his, and right now, she hated him.

"Fuck," she said, pulling on her heavy winter coat before shoving her favorite winter hat over her unruly red hair. Then she shouldered her bag and walked out of the garage without closing it behind her. Her phone vibrated, but she ignored it. When it stopped, she pulled it out of her pocket, ignored the caller ID, and turned it off.

Then she started walking.

It was a cold night, and the dark streets were empty. Their neighborhood was up and coming and relatively safe during the day, but nighttime was a different story. Blackman would be livid when he found out she had set out on foot, but she didn't care.

Or maybe she did.

Fuck him. Let him worry for once.

Stopping at a red light, she considered her limited options. She could turn south and head to Fitz's place, but she suspected he would send her back home to hash it out with Blackman. Fitz, in typical Fitz fashion, would not approve of Maggie's decision to leave her husband without having an actual discussion, and he would probably be angry about the broken crockery. He'd find the whole thing undignified, as any reasonable and happy person would. There was a time when she was a reasonable and happy woman, and she, too, would have found the whole thing distasteful.

But she was not presently reasonable.

And she had not been happy in a very longtime.

So, she turned west and started walking.

***

Blackman stood in the middle of what was left of his wedding dishes, sipping his wife's favorite Zinfandel out of a glass they'd bought the last time they were in Oregon.

His wife.

Maggie.

Maggie, his wife.

He picked at the kabob, but his heart wasn't in it. He wasn't hungry, but he was thirsty, and he wanted – in fact *all* he wanted – was to be drunk. Like college drunk, like fraternity party on a Saturday night drunk. Like a woman whose name he didn't know beneath him drunk. He looked at the smashed bottle of bourbon in the corner and sighed.

He should have thrown the fucking wine. Absently, he picked up some lamb with his fingers, put it in his mouth, chewed, and chased it with another mouthful of wine. He could taste neither the lamb nor the wine.

His iPhone buzzed in his pocket, and he dug it out without looking at the caller ID. No need to be disappointed.

"Smith," he said automatically.

"Hey, Dad. Is this a bad time?"

"Yes, Jamie, this is a terrible time," Blackman said, pouring more wine into his glass.

"Oh, is everything okay?"

"No, Jamie, it isn't. What do you need?"

"Umm– okay. Do you know where Mom is? She's not answering her texts. Or picking up her phone, and I need a ride."

"No, I don't know where your mom is. If you need a ride, call Uncle Fitz or Gabe. I'm in the middle of... something," Blackman said as he looked around the kitchen. He was in the middle of something alright, the dissolution of his fucking marriage.

"Dad," Jamie said awkwardly. "You sound weird. Are you sure everything is okay?"

Blackman closed his eyes and pinched the bridge of his nose. Every other conversation with his son was like this. Jamie asked a question, didn't listen to the answer, then asked the same question again. Blackman wondered if he had been the same way with Fatimah.

Christ, Fatimah.

She was probably rolling over in her grave or, worse, looking down on him with that look of disappointment he had so rarely earned.

"Dad?"

"Call Uncle Fitz or Gabe. One of them will give you a ride," Blackman repeated.

"Okay, Dad. Umm... see you later."

Blackman ended the call, wondering how much of this mess he could clean up before his son or brother-in-law got home, but he didn't move. He just drank more wine and did nothing.

Blackman was opening the second bottle of wine when he heard the front door open and shut. He poured another glass and waited for the inevitable.

"Holy shit," Fitz said, stopping in the entryway to the kitchen, much like Blackman had done an hour ago. He took in the scene as Blackman poured him a glass of wine.

"Wow," Fitz said, taking the proffered glass.

"Yes. *Wow*," Blackman said tonelessly.

"Is that *all* the wedding dishes?"

"She didn't get to the dessert plates or the coffee service. So, no, not all of it."

"I see she spared the champagne flutes."

"Not for lack of trying," Blackman said. He took another drink of wine.

Fitz picked his way carefully across the kitchen and stood next to Blackman. He sniffed the air and made a face.

"Is that bourbon?" he asked.

"*I* broke that."

"Ah," Fitz said before he drained the wineglass and poured himself another.

"Can you fix this?" Fitz asked, looking at Blackman, who pointedly avoided his eyes.

"I don't think we have that much crazy glue," Blackman said with a dry chuckle. His eyes stung, and his throat felt tight. It was getting hard to breathe.

"Are you drunk?" Fitz asked with raised eyebrows.

"Not even fucking close."

"Okay, mate, then let me ask you again. Can you fix this?" Fitz's voice was firm as he repeated himself.

Blackman's hands were shaking, and he gripped the counter as he considered the question. The fact of the matter was he didn't think he could fix this. The broken wedding dishes were quite the gesture from a woman who wasn't prone to making grand gestures, but he couldn't give voice to the thoughts because that would give them life. To say *no, I can't fix this* would mean his marriage to the only woman he had ever loved was over, and he wasn't ready to admit that.

To admit that he'd lost her.

Fitz put his hand on Blackman's shoulder, and Blackman let the tears come. Then he heard his son's footsteps. He'd recognize those footsteps anywhere and quickly swiped at his eyes as he heard his son say, "What the hell?"

Blackman turned around and looked at James Rhymer-Smith. He and Maggie decided the Blackman tradition would end with Blackman himself, which seemed appropriate since Jamie was much more his mother than his father, except for his height. When it came to height, Jamie was all Blackman.

At fourteen, Jamie already stood six foot four, on track to stand six foot eight or six foot nine. Height aside, Jamie was redheaded like his mom, with the same pale skin and icy hazel eyes, but most of all, he'd inherited his mother's fierce temper. Which, more often than not, left him and his mother at loggerheads as the high school freshmen tried to find his own voice. And, God, the kid was smart. Maybe more intelligent than both his parents, so maybe Blackman had contributed a little bit on that front, too. Because Blackman used to be a smart man.

Slowly, Blackman turned and looked at his son, instantly aching for his wife.

"What the fuck happened?" Jamie asked sharply. "Where's Mom?" His eyes grew dark, and Blackman couldn't determine whether he was alarmed or angry. Blackman flinched at Jamie's use of the word *fuck*. Blackman had never used such language in front of Fatimah, and before this moment, Jamie had never used the F-word around his parents. However, if anything might warrant his son dropping the work *fuck* in front of his father, the state of the kitchen would be it. Blackman wanted to tell his son to watch his language, but as per usual, words failed him.

"Jamie," Fitz said quietly, "mind your language with your father."

Jamie shot his uncle a withering look, or as withering a look as an angry American teenage boy could shoot, which wasn't very.

"Where's Mom?" Jamie asked again.

"I don't know," Blackman admitted weakly.

"What do you mean you don't know?" Jamie looked away from his father to the carnage in the kitchen. "Are those the good dishes?"

"Jamie," Fitz said a little more forcefully.

"She left," Blackman said, trying to swallow the lump in his throat that threatened to choke him. "Your mother left."

"Left?" Jamie was incredulous. "Left to go where? When's she coming back?"

Blackman took a steadying breath. "I don't know where she went or when she's coming back."

If she's coming back.

"And you're just standing there drinking fucking wine?"

Blackman wasn't sure if Jamie's voice was angry or panicked. Either emotion was good. The boy had been a nightmare for weeks since Maggie had taken away his X-Box for one transgression or another.

Blackman couldn't respond.

Again.

Fuck. No one would ever believe I'm a competent lawyer.

"Come on, Jamie, you're staying with me and Gabe tonight. Go get your stuff."

Jamie opened his mouth to argue, but Fitz shot him a withering look, and Fitz did withering looks like only a gay British man of a certain age could, and the boy fell silent. Jamie gave his father one more hard stare, then walked out of the kitchen, leaving Fitz and Blackman alone.

"Fix this, brother," Fitz said, touching Blackman's arm one last time.

"I don't know if I can," Blackman admitted, tears burning the back of his eyes again.

"Nonsense. Of course, you can, but best you come up with a plan soon. I'm not going to be able to keep the family out of this for very long," Fitz said not unkindly.

Blackman nodded, and Fitz gave him one more pat on the arm before he walked out of the kitchen. He heard Jamie's footsteps, a few muffled curses, and the front door open and close again.

Blackman was alone.

Again.

Just him and the broken dishes.

***

It was almost eleven when Maggie arrived at the renovated row house a few blocks from campus. She was tired, cold, and sore. If she knew she was going to walk so far, she would have worn her hiking boots, but she had forgotten about the goddamn check engine light. When she saw the lights still on in the front windows, she was so grateful tears pricked at the corners of her eyes.

She climbed the stairs to the front porch and knocked on the door, waiting patiently until a tall, slender, redheaded woman opened the door.

Dr. Tilly MacPherson was dressed for bed in a gray t-shirt with Chinese characters beneath a cartoon panda bear cheerfully munching bamboo, and a pair of bright orange soccer shorts that showed off her shapely legs.

"Maggie?" Tilly asked surprised as she took in Maggie's appearance and the fact that she was alone in this neighborhood at eleven o'clock at night. Alone with a big hiking pack on her back. The kind of pack she used on multi-day camping trips. The same backpack she'd used when they went to Canada a couple of years ago. You could practically put a body in that backpack.

"I did something terrible," Maggie said in a soft, choked voice.

Tilly blinked, then looked around quickly before pulling Maggie into the house and shutting and locking the door behind them. As she pushed Maggie gently toward the front room, a tall man with shoulder length black hair and a black beard with strands of gray shooting through it stood on the far side of the room holding a watering can as if he had been interrupted during his evening chores. He, too, was dressed for bed in a black Philadelphia Flyers t-shirt and flannel pajama bottoms. Tilly exchanged a meaningful look with her husband, who set the watering can on the nearest table.

"What do you mean by *terrible*, honey? Like we need to break out the tarp and the shovels *terrible*, or we need to break out the good whiskey *terrible*?" Tilly asked, cupping her friend's shoulders in her hands.

"I told Blackman I wanted a divorce, and..." Maggie tried unsuccessfully to choke back a sob.

Tilly waited patiently, then asked, "And?"

"I broke all our wedding dishes," Maggie sobbed pitifully as she buried her face in her trembling hands.

Tilly looked at John, who turned toward the kitchen.

"I'll get the whiskey."

Tilly took Maggie's backpack and set it next to the stairs. She helped her out of her coat and hung it on the banister, then led a sobbing Maggie to an overstuffed sofa. Tilly sat down alongside Maggie and waited for her friend to compose herself.

John returned with the whiskey and three cut glass tumblers and set them on the coffee table. He poured three measures, giving Maggie the lion's share, then sat on a matching chair. He held the tumbler in his long fingers but didn't drink. Like his wife, he waited patiently for Maggie to compose herself.

Tilly said nothing as she handed Maggie a tumbler of whiskey, which Maggie downed in one. When Maggie set the tumbler back on the coffee table, John leaned over and poured her another.

"Maggie, honey, what happened?" Tilly asked gently.

Maggie looked at the tumbler on the table, then at her hands where her wedding set shone in the light of the room. She took several deep breaths.

"I don't know," she said quietly. She had no idea how to explain the events of the last five hours. Tilly just waited. She, too, was a college professor, and knew how to wait for an answer.

"Things have been... difficult," Maggie started as she reached for the tumbler. "Since the shooting... between me and Blackman." She sipped her drink and thought about what she wanted to say. "We had talked about going away this winter, just the two of us, maybe try to – I don't know – salvage things?" she said with a shrug. "I don't know. I don't even think we were going to do it, anyway, so I suppose it doesn't matter."

Tilly and John exchanged looks. John was sitting and waiting for the part of the story where Maggie confirmed that her *terrible thing* was limited to the breaking of the dishes and not the breaking of her husband's neck. Otherwise, he was going to have to change his clothes, break out the shovels and tarp, and then drive to New Jersey, which was not what he wanted to do tonight.

"Some guy dropped off a bottle of bourbon and a note," Maggie said softly. "Just something from the office, you know, but I was curious, so I read the note."

"And?" Tilly prompted.

"And it was from his old boss, Jon Pierce, congratulating him on getting the Zachary Dixon case." Maggie paused, and more tears fell down her face. "That case is going to be a circus, but I guess it's also going to be a career maker."

Tilly and John exchanged looks.

The Zachary Dixon story was everywhere. The newspapers were obsessed with his victims, and the tabloids were obsessed with him. Zachary Dixon was the American Dream incarnate. A rags-to-riches self-made multi-millionaire with the perfect wife and children, and a tendency toward philanthropy that made him look like the Evangelical version of Mother Theresa. He also had a string of dead mistresses or alleged mistresses that made him look like Jack the Ripper. It was a Hallmark movie meets Karin Slaughter novel, and the prosecution was going to have its hands full.

This case was bringing out all the crazies, including the religious nuts, and it was the celebrity trial that Philadelphia had always wanted. It would bring millions of dollars of tourist money into the city between the murder tourists and the journalists, both reputable and disreputable. Like any high-profile celebrity murder case, the winning team would be immortalized in case studies, podcasts, and Netflix documentaries, whereas the losing team would spend the rest of their careers being punch lines to tasteless jokes.

This was the kind of case that made careers and broke them.

Destroyed them.

"And I can't do a case like that, not after all that's happened," Maggie said.

"And you told Blackman that?" Tilly asked, feeling like she already knew the answer. She shared a look with her husband.

Maggie looked at her feet noncommittally. To tell Blackman anything would require a level of communication that was beyond them now.

Tilly tried again.

"So, you confronted Blackman tonight? What did he say?"

"There wasn't really a confrontation per se. He came home, and I told him I wanted a divorce, and then I threw the wedding dishes at the wall."

"Why?" Tilly asked.

"Why what? Why did I break the dishes?" Maggie asked, a little confused.

Tilly nodded.

Maggie shrugged.

"I was angry."

John stood up and ran a hand through his hair.

"I'll put fresh sheets on the guest bed," he said as he kissed the top of Tilly's head. "I'm going to let Cujo down, okay?"

"Thanks, honey. I won't be late," Tilly said softly as she leaned into John for the briefest of moments. Maggie watched them and remembered when things had been like that. Easy. Tender. Loving. Now everything was too hard, and they'd gotten so lost, and with Zachary Dixon in the picture, maybe the best thing for them as people – not as a couple – but as two independent adults, was to stay lost.

Maybe their time together was coming to an end.

They wouldn't be the first couple not to make it.

And she was sure she wasn't the first spouse to read the writing on the wall and make decisions that were best for both of them.

Whether her husband understood those decisions or not.

John left the whiskey behind and walked upstairs with Maggie's backpack.

A few minutes later, a Burmese Mountain dog the size of a small bear came bounding down the stairs and into the living room. Cujo threw himself into Maggie's arms, and she pulled the dog tightly against her and began to cry again while Tilly walked into the kitchen and put the kettle on.

Chapter 13

Maggie woke up the next morning with a start. Early morning sunlight filtered through the blue patterned curtains that complimented the soft blue walls of the guest room. Turning over, she groaned and rolled back on the too soft bed. The small guest room housed only a bed, a nightstand, and bookshelves. Heavy handmade bookshelves. The walls were filled with nature photographs and photographs of Tilly grinning broadly in a variety of exotic environs. Zoologists, and Tilly in particular, were always better traveled than literature professors and most likely better paid.

In the publish or perish world of academia, Maggie had always held her own, but Tilly, who hadn't married until recently and had no children, was the Stephen King of academia. She had written dozens of books and co-authored or contributed to dozens more, some not even in her field. She and Maggie met in undergrad and stayed in touch as Maggie's life unfurled itself in Philadelphia while Tilly's life took her all over the globe until a tenured faculty position opened up and brought her back to Philadelphia.

Now married, Tilly still traveled, but not as much as she used to. Her husband John, a kindhearted and attentive man with a rather mysterious past, either traveled with her or took care of Cujo and the house while Tilly was abroad.

They were disgustingly happy, and Maggie throbbed with jealousy.

Maggie sat up in bed and ran a hand through her hair and over her neck as if her fingers could ease the tension in her muscles. That used to be Blackman's job once upon a time. Maggie slowly slipped out of bed and made her way to the guest bathroom, where she took a quick shower and brushed her teeth. She dressed in her jeans from the night before, a green cable knit sweater, and her boots. She grabbed her phone, then stepped back into the hallway. She could smell fresh coffee and bacon.

When she entered the kitchen, she wasn't surprised to see John at the stove, still dressed in his Flyers shirt and flannel pajama bottoms. Cujo was asleep on a giant dog bed, almost as big as the rough wood table that dominated the airy kitchen. Maggie bent down to give the pup a scratch behind the ears before she settled down at the table.

"Good morning," John said as he poured Maggie a mug of coffee and carried it to the table. "Do you need a side of aspirin with that?" He walked over to the stainless steel refrigerator, pulled out a carton of French vanilla creamer, and brought it over to the table and set it in front of Maggie. There was no judgment in his voice; it was simply a question from a man who'd been there before.

"Just coffee. We switched to tea after you went to bed," Maggie said as she poured a healthy shot of creamer into her coffee. Then she swirled it around in her cup and blew on it gently.

John grabbed another mug from the cabinet and poured himself some coffee. He drank it black as he turned back to the stove and cracked some eggs over a skillet.

Maggie sipped her coffee quietly. When she and Blackman were looking for their first house, they'd considered this neighborhood, but they wanted to be closer to the river. They'd always liked walking along the river and through the Old City neighborhoods with the cobblestone streets and the quiet restaurants. Tears pricked the back of her eyes, and she blinked them away. She'd lost her temper last night and thrown down a gauntlet she didn't think she could pick up.

And she'd broken the dishes.

Christ, her fucking temper.

Maggie watched John as he plated breakfast. When she first met John, she found him utterly charming. He was kind but reserved and reminded Maggie a little of Blackman during his college days; however, in the right light, he reminded her more of her father and brothers than Blackman.

Whenever Maggie asked about John's past, Tilly's answers were always vague. He'd grown up in Europe, but she never mentioned where. He came to the United States in his twenties and worked as a military contractor in the Middle East, but she didn't seem to know what he did overseas. For someone who lived in Europe until his twenties, he had no discernable accent, which was interesting to a woman who had never shed her own.

In Maggie's experience, *military contractor* was a catch-all term for all sorts of nefarious work. After all, she was her father's daughter, and she knew a player when she saw one. It was likely John had been a mercenary or a contract killer. She'd met her fair share of both while living at home, and they always looked a little bit alike and carried themselves similarly. Still, whenever she saw John sitting in that small lakeside town reading a paperback book on a bench, he struck her as a guy looking for an excuse to walk away from a job that had suited him once but didn't suit him all that much anymore.

Now, standing in the kitchen cooking breakfast, it was clear he'd found whatever he had been looking for because the man in front of her seemed very much removed from his violent past. Still, she wondered if anyone ever really left that kind of life behind. She thought about what Tilly had said last night.

What do you mean by terrible, honey? Like we need to break out the tarp and the shovels terrible, or we need to break out the good whiskey terrible?

Maggie hadn't thought much of the comment last night, but now she couldn't get it out of her head. Did Tilly think Maggie was the kind of woman who lost it and murdered her husband? And were Tilly and John the kind of friends who got rid of bodies?

Jesus. Her fucking life.

Of course, considering her own family, Maggie had no right to judge. Whatever John had done in his past, at least he didn't seem like the kind of man who would scream *I want a divorce* at his wife in a fit of temper while throwing the good dishes against the wall.

She was a fucking disaster.

Shame burned in her stomach like acid. She looked at her phone, sitting face down on the table. She had turned it off last night and had no desire to turn it back on this morning. She wasn't about to call Blackman, and as much as she knew she should text Jamie, she didn't want to do that either. She had no interest in talking or texting with either one of them. Jamie, especially. So, the phone stayed off.

Jamie had been a bloody nightmare the last few weeks as he settled into full tortured teenager mode. When he wasn't being short or snippy with her – or to call a spade a spade, when he wasn't being a complete asshole – he was sulky and silent, and since she spent the most time with him, she found herself taking the brunt of his teenage dumbassery.

Well, let his father deal with him for a while.

And, of course, there was Fitz. As much as she wanted to talk to her brother, she didn't have that kind of energy this morning. He was going to be incandescent with rage.

"Eat up," John said, setting a plate of bacon, eggs, and what looked suspiciously like homemade toast in front of her. She just stared at her plate.

How did all these fucking men know how to cook?

She hated cooking. In the beginning, she tried to help Blackman in the kitchen, but eventually, she was more of a hindrance than a help, so he relegated her to wine duty, which was definitely more her wheelhouse. She was forever cutting herself with his ridiculously sharp knives, and instead of having to risk an ER visit every time he cooked, it was easier to sit at the kitchen table or the far section of the counter where she couldn't distract him so much that he'd cut himself. There's had always been a unique relationship.

"You're welcome to stay here as long as you want," John said bringing her back from her scattered musings.

"Thanks," Maggie said, picking up her toast and putting it down again. "I don't want to put you out."

"It's not a problem. You can earn your keep by walking Cujo," he said with that easy smile. Cujo looked up at the sound of his name and waited to see if there was a treat in his future. When no treat was offered, he went back to sleep.

"I can do that." Maggie picked up the toast again, and this time, she got it all the way to her mouth. She wasn't hungry, but she wasn't entirely sure when she last ate. The last thing she needed to do was compound her problems by passing out in front of one of her classes.

"Good, but I *am* going to ask one thing of you in return." His brown eyes bore into her with such intensity it left her feeling exposed and uncomfortable.

Maggie didn't say anything as she returned the half eaten toast to her plate and reached for her coffee. She knew what he was going to say. It was what she would say if Tilly was sitting in her kitchen drinking coffee and eating store bought toast after torching her marriage in a spectacular fit of temper.

"I'm not ready to talk to Blackman," Maggie said simply.

"I understand." John's voice was a study in understanding. "But your husband deserves to know you're okay. You don't even have to talk to him. Just send him a text."

He cast her a pleading look, and she could sense that he was as sympathetic to Blackman's position as he was to hers. He might have been willing to get rid of her husband's body last night, but he was goddamn Switzerland this morning.

"At least let him know you're not dead in an alley," he said with an all too serious look because her being dead in an alley wasn't out of the realm of possibility considering the neighborhoods she had walked through last night. Maggie put her coffee down and picked up a piece of perfectly cooked bacon. She bit it in half and chewed slowly hoping to buy herself some time.

"If you don't call him, I will." It wasn't a threat, just a statement. Maggie continued to chew and avoided John's eyes. John was undeterred. "Your husband's a nice guy, and I understand you're having problems, but last night sounded like it was a bit... intense, so letting him know–"

"I understand," Maggie interrupted him. "I'll text him."

John nodded, and she suspected they both knew she was lying, but he was kind enough to let the lie go. They finished their breakfast in silence, and then John cleaned up while Maggie got her things ready for work.

***

Blackman's alarm went off at 5:30 signaling the end of a miserable night on the sofa. It had taken him until after midnight to clean up the broken dishes and the shattered bottle of bourbon. He mixed the cleaning solution Fatimah had taught him to make when he was still a boy who helped her clean the kitchen. He scrubbed the kitchen from top to bottom, and by the time he was finished, the smell reminded him so much of Fatimah he sat on the floor and cried. Then he stretched out on the sofa in the living room because he couldn't bear to sleep in his marital bed without his wife.

Since the early days of their relationship, he had never slept well when she was away, but after last night, he couldn't imagine crawling into their bed between the sheets that smelled of her favorite shampoo and soap with her demands for a divorce echoing in his head. And he wanted to be in the living room in case she decided to come home and talk or yell some more. Hell, she could have even come home and break more dishes, or anything else she wanted, as long as she was home.

Safe.

With him.

But she didn't come home.

Blackman slowly swung his long legs around and rested his half numb feet on the floor. Everything hurt: his back, his shoulders, his bad leg. He levered himself upright and limped upstairs. The house was painfully silent, and for the first time in his life, he understood how silence could be deafening.

He took a long shower and tried unsuccessfully to wash away the aches and pains a man of his age and size experienced after a night on the sofa. Then he shaved carefully, brushed his teeth, and ran a brush through his thick brown hair, which needed a cut. He dressed slowly in his best black suit, a crisp white shirt, and a red striped tie.

"Oh Auntie," he said quietly in Arabic as he stared at his reflection in the mirror, straightening his tie. "I have made such a mess."

He listened for her voice, but there was only silence. Even Fatimah was too angry to talk with him that morning. After he dressed, he moved around the house stiffly, gathering his things as if it were a typical weekday morning, imagining Jamie and Maggie's playful banter instead of listening to the oppressive silence of the empty house. A banter that had taken on more of an edge lately.

Jamie was feeling his oats, and Blackman should have done more to put the boy in his place, but he hadn't. In fact, he wasn't entirely sure how to. He had never gone through such a stage with Fatimah. He had always just been grateful to have someone who loved him after his mother's death. Jamie took Maggie for granted, and Blackman would fix that as soon as he brought Maggie home.

Blackman was looking at his work email on his phone when he opened the door to the garage and was hit with the cold chill of early morning air. He looked up, startled to see Maggie's Jeep on her side of the garage, and the garage door opened. For one desperate moment, he hoped she had slept in the Jeep to put the fear of God in him, just in case breaking the dishes hadn't been enough, but when he pulled open the back door, it was empty.

"Fuck," he groaned. He pulled out his phone and checked their family Uber account and then their debit card to see if there were any new charges. Maggie never had cash.

"Shit." There were no new charges. Had she walked out on him and then literally walked somewhere? At night? In this neighborhood? He tapped the *Find My iPhone* icon, but Maggie's phone didn't show up, meaning it was either turned off, was on airplane mode, or was laying shattered next to her dead body in a back alley.

"Mother *fuck*," he said as he threw his stuff into his SUV and drove out of the garage. He turned west toward the university. If she wasn't, God forbid dead, she'd be at work because no matter what was going on in their personal lives, Maggie rarely missed a class.

Blackman felt uncomfortable sitting on the bench on the far side of the winter dead lawn that separated the humanities building that housed Maggie's tiny office and most of her classes from the student union.

It was a bitter morning that started sunny only to go gray with the suggestion of an early snow. In fact, it smelled of snow, which was one of Blackman's favorite smells. He wore his heavy wool overcoat buttoned up tight and a red scarf that Jamie had given him one Christmas knotted at his neck, and a pair of heavy black gloves. Blackman liked the cold, and typically it didn't bother him, but this morning it did. Despite the overcast day, he wore dark sunglasses and stared at the entrance of Maggie's building.

He looked like a stalker.

To the college kids walking by, he probably looked like a cop or mafia hitman, depending on what video games they played.

He felt like an idiot.

He sat there ignoring his iPhone, which buzzed incessantly. He knew it wasn't Maggie because he had a special vibration for her, so he ignored the texts and the calls. Jamie texted him serval times, but Blackman ignored him. Blackman had a special vibration for him, too, but Blackman wasn't up to texting with Jamie. The boy probably wanted to know where his mother was, but since Blackman couldn't answer that question, it seemed easier to dodge his son.

Father of the fucking year right here, ladies and gentlemen.

The texts were most likely work related, undoubtedly because he was missing a meeting. In fact, he was going to miss several meetings this morning, some of which were important, but he didn't care. Right now, he needed to talk to his wife. Or, at the very least, he needed to see her so he knew she was alive.

As he sat on the bench, Blackman tried to keep his mind from wandering too far afield. If he got distracted, he might miss Maggie, and he didn't want that to happen. It was one thing to sit across from her building looking like a stalker, but it would be another thing to show up at her office door playing the role of the deranged husband.

He could already hear that 911 call.

It was close to eight o'clock when Blackman finally caught sight of his wife walking toward her building with a man he didn't recognize. Unlike Blackman, Maggie looked well rested, and as she walked alongside the dark haired man, she appeated to be smiling.

Smiling.

Blackman wasn't sure if he'd ever been filled with as much blinding rage as he was at that moment. He was exhausted, miserable, in physical and emotional pain, and she was fucking smiling.

At some fucking guy.

Christ, was she having an affair? Panic tightened his chest so much he thought he might be having a heart attack. When was the last time they'd had sex? When was the last time she *wanted* to have sex? With him? He didn't even want to think about how long it had been since she let him hold her. The last time she'd held him. God, she had always been amazing in bed. Was she being amazing in bed with someone else? Blackman felt sick.

Maggie and the guy paused and exchanged a few words, and then she gave him a quick hug and walked away. The man stood there for a moment as if he was waiting for her to get into her building safely. Blackman got to his feet, took off his sunglasses, and slid them into his pocket.

The man turned and walked across the lawn toward Blackman as if he had already known that Blackman was sitting on the bench. Blackman glared at the man, who was starting to look vaguely familiar and a bit menacing.

The man had long dark hair that hung nearly to his shoulders. He was dressed in dark jeans and a heavy green North Face jacket. His hands were in his pockets, and he carried himself like Maggie's brothers back in England.

Christ, had he seen this guy in court? Maybe even convicted him, and now he was fucking Blackman's wife as some kind of twisted revenge?

As the man closed the distance, Blackman could see he only just cracked six feet tall, which made Blackman feel good. Maybe this guy carried himself like he knew how to brawl, but Blackman easily had six inches on him and probably twenty pounds. Sure, his hockey days were a couple of decades behind him, but Blackman was sure he remembered how to hit. How to throw a punch so it left a mark, and that was something he wanted to do more than anything right then. Blackman wanted to get into a fight; he wanted to punch this guy in the face, get him on the ground, and beat him until he broke every bone in the man's face or every bone in his own hands. Blackman balled his shaking hands into fists as the man stopped a couple of feet away. Blackman clocked the distance, knowing he could cover it in two strides and land the first punch before the guy even moved.

"Morning, counselor," the man said pleasantly. His hands were still in his pockets, his face open and pleasant.

"Who the fuck are you?" Blackman spat. He'd never been a jealous man, not really, but the way Maggie smiled at this guy before she walked into her building was eating him alive. Blackman was supposed to be the man who walked his wife to work, the man she hugged before she started her day, the man she smiled at before she slid into her teacher persona. Not this fuckwit who needed a haircut more than Blackman.

"John Kovac. Dr. Tilly MacPherson's husband. You and Maggie were at our wedding a couple of years ago. Down in Key West," John said with a friendly smile.

Blackman glared at him as he tried to remember a Key West wedding. Slowly, recognition dawned. Tilly MacPherson was the zoologist Maggie went hiking with in the summers, and John was the guy with the shady past, the defense contractor *not* defense contractor Tilly met while they were on a hiking trip in Canada. Maggie had found the whole thing incredibly romantic, and she texted Blackman a blow by blow of John and Tilly falling in love over the course of a week. It had gotten to the point where Blackman felt compelled to remind Maggie of their own romantic beginnings. He might even have sent her a YouTube link, or two, after a few drinks one night. Just to jog her memory.

"Oh, yeah. I remember," Blackman said churlishly. The information did nothing to assuage his anger or lessen his desire to punch John Kovac in the face.

"It's a cold day. Looks like snow," John said, looking around casually. "Why don't you let me buy you a cup of coffee?"

"I don't want a cup of fucking coffee. I want to know why you're walking my wife to work," Blackman said coldly.

"I'm sure you want to know more than that," John said diplomatically. "There's a nice coffee shop just off campus. Come on, counselor, let's get out of the cold."

Blackman glared, but John looked serene, his body loose and relaxed. He was a study in calm equanimity compared to Blackman's barely contained rage. Blackman, very aware of the students walking past them, finally nodded. John turned and led Blackman through a crowd of students headed to their early classes. Their cheerful hope filled eyes a cruel reminder of what Blackman feared he had lost.

Chapter 14

Maggie stood at the wall of windows just inside her too warm building watching Blackman get to his feet and ball his hands into fists. It had been years since she'd seen him so angry.

So jealous.

When they were in school, she used to watch him sit on that bench and read books or talk to pretty girls. She used to think of it as his bench. She would imagine walking over to him, holding a coffee, and striking up a conversation. She would run these imaginary conversations through her head on endless loops. They would talk about school and commiserate about boring classes, demanding professors, and the crushing work that came with heavy course loads. They would talk about music and art and books and the few bars that would let her in because the bartenders knew Fitz, and they wouldn't put any rum in her Coke. However, she never made the short walk to that bench, never started a conversation with him, never told him that she couldn't stop thinking about him. She only watched him from a distance.

He was just too handsome, and she was just too plain. He was heading toward a promising future while she was trying to outrun a shameful past. After he was hurt, she used to sit on that bench, her bare hands pressed against the wood as if she could still feel him there.

She missed him so much that her longing was a physical thing, a weight pressing down on her chest, making it hard for her to breathe. Then, instead of running their imaginary conversations on an endless loop in her mind, she replayed the night of the hockey game. She saw his smile through the plexiglass, saw him move over that ice like a man made for ice, saw him make that goal, then come to her as if she was the only person in that arena he cared about. She heard him call her sweetheart in that deep, beautiful voice of his. She wanted the movie in her mind to end there. She wanted the last thing she remembered to be how he made her feel when he grinned at her, but she couldn't. All those beautiful moments were always followed by the sound of Blackman's head bouncing off the glass, the smear of blood on his mask, the sound of his leg snapping.

The blood.

The sound of his scream.

She'd written a dozen poems in the months after the injury trying to process what she had seen, how she felt about it, and the crippling guilt that left her feeling lost. If he hadn't been showing off for her, trying to impress her, he never would have gotten hurt.

But God forgive her, she had been so very much impressed.

And so very much in love.

She'd allowed herself to be charmed by him, to be distracted from her schoolwork by him. To be tempted by the idea of a life beyond academics, and something terrible had happened. She wasn't meant for love or relationships with tall, handsome boys.

She was meant for school and books and papers because all those things were safe.

Blackman Smith was not safe.

And now here she was all these years later, or maybe it was better to say there they were all these years later, both hurt and angry and a dozen other things. Neither of them safe.

Even from a distance she could see the tension in his shoulders, the cold look on his face. The way he stood tall and loose radiating anger. It was the stance of someone looking to start a fight. She should know, she was usually the one starting fights.

A snippet of a Taylor Swift song skittered across her mind.

I can see you starin', honey
Like he's just your understudy

Like you'd get your knuckles bloody for me...
He'd done that once, hurt someone for her.

***

They were in London for Christmas, and the family had gathered in one of Nick's favorite pubs. All the brothers were there with their wives or girlfriends. Fitz was dating someone at the time, but the boyfriend hadn't been able to make the trip, and Fitz had been unusually maudlin. There was a football match on, and a band playing loudly in one corner. People were dancing and drinking and laughing, and Maggie was having such a wonderful time. Her brothers had folded Blackman into the family, and Blackman had gone from being a lonely only child to being one of dozens of Harringtons. The joy Maggie saw on his face was always worth the trans-Atlantic trip.

Even now, she wasn't sure how everything had gone pear shaped that night. It had all happened so fast. There had been a guy paying too much attention to her, one of the many hangers on who always seemed to follow her younger brother Joseph about. A short guy with a buzz cut and a skin-head sort of vibe: polished Doc Martens, cargo pants, and a buttoned-up polo shirt. He'd approached her a few times when she was at the bar, and although he always stood a little close, he never got *too* close.

He tried chatting her up, but his thick Scottish accent was difficult to understand in the noise of the bar. She'd been growing impatient with him during the night, but she knew if she lost her temper or, God forbid, hit him, her brothers might kill him. The beer and the whiskey had been flowing freely, and she suspected her brothers' blood alcohol was well past the beat the shit out of him limit and more into the body in the boot of the car limit.

But the guy wouldn't take the hint, and when Maggie was on her way to the loo, he made his move. He'd maneuvered her into a shallow alcove, and the more she tried to step around him without touching him, the closer he got. His hands were on her waist, and then they weren't.

Blackman grabbed him by his shoulders, spun him around, and slammed him into the opposite wall. The man's head hit the exposed stone with a crack. He started to say something, but one of Blackman's huge hands closed around the man's throat and started to squeeze.

Maggie lunged for Blackman's arm and tried to move him, but he was immovable. The man's face started to go red, and he pawed at Blackman's hand, panic shining in his eyes.

"If you ever touch my wife again, I will fucking kill you," Blackman said, his voice low and dangerous, deadly. The man's eyes widened as Maggie assumed Blackman increased the pressure on his throat.

"Everything okay?" Nick asked casually as if Blackman throttling a drunken Scotsman wasn't cause for concern. Maggie glared at her brother, practically her twin with the red hair and the hazel eyes. She, like the drunken Scotsman getting throttled, was starting to panic. Nick, however, was a study in calm.

And curiosity.

Joseph, Oliver, and Fitz stood behind Nick, taking in the scene with interested eyes. They knew Blackman as the easygoing guy who enjoyed a nice night at the pub and a proper football match. Even Fitz, who spent the most time with Blackman, was surprised by the scene. They had never seen Blackman angry, and as far as they were concerned, Maggie was the dangerous one.

"Nick, please, *do something*," Maggie pleaded, her hands wrapped around Blackman's rock hard forearms. This was a side of Blackman she'd never seen before, and for the first time since they'd started their relationship, she saw how his size could be a problem. As it turned out, tall and broad was not only sexy, it was also damn near impossible to move.

Nick tilted his head and looked at the man who had stopped pawing at Blackman's hand and appeared to be losing consciousness. Then Nick put his hand on Blackman's shoulder.

"That's enough, brother. You've made your point," he said respectfully.

Blackman waited another half second, then let go of the man who hit the ground with a thud. Nick watched as the man gasped for air and rubbed his throat, looking appropriately terrified.

"Party's over, mate. Off you fuck," Nick said, his voice light but his face hard. After all, this man had put his hands on Lennie Harrington's little girl, Nick Harrington's little sister, so there would be repercussions. Blackman's hands wouldn't be the last set of hands around the drunken Scotsman's neck that night, and although he wouldn't find himself in the boot of Nick Harrington's car, he would find himself at the bottom of the Thames by dawn.

The guy scrambled to his feet and stumbled toward the door. Blackman turned back to Maggie.

"Are you okay, sweetheart?" Blackman asked softly. The anger was gone, replaced by a tender concern. Maggie nodded, and he pulled her into a tight hug and kissed the top of her head. She closed her eyes and leaned her head against his chest. His breathing was calm, his heart not beating any faster than normal. As if he hadn't just throttled a man in a Notting Hill pub. On the other hand, Maggie's heart was pounding so hard in her chest it hurt. She had no idea what to do with the knowledge that Blackman had that kind of violence locked away somewhere inside him. She knew he'd been a fighter back in his hockey days, but she'd always thought about that violence in abstract terms. Sure, he'd gotten into fights, and yes, he had hurt other players, but that was on the ice, in the context of the game.

This, however, wasn't a game; it was a pub.

For the rest of the night, Blackman stayed close to her as if he didn't want to leave her alone. As if he thought that Maggie was someone who needed protecting, and Maggie was conflicted. On one hand, she didn't need to be protected, but on the other hand...

That demonstration of strength on her behalf – no one had ever done that for her before. She'd nearly beaten a man to death in her teens to protect Fitz, and then she'd beaten a man in her twenties because he'd frightened her friend in a bar, and she'd have done worse to him if Blackman hadn't pulled her away. Now Blackman had nearly throttled a man for getting handsy with *her* in a bar, which was something she should have done for herself.

It was late when they finally got back to their hotel. They were quiet as they took turns in the oversized bathroom. First one and then the other, showering and brushing their teeth, completing their nightly ablutions. Maggie wanted to talk to Blackman about what had happened in the pub, but she didn't know how. She wanted to tell him she could take care of herself, that he didn't need to defend her. He didn't need to risk his career for her, or his life for that matter. He was too precious to take such risks.

Because...

Because, at the end of the day, she wasn't worth it. She wasn't worth the risk. Of course, she couldn't say that to him because he would never understand. Because when he looked at her, he saw something that she herself couldn't see.

Something she didn't want to see.

Blackman, however, hadn't seemed to give the incident in the pub a second thought. As if almost throttling a man to death was not worth talking about. Instead, Blackman played some Nina Simone, turned on the gas fireplace, and waited for his wife to come to bed.

The hotel suite was beautifully appointed. The first time they came to London to see the family, Lennie insisted Blackman and Maggie stay at the Kensington townhouse, which was fine with Blackman. Blackman loved the townhouse, and he loved Maggie's childhood bedroom, decorated in shades of peaches and cream. He loved Maggie's four poster bed with the canopy, a testament to her once passionate devotion to all things Jane Austin.

The four poster bed, however, turned out to be *comically* small for Blackman.

After the first night, Maggie quietly explained to her father that a man Blackman's size needed more space than her childhood bed could provide, and Blackman's painful limp the next morning seemed to emphasize the point. From that point forward, Lennie Harrington made arrangements for Maggie and Blackman to stay in a hotel not far from the townhouse.

When Maggie emerged from the bathroom, she paused in the doorway, taking in the fire and the Nina Simone. She smiled at Blackman, who was stretched out on top of the covers, wearing only his boxer shorts, which was all her husband ever wore to bed. The man was impervious to cold; the fire was for her. Maggie, dressed in one of Blackman's t-shirts, sat down on the bed. She wanted to talk about what had happened, about what he had done, but before she could find the words, Blackman reached for her and pulled her down. Without a word, he pulled the t-shirt over her head, then pushed down his boxers.

He pulled her body close to his, and she could already feel him growing hard against her bare thigh. He watched her with attentive brown eyes that went on forever, as he ran his thick fingers along her cheek, along her jawline. He'd die for her and, God forbid, kill for her. He'd ruin his life for her because that was how much he loved her.

He brushed his lips over hers as he ran his fingers over her neck, pausing on her pulse point. Her pulse quickened beneath his fingers. His lips followed the same path, his teeth scraping over sensitive skin. She shivered as he nipped at her neck while his fingers ran slowly over her breasts, pausing long enough to caress her stiffening nipples. She moaned as she slid her fingers through his hair.

By the time his fingers reached the gentle slope of her stomach, she was panting. He ran his tongue slowly up her neck until he was once again looking into her heavy lidded hazel eyes. He watched her as he slipped a finger inside her, stroking her gently. She was soaked and ready for him, but unlike other times, she couldn't hold his gaze. There was too much there tonight, too much laid bare on his face – the depth of his love for her and the pleasure he wanted to bring her.

He whispered against her lips, "Tell me you love me."

"I love you," she gasped as he slipped another finger into her, stroking her slowly. He always touched her the way she liked, the way she needed. He knew her body as well as he knew his own.

"Tell me," he whispered, moving deeper inside of her. "That you want me."

She whimpered as he slid his tongue over her lips, teasing her.

"I – I want you," she gasped as she arched against him.

He gently pulled his fingers from her as he moved his body closer to hers, slipping his slick fingers into his mouth and sucking them clean. Maggie moaned as she desperately pushed herself against him.

"Tell me," he said taking her wrists in the hand that throttled the Scotsman, and pushed them over her head. Her body stretched taught against his. "That you need me."

"Blackman," she begged. She vibrated with need, like a piano string, but she didn't want to do it this way. She didn't want to talk, she didn't want things to be slow, she wanted him inside of her. She wanted to feel the weight of him on top of her. She wanted him to push her down into this hotel room bed and make her forget how frightened she had been tonight. How scared she was still.

"Tell me," he repeated, running his fingers over the swell of her breasts, caressing her taut nipples with his thumb, moving like he was a man with all the time in the world, while she was coming apart.

"I – I need you... please... I need you so much... my love... my only love," she panted desperately. Tears prickled her eyes. Everything felt so raw, like she was ground down to the bone, and she needed him to make her feel safe and loved like only he knew how. He was her everything, and it scared her so much.

Finally, he covered her mouth with his, breathing in her moan as he entered her. He teased her with his lips and his tongue but didn't give her the kiss she wanted. He moved slowly, filling her, stretching her. He let go of her wrists, and she ran her hands down the length of his back. He dipped his head and swirled a tongue over her nipple so softly she had to bite back a scream. She tried to quicken their pace, but he wouldn't move faster, instead keeping his strokes slow and deliberate. Soon he was covered in a sheen of sweat as he restrained himself.

"Look at me, Maggie," he whispered. Commanded. She opened her eyes and met his. He moved faster, and she met his thrusts fiercely. She moved her hands to his ass and gripped him tightly, pulling him deeper into her.

"Let me hear you," he panted. His voice raw with want, with need, with desire.

She chanted his name like a prayer, telling him she loved him and needed him, that she wanted to please him, that she needed to feel him come for her, to make a mess in her. Her pleasure was volcanic, her need for him all consuming. She wrapped her arms around him, splayed her hands over the hard muscles of his back, bit into him as he pushed her closer and closer toward the edge of everything.

"Blackman," she panted. "God... please... I'm..."

She cried out loudly, knowing that was what he wanted. He wanted to hear her call his name. He pulled back so he could watch her eyes go hazy with the pleasure he gave her. As she spasmed around his cock, she looked at him with those icy hazel eyes he adored, and he buried himself in her with a hoarse cry.

Nine months later, Jamie was born.

Chapter 15

Blackman sat in the window seat of a cafe he'd eaten in several times. He wasn't exactly a regular, but he didn't think of himself as a stranger either. But compared to the effusive welcome John, the former military contractor *not* military contractor, received, Blackman was once again reminded that despite his impressive height, he was evidently not a memorable man. John, on the other hand, the probable perpetrator of war crimes, was not only memorable but also well liked.

Blackman watched as John chatted with the barista, asking about the young woman's girlfriend, "doing well, thank you," her organic chemistry class, "It's a nightmare, but I'm hanging on," and if she was heading home for Christmas, "Yes, and I'm taking Jenna home with me to meet the parents." John paid for the coffees and a sack of pastries and greeted more people by name and with some small personal detail as he made his way to their table.

Blackman hated him.

Almost as much as Blackman hated himself.

John unzipped his heavy coat and shrugged it off after he set the coffee and the sack of pastries on the table. Underneath the jacket, John had on a gray university hoodie.

"The corn muffins are delicious, and there are a couple of blueberry scones in there. You look like you could use a little food," John said in the same affable voice he used with the barista. A friendly man being friendly with everyone.

"I'm not hungry," Blackman said coldly.

John shrugged and pulled out a corn muffin, then proceeded to break it into pieces on top of a napkin. He leaned back in his chair and watched people walking by on the street, clearly comfortable with Blackman's silence. John sipped his coffee and ate his muffin and waited.

After a few minutes, Blackman reached for the coffee John had set in front of him and pulled one of the scones out of the sack. Like John, Blackman broke the scone into pieces over a napkin and started to eat. He was famished, and the scone tasted as good as anything could taste, all things considered.

"Maggie knocked on our door about eleven o'clock last night. She walked from your place," John said as Blackman finished one scone and reached for another.

Blackman winced.

"She was pretty upset," John continued. There was no judgment in his voice. He could have been telling Blackman about last night's hockey game. "She said she'd done something terrible."

Blackman looked at him blankly.

"I thought she meant like shovel and tarp terrible, and I'm not saying that what happened last night wasn't terrible, counselor. But at least I didn't have to drive to Jersey."

"Stop calling me that," Blackman snapped.

"Okay, *Blackman*," John said. "I'm glad to see you're okay."

Blackman glared at John with the same icy stare that had been using to scare defense witnesses for years, but John, the probable war criminal, was impervious.

"Did she tell you what happened?" Blackman asked.

John picked up a piece of corn muffin and popped it into his mouth. He chewed thoughtfully. He seemed to be considering his words. "A little," he finally said. "She seemed upset that you'd taken the Dixon case."

Blackman said nothing. In all fairness, he had been *assigned* the Dixon case, which was most likely a distinction his angry wife had chosen to ignore.

"She told Tilly more. I just stuck around long enough to make sure you were physically okay. Maggie's got a temper."

"That's why she broke the dishes," Blackman said quietly.

"Yes, well, you can always walk back broken dishes; other things aren't so easy."

"Yet, you were willing to dispose of my body," Blackman said, meeting the other man's eyes. They were a shade darker than Blackman's. There was a sharp intelligence in them that reminded Blackman of Lennie Harrington.

John shrugged. "I doubt you'd want your wife in jail even if she killed you."

Blackman conceded the point.

"We told her she could stay with us for as long as she needed, but I insisted she call you or at least text you this morning to let you know she was okay."

Blackman dug out his phone and showed it to John.

"Thirty-seven text messages and a dozen missed calls. None from my wife."

John didn't say anything, and Blackman put the phone on the table between them as if the physical location of the phone might compel Maggie to call. He sipped his coffee, and John looked down at the phone as an incoming text lit up the screen. The lock screen was a picture of Maggie wearing her doctoral robes and the matching floppy hat that barely contained her wavy red hair. She was glowing with joy.

"This can be fixed," John said when the screen went dark again. It wasn't a question.

Even Fitz had posed it as a question when he was standing in the unnatural disaster of their kitchen. Blackman tried to say something, but a painful constriction in his throat silenced him. He tried to clear it.

"How can you be so sure?" he asked unsteadily.

John leaned forward and met Blackman's gaze with his own unwavering brown eyes.

"I don't know, but – I mean, I'm no expert on relationships, but this doesn't feel like the end of the things. It feels more like something coming to a head."

Blackman said nothing.

"Also, when she showed up last night, she led with *I did something terrible*, not *he did something terrible.* Whatever happened last night, she felt badly about it," John said as he finished his coffee. Then he excused himself and walked back to the counter to get two more coffees.

Blackman reached for his phone but didn't touch it. He just stared at it while the screen lit up with more text messages. Every time it lit up, he saw Maggie's face, his wife's face.

I want a divorce.

She had yelled those words because she was angry, but what he did not understand was *why* she was so angry. Sure, they were going through a rough patch, a really rough patch, but was it rough enough to end an eighteen year marriage? A twenty-year relationship? The other four years he'd spent trying to have a relationship with her?

"I don't know what I'm supposed to do," Blackman admitted when John put the second cup of coffee in front of him.

"I think the short answer is you have to talk to her," John said as he resumed his seat.

"How? She won't answer my calls?"

"Her phone's off, so she's not taking anyone's calls. Maybe she just needs to cool down. Maybe give her a day or two," John offered.

Fuck, I already gave her a goddamn year.

Blackman looked at his coffee cup and thought about Fatimah. Fatimah would have known what to do. She would never have let him make such a mess of things. She would have made him and Maggie sit down and talk; she would have never let them hide behind their pride and their stoicism. Fatimah would never have allowed him to be such a coward, but she was gone, and he was alone. His face burned with shame as he longed for his beloved auntie, his mother, the woman who taught him how to be a man. How to be a good man, a decent man. Now with his marriage in tatters, he felt as if he had failed Fatimah as much as he had failed Maggie.

Blackman cleared his throat and got to his feet.

"I need to get to work," he said gruffly. He reached into his pocket and pulled out a business card. He handed it to John. "My cell's on there. Call me anytime," Blackman said, picking up his coat. John looked at it, then slipped it into the back pocket of his jeans.

"Thanks for the coffee," Blackman said stiffly.

John nodded. "You're welcome. We'll look after Maggie for you. I'm sure you'll be able to work through this."

Blackman turned away and walked through the coffee shop and into the cold late morning. His phone buzzed again, and this time, he pulled it out and looked at the caller ID.

It was Jamie's school.

Shit.

"Smith," he said automatically.

"Mr. Smith, this is Father Scott Wisniewski. Is this a bad time?"

Blackman closed his eyes and inhaled deeply. He wanted to tell the priest that, *yes, this was indeed a very bad time*, but instead, he said, "No, Father. What can I do for you?"

"Well, Mr. Smith, we had an incident with Jamie this morning, and I need you to come to school. I tried your wife –"

"I'll be there in thirty minutes," he said quickly. Ending his call, he buried his hands in his pocket and walked to his car.

Jamie's school sat on the corner of a busy intersection not far from Blackman's office. Parking was impossible, so Blackman drove to work, parked in a nearby garage that charged the most exorbitant rates in the city and walked back to Jamie's school. It took him almost an hour, and by the time he arrived, his bad leg was aching, and his limp was more pronounced than usual.

He waited to be buzzed through the heavy wooden doors at the front of the building that gave the school a distinctly Catholic school feel. When the door unlocked, he stepped into the old but immaculately maintained building. Blackman had initially balked when Maggie insisted on sending Jamie here. Blackman had terrible memories of playing this hockey team when he was in high school. They had always been brawlers and boasted some of the biggest players in the city, and no matter how rough those boys were, they knew how to shoot, and they always found the back of the net. No Catholic school was allowed to recruit, but this school seemed to get around the rules that held other schools in check. Blackman's school lost every time. In the beginning, Blackman's biggest fear was that Jamie would switch from football to hockey, and then Blackman would have to root for these purple and gold delinquents on the ice.

Of course, after last night, he'd have to rethink what really scared him in this world: his son wearing the dreaded purple and gold hockey uniform or his wife serving him with divorce papers.

Blackman walked into the brightly lit main office and told the administrative assistant at the front desk his name. She gave him a sympathetic look, and his stomach tightened.

"Father Scott's waiting for you," she said, nodding toward another heavy wooden door with the word principal etched across it. In all Blackman's time in school, he had never been called to the principal's office. Now as an accomplished adult and tuition paying parent, and the tuition wasn't cheap, mind you, he felt like little more than a wayward sixteen year old as he made his way toward the closed door.

He tried not to limp.

Just as he was about to knock, a stocky priest with male pattern baldness and a boxer's nose opened the door. His face was solemn, and Blackman felt nauseous.

"Mr. Smith," the priest said, extending his hand. "Thank you for taking the time out of your busy schedule to come in. I appreciate it."

Blackman shook the priest's hand and stepped into the brightly lit office, which looked as if it hadn't been updated since the building opened over a century ago. Father Scott pointed toward one of the high back chairs on the business side of his desk, and then before he shut the door he said, "Amanda, hold my calls, please."

"Yes, Father," Amanda replied dutifully.

The office door closed with an audible click. Blackman sat down and stifled a groan; his leg was killing him.

Father Scott took the seat opposite Blackman instead of the more comfortable chair on the other side of the large mahogany desk. So, it was going to be that kind of conversation. Blackman schooled his face, crossed his legs, which hurt like a motherfucker, and folded his hands on his lap. He steadied his breathing and hoped he looked like a study in calm equanimity, like John Kovac, instead of the terrified mess he was.

"Let me start by saying how much we all like Jamie. He's a hardworking young man who is as talented off the field as he is on it. I can't remember the last time we had a freshman playing on the varsity football team, let alone as the starting quarterback."

1984.

1984 was the last time.

Blackman had looked it up.

Instead of saying anything, Blackman nodded. How many times had he delivered a similar opening line? *Yes, your client is a pillar of the community, and we understand how much good he has done over the years, and we appreciate that he's going through some difficult times, but we* will *be seeking the death penalty.*

"And he's never been in any trouble before..." the priest continued.

Blackman looked at a point just to the left of the priest's ocean blue eyes. He hadn't noticed his eyes until he sat down, and he and the priest were at eye level.

"...which is why we were so surprised when he got into a – scuffle – in the cafeteria this morning."

Blackman's face didn't change, but his mind raced. Ok, scuffle wasn't *fight*. A fight meant expulsion, but a scuffle meant what? Suspension? Detention? That restorative justice bullshit he'd been reading about? The priest stopped talking, and Blackman had the distinct impression he had missed something. He tried to replay the last few things the priest said and failed.

"Was the other boy hurt?" Blackman bit back the word *badly*. Jamie was a six foot four football player built like Blackman himself had once been built. Blackman dreaded the answer.

"No, not at all. Just some shoving – and we'll call it *spirited* language. The other boy, Owen Nguyen – seemed rather shocked by the whole thing."

Blackman tried to place the name. Owen Nguyen? Maggie was always better at keeping track of Jamie's friends.

Fuck, Blackman thought as he finally pulled up a face to go with the name. Owen was one of Jamie's friends from elementary school. He was a sweet kid about a foot shorter than Jamie and thin as a rail. He played the violin in the orchestra. The kid didn't have a mean bone in his body or an athletic one.

"It seemed," the priest continued, "that it might have had something to do with Jamie's phone, which I should remind you, Jamie isn't supposed to have on his person during the school day."

Blackman nodded seriously.

"Now, bearing in mind that Coach Dennison was able to intervene quickly so that the event didn't escalate, there will be no need to suspend Jamie."

Blackman let out a slow breath.

"But," the priest said, finding Blackman's eyes and holding them, "he will have to write a formal letter of apology to Owen, and he'll have to sit detention for one week."

Fucking right, Jamie would write a letter of apology to Owen Nguyen, and detention better include cleaning bathrooms with a fucking toothbrush.

"That sounds quite reasonable, Father," Blackman said, hoping his voice didn't betray the relief he felt. Father Scott looked at Blackman as if he expected him to say more, but Blackman said nothing. He knew how this game was played.

"Mr. Smith," the priest said slowly, "usually I would deal with something like this with a phone call, but Jamie seemed very upset this morning. In fact, he's still upset."

The priest paused.

Waited.

Blackman said nothing.

The priest held Blackman's gaze.

"We sent him back to class after meeting with the Dean of Students, Mr. Walker, but his Latin teacher and science teacher have both reached out to say that he's still unusually quiet and dispirited. Something is clearly bothering him, and I don't think it has anything to do with what happened this morning with Owen."

Please. Please don't.

"Is everything okay at home?"

And there it was.

Blackman looked at the priest for a moment, then shifted his eyes to the window that overlooked the busy city street outside, and then he looked down at his hands where his eyes snagged on the thick platinum wedding ring he had been absently running his thumb over.

Probably to remind himself that at least he still had that.

The priest waited patiently, a study in calm equanimity that everyone but Blackman seemed to be able to achieve this morning.

"My wife," Blackman began, then stopped.

"My wife," he started again but stopped again and cleared his throat.

"My wife and I are experiencing some," he searched for the word that could adequately convey the level of clusterfuck that was happening in his life right now, then settled on, "problems."

He paused. Then he cleared his throat again.

"She's decided to stay with friends for a few days while we," he paused again to swallow whatever it was in his throat that was trying to choke him to death. He cleared his throat yet again, and then concluded, "consider the best way to move forward."

The look of concern on the priest's face made Blackman want to crawl under a rock and disappear entirely. Blackman knew at that moment the priest was not looking at Blackman Emerson Smith, Esquire, assistant DA, loving father, and husband, which he was, goddamn it, but as a six foot six, 220-pound former collegiate hockey player and potential wife beater, and a possible murderer because statistically speaking, Blackman was more likely to kill his wife than a random stranger on the street.

Just ask his father.

Of course, you'd need a Ouija board to do that.

Then, suddenly Blackman was ten years old again, and none of his mother's relatives wanted him because he looked surly because big kids couldn't just be fucking shy.

"I'm very sorry to hear that, Mr. Smith," the priest said quietly.

"Thank you," Blackman replied.

The priest leaned back in his chair and looked at Blackman for a long. "Marriage can be difficult."

Fuck. My. Fucking. Life.

Blackman fought the urge to close his eyes and rub his temples or to just get up and leave.

This could not be happening. This day could not possibly be getting worse.

"I was married for ten years before entering the priesthood. My wife died. Cancer," the priest added as if reading Blackman's mind. Blackman looked at his ring, unable or unwilling to meet the priest's eyes. He had no idea which it was.

"She was a wonderful woman, my Cath. We'd been together since high school. She was a --- shall we say a spirited woman. High energy. Typical Irish redhead."

Blackman continued staring at his ring. He said nothing.

"We were both stubborn people. Our parents immigrated to this country, so we came from families of hard workers. Sometimes, our stubbornness – our pride, really – made it hard for us as a couple, and we couldn't have kids. That took its toll, of course, but we kept trying right up until we ran out of time," the priest said quietly.

Blackman remained silent.

"I was at the last game you played in college. The night you scored that hat trick."

Blackman looked up slowly and met the priest's eyes.

"My cousin played with you. Pete Murphy."

Blackman remembered Murphy. He had been younger than Blackman. He was a good kid, funny as hell, majoring in girls, hockey, and chemistry, in that order. He left college after his sophomore year and enlisted in the Marines. He died in Iraq a year or so later. IED explosion. Blackman had gone to the funeral.

"I'm sorry for your loss. Murphy was a great kid," Blackman said softly.

The priest chuckled.

"He was." He paused again as if weighing his words carefully. "He said you scored those goals for your future wife. He didn't seem to understand because he said you were dating someone else, but she wasn't there, at the game. But he said whoever you were doing it for had gotten under your skin. Your future wife."

Blackman's eyes went back to the busy street outside.

"I did. She did," he said absently. His voice was too low, but he didn't have the strength to make it louder.

"And you married that girl?"

"Yes," Blackman's voice was barely a whisper. He cleared his throat again and searched for his composure.

The priest nodded.

"Then I'm sure you're applying the same determination that helped you win her to working through your problems now. God doesn't give us a love like that just so we can give up and walk away from it."

Blackman's face tightened. *He* hadn't walked away. *He* hadn't asked for a divorce. *He* hadn't broken all the fucking dishes and walked out of the house. *He* hadn't done any of those things. *He* was the one who had been left. *He* was the one who had to clean up the detritus of Maggie's destructive anger.

But it wasn't like he was blameless, either.

"Do you love her, son?"

"Yes." Blackman met the priest's blue eyes.

"Good. I'll pray to Saint Joseph for you and your wife. He's the Patron Saint of Marriage. With his help and some determination, I'm sure you'll be able to weather this difficult time," the priest said with a kind smile.

"Thank you, Father," Blackman said quietly. Since he didn't have Fatimah to pray for him anymore, maybe she had sent the old priest to pray for him; it felt like something Fatimah would do.

Father Scott pulled his iPhone out of his pocket and sent a text, which looked oddly anachronistic: this old priest in his traditional garb sitting in this hundred year old office texting on an iPhone. Blackman watched as the priest waited for a response, then pocketed the phone again. Then, the two men sat in silence, both seemingly lost in their own thoughts until there was a knock at the door, and Jamie entered. Blackman looked at his son, tall and handsome in his school uniform, the tie with the Windsor knot Fitz had taught him how to tie because Blackman had never mastered the

Windsor knot. Jamie's red hair, which was a little longer than it should be, it seemed that all the Smith men needed a haircut, was combed neatly. His hazel eyes were especially cold when they settled on his father. Then they moved to Father Scott, who stood up and motioned for Jamie to take the seat he himself had just vacated.

Jamie didn't move.

"Jamie," Father Scott said gently. "Have a seat, please."

"Why are you here?" Jamie asked, looking at Blackman. The coldness in Jamie's voice stung, and Blackman tried not to react.

"I called your father, Jamie. I wanted to talk to him about this morning," Father Scott said patiently. Jamie continued to glare at Blackman. His defiant stare was so much his mother's that Blackman found it hard to breathe. Again.

"Because my mom wouldn't answer her phone?" Jamie asked, glaring at his father. Blackman didn't say anything. He wasn't up for making excuses for Maggie; he had his own excuses to make. He couldn't decide if he should stand up or remain seated. If he remained in the chair, Jamie could hold the high ground. Literally and metaphorically, as it were.

"Your mother was probably in class, Jamie," Father Scott said gently. Evidently, *he* was up to making excuses for Maggie.

"Bullshit," Jamie exploded, but he wasn't yelling at the priest, he was yelling at his father. "I've been calling and texting her since last night, and she's not answering anything. She's not busy. She left. She walked out on us, and she's not coming back!" Jamie's voice rose into a hysteria Blackman hadn't heard since Jamie was six years old, and he'd left his favorite teddy bear, Blackman's teddy bear, on a train going from Rome to Venice. As Jamie waited for Blackman's reaction, the tears came. First, his eyes shone brightly, and then the tears streamed down his cheeks in hot rivers. Blackman levered himself out of the chair and grabbed his son, pulling him into a tight hug as the sobs came.

"I've been an awful son," Jamie sobbed pitifully into Blackman's shoulder. "And she hates me, and she's never coming back."

Blackman closed his eyes, leaned his cheek against his son's hair, and inhaled the clean scent of the boy's shampoo, some ridiculous thing with an oversized octopus on it.

"I've been so mean... all the time... she – she's just being mom. But I've been such an asshole. I'm so sorry, I just want to tell her I'm sorry," Jamie wailed. Blackman just held him, waiting for the sobs to subside. Mercifully, the priest said nothing. He, too, seemed to be waiting.

"Habibi," Blackman said, still holding Jamie's strong body against his own, "you haven't been an awful son, and she didn't leave us. Not forever. She's coming back, I promise you. I'll bring her home," Blackman said, hoping to God he wasn't making a promise he couldn't keep.

"But she broke all the dishes," Jamie sobbed.

Blackman could feel the priest's eyes on him, and he felt an odd sense of vindication.

See! She broke the dishes. Not me. I didn't break anything.

"It's okay, Habibi, they're just dishes, and Mom was angry, but I'm going to talk to her, and everything is going to be okay," Blackman said, holding his son tightly, maybe too tightly, but he needed to be the father to Jamie his own father had never been to him. The few times Blackman ever shed tears in front of his father, the old man had just stared at him curiously, as if he couldn't fathom a boy his size crying. Fatimah had always been the one to comfort him when he needed comfort, but sometimes, a boy needed his father to tell him everything would be okay. Blackman felt tears prick the back of his eyes and blinked them away.

"Tell her I love her," Jamie said in an almost little boy voice. "Tell her I'm sorry."

"Yes, Habibi, I will," Blackman said, giving his son one final kiss on the head. Then he let go of his son, and Jamie, his tears subsiding, stepped away from his father as if suddenly self-conscious about the display of emotion. Blackman was fascinated to watch his son transform from the scared little boy who had a moment ago been crying back to the teenager who exuded a self-confidence Blackman couldn't have imagined possessing at that age. Further, he understood that self-confidence was as much a façade as the defiant nature he had adopted with his mother as of late. Jamie was just as scared and confused as Blackman had been at that age.

As Blackman was now.

Blackman smoothed down his rumpled suit and looked at the priest uncomfortably.

"I – umm – if everything is settled here, I think that I should get back to work. Jamie, I'll see you at home for dinner. After basketball practice," Blackman said, feeling awkward and exposed in front of the old priest. Jamie nodded stiffly and looked to Father Scott who nodded toward the door.

"Miss Blakely will give you a pass back to class if you're ready to return."

"Thank you, Father," Jamie said deferentially. He looked back at Blackman, who smiled at him. Jamie nodded back, and as he opened the door, Blackman said, "I love you, Jamie."

"I love you, too, Dad," Jamie said gruffly as he turned back and took one more look at his father. Then Jamie was gone, and Blackman was once again alone with the priest.

"I need to get to work," Blackman said stiffly.

"Of course," the priest said, extending a hand that Blackman took. "Thank you for coming in. I hope that you're able to get everything sorted out."

Blackman nodded, released the priest's hand, limped out of the office, and walked to work.

Chapter 16

Maggie sat in her small office, her feet propped up on the windowsill, staring into the late afternoon gloom. She was done teaching but was too tired to walk back to Tilly's just yet. Clouds hung low and expectant in the sky. Temperatures had fallen precipitously during the day, and it seemed an unusual December snowstorm might be blowing in. Her undergrads had been ridiculously excited about the prospect of a storm the week before final exams. But she didn't know if the potential of snow was what excited them or if it was the fantasy the snowstorm could morph into some blizzard that would cancel finals.

As if Philadelphia ever got that much snow in the age of climate change.

However, snow always held so much potential, so much promise.

Maggie leaned further back in her chair and thought about the times she had watched Blackman in the snow.

God, that man loved snow.

A small smile danced across her lips as she thought about a day when she watched Blackman and his teammates have a snowball fight on the quad. They had taken food trays from the cafeteria and were alternating between using the trays as shields and sleds. It was a Sunday afternoon, maybe a month before the game that ended Blackman's career. Maggie had been on her way to the library when she saw them. It was a bitter day, and she had been bundled up in what felt like a dozen layers of clothes. Blackman, however, was dressed in jeans, hiking boots, and a hoodie. His face had been ruddy and so handsome she could hardly bear to look at him. His laughter, distinct from the laughter of his friends, was a deep rumble. It echoed off the buildings around the quad, and she ached for him so badly. If she had been a better woman, a braver woman, she would have gone to him and said something pithy. Something flirty and witty.

I'm Maggie Rhymer, the girl from the bar, so this is what you look like when you're not an asshole. Wanna get a coffee?

But she didn't do that. She just turned and continued her walk to the library, where she would spend the afternoon reading and writing and studying, preparing herself for a future she never once imagined correctly. Now, here she was, sitting in this small office, behind a messy desk, watching a bench she hadn't watched in years, staring at the falling snow, and thinking about the man she'd married, the father of her son, the love of her life.

***

The day Maggie found out she was pregnant was a day just like this. The clouds hung heavy and low and full of potential. Maggie, who had been feeling under the weather since she and Blackman had come back from London, took the pregnancy test at work. In retrospect, she had no idea why she hadn't waited until she got home, but like so many decisions in Maggie's life, this one had seemed like a good one at the time. When the test came back with the requisite pink lines, she threw up.

After her classes finished for the day, she called Fatimah in tears. They met late in the afternoon in the small park across from Fatimah's apartment. The first snowflakes drifting down around them. Fatimah held Maggie's hands while Maggie cried hot, terrified tears, and outlined all the ways she wasn't prepared to be a mother. All the ways in which she would never be prepared to be a mother. Fatimah simply sat on the bench next to Maggie and listened to her without judgment, holding Maggie's shaking hands in her own steady ones.

When Maggie stopped talking, Fatimah wrapped her arms around her and pulled Maggie into a long hug. When she let go, Fatimah lifted her hands to cup Maggie's face and smiled.

"My dear," Fatimah began gently, soothingly. "No woman is ever prepared to become a mother, even the women who have dreamed of children since they themselves were children." Fatimah let go of Maggie's cheeks and held her hands again.

"Even I was not prepared to be a mother when Allah blessed me with my first child," she said softly, her smile soft and sad. Maggie looked at the older woman's pale face and brilliant blue eyes and wondered what Fatimah's hair looked like beneath her hijab. Was it still lush and dark or fine and gray? Fatimah's skin was beautiful, and her face had so few lines. She looked timeless. She *was* timeless. Maggie had no more idea how old Fatimah was than Blackman, and he had known her almost his entire life. It was easy to forget that Fatimah had lived a whole life before she came into Blackman's life. She had once been young, in love, married, and a mother, and then she had been none of those things. Maggie marveled at how this woman, who had lost so much in such tragic circumstances, still possessed such a great capacity for love. At ten years of age, Blackman had found a second chance at a mother's love with Fatimah; now Fatimah was giving Maggie that same gift.

The gift of a mother's love.

Maggie wondered what kind of woman she might have become if she hadn't been sent to a boarding where no one had been interested in her loneliness because they were all lonely. Who might she have grown into if she hadn't been sent half a world away from her family? Maybe she would have been better, less impulsive, less angry.

Fatimah patted Maggie's hand and waited for her to focus.

"My dear," Fatimah said kindly. "You will not be alone in this journey. You have been blessed with a good hearted man who loves you, and who will love this child," she said proudly. "Blackman is a good man, a blessing, just like you. You are a good woman, and you will be a good mother. There is no need to worry so much."

Maggie desperately wanted to tell Fatimah she was wrong about her. Maggie was not a good woman, and she had known from the beginning Blackman could do better than her, but he was blind when it came to her, and she was weak when it came to him.

"You and Blackman take care of each other," Fatimah continued. "And now it is time for you both to care for this blessed child. Everything will work out the way it is supposed to work out."

"And what if it doesn't?" Maggie asked, her voice small.

Fatimah looked sad for a moment, and then her indomitable smile returned.

"We cannot know the future, dearest, and we cannot live our present burdened with the fears of what might happen. We must have faith." Fatimah squeezed Maggie's hands and waited for Maggie to meet her eyes.

"Everything that happens to us in this life has a purpose, every one of our mistakes and *all* our pain. We must use even the most painful lessons to help us forge a good life and make the world a better place in our own small way. You and my--," Fatimah's voice caught for a moment, and her eyes shone with a mother's pride. "My beloved son – have dedicated your lives to service. Service to others and service to Allah, and now it is time for you to bring forth another generation to do the same, to serve an uncertain world. That is what good people do."

Maggie leaned forward and let Fatimah wrap her strong arms around her again.

"How are you so certain of everything, Auntie?" Maggie asked quietly.

Fatimah kissed Maggie on the head and whispered, "Because I have faith, my child."

***

After her last class, Maggie took a long walk around campus despite the cold temperatures. She stopped next to a small duck pond and watched the water for a little while. She turned her phone on for the first time since she'd left the house the night before. After a minute, she saw that she had over thirty texts from her son, another twenty from an increasingly angry Fitz, and a dozen of the usual texts from her other brothers and sisters-in-law. None of whom seemed to be aware of what was going on between her and

Blackman. She had one text from John asking if she wanted chicken or beef in her ramen.

His was the only text she answered: Beef, please.

The rest she ignored.

Blackman hadn't texted or called. Though, he had come to her work and sat on their bench. Well, not *their* bench per se. It was more like his bench and her bench. Separately. Not together.

He probably had no idea about the bench.

Before she started the long walk back to her office, she stared at her phone, which had started to vibrate with another text from Jamie. Without thinking, she picked up a rock and smashed the phone. Then she stood up and walked back to her office. Even though she knew better, she didn't pick up the pieces of glass and plastic. She just left them behind, much like the broken dishes in the kitchen. She just wasn't in the mood to clean up after herself.

Leaning back in her office chair, she closed her eyes and willed herself not to think. She had taught four classes, sat through two hours of office hours, and focused all her energy and attention on her lectures, her students, and being the best teacher she could under the circumstances. She'd tried not to think about Blackman, Jamie, broken dishes, or Fatimah, whose voice she couldn't get out of her head.

Promise me that you will never break my boy's heart, dearest. Please do that for me. I know he is a big man, too big, but he is sensitive, and his heart is soft.

I promise, Auntie. His heart will be safe with me.

One more lie told because it was easier to lie than tell the truth.

"Well, you've made a right tit of yourself, haven't you?"

"Fuck me," Maggie groaned under her breath. She slowly lowered her feet to the floor and turned around to face her angry brother. Fitz leaned against the door jamb. Short, lean, and clearly angry, he was an incredibly handsome man, the only blonde out of all of them. Snow melted on the shoulders of his wool coat, which hung open over a nicely tailored black wool suit, pale blue shirt, and paisley tie. A black cashmere scarf, worth more than all the clothes Maggie was wearing, was wrapped around his slender neck. Fitz's only concession to the weather was a pair of black leather snow boots. He radiated righteous indignation.

"I'm busy," Maggie said, sitting up straighter in her chair.

"Hopefully, you're busy trying to figure out how to fix this fucking mess. Breaking the dishes is one thing, but asking for a divorce is another. Christ, Maggie, those are hard words to walk back," Fitz said as he pulled off a pair of black leather gloves one finger at a time like some Bond villain.

Maggie met her brother's blue eyes.

"I don't intend to walk them back. I'm leaving Blackman," she said slowly and clearly.

"The fuck you are," Fitz snapped as he shoved his gloves into his coat pocket.

Maggie said nothing.

"Oh, and your son? Are you leaving him, too?" Fitz snapped.

"Yes." Even Maggie was surprised by the speed of her response.

Fitz walked into the tiny office and slammed the door so forcefully everything in the room shook. Maggie didn't flinch. She knew her brother would show up in a snit sooner or later, and she needed him to understand what she was doing, and she was certain she could make him understand. She had to. It didn't matter if he agreed with her or not; he simply had to *understand*. Because she was doing the right thing. Wasn't that what their father had taught them: one had to do the right thing no matter how much damage it caused?

Or to whom?

"What the fuck is wrong with you? Is this some weird midlife crisis? Christ, are you having an affair? Is that it? You're having an affair?" Fitz was bordering on apoplexy, but even apoplectic, Fitz shrugged out of his expensive wool overcoat and folded it neatly over the other chair in Maggie's office.

"I'm not having an affair, and I'm not having a midlife crisis." Maggie sighed.

"Then you must have a bloody brain tumor to be talking nonsense like this," Fitz said as he dropped into one of the uncomfortable chairs reserved for her students. He was still angry, seething in fact, but he was also curious and concerned, and it seemed that at least for the moment, his curiosity was winning out over his anger.

He took a deep breath and said gently, "Maggie, talk to me. What's going on?"

Maggie leaned forward and set her elbows on her desk. She focused on Fitz instead of the silver picture frames lying face down to her left. She couldn't do what she needed to do if she had to look at their faces.

"Blackman and I have been having problems – since the shooting. Things have – been different," she began.

"Of course, things are different. Your husband was nearly murdered," Fitz said almost dismissively as if people's husbands were murdered every day. Of course, considering the city's murder rate, a murdered husband was probably not that out of the ordinary.

Maggie chose her words carefully.

"Yes, I know, but in the last several months, we've grown apart."

"Christ," Fitz breathed dramatically, pressing his hand to his chest, "you *are* having an affair."

"I'm –"

"People always use *grown apart* when they're having affairs. Look, just end it and ask Blackman to forgive you."

"Jesus Christ, Fitzwilliam, I'm not having a fucking affair," Maggie yelled.

Fitz narrowed his eyes at the sound of his full name.

"Then what's going on? Because I sure as shit know your *husband* isn't having an affair."

"Marriages have their –"

"October, cut the bullshit," Fitz said, raising his voice. His sister wasn't the only one who could whip out the formal Christian names. Maggie looked at Fitz for a long time before she finally softened her eyes.

"I have to leave," she said softly.

"Why?" Fitz asked, his voice laced with curiosity and concern.

"Blackman took the Dixon case," Maggie said meaningfully.

"So?" Fitz looked at her blankly.

"So, that's a high profile case. The biggest one he's had since the shooting." Maggie willed her brother to connect the dots he didn't seem like he wanted to connect.

"So?" Fitz repeated. "If you're worried about the time he's going to be spending on it, talk to him about it. Don't end an eighteen year marriage–"

"You don't understand," Maggie said, trying to keep the frustration out of her voice.

"Then enlighten me."

"His attorneys – Dixon's attorneys – will dig into our lives to find Blackman's weaknesses. Anything that they can exploit."

"Who cares," Fitz said, exasperated. "Blackman's a Boy Scout. He's..." Fitz's voice trailed off, and he looked at his sister more closely. Then he said very quietly and very carefully, "*That* can never be traced back to you. Ever. That was a family decision. Family business."

"Dixon has money," Maggie answered.

"*We*," Fitz said slowly, "have money and... other resources."

Fucking *other resources* was what had gotten her into this position in the first place. That and her goddamn temper, and Nick's goddamn tendency to indulge her.

"I can't have him finding out what I did," Maggie said, meeting her brother's eyes.

"What *we* did," Fitz corrected. "And by he, do you mean Dixon's people? Blackman? Or Jamie?"

"That doesn't matter," Maggie deflected.

"Oh, yes, it does," Fitz said. He took a deep, steadying breath. "Maggie, darling, there's nothing that connects you to what happened."

"There were suspicions," Maggie said. She folded her hands and tried not to look at her wedding set.

"Fuck suspicions. One person–"

"Not just one person. A cop. A cop with cop friends."

Maggie and Fitz stared at one another. Blue eyes versus hazel, two of Lennie Harrington's most stubborn children.

"It doesn't matter," Maggie said, leaning back in her chair as if she wanted to put as much distance between her and Fitz as she could manage in the small space. "If I'm out of the equation, that's one less thing to worry about. One less angle for them to play. We both know suspicion is enough to ruin a career, especially a career like Blackman's, a life like Blackman's."

"Then," Fitz countered, "tell Blackman what *we* did. Not you, but the family."

Tears pricked Maggie's eyes, and she shook her head.

Fitz got to his feet like he wanted to pace, but the space was too small. His face was bright red, and Maggie worried about his blood pressure. The last thing she needed was for him to have a stroke.

"So, you're going to blow up your family because of your fucking pride?" Fitz hissed.

"Not my pride, Fitz. He's an officer of the court. If I tell him what I did – we did – then he's obligated to report it."

Fitz looked at her as if she were deranged. "Your husband, with his eyes wide open, mind you, married into our family. *Our* family when he was already an officer of the fucking court. He knew from the beginning what dad and the boys did – do."

"We've shielded him," Maggie countered.

"Jesus Christ, Maggie, the man carried Dad's casket at the funeral, for fuck's sake. We certainly weren't shielding him that day," Fitz said, warming to his theme. "Your husband's not stupid. He knows that the villa in Greece, which he loves, *and* the ski chalet, *and* the estate in Scotland were all bought with family money. Doesn't stop him from getting on a plane four times a year to drink beers with us and watch a proper football match."

Fitz put his hands flat on Maggie's desk, leaned forward, and glared at her.

"But, no, it's going to be the mischief his wife got up to when he was in a fucking coma that's going to prick his conscience?" Fitz asked with an arched eyebrow.

"This is different," Maggie said, her voice a little quieter. A little more subdued. A little unsure.

"Why? Because it's you, and you're supposed to be some paragon of civility," Fitz asked sarcastically.

"Fuck you, Fitz!" Maggie said, getting to her feet. Fitz pushed off the desk and took a step back. "I almost beat a man to death to protect you. Don't think I won't walk out on my marriage to protect my family."

"Our family, Maggie. *Ours* not *yours*. And is that what you're doing? Protecting your family? Are you even listening to yourself?" Fitz asked incredulously. Suddenly, he felt guilty about asking Blackman the other night if he could fix this mess. Clearly, Blackman didn't even understand what this fucking mess was about.

"Look," Maggie said, trying to regain her composure. "I've decided. This is what I'm doing," Maggie said with a decisiveness she no longer felt. Everything had made sense in her head, and then Fitz showed up, and now everything felt jumbled as if she was trying to solve a puzzle without all the pieces or too many pieces. "Finals are next week, and then I'm going to leave."

"Leave? Just like that? And go where?" Fitz asked skeptically. "And you're doing all this right before Christmas? To. Your. Son."

Maggie swallowed. "He'll have Blackman; he'll have the family. He won't be alone."

Fitz shook his head and stepped closer to the desk, which stood like an insurmountable obstacle between them.

"Look, Dad was wrong when he sent you away. I know he thought he was doing the right thing, but he was wrong, and he knew it, and he always regretted it."

"This has–"

Fitz exploded. "Your whole fucking life has everything to do with Dad sending you away, and now you're going to inflict that same pain on Jamie? You're going to leave him with the same abandonment issues *you* can't get over."

"He'll be fine," she said stubbornly, digging in.

Fitz laughed mirthlessly. "That is exactly what Dad said about you. *Oh, she'll be fine, Fitzy, don't worry about our October*. And look at you, you're a fucking train wreck."

"Get out," Maggie said. Her voice was low and menacing.

"Or what? You're going to beat me up? Break my toys and make me cry?"

"Fuck you, Fitzwilliam," Maggie said. Her voice was hard, edged in ice and anger and reproach, but the tears in her eyes betrayed her. "Get out of my office and stay the fuck out of my life."

Fitz's face, on the other hand, was filled with disappointment and maybe a touch of disgust. He gathered up his coat and straightened to his full, unimpressive height. He sniffed, and said, "I'm calling London."

Maggie blinked.

Then Fitz, in total Fitz fashion, turned on his heel, opened the door, and left the office having not only the last word but backing her into a corner she couldn't get out of.

He was calling the family.

Maggie sighed, turned back to the window, and watched the snowfall. All avalanches started like this: small moments that spun out of control and buried everything and everyone in its path.

Chapter 17

Blackman sat at his desk staring at the files in front of him, his computer open and expectant. He had gotten to work nearly an hour ago, and so far, no one had come near him. After he shut his office door, he dropped his things on the ground, limped to his desk, and dry swallowed four Motrin. At some point, his administrative assistant Julia brought him coffee but didn't say anything. Before she left the office, he picked his things off the floor and put them where they belonged—the coat on the coat tree, his backpack beneath it. Blackman was never late for work or missed meetings, so whatever was going on in his life was clearly important. His deep scowl communicated quite clearly that he wanted to be left alone.

As he returned phone calls, he apologized for the missed meetings and delays, blaming his absence on an array of fictitious meetings in judges' chambers, last minute doctor's appointments, and a meeting at his son's school, which was mostly true, citing an issue with tuition payments. He saved that excuse for the people he knew who had children in private school because, for them, that excuse was not only the most plausible but the most relatable. After almost twenty years at the DA's office, Blackman was a capable and practiced liar. He was not quite as good as his father, who was an expert at lying to everyone around him, including himself. When he became a prosecutor, Blackman never imagined having to be the type of lawyer who would have to lie. He'd always thought lying was a defense attorney's lifeblood, but as he grew older, he realized that some days he was no better than his father.

As he returned the phone calls, he realized no one was terribly interested in his excuses. All they seemed to care about was that he was finally calling them back and that he was going to do what they wanted him to do or that he was telling them that he was going to do what they wanted him to do. Then, Blackman settled into the business of working.

As he took case notes, he lost himself in the law, in the challenges it promised. He'd always liked a challenge: the challenge of hockey, the challenge of his wife. He forced Maggie out of his mind, then waited to see if Fatimah would chide him for ignoring the one thing he ought not ignore, but her disappointed voice remained stubbornly silent. For all the times in his life for Fatimah to abandon him, he couldn't believe she had chosen now.

He shook his head and ran a hand through his hair, and again focused on his notes. At 4:45 his boss came into his office and asked for an update on Blackman's cases. Blackman dutifully provided the information. His boss, Jon Pierce's replacement, was *only* his boss. He wasn't a mentor, a confidant, or a friend. He was just another guy using the DA's office as a springboard to something better. Something sexier. Blackman wasn't a ladder climber, which was why he'd been surprised to be handed the Dixon case.

Much like his final hockey game, other men and women in the office would benefit much more than he from running point on a high profile case like this. So why the case had been assigned to Blackman remained a mystery to him. Contrary to what Jon had written on the note, words intended to be ironic, he was sure, Blackman had no desire to be the DA or the state AG or, God forbid, a judge. What Blackman wanted was to put more bad guys away than his father had set free. It was a lofty goal considering the length of his father's career and his rate of success, but Blackman was a goal oriented man.

He worked until Jamie texted him at 6:30.

Jamie:

BB practice over. Heading home.

Want me to pick up food?

Blackman looked at his desk; he really should keep working, but he thought about Maggie, and the broken dishes, and his son's angry tears in the priest's office that morning.

Fuck work.

Dad:

Pizza or Thai.

Jamie:

Thai

Jamie was the only kid Blackman ever knew who preferred Thai to pizza. He was like his mother that way. Maggie preferred Thai to just about anything.

Dad:

Leaving now

Jamie texted a thumbs up.

Blackman stood up and winced. His bad leg hurt despite the additional Motrin he'd taken an hour ago, and now his back hurt, too. When he could find a minute, he promised himself he'd make an appointment with the chiropractor. Being so tall had been great in his teens and his twenties because women loved a tall guy, but in his forties, the only thing his height brought him was aches and pains. He needed to go to the pool this week to loosen up his back, or he'd have to start taking more than Motrin.

He was getting old.

He gathered his things, pulled on his overcoat, and walked to the elevator.

He tried his best never to limp while he was at work.

After a slow drive through the unplowed streets, Blackman made it home as Jamie unpacked the Thai and set it out. He'd ordered all his mother's favorites, either consciously or unconsciously, but didn't bring up her absence or acknowledge the spotless kitchen. Father and son ate dinner in front of the television and watched a college basketball game. Blackman wondered if college basketball was in his son's future.

They didn't talk much, and neither of them brought up the elephant in the room. Instead of doing his homework upstairs in his bedroom behind a closed door, Jamie spread his books around him on the floor and did his work with one eye on the television. Blackman unpacked his own work and sat on the sofa with his feet up. When Jamie fell asleep on the floor, Blackman covered him with a blanket and turned on a West Coast hockey game.

Not wanting to go to bed, he made himself as comfortable as possible on the extra long, couch and watched the game until he eventually fell asleep. When Blackman woke up around four, he found the blanket that had covered Jamie was now covering him. The television was off, and the only light in the room came from a lamp Jamie had left on when he went to bed.

Blackman looked at the ceiling. He wanted to go back to sleep, but he figured he was probably awake. He blinked his eyes and rubbed a hand over his stubbled jaw.

Maggie had left him over the Dixon case, so afraid that the unspoken truth slowly destroying their marriage would finally be spoken, and they'd have their *Crime and Punishment* moment. And then maybe they could lance the gangrenous wound that was slowly poisoning them. Of course, he wasn't sure if one actually lanced something gangrenous, but he didn't care. If they had to metaphorically lance the wound or just cut it the fuck out of their dying marriage, the semantics didn't matter.

Maybe John had been right. Maybe last night was just everything coming to a head.

Maybe this disaster would save them all.

Blackman pushed himself slowly to a seated position and ran a hand over his face. He got to his feet and limped upstairs. In his cold, empty bedroom, he left his clothes crumpled on the floor, walked into the bathroom, and turned on the shower. He sat on the marble shower bench and let the hot water pour over him.

Maggie always thought she was stronger than him, more worldly, and less naïve because she had attended an expensive boarding school. As if going to boarding school made her more experienced, and being sent away made her more tragic.

Fuck that.

Maybe she went to boarding school, but he'd gone to a big money prep school where the average student had more money than brains. He'd been an elite athlete, his dad was an asshole, and he'd lost his virginity in the back of some girl's car when he was sixteen. Maggie had been in her twenties, when *he* took her virginity in *his* bed. And she wasn't the only one who could throw a goddamn punch.

What made her so fucking special?

She was nothing more than an impulsive, bad tempered bitch, who was running away from their marriage because she was too much of a pussy to fight for it.

Blackman Emerson Smith!

Fatimah had only called him by his full name once, and it was because he called a girl he was angry with a bitch. Fatimah said his name in shock and then slapped him so hard that she nearly knocked him off his feet. It was the one and only time she ever struck him, and he had never imagined that such a diminutive woman could possess such physical strength.

Just like Maggie.

Blackman closed his eyes and tilted his head into the spray. "Finally, mother, I knew you would not forsake me."

***

Although the evening before had been pleasant enough, Maggie barely slept, unable to turn her brain off. Dinner had been lovely. John made ramen, and Maggie had the distinct impression he made the noodles himself. She wondered what kind of divine or universal force had led Tilly to find such a skilled man in a lakeside town in Canada. Over wine, Tilly talked about the exciting day she'd had in the lab working on a proposal with her grad students, and John talked about his day at the museum, where he spent most of the morning studying a Jackson Pollock exhibit. Maggie discussed the challenges of exploring existential ennui while snow fell outside her classroom window.

The conversation was pleasant and adult, and it was nice to have dinner at a normal time and at a normal speed, knowing there was nowhere to go, nowhere to be. Everything felt casual and calm. It was a nice change to talk with people who weren't perpetually angry with her. And she didn't miss feeling like she had to pull teeth to hear about her teenager's day or, worse, to sit around a table in a painful silence that hurt her soul.

Those were the most miserable dinners.

Still, as she sipped her wine and listened to John expound on art, she missed Jamie and Blackman. At least a little bit. She would probably miss them more once she left, and despite what Fitz believed, she was doing the right thing. Fitz would understand eventually, and so would Blackman.

Jamie, however...

After dinner, Maggie took a pot of tea to her bedroom and graded until she couldn't keep her eyes open. Her sleep had been deep and dreamless for an hour or two, and then her eyes opened and stayed open for the rest of the night.

When Maggie arrived at her building the following day, she was alone. Tilly had walked part of the way with her but peeled off when they passed the building that housed Zoology.

Maggie was exhausted.

She didn't look at the bench until she was inside the building, until there were walls of brick and glass between her and it. He was there again, sitting on the bench with a travel mug of coffee. He looked at her, but he didn't get up. He just sat there. If Blackman had been a different kind of man, if a different woman had raised him, his presence could have been construed as threatening. But he was Blackman Smith, Fatimah's pride and joy, and Maggie could never be afraid of him.

Even that night in that college dive bar when he'd gone for menacing, he'd failed. She'd almost laughed at him when he told her that plenty of girls wanted to go home with him, but she didn't. Even sad and drunk, he was too easy a target. Too vulnerable. Moreover, in a bar full of women, some of them drunk, she was the only one who had approached him. It seemed that, for that night, at least, he was the hockey player least likely to get laid. Something campus gossip later confirmed. He wasn't a monk, but he wasn't much of a player either.

No, Blackman sitting on the bench dressed for work, holding his favorite travel mug, the pirate one Jamie had given him one Father's Day, wasn't a threat. If anything, Maggie understood, it was a promise. He'd promised to love her always, to love her without reservations or limits. To love her even when she didn't want to be loved. She, in return, had promised him the same thing.

And, evidently, he was going to hold her to those promises.

Whether it was good for him or not.

Chapter 18

Blackman wasn't on the bench the next day or the day after, and his absence filled Maggie with an overwhelming melancholy. Obviously, she had no right to expect him to sit on their bench every day and wait for her to come to her senses or change her mind, but the fact that she wanted him to be there hurt deeply. She missed him so much, but it didn't matter because she was doing the right thing, and maybe since he wasn't there, *he* knew she was doing the right thing, too. Perhaps he had accepted the inevitability of their end.

Still, her eyes continued to be drawn to the bench.

Late in the afternoon, after her final class, she walked to the bench and stared down at it. It was another cold day; this time, freezing rain was in the forecast. Maggie knew she should get back to John and Tilly's house before the rain came, but her legs wouldn't work.

She liked being with John and Tilly, hiding in their warm house, but she was wearing out her welcome, not so much because she was still there but because she seemed unwilling or unable to move forward with Blackman. Her avoidance strategy wasn't something that people like John and Tilly understood or appreciated. They thought she was being cowardly, but at least John was too polite to say it.

Whereas Tilly was more than willing to say it.

"Maggie, you know I love you, and I really like Blackman, too, so I say this with complete and total affection: shit or get off the pot."

And, of course, Maggie couldn't argue because Tilly was right. Maggie did indeed need to shit or get off the pot. Blackman wasn't the only one twisting in the wind.

There was Jamie, too.

Maggie sighed and sat down on the cold bench.

Settling in, she waited for the feel of the cold wood to seep through her jeans. She let her eyes drift over the nearly empty campus as if she would somehow stumble over a young Blackman dressed in those worn jeans he loved and one of those dark wool sweaters he always wore beneath that tan barn coat. He still had that barn coat hanging in the bedroom closet at home.

Their bedroom closet.

Their bedroom.

She closed her eyes against the sting of tears.

Shortly after they got engaged, they were sitting on the sofa in front of the fireplace in their apartment drinking wine, drinking too much wine, in fact. They had been half planning the wedding as they finished one bottle of wine and opened another. Maggie was drunk, and she told Blackman, who wasn't drunk, about the daydreams she used to have about him in college and how she used to imagine him coming up to her and saying all sorts of corny pickup lines. Drunken Maggie thought Blackman would find the story funny, but the smile he gave her didn't quite reach his eyes. Instead, his face grew serious, and she immediately regretted saying anything.

"I know," she said, reclining against her corner of the sofa. "It sounds silly." She felt her face go red as she searched for something else to talk about.

"No," Blackman said, looking at her from his end of the sofa. Her legs were stretched out, and he reached for one of her bare feet after setting his wine glass on the coffee table. He started to massage her arch gently, and she groaned in pleasure.

"It's not silly at all. It's just that I used to look for you all the time, but I never saw you."

"I was just good at blending in, I suppose. Whenever I did see you, you were always heading somewhere with a purpose," she lied. "You were a very studious student."

Blackman met her eyes and considered the lie. She was a terrible liar. He reached for her other foot. Her engagement ring shone in the firelight.

"I think you were avoiding me," he said with a mischievous smile.

"And why would I avoid you?" she asked quietly, wondering what kind of answer he would give. Would he drive the conversation into deeper, more serious waters, or would he keep it light? She wasn't sure which one she preferred. If she had been sober, she never would have taken them down this road where her intense, all consuming love for him was too close to the surface. She never wanted him to know just how much she loved him, how much she wanted him. How much she couldn't go back to a life without him.

That, however, was a level of honesty and emotional intimacy she wasn't capable of. She could do physical intimacy with him. She could let him look at her and hold her eyes during their most intimate moments, but the emotional intimacy he was so comfortable with was beyond her. She thought he was capable of that because of Fatimah and the uninhibited love she had shown him in his youth and continued to show him in adulthood. Maggie wondered what kind of woman she could have grown into if she hadn't been sent abroad, if her mother hadn't died, if she had found her Fatimah in boarding school.

Blackman, as intuitive as always, seemed to understand that the mood in the fire-lit room had shifted. In true Blackman form, he lifted her foot and kissed it gently. Maggie shivered.

"I think you avoided me because you knew that you'd never be able to resist all of my amazing pickup lines," he said with a grin.

"Really? Lines better than your bar lines?" she asked playfully.

"First, that was a quality pickup line," he said, putting her foot down and reaching for his wine glass.

"Try again, counselor," Maggie laughed.

"Okay," Blackman said as he pulled his Blackberry out of his pocket and tapped some buttons. "I bet you couldn't resist this one." He paused dramatically. "Are you Australian? Because you meet all my koalafications."

Maggie snorted.

Blackman's grin widened. "Okay, how about this one? Do you believe in love at first sight, or should I walk by again?"

Maggie groaned, and Blackman started to move over her slowly. "I would've said God bless you after you sneezed, but it's clear he already has."

"Stop!" Maggie cried as she dissolved into giggles. Blackman nuzzled her ear and whispered, "Are you a parking ticket? Because you have fine written all over you."

"Dr. Rhymer?"

Maggie's eyes snapped open, and the warmth of the long-ago apartment with its fireplace, its windows, their youth, and all the promises it held was gone.

"Yes," Maggie asked as she quickly blinked away the wetness of her eyes.

"Do you have a sec?" the undergrad standing before her asked.

Maggie forced a smile and patted the empty place beside her on the bench.

"Sure. What can I do for you?"

No matter what was going on in a teacher's personal life, God forbid they not have a moment for their students, no matter how awkward the timing.

Chapter 19

Blackman leaned against the cold tiles of the shower as he let the scalding hot water fall forcefully against his aching shoulders. Since he couldn't sleep worth a damn on that fucking sofa, he'd gone swimming the last two mornings. He had to do something with the restless energy that was making it impossible for him to think or complete simple tasks.

Like making palatable coffee.

Or operating a rice cooker.

Or doing his fucking job.

Earlier in the day, his boss had entered Blackman's office without knocking or an invitation. As if the asshat had the right to breeze into Blackman's office whenever he wanted. Then the asshat in question took a seat in one of the chairs across from Blackman's desk and said without preamble, "What the fuck is wrong with you?"

Blackman leaned back in his chair, schooled his face, and counted to ten. "Nothing."

"You sure about that?"

"Yes. I. am." Blackman enunciated every word. Then he shut his mouth, ground his molars, and tried not to think about how easy it would be to put this man through a wall. They looked at one another, both waiting for the other to say something more. Finally, his boss shrugged his shoulders, making it clear to Blackman that if something was wrong, he didn't give a shit.

"Fine, whatever. Just make sure you take care of *nothing* before Dixon's in a courtroom."

Blackman remained silent. His boss tried to stare him down, to intimidate him, but the man was an idiot, a politically connected idiot, but an idiot nonetheless. And since Blackman wasn't interested in anything beyond his job as an ADA, there was nothing the other man could do to him. No way for him to intimidate him.

"Good."

When his boss walked out of the room, he left Blackman's door open behind him.

Blackman fucking hated the guy, and he hated working for him. He would have followed Jon Pierce anywhere, would have done anything for him, but he wouldn't piss on this guy if he were on fire.

And Blackman very much wanted to see him on fire.

Literally.

"Dad?"

"Yeah, Jamie, what do you need?" Blackman said, taking his head off the tile and standing up straight. His muscles groaned in protest.

"Uncle Nick's on the phone," Jamie called from the bedroom.

"Well, tell him I'm in the shower, and I'll call him back when I get out."

"He says he needs to talk to you now. He says it's important."

Blackman groaned.

"Okay, tell him to give me two minutes."

"Ok."

Jamie shut the door, and Blackman sighed. Fitz had called London. Now, the family was involved, and once the Harringtons got involved, shit was going to get dealt with.

"Fuck," Blackman hissed as he shut off the water and reached for a towel. He dried himself as he walked into the bedroom and pulled on a t-shirt and joggers. He reached for his iPhone, and the display showed several missed calls from Nick.

Christ, Blackman thought, *he'd only been in the shower for ten minutes.*

Maybe.

He unlocked his phone and started to tap the phone icon when he paused and looked up at the 8x10 photo of himself and the Harrington brothers on his bureau. It had been taken at Lennie's funeral. They were in their funeral finery, their eyes bright and their faces flushed because they had been drinking for hours before the picture was snapped. Fitz and Nick stood to Blackman's right, and Joseph and Oliver stood to his left. They were a handsome group of men in their best black suits, starched black shirts, and black silk ties. Fitz's blond hair was still thick, but Nick's red hair was starting to thin. Joseph and Oliver had dark brown hair and brown eyes like Blackman; if not for Blackman's towering height, he could have been one of them. He *was* one of them. From the first time Maggie brought Blackman home to meet the family, he had been shown nothing but love, and he was so grateful for it. So thankful for the Harrington men.

With a resigned sigh, he dialed Nick.

"Blackman, I've been calling you!" Nick shouted. It sounded like he was somewhere crowded and loud. Someone in the background laughed loudly.

"I was in the shower."

"Long fucking shower," Nick quipped.

"Long fucking day," Blackman said as he ran a hand through his damp hair. The silence between them was long and awkward, and Blackman didn't want to break it or start the conversation he didn't want to have. Nick, however, knew Blackman, and he waited him out until Blackman finally gave in.

"Where are you?" Blackman asked, sitting down on the bed.

"Hawaii."

"What are you doing in Hawaii?"

"Conference."

"Conference?" Blackman asked.

"Yes, Blackman, we have conferences; I go to conferences," Nick snapped, clearly annoyed. "Fitz called."

Shit, Blackman thought. He prayed Fitz hadn't included all the sordid details from the other night.

"Did she really break all the dishes?" Nick asked.

Blackman closed his eyes and silently cursed Fitz.

"Not all," Blackman answered carefully.

"But most?"

"Yes," Blackman said through clenched teeth. "I'm handling it, Nick."

"Handling my sister? Well, that takes a load off my mind. Can you put her on the phone because she's not answering hers," Nick said, his voice artificially cheerful. Blackman tried to think of something to say, but his mind was blank.

Painfully blank.

Again.

"Blackman, my sister. Put her on the phone, mate." Again, with the false cheerfulness.

"I can't," Blackman admitted slowly.

"Yeah, because she's not there, you twat. Handling Maggie Rhymer my ass. How long has she been gone?"

He'd briefly considered lying to Nick, but he was in enough trouble as it was. He didn't need to add Nick's considerable ire to the mix.

"Four days," Blackman answered.

"My sister left you *four* fucking days ago, and you haven't called me?"

Blackman recognized the rhetorical nature of the question and remained silent.

"Blackman?" Nick asked.

"I'm handling it," Blackman repeated. Weakly.

"Not very well, brother," Nick snapped.

"Nick –"

"The wives are coming over. They have the first flight out of Heathrow in the morning."

Blackman put his face in his hand and groaned.

"Nick," Blackman said wearily, hating the whine in his voice.

"Don't 'Nick' me. It's been decided. Sherry's livid with you for not calling us."

"Of course she is," Blackman sighed because this was all about Sherry, and then Blackman instantly regretted the unkind thought. Sherry was wonderful, and she only wanted to help. Of course, she was going to tear Blackman a new asshole, then she'd find Maggie and tear her a new asshole, and then the helping part would begin.

"Four days is a long time. When's the last time you've gone four days without talking to your wife?"

Blackman didn't say anything, but the answer was four days before he saw her standing in that lawyer bar looking like everything he'd ever wanted in life.

"I'm giving her space."

"How's that working for you?" Nick asked sarcastically.

"Well," Blackman said slowly, "she hasn't served me with divorce papers, so not as bad as it could be."

Nick lost his mind in the middle of whatever conference hall he was standing. His voice was so loud Blackman held the iPhone away from his ear and looked at the door as if Jamie was going to walk in and add to the misery.

"No one in this family is getting divorced. Da would roll over in his grave," Nick yelled.

Blackman sighed again. He had nothing to say; literally, there was nothing in his head.

When had his life spiraled so far out of control? When had his goddamn brain stopped working?

"Nick," Blackman said softly, "the wives showing up is not going to make things any better."

"Well, it sure as shit isn't going to make anything worse. When's the last time my sister talked to her son?"

Blackman closed his eyes and pinched the bridge of his nose. Nick knew the answer, so Blackman opted to say nothing.

"I can't believe you didn't call us," Nick said, and the sound of disappointment in his voice was almost more than Blackman could bear.

"Nick –"

"When Sherry threatened to put me out, whom did I call?"

"Me," Blackman answered quietly.

"And when Pippa threw Oliver out, whom did I call?"

"Me."

"And when Joey had to go to rehab, whom did I call, *and* who got on the first fucking flight he could find? Correct me if I'm wrong, but you had to drive to New York at like two in the morning."

"Fine," Blackman snapped. "I get it. I should have called, but in my defense, I didn't think that it'd go on for so long. I thought if I gave her some time to calm down, she'd see reason and come home."

"Brother, my sister was beyond reason when she broke the crockery," Nick said, a note of sympathy creeping into his voice.

Blackman said nothing; Nick wasn't wrong.

"Yes, well," Nick said, clearing his throat. "Sherry's coming. Things will get sorted now."

Nick wasn't wrong there, either. Once Sherry and the others showed up, shit was definitely going to get sorted. Blackman tried to say something, but he closed his mouth. As if having his wife walk out on him wasn't humiliating enough, the Harrington women were going to fly trans-Atlantic to do precisely what he hadn't been able to do with his wife for over a year: talk. Clear the fucking air. The hollow ache of embarrassment filled his chest with lead, making it hard for him to breathe. Again.

"Blackman," Nick said. His voice was kind, too kind. "My sister is a difficult and stubborn woman, and she's always been that way. Even when she was young, and all of us know that marriage is fucking hard. You've always been there for us. *Always*. Now, let us be there for you."

Blackman's throat closed, and his eyes stung. What was there to say? After four days, he still didn't understand why Maggie was angry, why she'd broken the dishes, or why she'd asked for a divorce while essentially walking out the door. Sure, they were going through a tough time, but was that grounds for a divorce? Marriage counseling, sure. A vacation, at the very least. They were due to return to London for the holiday, then they'd get some time together. They could go to the coast, just the two of them, or maybe Paris or Barcelona. Christ, they could go to Greece if she wanted. Could all this really be about the Dixon case? If he'd known she'd react so badly, he could have suggested someone else take it. It wasn't like he was the only lawyer in the office. Or was this about her unresolved feelings about the shooting? About him *and* the shooting? Or was it about Jamie, or was it about all of it?

"You still there, Blackman?" Nick asked.

"Yes," Blackman managed to say, his voice thick with emotion.

"Okay, look, I have to go, but Sherry will text you the airline information when she has it sorted. I believe they're staying at the hotel they like near the river. I'll have her send that information, too."

"Okay."

"Blackman, it's all going to be okay. I promise you. I love you, brother."

"Love you, too, Nick."

The call ended, and Blackman flopped back on the bed. After a minute, Jamie knocked on the door.

"Game's starting soon. Want to watch it?"

"Yeah, I'll be down in a minute," Blackman said, staring at the ceiling.

"Okay," Jamie said, but he didn't move. "Uncle Nick said the aunts are coming."

"Yes. Yes, he did."

Jamie seemed like he wanted to say something more but decided against it. Instead, he turned around and shut the door. Blackman listened to him walk downstairs. Then he stared at the ceiling and wondered what the absolute fuck he was supposed to do.

Chapter 20

Maggie stared at the ceiling, having passed another sleepless night, but at least it was the last night she would spend at Tilly and John's. They had been nothing by gracious and understanding, and John was a fantastic cook, almost as good as Blackman, but she needed some space of her own, and she needed to think, which she couldn't do in this house. She could barely breathe with John and Tilly's marital bliss crushing her, and on top of everything else, their fucking bed squeaked, and the noise was driving her out of her mind. She hadn't had sex in months, and it felt more like years.

Fucking dog years.

She groaned and buried her head in the pillows as she heard Cujo get up and shake, signaling the start of another interminable day. Yesterday, she had almost called Blackman on her office phone, but she couldn't bring herself to do it. Then she almost emailed him, but she didn't do that either. What the hell was she going to say?

Sorry?

Sorry, I lost my temper.

Sorry, I broke the dishes.

God, the fucking dishes.

Sorry, I asked for a divorce.

Sorry, I walked out.

Sorry, I used a really big rock to break my iPhone.

Honestly, why couldn't she be cool and calm like other people? Why did she have to lash out when she got mad? Why'd she have to break the fucking detective's nose? If she didn't piss him off and humiliate him in front of the other officers in the waiting room, he wouldn't have such a hard on for her.

This is your Raskolnikov moment. I hope you choke on it.

Well, she wasn't going to choke on it. What was done was done. When she asked Nick, or better *told* Nick, to find the man who shot her husband and kill him, she honestly thought Blackman was going to die. Also, in her defense, she didn't expect her brother to kill so many people in one week.

Then Blackman woke up, and she knew he would find out what the family had done to get Maggie her pound of flesh. Now, the only reasonable thing for her to do was leave and hope Semple wouldn't go after Blackman if she were gone, that Semple wouldn't tell Jamie what the family had done at her behest. If her decision to leave hurt Jamie and Blackman, then they'd have to learn to live with that, and maybe they'd eventually forgive her.

At least, maybe Blackman would forgive her.

Jamie wouldn't.

Children never forgave their parents, not really. She was living proof of that. If the last few months were any indicator, Jamie would probably be happier with her being gone. Now he could go blind playing that fucking X-Box.

Fuck. Her. Fucking. Life.

She got out of bed and started her day.

When Maggie walked downstairs, she was already working through her excuses for leaving. The whole *it's me, not you* spiel, and then she could spend the rest of the morning finding a hotel. Maybe something with a pool and a gym because she needed a workout. Maybe a sauna. She hadn't packed any gym clothes or a bathing suit, but she could stop by Dick's Sporting Goods or maybe that new Lululemon that opened near Rittenhouse Square. She was pretty sure they sold bathing suits. For their prices, they should probably sell the whole damn pool. She wondered if they carried trainers, too. Maybe those HOKA trainers everyone raved about, even though they were a little bit ugly.

Maggie was so lost in her thoughts that she almost didn't notice Blackman when she walked into the living room. She came up short when she saw him sitting on the sofa in his best black suit and that purple tie she had given him a lifetime ago. He was leaning back, his legs crossed, hands folded over one knee. His hair was neatly combed, but it needed a cut. He had the beginnings of a dark beard. He hadn't had a beard in years. There was an empty coffee cup in front of him.

His brown eyes were dark and angry. In fact, he looked positively furious.

Possibly more furious than he'd looked in years, or quite possibly ever.

Blackman looked her up and down, at once looking incredibly relieved that she was standing in front of him while also incredibly angry that she was standing in front of him in another man's living room. Blackman got to his feet, rising to his full and formidable height.

She tried to return his look of... contempt? Disgust? Whatever it was, he was definitely pissed. She shifted her eyes from Blackman to John, who was slowly unfolding himself from one of the chairs on the far side of the room, dressed for a run.

Probably a long run.

Like a marathon long run.

John looked from Blackman to Maggie, and he didn't have the decency to look even slightly concerned. In fact, he seemed positively serene.

"So," John said bending over. He picked up a leash from the floor and gave it a shake. After a moment, Cujo came bounding into the room, ignoring both Maggie and Blackman. The dog went to John, sat down patiently, and allowed the leash to be clipped to his collar. He was, after all, a very good boy.

"I'm going to take Cujo here for a walk. A long walk," John added. "I'm sure you two have plenty to talk about."

Maggie glared at John while Blackman glared at her. John nodded, clicked his tongue at the oversized dog, and said, "Come on, boy, let's give these two some privacy."

Maggie watched John leave the room and didn't turn back to Blackman until she heard the front door click shut. Then, after calling John every combination of swear words she could think of, she slowly, deliberately, turned and faced her husband.

The father of her only child.

Her son. *Their* son.

She took a deep breath.

"You're supposed to be at work," she said because she had no idea what else to say. She wasn't exactly great with words anymore. Blackman looked down at his watch, a heavy silver Swiss Army watch she had given him their first Christmas together, which he wore face down on his right wrist, the only habit he'd picked up from his father. Jamie, the only high school student who wore a proper watch instead of an Apple watch or some such nonsense, wore his watch the same way.

Jamie might resemble her, but he was 100% Blackman.

Thank God.

"Actually," Blackman said, "I should be in court."

Maggie blanched.

"Why are you here, then?" she asked, trying to sound sharp but failing. His appearing in John and Tilly's living room without notice had wrong footed her. She wondered if he had called to warn her that he was coming over this morning, but she wouldn't know because she had broken her fucking phone with a motherfucking rock.

"Because," Blackman said, taking a step forward, radiating rage like waves of heat off a campfire, or a forest fire, or some other conflagration that consumed everything in its path without mercy. "My wife's blowing up an eighteen year marriage over God knows what. So, I decided talking to you might be a little bit more important than going to court."

Maggie blinked. Her mouth went dry, and her stomach pitched. Weren't there consequences for missing court? Like contempt charges? Christ, was he going to be arrested? Maybe go to jail? This whole fucking disaster she'd started just kept getting worse and worse.

"Court's important," she said, going for defiance but coming up short. Again. "Your job is important," she added weakly. Blackman's eyes flashed, and his already stiff body went rigid.

She wasn't prepared for a fight; she hadn't even had a cup of coffee, and she was exhausted, and Blackman, who vibrated with anger like a goddamn tuning fork, looked well rested, confident, and prepared to annihilate her. If he was the prosecutor, and she was the defendant in his court, she'd just change her plea and take the jail time simply so she wouldn't have to be in the same room with him.

"No, Maggie," Blackman said, his voice a deep, low growl – something entirely unfamiliar to her. "This – *us* – is important to me – more important than a case, or my job, or fucking court." He took another step toward her, and she instinctively took a step back.

"Your bag is packed. So where are you going this time? Because I doubt it's home," he said sharply. His eyes were stormy and dark and almost impossible to look at for long. It was like looking into an angry and unforgiving sun.

"Were you going to let me know? Maybe drop me a postcard? Maybe write me a fucking poem?" he sneered. Maggie dropped her eyes. There was no way for her to hold his gaze; it just hurt too much. All the anger and the pain she'd caused him shone brightly in those eyes. She'd hurt him and then run away like a coward. Now he was there, and he was going to make her face him, and he wasn't going to pull his punches because she hadn't pulled hers. The first blow, the shot about the poem, landed especially hard because she hadn't written in over a year.

Not that he knew that.

Or maybe he did know.

Blackman always seemed to know more about her than she realized.

Maggie stared at the floor and tried unsuccessfully to control her breathing, to still her trembling hands.

"Well?" he demanded.

She couldn't think of anything to say, and Blackman exploded.

"Jesus fucking Christ, Maggie!" His voice echoed in the small space. She had never heard him yell before, not *really* yell, not like this, and never at her. He took another step forward but stopped as if he didn't trust himself to get any closer.

Maggie forced herself to stand still, to hold her ground. She could see he was struggling to keep his hands loose by his sides instead of balling them into fists. He'd never hit her, she knew that, but not hitting her didn't mean he didn't want to grab her and shake some sense into her.

"Is it me? Are you ashamed of me?" he finally asked, his voice loud, accusatory, filled with hurt and bone-deep betrayal. Maggie's head snapped up; her eyes went wide. She stared at him incredulously.

"Because --" he continued, "because I got shot? Because I didn't stop it? Because I couldn't? Because it hurt so much? Because I'm not brave or strong like Nick? Because something like this would never happen to one of your brothers?"

Maggie didn't move. Bile churned in her stomach, and she was afraid she would throw up. She looked away, unable to hold his eyes, which were growing wet.

"Do you think I'm a coward? Is that it, Maggie?" Blackman asked, his voice edged with pain and humiliation.

Maggie just shook her head, unable to speak.

"Fucking talk to me, Maggie!" Blackman yelled again. This time, he took a small step forward, closing the distance between them a fraction.

"No," Maggie managed weakly. She felt lightheaded. She was going to be sick all over Tilly and John's floor. She had broken the good dishes in a rage, and he had barely said a word, and she had taken his dignified silence for granted. In all their years together, he had never raised his voice to her, never spoken to her so harshly, so angrily, so scornfully. She thought that by walking away from him, she was sparing him something – what exactly, she wasn't entirely sure. But in the last few days, he'd gotten everything wrong, which she couldn't understand. He was the lawyer, the logical one. If anyone was supposed to understand what she was doing, it was him.

"No? Really? You can barely look at me, let alone touch me," he spat.

Maggie tried again to meet his eyes but settled on a point just above his left shoulder. She opened her mouth to speak, but Blackman plowed on.

"And then you run off to John-whoever-the fuck-he-is. Military contractor, my ass. He's probably some fucking war criminal."

"I went to –" Maggie tried to interrupt Blackman, but he was on a roll unloading everything that had been crushing him since she'd left him alone to deal with the wreckage of their marriage.

"Is that who you wish I was?" he hissed. "Do you wish I was more like him? More like your brothers? Am I suddenly not enough for you? With my..."

"No," she wailed, crossing the space between them in three strides, pushing against Blackman's chest as hard as she could. He looked down at her, but he didn't move, and then she bladed her body, planted her back foot, and shoved him again. This time, he took a step back, but whether it was because of the force of her blow or because he wanted to give her space, she couldn't be sure. She was just grateful for the movement.

"How dare you?" she cried. "How dare you? I love you, and my brothers have nothing to do with this, and I went to *Tilly,* not John, you idiot."

Tears shone in her eyes.

"I – I –" She pushed a hand through her hair, "I can't touch you because it's my fault."

"What the hell is your fault?" He glared at her, his brown eyes nearly black.

"You – you were out looking at gifts for me. The jewelry store, the lingerie shop, you – he shot you because you were out of the office because of me." She could tell from the look on his face that he didn't understand. He couldn't follow her logic.

"So, if I was shot at Staples, we'd be fine?" he asked sarcastically. He wouldn't give her an inch, and that was okay. She didn't deserve an inch; she deserved his anger and sarcasm. Maggie spun away from him and walked to the far side of the small room, which was barely large enough to contain all of Blackman's hurt and fury.

"You're not listening to me," she said, turning back and looking at him from a safer distance.

"You're not making a lot of sense," he snapped.

She met his eyes and chewed on her bottom lip for a moment.

"There had been threats," she began slowly.

"There are always threats," he replied.

"There aren't always threats," she shouted, frustrated with his dismissiveness.

"Yes, Maggie," Blackman said a little more calmly. "There are. I just never tell you about them."

Maggie narrowed her eyes, her cheeks reddened.

"What do you mean there are always threats?" she asked incredulously. Twenty years together, and she was only now hearing about this?

"Christ, Maggie, I put bad people in jail for a living. You don't think that pisses people off? Or their friends? Or their fucking families?" Blackman asked, unsure of how this was news to her. Of course, there were threats. He worked in a building with metal detectors and guards. It wasn't like they were there for decoration.

"Most of the time, the threats aren't anything to worry about, just people talking shit, letting off steam. I don't tell you because there's no need to worry you about it, and you weren't supposed to know about this one either. Semple should have been more discreet, and *you* shouldn't eavesdrop."

Maggie didn't say anything but privately conceded the point. She did tend to eavesdrop, a bad habit from childhood. And, yes, she shouldn't have eavesdropped on him at work, but the office door had been ajar, and she'd only nudged it open a little bit with the toe of her boot, but she hadn't *actually* knocked. Blackman had looked more than a little annoyed that day when he looked up and saw her standing in the doorway, the picture of innocence.

"So," Blackman said, attempting a reasonable tone. "Like the other hundred times I've been threatened over the years, this was most likely going to come to nothing."

"You were shot!" Maggie yelled, anger creeping into her voice, although she couldn't exactly pinpoint why she was angry. Maybe because strangers had been threatening her husband for years, and he'd never bothered to tell her. Or maybe because strangers had been threatening him for years, and he never took it seriously. Honestly, had all these years with her brothers, with her family, taught him nothing? What the hell?

"Yes," Blackman yelled back at her. "But not by the guy who threatened me!"

Maggie opened her mouth and then snapped it shut. She settled for glaring at Blackman, who glared right back at her.

Blackman took a deep, calming breath that did nothing to calm him. Then he met Maggie's eyes.

"I know what happened while I was in the hospital, while I was unconscious." Blackman always said unconscious; he hated the word *coma*. It reminded him of an old horror movie.

Maggie said nothing. Her face was inscrutable.

"Nick told me," Blackman said quietly.

Maggie didn't so much as blink.

"He told me things were... handled; he called it a family matter. He spared me the details," Blackman said carefully. Maggie clocked the lie. Blackman was Nick's brother, his equal, and Nick wouldn't keep secrets from him or spare him the details of what the *family* had done, unlike Maggie, who, as it turned out, was keeping secrets that weren't actually secrets.

"I told him to do it. He did it because of me," Maggie said defiantly. She held Blackman's eyes and waited. Waited for him to respond. Waited for him to be shocked or disgusted or horrified at what she had allowed to happen while he was unconscious, at the events she set in motion.

"No, Maggie." Blackman sighed. He almost rolled his eyes. Honestly, it was like she didn't know her brother. "Nick was going to do what he did anyway. Nick answers to no one but himself. He might have wanted your blessing, but he certainly wasn't asking for your permission."

Maggie wanted to argue, wanted to take responsibility for what had happened, for the carnage, but Blackman wasn't wrong. Nick might have asked her what she wanted him to do, but he would do what he wanted regardless. The only person Nick had ever sought permission from was long since dead and buried in the family plot.

"Semple knows," Maggie said quietly. Looking away from Blackman, she let her eyes settle on a large painting above the sofa. In it, a young girl in a dress held her hands toward a sea of colorful butterflies as if she was sending them into the world to bring joy to people in desperate need of it.

Blackman shook his head.

"No, Semple has a theory he can't prove and a grudge he can't act on. Semple isn't half as smart as he thinks he is," Blackman said, trying to catch Maggie's eyes, but she was focused on the canvas. Maggie stared at the butterflies for a long time before she spoke again.

"He told me what Nick did. He called it my Raskolnikov moment. He said he hoped I choked on it," Maggie said softly.

Blackman thought back to that night at the bar, to Semple leering at Maggie as if Semple had the privilege of even looking at Blackman's wife. Blackman remembered the anger he'd felt that night when he saw Maggie flinch at whatever Semple had said. He'd wanted to kill Semple, but he settled for honesty.

If I ever see you talking to my wife again, I will bury you so deep in shit, the only way you'll be able to get out will be to eat your gun.

Now Blackman regretted not beating the shit out of Semple when he had the chance—regretted not pounding the man's head into the exposed brick wall until Semple couldn't stand. Now he thought about how many bad things could happen to a bad cop in a dark alley in a bad part of town.

"It doesn't matter," Blackman said with a shrug. At least it didn't matter in the way Maggie wanted it to matter. He'd deal with Semple.

"It *does* matter," Maggie insisted. She finally looked at Blackman. "Semple will go to Dixon's lawyers and tell them what he knows, and they'll use this to bury you."

Blackman's eyes softened as puzzle pieces finally started to slot into place.

"Is that what this is about? Dixon's lawyers?" he asked, his voice gentle.

"Yes!" Maggie exclaimed, finally feeling like she was getting somewhere. "His lawyers will dig into your life, into *our* lives, and they'll use it to ruin you."

"Jesus, Maggie, he's a tech guy, not a Marvel supervillain. If he goes after anyone, he'll go after the victims or their families. And either way, it's not like our family is a big secret. I was named in articles about Dad's passing. My picture was in the newspapers."

Maggie ignored him and his fucking logic.

"This is a high profile case," she countered. "A career maker. Even Jon Pierce said it. This could set you up for a run for DA or AG. You win this case, and you can do whatever you want. Christ, you could probably position yourself for a judiciary appointment. You have to start thinking about yourself." Maggie's voice held a pleading note he'd heard too many times before. She took a step towards him, but Blackman stepped back.

"God, Maggie," Blackman said, his voice weary. He couldn't bear to hear another speech about how he had to start putting his career ahead of his family. He swore he was the only man he'd ever known whose partner complained about how little he prioritized his job. He dug his hands into his pants pockets and paced the small room, stopping in front of the window that overlooked the tree lined street. Staring into the early morning light, he rubbed his wedding ring with his thumb.

"I–" he started to speak, then stopped. His voice was thick with emotion, and he had to clear his throat before he began again. "I've been in love with you since I was twenty-one years old. That night in the bar, you were wearing those jeans and that little green t-shirt, and every time you bent over that pool table – God," he said softly. Even now he could still see her that night, still hear the way she teased him, the way she insulted him. The kindness she showed him when he didn't deserve anyone's kindness.

"You were gorgeous," Blackman said, his voice unsteady. "And I was such a jackass. I was so ashamed for hurting that kid. And I made a fool out of myself with you, and you could have just laughed in my face, but you didn't. You were so kind, and I didn't deserve it. Do you remember what you said to me that night? When I came on to you?"

Maggie was silent for so long Blackman worried she had forgotten about a night that had meant so much to him. A night that had changed his life forever.

"I said," Maggie said slowly. "It would have been nice to meet the non-asshole version of you."

Blackman smiled thinly and tears filled his eyes. He let them fall.

"I dreamt about you for years – fantasized about you – Christ, that night outside my apartment, the way you whispered my name — no one had ever said my name like that – I still get hard when I think about that night," he said feeling his cheeks heat from the memory. "I've spent my entire adult life trying to be a better man than the boy you met in the bar. You and Jamie and your family are all I have, and you're all I want."

He turned and looked at her, his face wet. "I don't want to be DA or AG, and God knows I don't want to be a goddamn judge. I just want to do my job and come home to you and Jamie."

And he wasn't even sure he wanted to do his job anymore.

"I didn't ask for the Dixon case," he said, taking a step toward Maggie. "It was assigned to me. I don't even have to take it. I can still get out of it. If you were so afraid, you should have talked to me."

Maggie looked away and tried to collect her thoughts.

"What did you think would happen when you broke the dishes? That I was just going to let you go? Give you a divorce without at least talking to you?" Blackman asked. He wiped his eyes with the back of his hand. "Do you think you're so easy to walk away from? Am *I* that easy to walk away from?" he asked as if he genuinely needed to know the answer. Maggie stared at the floor, her wavy hair hiding her wet eyes, her breaking heart. Blackman took another step towards her.

"I get that your dad's decision to send you away messed with your head irrevocably," Blackman continued. "I understand that it made you feel expendable, and it made you believe everyone else is more important than you. And that sort of torturous thinking has been great for your poetry and great for your career, but I'm not your poetry." More tears slid from Blackman's eyes, and he wiped them away. "We – Jamie and I – aren't your poetry. We're your family, and we love you, and we *need* you. And you just can't leave us behind because you either don't think you're worth the effort or because you think we'd be better off without you. You can't just decide that the best way to keep us safe is to torch our lives," Blackman said softly.

"I'm sorry," Maggie whispered to the floor. Blackman stepped toward her, but Maggie stepped back and held up her hands. Blackman stopped, his face guarded, wary.

"I spent so much time and energy trying not to fall in love with you," she said, lifting her head to look at him. She pushed her hair back, and the emotions playing across her pale features worried him because the prevailing one was shame. Deep, deep shame.

"That night in the bar, I would have gone home with you," she said with a nostalgic smile. She, too, still thought about that night, about a young man barely out of boyhood drowning his sorrows in a dingy bar, alone. A man whose good looks weren't enough to get someone to pay attention to him that night, and God, did she love the way he looked that night. The hair, the eyes she saw a time or two checking out her ass, those cheekbones that could cut glass, and those fucking shoulders. She'd always loved big guys, and Blackman was a *big* guy.

"There was something so vulnerable about you, so sweet despite the bravado and ridiculousness. When you were still sober, I saw you, and I thought maybe you'd come and talk to me, but I think you were too shy, and then you were too drunk." Her chuckle turned into a soft sob. "Then I used to see you everywhere on campus, everywhere, and it was torture because I wasn't ready for you, for us. Then, the game and that smile. Everything about you – I wanted you so badly it hurt, and it was frightening because I'd never felt that way before. To ache for a man I barely knew... it was too much, but you made me so happy. But then you got hurt, and I felt responsible. You were showing off." She shook her head at the memory.

"You weren't responsible."

"I was distracting you."

"It was a bad hit. I'd done the same thing a hundred times. Hockey's a rough game. People get hurt... *I* hurt people," he said, his voice quiet and sad.

"It's always been so hard to resist you," Maggie said, looking back at the painting of the girl and the butterflies as if the words she needed were somehow hidden in the brush strokes. "The night I walked away from you after the coffee shop, I thought I'd die, that I'd never be whole again because I had never been whole before, except when you touched me." Her voice was so low he could barely hear her. He took a small step toward her. Slowly, as if he was afraid of scaring her. As if clocking the movement, she swung her gaze back to him and pinned him with those icy hazel eyes he had missed so much.

"And then you saw what I could do, that I could hurt people, too, and still, you just wouldn't go away. You were so fucking kind to me that night – and when you put me in that cab, I thought that was the end of things. You'd seen the real me, and I mean, who wants a woman with that sort of off-the-rails temper?" Again, her chuckle broke into a sob. She wiped her eyes and her nose with the sleeve of her shirt.

Blackman didn't say anything because she already knew the answer.

He did.

Because even after she'd broken the dishes and asked for a divorce, he still came to campus to see if she was okay. He sat on their bench so she would know he still loved her despite whatever was happening.

That he'd always love her.

That the last year hadn't diminished how much he loved her.

"Sometimes – I don't think you understand how much I love you, how much I *feel* for you, how much I don't want to go back to a life without you," Maggie said. Her voice was quiet, and she slipped her hands into the back pockets of her jeans as if she didn't know what to do with them anymore.

"Then why did you leave?" he asked gently.

Maggie lowered her gaze again and took some time to collect her thoughts. She took a deep breath and met Blackman's eyes again.

"After you were shot," Maggie said. "Everyone kept telling me you weren't going to make it. They wanted me to be prepared to say goodbye. Even Jon didn't think you were going to pull through."

She started to cry.

"Sweetheart," Blackman said as he took another step toward her, but Maggie shook her head and took another step back. She swung her head around the room as if looking for a way out. The room was so goddamn small. She wished they were doing this anywhere but in this tiny fucking room. With another deep breath, she looked back to Blackman.

"I understand love can be finite, that bad things happen. People die. People leave. People get sent away." She paused and wiped her nose with the back of her hand. "Da didn't send me away because of what I did to that boy. I mean, that was part of it, but that wasn't really the deciding factor."

Maggie paused and sighed deeply. She pulled her hands out of her pockets, wiped her face again, and pushed her hair back behind her ears. "If it was just that I needed structure," she began again. "Da could have sent me to a convent school in Paris or Barcelona or Ireland, for God's sake, but he didn't. He needed an ocean between us because I looked so much like my mother, it was driving him mad. Every time he looked at me, he saw her before he saw me."

She willed Blackman to understand, to follow her own fucked up logic.

"He loved my mum so much he had to send me away because seeing me every day hurt too much. It was killing him," she said pointedly.

Blackman waited patiently, but Maggie could tell he didn't understand what she was saying. He wasn't hearing what she needed him to hear.

"And I feel that way about you, and you were *going to die*, and I didn't know what I was going to do." More tears ran down her face, falling from her chin and dampening the front of her shirt. All Blackman wanted to do was take her in his arms and hold her, but that wasn't what she needed. So, he didn't move. He knew there was something she wanted to tell him, needed to tell him. Something that would explain why she was so ashamed.

"I should have been braver for Jamie, but I wasn't," she started again. "The family arrived, and everyone was taking care of him but me, and they were doing a better job of it. Every day I sat by your hospital bed felt like it would be the last, and the family was whispering about funeral arrangements and organ donation. They didn't think I could hear, but I could. I heard everything they said." She paused and lowered her eyes to Blackman's chest.

She was crying again.

"And all I wanted to do was die right along with you," she said, wiping at the tears that wouldn't stop falling. "I couldn't imagine a life without you or how I was supposed to raise Jamie alone. And I wasn't eating, and I wasn't sleeping, and I couldn't fucking think. Nick finally made me go home so I could get some sleep and maybe eat a meal."

She stopped talking. She wiped at her face again with her sleeve and sniffled. Blackman took a half step toward her.

"I didn't know we had a gun," she said quietly. Her eyes were sharp, almost accusatory, because a gun wasn't a secret you kept from your wife. Blackman stopped moving and went still; the room around him went cold. Maggie held his eyes.

"I was in the closet going through a box of your old jerseys. I wanted something of yours to sleep in, and I found a box. A lockbox. It had a combination." She paused as if to give Blackman the chance to say something. Anything, but Blackman was silent. He'd stopped breathing.

"The combination was the date of the hockey game. It was easy to figure out." Maggie lowered her gaze to the floor as if she was unable or unwilling to hold his gaze for this part of her story. "I'd never held a gun before. I know the boys have, but they never showed me how to shoot or anything. I mean, I wasn't even sure how to check to see if it was loaded."

"Jesus," Blackman breathed. He began to shake. He started to cross the room slowly.

"Nick came in, and I was sitting on the bed with it in my lap, and I thought he was going to shit himself. I've never seen him so terrified. He held up his hands and started babbling on about... I'm not even sure what – I wasn't listening. I – I --," Maggie's voice faltered. "I don't think it was loaded, or maybe the safety was on. I – I couldn't make it work, and Nick – fuck, he hadn't hit me since we were kids, and he'd never hit me that hard before. He knocked me clear off the bed and... I don't know what happened next. I remember Sherry coming in, but I don't think she saw the gun, and then I was in the bath, and then I think Sherry gave me sleeping tablets because the next thing I knew, it was thirty hours later, and you weren't dead."

Blackman was standing so close to her that he could smell the soap she had used that morning. Another man's soap and a twinge of jealousy coursed through him like an electrical current.

"Then you started to improve, and then you woke up, and I was so ashamed of myself. I mean, what kind of wife does that? What kind of mother? When you looked at me that first time, something inside me broke because you were so strong, and I..."

Blackman caught her before her legs gave out, and she fell to the floor. He pulled her tightly against him and moved them toward the chair John had been sitting on earlier. Blackman sat down and pulled Maggie onto his lap. He wrapped one arm around her waist, settling the other at the base of her skull. She sobbed uncontrollably into his chest, her body convulsing with the force of her sorrow and shame.

"How," she wept, "can you love a woman like that? You were so strong, and I should have been strong and brave, but I wasn't. I was a coward, and I can't bear it. I can't bear the shame of it."

Blackman buried his face in her hair and let her cry.

"Sweetheart," he said softly. "It's okay. I'm here, I'm fine, we're fine. I love you so much, and I could never be ashamed of you. I wasn't there when you needed me, but I'm here now, and I'm not going anywhere, ever again." He pressed his lips against her hair.

He waited as more sobs racked her body, her tears soaking through his shirt, her breath hot against his chest. And he held her tighter, so tightly he was afraid he was going to hurt her, but he needed to feel her against him. Her solidity, her breath, her life. It terrified him on a molecular level that he'd almost lost her, and he hadn't even known it.

For more than a year, this had been eating her alive, and she hadn't told him, hadn't confided in him. Maybe she hadn't let him in, but he could have done so much more, tried so much harder. He thought back to the night after the altercation with Semple. He should have forced the issue then. He should have taken her upstairs and made her tell him everything.

He should have been a braver man.

Then there was the gun.

He'd almost forgotten about that fucking gun.

When they bought the house in that neighborhood, Nick insisted he get a gun for protection. Actually, first, he insisted that Blackman learn how to use a gun.

"You're a fucking American, Blackman. How do you not *know how to use a gun?"*

"I'm a fucking lawyer, Nick. Why would I know shit about guns?"

"Every American knows how to use a gun. It's like a requirement or something. I mean, it's in your bloody Constitution. It's like the OK Corral over there."

"This is Philly, Nick. Not Texas."

"The OK Corral was in Arizona, you twat. You're a prosecutor. You know just how rough the city is, and now you're in that house in that neighborhood. A gun might not go amiss."

"I'm not getting a gun, Nick. End of discussion."

And then there were some break-ins and a carjacking, and then Lennie brought it up while they were in London for the holidays, and the next thing Blackman knew, he'd not only learned how to shoot a gun, he'd bought a gun, which he regretted as soon as he brought it home. Then he decided not to tell Maggie because he already knew what she was going to say, so he put it in a lockbox and buried it in a box of his old jerseys. Then he forgot about it. He couldn't even remember where he'd put the bullets or if he'd even purchased bullets. It had been so long ago.

"And Jamie hates me," she sobbed bringing him out of his thoughts.

Blackman sighed.

"Jamie doesn't hate you, honey," he said against her hair. "He's just being a teenager and a bit of an asshole, and he takes you for granted, but we can fix that. *I* can fix that. Trust me, the only thing Jamie wants is for you to come home. He wants us to be together again."

Maggie cried harder.

"I want to go home," she sobbed.

"Then," Blackman said, and he kissed her head again. "Let me take you home, sweetheart."

Chapter 21

For the first time in a long time, Blackman watched his wife sleep. When they had gotten home, Maggie had gone right to bed – their bed – and curled up on her side. She was asleep in minutes, curled up tightly using her arm as a pillow. She looked like a woman who hadn't slept in days, weeks, maybe months. Blackman covered her with the duvet and sat on one of the brown leather chairs next to the windows overlooking their small backyard. He watched his wife for a long time. He felt like he hadn't seen her in years.

And maybe he hadn't.

Until she was safely tucked into their bed, it had never really occurred to him how close he had come to losing her. For the last four nights he'd gone to sleep telling himself she'd come back, that he could fix things. *They* could fix things. That there would be a happily ever after because anything else was unimaginable. Because he loved her so much, and he knew she loved him. Yet, he had foolishly discounted her pride, her pathological need to keep everyone around her safe. Her deep-rooted fear of disappointing the people she loved. Maggie could beat a man senseless, break a cop's nose, and then apologize to the witnesses for subjecting them to the indignity of her violence, and despite what she thought, she wasn't violent by nature. Her temper aside, she was just passionate and occasionally unpredictable, and sometimes, her better angels weren't quite loud enough for her to hear.

Blackman resisted the urge to touch her; she needed to sleep, and for now, being in the same room as her would have to be enough. He changed out of his work clothes into an old law school t-shirt and loose-fitting running pants. Then he pulled out his iPhone and texted Nick.

Blackman

Call off the sisters. Maggie is home. We're talking.

Before he could put his phone away, Nick texted back.

Brother Nick

Good man. They'll go shopping today. They'll expect a proper family dinner tomorrow. Text Sherry and check in. Don't forget to grovel.

Blackman sighed, texted a thumbs up emoji, and dropped the phone on his bedside table. After a few minutes of indecision, he climbed into bed, which felt like heaven to his tortured muscles. He rearranged the pillows so he could settle next to Maggie without disturbing her. Then he reached for the Marlon James book he'd been neglecting for weeks and started to read.

***

It was late afternoon when Maggie finally woke up. She blinked the sleep out of her eyes and looked at Blackman's sleeping form. He had fallen asleep with his book open across his chest, his reading glasses perched on the edge of his nose. His face was illuminated by a shaft of weak light that came through the skylight above their bed.

He was the most beautiful man in the world.

As they grew older, Maggie was amazed by how much more attractive an already attractive man could be with a bit of gray in his hair and the lines that came with time and experience. She reached up and brushed a lock of dark hair from his forehead. He had a point at Tilly's house. What *had* she expected? That he would just walk away? Let her throw away their lives together without a fight? Blackman had never backed away from a fight in his life, not on the ice, not in the courtroom, and not with her, but like every other time in her life, when her temper or pride had gotten the best of her, she hadn't been thinking.

She'd simply been reacting.

She slipped off his glasses and put them on his nightstand along with his copy of *A Brief History of Seven Killings,* then ran her fingers down the curve of his face, over his full, soft lips. She paused on the hard angle of his chin, where she could still see the faint scar from a high stick he took in high school. He opened those beautiful brown eyes and looked at her.

"Hey," he said softly.

"Hey," she answered.

She pushed the duvet away and moved closer to him. Before the shooting, he had always slept in only a pair of boxers, no matter how cold it was. Since the shooting, however, he'd started sleeping in a t-shirt and pajama bottoms as if he was trying to hide all his new scars from her. Now, she rarely saw him without a t-shirt, and when they made love, it was always in the dark and beneath the sheets. Maggie wasn't entirely sure when she had last seen her husband naked or when he had last seen her naked. It was so unfair. She had been so unfair to him.

She moved her hand to the hem of his shirt and then beneath it. He breathed in sharply as she moved her hand over the strong plain of his stomach. She sat up and pulled off his t-shirt. Then pulled off her own shirt and jeans in quick succession, leaving her in only a utilitarian bra – a hideous black thing that had seen better days – and a pair of old, faded boy cut briefs that were a world away from the sexy lace panties she used to wear.

Maggie moved her body over her husband's and brushed her lips over his as he wrapped his arms around her and pulled her against him. She could feel his heart pounding in his chest. She deepened the kiss and slipped her tongue into his mouth. They moved together tentatively, nervously. As if they were both afraid something that had been lost might not be found.

He ran trembling hands down her back, over the bumps of her spine, and cupped her backside. She moaned into his mouth as she felt his erection press against her thigh. She tunneled her hands through his hair, and they lost themselves in the kind of kiss they hadn't shared in over a year.

A long fucking year.

She felt Blackman unhook her bra and pull it from her body, so her soft breasts could press against his chest, her nipples hard against his skin. She broke the kiss and slid her lips over his jawline and down his throat, where her tongue slid against his hot, sensitive skin. She peppered his chest with soft open mouthed kisses and felt the thrill of his pleasure as he moaned when she slid her tongue over one of his nipples. She took her time there, licking and teasing in the way he liked, the way he needed. Slowly, she moved her lips down his trembling body until she reached the Frankenstein scar on his side.

"Oh, God, Maggie," he panted as she ran her tongue over the knotted flesh. The first bullet wound. She took her time, exploring his scar thoroughly, tenderly. The same way she had explored his other scars the night she came home from Austin. The night she couldn't dump him. The night she realized her love for him was almost too much for her to bear.

She settled her body between his thighs as her mouth moved to the small entry wound the second bullet left behind, and as she slid her tongue over the indentation, she gently stroked the knotted flesh of the exit wound in his back.

Tears filled her eyes as he arched into her.

Tears filled his eyes as she tasted him.

She moved her mouth over the final set of scars: the bullet wound that nearly killed him and the scars from the subsequent surgeries that saved him. He shook beneath her, arched into her, and lost himself in the feel of her mouth while he ran his fingers through the silky waves of her red hair. When she finished exploring his damaged body, when he couldn't take it anymore, he pulled her up and rolled over, so she was beneath him. He kissed her hard, pushed her into the bed, and ran his hand down her body, pushing apart her thighs. She gasped as she moved his fingers over the hot wetness of her panties. Blackman groaned against her mouth. He had been so afraid to touch her, so afraid he'd find her dry and unyielding like the other times they'd been together over the last year. Those nights when she had barely been wet, unmoved by his kisses and caresses, that made everything that transpired between them awkward and uncomfortable, more obligatory and transactional than loving.

Or intimate.

Now, she pressed her body against him, pushing herself against his hand. Wanting. Needing. He rubbed her gently through her panties as he kissed her, swallowing her moans of pleasure. She broke the kiss and pressed her face against his neck as he hooked his fingers into the waistband of her panties. She lifted her hips so he could pull them off. Finally naked, he propped himself up on one elbow so he could take in the full beauty of her: her strong arms, her beautiful breasts, the slope of her stomach, her long, strong legs. She was the most beautiful woman he had ever seen.

His wife.

His world.

She looked up at him with soft, loving eyes swimming in tears.

"I missed you," she whispered as she reached for the running pants he was still wearing. He helped her push them down until he could kick them off. She reached for him and gently took his aching cock into her hand.

"Maggie," he whimpered.

She stroked him gently, up and down, the way he liked. She cupped his balls and teased him where he needed. He groaned helplessly in her grip. "Jesus, Maggie," he said, gently pulling her hand away. She started to say something, but he covered her mouth with his own. He slipped his tongue deep into her mouth as his warm fingers slid over her breasts, then her stomach, down between her legs. He ran his fingers over the inside of her thighs and then into the hot wetness of her. She cried out, arched against him. She reached for him, but he shifted away from her.

"Blackman," she begged, her breath hot against his mouth.

He moved away so he could see her, watch her. He slipped a second finger into her and stroked her deeply. She pushed against him, desperately panting his name.

"I have to feel you come, sweetheart. It's been so long, I need to see you," he whispered.

"I – I – please – I need you," she whimpered. Her eyes were wide, her face flushed with desire. Need. "I need you inside of me... please..." Her voice held a note of desperation he hadn't heard in too long.

"And I need you. I love you, and I'm going to give you everything, but you have to give me this first," he said softly. He moved his fingers deeper, and she was so incredibly wet he wanted to cry. He slid his thumb over her clit and moved the way he knew she needed. She gripped his shoulders tightly and buried her nails into his hot skin. She closed her eyes and cried out as he increased his pace, his pressure on her clit.

"That's it, Maggie, let it go... give me what I need," he whispered against her open mouth. She tried to kiss him, but she couldn't manage. She just pressed her mouth against his, panted against his lips. She tried to say something but couldn't. Everything was too much. The pleasure she felt at his touch, the safety she felt pressed against his long, strong body, the love she felt welling up in her soul. She felt his lips ghost her ear, his breath hot against her too sensitive skin.

"Come for me, Maggie." His voice held an edge of demand, the slightest hint of an order given, and her body knew instinctively what it had to do because, for the rest of her life, she would deny this man nothing. She pressed her head back against the pillow and screamed. Blackman, his eyes hazy with his own pleasure, moved with her, staying with her as she slipped over the edge.

"That's it, sweetheart, you're doing so well," he whispered, his forehead pressed to her so he could watch the pleasure on her face. She cried his name over and over as she spasmed around his fingers, the waves of her orgasm washing over him. He didn't stop moving, just slowed down, drawing out her pleasure, watching her intensely.

"Look at me, Maggie," he said, and she opened her eyes and slowly focused on his face.

"I love you," she whispered.

"I love you," he said, brushing his lips against hers. Slowly, sensually, lovingly. Still trembling from the aftershocks of her orgasm, she wrapped her arms around him and pulled him against her. Rolling over, she pushed him onto his back, swung her leg over his waist, and settled on top of him. He watched her, his face eager with anticipation, as she slowly guided him to her entrance.

"Maggie," he breathed. "My love, my wife." He reached up and cupped her face as she slowly took him inside her. He had to shut his eyes against the intensity of his pleasure. She was hot and wet, and so tight around him. She covered his hand with her own and whispered, "Look at me, Blackman."

He opened his eyes and held her gaze. Her icy hazel eyes shone in the dim light of the room. He ran his thumb over her lips, and she opened her mouth. He slipped his thumb inside and marveled at the feel of her tongue against his skin. She settled her other hand flat against his chest as she started to move. Slowly at first, rolling her hips tentatively, adjusting herself, taking him deeper until he was fully seated inside of her. He moved his hand away from her face, settling it on the back of her neck. She leaned back, and he moved his hands down her back, over the swell of her backside. He slipped his fingers into her most secret places, and she watched him closely until his eyes fell shut, and he lost himself in the feel of her. She set the pace, moving slowly at first, then increased their pace when he moved his hands over her hips. He gripped her tightly, possessively, breathing her name, worshiping it. Worshipping her.

"Maggie... Maggie..."

She moved faster, listening to his breathing, his cock thickening inside her. She leaned forward, pressed her body against his, and he wrapped his arms around her. She could feel his heart pounding in his chest.

"Blackman," she gasped.

She could feel his control slipping.

"Blackman, please," she begged.

He groaned as he rolled her over and drove himself into her. She wrapped her legs around him, matched his frantic pace, and lost control with him as he filled her with everything he had to give. Afterward, sweaty and breathless, they held each other tightly, and he whispered into her ear, "You're my entire world, Maggie."

"And you're mine," Maggie murmured as she closed her eyes. He kissed her temple and breathed in the scent of her. He closed his eyes, too. Grateful that she was his again, and he was hers.

Chapter 22

Blackman opened his eyes with a start and reached for Maggie, but she wasn't there. He had been deep in a dream, and as he came around, he couldn't quite orient his confused mind. There had been a noise that woke him up. A bang? Something dropping or breaking?

He sat up and looked around, almost surprised to see that he was in his bed, naked, sticky, and smelling of sex. He had been dreaming, but the memory was fading. He'd been in this room, and Maggie had been here, too. It was dark and cold, but it had been during the day. Maybe it had been raining? Probably. There had been a distant rumble of thunder, so it must have been raining.

Maggie had been sitting on the bed dressed in a hoodie and jeans, her feet bare. She'd been wet, like she'd gotten caught in the rain, something black and heavy in her hand. Blackman was in the closet doorway, reaching out to her, trying to talk to her, but no words would come out. Semple was standing in the doorway to the bedroom in a cheap, rumpled suit, a sneer on his face, and something in his hand. Maggie looked at Semple as if she could only hear what he was saying. Blackman couldn't get her attention, couldn't get her to look away from the detective. He couldn't get her to look at him, to listen to him, to focus on him.

Then he saw Maggie's hand move, and he saw the...

Blackman looked around the empty room as panic settled heavy on his chest. Maggie. Maggie had been there. They had been together; they had made love, and it had been incredible. Now, though, she was gone. He tried to listen to the house, to hear her moving around somewhere, but blood pounded in his ears, and he could hear nothing except the sound of his pounding heart. He scrambled out of the bed, his bad leg almost buckled beneath him. Naked and confused, he searched for his clothes. He had no idea how long he'd been asleep, but the light coming through the skylight said it was maybe late afternoon or early evening. How long could she have been gone? Blackman was just about to pull on his pants when Maggie breezed into the room, holding a plate of food and a heavy green hydro flask covered in stickers, wearing his law school t-shirt and nothing else.

"We really need to go to the store, love. Hope you're in the mood for peanut butter and overripe blackberries. And this apple has seen better days," Maggie said, completely unaware of Blackman's panicked look as she sat on the bed.

Blackman stood still for a moment, awkward in his nakedness. Once he could finally move his legs, he climbed back into bed and pulled the sheet over his waist. He reached for one of the sandwiches and leaned back against the headboard. His hands were shaking. He was shaking. His heart pounded like he'd just finished thirty laps in the pool.

Maggie took a bite of her sandwich, chewed, and looked at him curiously.

"Are you okay?" she asked. Her eyebrows raised.

"Just hungry." Blackman forced a smile. He settled on this version of the truth because he *was* hungry, but also because blurting out that he thought she'd walked out on him *again* sounded pathetic in light of what they had just done to each other, what he'd like to do to her again.

He took a bite of his sandwich, and Maggie looked at him for a beat longer.

"You know," she said a little sternly. "It's not nice that you keep calling John a war criminal. He's a nice guy who thinks very highly of you."

"You're right," Blackman admitted. "The war criminal comment was unkind." He reached for the hydro flask.

"Actually, I think he might have been some kind of organized crime hitman. He's got some crazy Eastern European ink. All sorts of interesting iconology," she said casually as if they were the kind of people who had friends who married men who had once been hitmen. Like being a hitman, either previously or currently, was an everyday thing.

Blackman choked on his water.

"You're shitting me," he blurted.

What the fuck?

Maggie smiled that smile that always drove him wild and shrugged her shoulders.

"Everyone's got a past, and whatever he used to do, he doesn't do it anymore. Now, he teaches self-defense classes to sorority girls. He's studying art, too. He paints, and he's quite good," Maggie said before she took another bite of her sandwich.

"Of course, he does," Blackman said, and a hint of bitterness slipped into his voice like he was jealous of the one time hitman now artist who everyone in the coffee shop seemed to love.

Maggie narrowed her eyes. "Be nice."

"I am being nice," Blackman protested, then popped the last of his sandwich into his mouth and reached for a section of apple. He was starving, and this wasn't going to cut it. He wondered if there was anything else in the fridge or the freezer. "Maybe we should introduce him to Fitz." Blackman was only half joking.

Maggie's face lit up.

"That's a fantastic idea! We should have a dinner party," she said as if the last week hadn't happened. Blackman had no earthly idea how to react to the suggestion of a dinner party. So, he chose to ignore it.

Maggie finished her sandwich and put her plate back on the duvet. Then she leveled Blackman with a serious look that he'd seen too many times before.

"I need to tell you something," Maggie said slowly.

"What?" Blackman looked at her warily.

"I broke my phone," she admitted, looking rather sheepish. As she did every time, she broke something expensive, which was, ironically, more often than their son.

Blackman let out a long suffering sigh.

"Did you drop it in the toilet again?" he asked because that was how she'd broken the last three phones. For the love of God and Steve Jobs, couldn't the women go to the bathroom without looking at Instagram? Or X? Or Threads? Or playing Wordle?

Maggie shook her head guiltily as a blush crept over her face. "No, I – I dropped a rock on it. Several times," she admitted.

"A rock?" he asked.

"Yes," she confirmed as she reached for another section of apple.

"You dropped a rock on it?" Blackman asked, hoping for additional information.

"Yes. Several times." Maggie nodded, still looking guilty.

"Do I want to know why you dropped a rock on your phone several times?"

"It wouldn't stop vibrating," she answered as if that was all the information he could possibly need.

"And," Blackman said patiently. "Why didn't you just turn it off?"

Maggie finished her sandwich and shrugged. "I was frustrated."

Blackman nodded and didn't ask any more questions. Sometimes, simple acceptance was the path of least resistance.

"Well, I think you're due for a new one anyway. We'll pick one up tomorrow when we go shopping," he said, reaching for the hydro flask.

"We're going shopping tomorrow?" Maggie asked, handing the hydro flask over.

"Yes."

"Why?"

"Because that bra and panty combination was hideous. We're getting you new underwear."

"Honey –"

"Don't honey me. You can either come with me, or I'll buy whatever catches my eye," Blackman said sternly.

Maggie sighed dramatically. "No weird bondage bras. I can never figure those things out."

"I make no promises," Blackman said with a wicked smile.

Maggie smiled and moved so she was tucked beneath Blackman's arm, which was warm and solid around her shoulders. He twirled a lock of her hair absently in his fingers. Maggie closed her eyes and enjoyed the moment; she'd missed his touch so much.

"Did you, by chance, drop my Jeep off at the dealer?" she asked.

"Nope, was a little busy," he answered as if the chaos of the last week hadn't happened.

"Yeah, I understand. I'll see if I can drop it off tomorrow."

They sat in a companionable silence and listened to the rain falling lazily against the windows.

"Maggie?" Blackman asked softly.

"Yes," she murmured, taking the hand that had been twirling her hair and bringing it to her mouth.

"I think we should go to London."

"We are, darling. For Christmas," Maggie answered quietly. She closed her eyes and enjoyed the warmth of Blackman's body pressed against hers.

"No," he said, leaning his head against hers. "I think we should go permanently. I think we should move to London to be closer to the family."

Maggie turned around and looked at him, her eyes curious. Cautious.

Blackman shifted against the headboard and took both of her hands in his. "Hear me out," he said.

"I'm listening."

"I think it's time. Time for you, for us, to go back. Jamie's getting older, and I think being closer to the family would be good for him."

Maggie said nothing.

"And," Blackman said carefully, "I think it's time for you to go home. You've been here long enough."

Maggie blinked, and for a long moment, her face was inscrutable.

"This is home," she said rather weakly, unconvinced of the words even as they came out of her mouth,

"No, sweetheart," Blackman said, placing his palm gently against her warm cheek. "*This* is exile."

Maggie looked down, but she didn't move away from his touch.

"What about your job?" she asked.

Not her job, *his* job.

Always his fucking job.

"I hate Calvin Nicholson," Blackman said. His voice a little angry, a little resigned. "I hate what he's doing at work. I hate the politics of it all. I think it's time to move on."

Maggie looked up and met his eyes, hers were shining.

"What about Jamie?" she asked because she couldn't agree to upend their lives again without considering its effects on their already angry son.

"Jamie loves his family," Blackman answered. "And I think moving so we can be closer to them will make him happy."

"We don't know that," she said uncertainly as if she was afraid that when this information was sprung on Jamie and he was displeased, she would once again bear the brunt of his anger. Blackman leaned forward until his forehead was against hers.

"It's time, sweetheart. It's time to go home."

Tears pooled in her eyes, and for the first time, he understood, *really understood*, how much she wanted to go back home. Just how much she might have *needed* to go home. He wondered if she had not broached the subject earlier because she didn't want to ask him to change his life for her, because she didn't want to inconvenience him or, God forbid, disappoint him. And some part of her, he understood now more than ever, might have been afraid he would say no, that he'd prioritize the DA's office over her. For such a brilliant woman, she could be so foolish.

"I don't know," she said softly, but he knew she was lying.

"Yes, you do."

"What about Fitz?"

"Maybe it's time for him to go home, too."

Maggie didn't say anything as she turned around and once again leaned against Blackman, pulling his arm more tightly around her shoulder.

"I have to think about it," she said in a voice that suggested she'd been thinking about this very thing for a very long time, even if she was unwilling to admit it out loud.

"I understand. You can talk to the sisters about it tomorrow night over dinner. See what they think," Blackman said with a nonchalance he didn't feel.

Maggie lurched forward, turned around, and stared at Blackman open mouthed.

"The sisters? Dinner? Here? The sisters are *here*? In Philadelphia?"

"Fitz called London," Blackman said, resigned.

"Of course, he did." Maggie groaned.

***

It was a little after six p.m. when basketball practice let out. Maggie, dressed in a heavy coat, blue jeans, and thick-soled Doc Marten boots, leaned against her Jeep. Her red hair gathered underneath a heavy purple and gold wool hat Blackman hated.

She waited patiently as the boys trickled through the gym door into the rainy December night. She knew most of the boys, and they greeted her as they walked past her, either to climb into other waiting cars or to head to the subway for their long trips across the city.

Jamie was the last to come through the door. He'd been like that since he was little: first to arrive and last to leave the field, the court, or the pool. He stopped when he saw her. He looked tired and disheveled, as if he, too, hadn't slept well all week. His jaw was covered in pale reddish blond stubble; he was so breathtakingly handsome, just like his father.

Maggie pushed herself off the Jeep, took a step toward him, and waited. He looked at her for a long time, or what felt like a long time, before he walked over to her. His stride so much like his father's. Then he dropped his bookbag and wrapped his arms around his mother.

"I'm sorry, Mom," he said gently. "I'm sorry I hurt your feelings." His voice was wet and young. So very young.

Maggie held onto him tightly and let the tears fall down her cheeks. "No, love, *I'm* sorry."

***

Blackman leaned against the bar and watched with quiet amusement as the sisters, in all their glory, grilled a chastened Maggie while Fitz, Gabe, and Jamie played a round of pool. The small neighborhood restaurant was a favorite haunt of the Harrington's whenever they came to town, especially if Jamie was with them. The pool tables, dart boards, and flat-screen televisions perpetually tuned to sports, showing everything from Australian rules football to cricket to college hockey, were the perfect distractions for young and old men alike.

But tonight, Jamie didn't seem too interested in the college hockey game, pro hockey game, or the English football game playing on each of the many screens. He seemed much more content just to be surrounded by his doting family, who took turns praising his stunning good looks, showing him pictures of their friend's daughters, and kicking his ass in pool and darts, respectively.

Blackman, like everyone else but Fitz, who was in his usual suit, was dressed casually in well worn jeans and a blue button down shirt that hung nicely on his broad swimmer's shoulders. He moved his eyes from his family to the college game on the television behind the bar as Sherry Driver Harrington excused herself from Maggie's excoriation and made her way toward Blackman.

Tall and loose limbed, Sherry Driver-Harrington had a way of moving that made her the center of attention in any space she occupied, all thanks to her natural beauty and formidable height. A former collegiate and almost Olympic diver, she met Nick at a fundraiser for childhood cancer not a week after the family vacation in Greece when Blackman told Nick he deserved better than the last girl. Well, Sherry Driver was definitely better, and unlike the girl before her, she had no problems with the family business. Nick and Sherry knew each other less than a month before they ran off to the Spanish coast to elope. The Driver family had been horrified, and as soon as Sherry and Nick returned from Spain, a hasty church wedding was arranged. The elopement story and the fact their first born came screaming into the world barely eight months later was relegated to the category of *things we don't talk about in front of the children*.

Now older and more mature, Nick and Sherry were the picture of respectability. They were the responsible and possibly boring parents of two impulsive boys. When Sherry wasn't trying to keep Brendan and Benjamin on the straight and narrow, she ran a south London woman's shelter with an iron fist. No one crossed Sherry Driver-Harrington partly because they knew who her husband was but more so because they knew who *she* was, and she was a force of fucking nature, with or without the Harrington name attached to hers.

Now in her forties, Sherry still had the long, lean build of an almost Olympic diver, which, along with her blonde hair and emerald eyes, made her as beautiful, if not more beautiful, than she'd been in her twenties. Her clothes were the kind of casual only the wealthy could wear, and Sherry Driver-Harrington wore them well.

Better than most.

But her outward appearance belied her barroom brawler attitude. She was probably the only woman alive who could keep Nick Harrington in line, and Nick knew it. Everyone knew it.

Sherry leaned against the bar and hit Blackman with those emerald green eyes.

"Buy a girl a drink?" she asked in an Irish accent that always seemed thicker when she was in the States because she knew Americans loved it even though they had difficulty understanding it. Blackman signaled to the bartender and waited for Sherry to start busting his balls for the chaos of the last week, but instead, she let her eyes go soft.

"How are you doing, love?" she asked with a depth of kindness Blackman had neither expected nor knew what to do with. He sighed. Sherry's sympathy cut far deeper than her anger could have. He opened his mouth to respond, but Sherry cut him off sharply.

"And don't lie to me, Blackman Smith," she warned with an arched eyebrow.

"I wouldn't dare," Blackman replied with a smile he couldn't quite hold. He looked down at his half empty pint glass. "I've barely slept in a week, but I think I haven't slept well for far longer than that. I'm exhausted, and I feel... whiplashed," he admitted honestly. There was no point in lying to Sherry. She'd simply call bullshit and demand the truth anyway. "She really hurt you." It wasn't a question, and there was no judgment in her voice. It was just an observation.

"She didn't mean to," Blackman replied picking up his beer.

"Doesn't matter whether she meant to. It's important that you recognize your own hurt, and once you do that, you'll find it easier to move forward," Sherry said knowingly. Clearly a woman who'd been in his shoes once. More than once.

"You learn that in marriage counseling?" he asked not unkindly. She and Nick had done more than one round of marriage counseling over the years, and they weren't shy about admitting it.

Sherry paused as the bartender handed her another glass of wine. She waited until the young man made his way back to the other end of the bar before she answered.

"I know you love Nick, but he's not the easiest man in the world to be married to," Sherry said with a smile. She slipped onto a barstool and got comfortable. Blackman nodded but didn't say anything. He remembered vividly when Sherry threatened to throw Nick out, take the kids, file for divorce, and go back to Dublin. In that order. Nick had called Blackman at two in the morning a drunken, crying mess, and Blackman had been grateful he'd been in the office working late, if for no other reason than he didn't have Maggie yelling into his ear about what an unforgivable asshole her brother was. Guilt churned in Blackman's gut; he should have called Nick the night Maggie left.

Blackman finished his beer and waved for another. He looked over at Maggie, who leaned forward in her chair, elbows planted on the table, a glass of red wine in her left hand as she gesticulated with her right. He wanted to be next to her, wanted her to lean against him, to rest her head on his shoulder, to wrap her arm around him. He wanted not to be terrified he was going to wake up alone. He wanted to know that they were really moving forward.

They'd had a wonderful evening the night before, making pasta with sausage together. They'd sat around the kitchen table and talked and ate like a family. Like a happy family. They talked about their week without talking about their week, and when dinner was done and the dishes put away, they went into the living room and watched a basketball game. The three of them on the sofa, Blackman and Jaime bookending Maggie as she leaned against Blackman and slept through most of the game. And then they went to bed, and Blackman couldn't fall asleep because he couldn't shake the panic he'd felt that afternoon. He'd finally drifted off around dawn, and for all his fretting, he still woke up alone, but at least there was a note on the pillow.

Went for a run. XX

"Are you going to be able to get past this?" Sherry asked, drawing him out of his thoughts. Blackman didn't look at her as he took the fresh beer from the bartender. Of course, he'd get past this. What else could he do? Maggie came back. She didn't divorce him. She didn't find a better man. She didn't run off to God knows where so she could fall on a sword that didn't need falling on.

Sherry waited patiently. She was always patient with Blackman. He was, after all, her favorite sibling-in-law, which was saying something because she had a baker's dozen of them.

"Yes," Blackman said after a long pull from his glass. Sherry drank her wine and waited to see if he would say more, but he remained silent. He let his eyes drift to Maggie and then to the game. Sherry gave him a few minutes to collect his thoughts.

"The Harringtons aren't easy people to love," she finally said, breaking the protracted silence.

Blackman shook his head. "No," he corrected, "my father wasn't an easy man to love."

"You hated your father," Sherry observed. She'd never met Blackman's father, but she'd attended the funeral. It was a well-attended affair where no one seemed to take much notice of the deceased. Instead, it seemed like one long networking exercise that just so happened to involve a coffin and a hole in a nicely manicured cemetery Blackman never visited.

Blackman chuckled mirthlessly as he reached for his beer, but his hand stalled, so instead, he turned the pint glass in lazy circles. "I love the Harringtons; I always have. From the minute I met them. All of them. You." He tilted his head toward Maggie and the sisters. "Them. *This* is the only family I have."

Sherry nodded. "I know, Blackman, and we love you, but –"

"This was as much my fault as hers," he blurted out. "We stopped talking, or maybe she stopped talking, and then I stopped talking, and I never asked why. I never asked why we stopped. I just ignored it."

"Why do you think that is? That you ignored it?" Sherry asked thoughtfully.

"Because." Blackman looked at Sherry and swallowed his pride. "I was afraid she was ashamed of me."

Sherry's face was inscrutable, but Blackman's was an open book of misery and self-reproach.

"Ashamed–" Blackman stopped and collected himself. "Ashamed that I –I'd been shot, that I hadn't handled it better. I was in so much pain – afterward – after I woke up. And I was useless," he said bitterly. His face burned with shame. Some days, the pain had been so bad he cried, and some days, it was so bad he couldn't make it to the bathroom in time. He was a proud man, but there were days when the only person in the world he wanted was Fatimah, and other days when he wished he'd died on that cold street because an early death would have been better than the indignity of shitting himself.

"So, I was a coward. I let things get out of hand. I'd been afraid she was going to leave me for months, and instead of confronting her, I worked late or avoided being alone with her." He looked into his beer glass. "When everything happened, when she broke the dishes and left – I was almost relieved," he admitted. "I – I thought about letting her go. Just for a second – you know – but – but I couldn't." Tears pricked his eyes.

"Because you love her, darling," Sherry said sympathetically. Because she knew what it was like to both want to let your spouse go while also not knowing how to live if they left.

"Love isn't always enough," he said softly. "Maybe she deserves better."

Sherry sipped her wine and watched Blackman thoughtfully. Her eyes were bright and curious when Blackman finally looked at her.

"I have never met two people so determined to believe that their partners married down. Maggie's been saying for years, literally years, that you deserve better than she. Now, must I listen to you say the same thing? I mean, you two are hopeless. Thank God you two married each other. No other family could deal with you."

Blackman picked up his beer and took a deep pull.

"You two need to talk to each other, really talk to each other, and you need to let her know how much she hurt you, and that you're afraid she's going to do it again. I know you two fucked the shit out of each other yesterday," Sherry said with a wicked grin. "But the last week isn't going to go away with a tumble in that ridiculously oversized bed of yours or wherever else you two fucked. *You need to talk.*"

"We talked," Blackman said, which was true. They'd said more in Tilly and John's sitting room than they'd said to each other in over a year.

"Congratulations. You talked. Now you need to talk some more," Sherry said, picking up her wine glass—the voice of inconvenient reason. Blackman looked over at Maggie, who slapped a hand over her mouth as she laughed at something Pippa said. He wondered if they, too, were talking about yesterday's make-up sex.

"Sherry –"

"Now you listen to me, Blackman Smith. I know you're happy she came back and that you two talked, but you're still not sleeping, so clearly, there are more things to discuss. There's no shame in getting a professional involved."

Blackman nodded. He thought about bringing up the incident with the gun but decided against it. If Sherry didn't know all the details of that story, Blackman didn't need to land Nick in the shit. Blackman looked back at Maggie and saw her staring at him. Watching him. She smiled shyly; he smiled back. His stomach clenched.

Christ, he loved her so much.

"Darling, Christmas break is coming soon. Why don't you let us take Jamie back to London early. Joey's boys are coming back from uni, and it'll be good for your boy to spend some time with some proper juvenile delinquents," Sherry said with a smile.

"I asked Maggie if she wants to go back to England."

"You what?" Sherry's eyebrows shot up.

Blackman met Sherry's eyes. "I asked Maggie if she wants to move back – for all of us to move back. For good. To leave Philadelphia."

"What about your job? I thought you loved your job," Sherry said, unable to hide her excitement over the prospect of this arm of the family returning to the fold.

Blackman shook his head, picked up his beer, and took a drink.

"Can I be honest with you?" he asked.

"Always, love," Sherry said with a smile.

"I fucking hate my job. When Jon Pierce was in charge, it was different, but this guy Nicholson's just a political flunky, and he's dumber than shit. He only gave me the Dixon case because he didn't want Marquetta Muhammed Abdullah to be the face of the DA's office when Fox News came into town. He's a stupid racist fuck," Blackman said quietly. He and Marquetta had been friends for years, but since he'd gotten the Dixon case, she'd been notably cooler towards him, as if he'd somehow gone out of his way to screw her over.

The Dixon case was a goddamn albatross around his neck.

"And my job aside," he said, amazed at how much the Harringtons cared about his job. "I think it would be good for Jamie to be closer to his cousins. The teenage years are hard, and he's turning into a bit of an asshole. The cousins might bring Mr. Freshmen Quarterback down a peg or two."

"What does Maggie think?"

"About the move or about Jamie being a dick?" Blackman asked with an arched eyebrow.

"Blackman," Sherry warned as she picked up her wine glass.

"She thinks it's a stress reaction," Blackman admitted.

"Is it?" Sherry asked. She seemed genuinely curious.

"No," Blackman said, draining his beer and signaling for another. He wasn't driving, so why not. Christ knew he earned an extra beer or two after the fucking week he'd had.

"Nick brought up the prospect of a job at Dad's funeral. I was considering it, but then the shooting happened, and I was distracted. But now..." His voice trailed off, and Sherry weighed her words carefully.

"You know, Blackman," Sherry said carefully, diplomatically, "with Fatimah gone – God rest her soul."

"Verily we belong to Allah and truly to him shall we return," Blackman automatically said in Arabic. Sherry waited a beat, always impressed by the beautiful Arabic that came out of Blackman Smith's very WASPish mouth.

"Indeed. Now you have no family here, Fitz aside, but it takes more than an uncle and a brother to get you through the hard times. Family is important, and honestly, we all wish you were closer. Fitz, too. Things are different in London. He could really flourish if he decided to come home," Sherry said gently but with an edge of eagerness to her voice. Blackman suddenly suspected this might have been something the family had been wanting for years. Blackman nodded. Out of the corner of his eye, he saw Maggie get up and walk toward him. Sherry looked back and smiled as Maggie neared.

"Maggie, love, would you mind if we took Jamie and popped out for some food?" Sherry asked as soon as Maggie was close enough.

"No, of course not," Maggie said.

"Splendid," Sherry said, slipping off her barstool. She leaned down and gave Maggie a kiss on the cheek. "We'll probably keep him for the night, too. He hasn't been spoiled by his aunties in months," Sherry said with a wink, then leaned over and kissed Blackman on the cheek before she walked away.

Maggie took the empty barstool on the other side of Blackman. She opened her legs and scooted forward so she was pressed against him, her cheek resting on his shoulder as she watched Sherry gather up the family, drop a pile of bills on the table, and hurry everyone toward the door. Everyone but Jamie, who seemed deep in conversation with Gabe, waved goodbye. Clearly, he had gotten over the events of the last week.

Once the Harringtons were gone, it felt as if the restaurant was practically empty. That was how much space the Harringtons seemed to take up literally and metaphysically. Maggie set a hand on Blackman's back and rubbed him gently. He closed his eyes against the rush of emotions that came with her touch.

"You're not okay," Maggie said gently.

"Just tired," Blackman answered knowing he was pushing them toward the same patterns that had gotten the dishes broken.

"You didn't sleep well?" she asked, a little surprised. She'd had the best sleep she'd had in months.

"No," he replied quietly.

Maggie looked at the side of his face and then reached for him. She hooked his chin with her fingers, his stubble rough against her skin, and gently turned his head so he was looking at her. She searched his dark brown eyes, which seemed to reflect so many emotions so quickly that she couldn't keep up with them.

"Talk to me, my love," she implored.

Blackman looked at eyes so filled with love he could barely breathe. He reached up and took her hand and brought it to his lips. He kissed her softly, then he moved her hand so he could look at her wedding set in the dim light. He'd never forget that drunken night he'd plopped down his credit card and impulsively purchased a two-caret diamond ring that was too big for her small hands and too ostentatious for a poor graduate student. None of her friends knew about her family's money, and when he'd put the ring on her finger, he wondered if he was trying to impress her, her family, or, God forbid, his father.

He wanted to say so many things to her, so many things about how much he loved her, how much he needed her. How much her story about the gun terrified him, how much the idea of Nick hitting her enraged him. How much making love to her yesterday meant to him, how much he wanted to see her in the new panties he'd bought for her that afternoon. How terrified he was of losing her, but nothing came out. This whole mess had happened because he couldn't talk to her, and now that he wanted to, there were too many thoughts running through his head, and he couldn't get a handle on any of them.

So, he took a deep breath, picked one, and started small.

"When I woke up yesterday, and you were downstairs making sandwiches, I thought maybe you'd left again, that maybe you'd come home with me, but changed your mind," he said, still staring at her hand.

Maggie wrapped her fingers around his and held tightly.

"That's why you were standing beside the bed looking upset?"

Blackman nodded.

Maggie leaned her head against his arm, pressed her cheek against his bicep, and ran her thumb over his wedding band.

"You're afraid you're going to wake up one morning, and I'm going to be gone *gone*. Not just making sandwiches in the kitchen gone."

"Yes," Blackman admitted. He hated the fragile quality of his voice.

"I understand. I hurt you badly," she said. A statement of fact. Because she had hurt him, she had hurt him and Jamie. She'd been angry and selfish and thoughtless to a man who had only loved her unconditionally since the night he met her.

"Yes. You did," he admitted because he had to admit it. He had to be honest with her even if it terrified him. Maggie didn't say anything. She just leaned her face against his arm and rubbed his back. They sat like that for a long time.

"Would you like to get something to eat? You hungry?" Maggie asked, breaking the silence.

"I could eat," he said quietly.

Maggie called the bartender over and ordered two cheeseburgers, one with a side salad and one with extra fries. "Make sure the one with the side salad is still mooing, but the one with the fries should be medium. Not medium rare but *medium*," she said clearly and a little sternly.

That bartender nodded and walked away.

"You're going to eat my fries," Blackman said, still watching the game on the television.

"Yes, but I'll let you have my pickles," she said, then pressed her lips against Blackman's arm and looked back at the television.

"Who's winning? Blue team or hideous green-we-need-to-fire-the-marketing-department team?" Maggie asked after a moment or two.

"Hideous green-we-need-to-fire-the-marketing-department team," Blackman answered with a chuckle.

"I'm rooting for the blue team."

"They're down by three," Blackman said.

"Well, you know me. I'm a sucker for a blue hockey jersey," Maggie said with a smile that he could feel against his arm.

***

The house was empty when they got home, and Maggie wondered briefly if Jamie had gone back to Fitz's to sleep or if the sisters had taken him back to whatever suite of rooms they had booked. Maggie followed Blackman into the house and closed and locked the door behind them. It wasn't that late, but she was tired, and she knew Blackman had to be beyond exhausted.

And sore.

She knew that her husband hadn't slept in their bed all week because he never slept in their bed when she was away.

Bed's too empty without you; I can't sleep...

Guilt knotted her stomach. She'd had a bed to sleep in, a dog to play with, and a former organized crime hitman making her homemade ramen.

Christ, she was a thoughtless bitch at times.

And that was after she'd broken all the dishes and walked out of the kitchen, leaving it looking like a not so natural disaster. Over their twenty years together, Maggie wasn't entirely sure if Blackman had so much as left an unwashed dish in the sink.

"Do you want me to make some tea?" she asked, stepping out of her boots, leaving them by the front door.

"No, let's go up. It's been a long day," Blackman said, stifling a yawn.

He stepped back and let Maggie walk up the stairs first, in part to be polite, but also so she didn't have to see the limp he hadn't quite been able to hide when he got off the barstool. When things settled down, she'd suggest another trip to the doctor, which he'd resist because he knew what the doctor was going to say: start using a cane.

And Blackman Smith was *not* going to use a cane.

When they reached their bedroom, Maggie gently pushed Blackman toward the bathroom, where she started the shower and then looked at him.

"Strip," she commanded.

He sighed.

"Sweetheart, I'm tired," he said on a sigh.

"And you'll sleep better after a hot shower with my best lavender body wash, and I promise: no funny business."

Blackman raised an eyebrow.

"Okay, minimal funny business. Now take off your clothes, 42," Maggie said with an innocent smile. Blackman sighed again, stepped out of his shoes, pulled the button down shirt over his head, and stepped out of his jeans. He stepped into the shower, yelped, and turned down the hot water. He could never understand how Maggie could endure such hot showers, which was part of the reason they rarely took them together. The few times they'd tried to make love in the shower in the early days, he'd always come out feeling slightly boiled and more than a little scalded.

He stood tall in the oversized stall with the pale yellow tile, the river stone floor Maggie loved so much, and the smoked glass door. The shower head was mounted high enough so Blackman had plenty of space to stand under the spray. Behind them was a stone bench that Maggie had insisted they have installed so that Blackman could sit down when his leg hurt too badly to make a shower enjoyable.

Blackman closed his eyes and tilted his head into the spray.

God, he was tired. So ridiculously tired.

He felt Maggie step behind him. He started to turn toward her, but she gripped his arms gently, so he remained facing away from her.

"Relax, darling," she said softly, her voice barely audible over the sound of falling water. She reached for the oatmeal and lavender soap she had loved since she was a barely eighteen-year-old girl flirting with an angry twenty-one-year-old boy back when they were both children playing adult. Maggie lathered her hands and started at Blackman's neck. She rubbed it gently, kneading the tense muscles with her strong hands. It felt so good Blackman had to brace his arms against the cool tile to maintain his balance.

He shifted his weight so his good leg steadied him. Maggie moved her hands to his shoulders, broad and strong, and worked on the tense muscles there. She took her time, not stopping until she felt the tension start to ease.

"That's it, love," she said softly, just loud enough to be heard over the water.

She moved her hands between his neck and shoulders, then ran them down the length of his back. She massaged his shoulder blades, then moved her hands along his spine. He groaned as she dug her palms into the space just above his backside.

"God, Maggie," he breathed. "That feels good."

She knelt behind him, running her hands gently over his long legs. Gentling the muscles she knew hurt him the most, just like she had done the night after he taught her how to ice skate. Like she had done so many nights after. As she ran her hands over his legs, she thought about how long it had been since she had done this for him. How long it had been since she had touched him, loved him. The unfairness of it all settled on her like a weight that made her heart ache.

Is it me? Are you ashamed of me?

She climbed back to her feet and pressed her naked body against his, her breasts soft against the firm muscles of his back. She wrapped her arms around him and listened to his breathing quicken as she ran her hands over his hard chest, through his dark hair, over his sensitive nipples.

"I am so sorry for what I did, for hurting you," she spoke clearly so he could hear her and be sure of what she was saying. "I will never hurt you like that again," she said, pressing her lips to his back, pressing her body against him. "I will never betray your trust again."

She felt Blackman cover her hands with his own.

"And I swear on everything I hold dear, you will never have to worry about waking up without me. I will never leave you, Blackman. Ever. You're all I want in this world."

She could feel his heart pounding beneath her hands.

"Do you believe me?" she asked.

"I believe you." His voice was thick with emotion.

"Can you forgive me?"

"Yes," he said, looking at her hands beneath his, the way their rings shone in the soft light of the shower.

"I love you, Blackman," she said, pressing her lips to his back.

They stood holding on to one another, the water streaming over them, hopefully washing away the pain and the hurt of the last week, of the last year.

Then Maggie slowly trailed her hands down the plain of his stomach until she found his erection. She wrapped her fingers around him, and he gasped as she stroked him.

"Maggie, God, Maggie," he panted.

She wrapped one hand around his waist and held him tightly.

"I love you, darling. I love you so much," she said, her voice soft.

He tried to say something, but he couldn't pull enough air into his lungs.

She moved over the length of him with long, firm strokes. He lost track of time as he lost himself in her touch, in the pleasure she gave him, in her love for him, in the way her touch still thrilled him.

"That's it, Blackman," she said, her face pressed against his back. Her own body growing warm and hot as she pleased him.

"Maggie," he panted, "Maggie, please, don't stop – God – I love you, I..." He thickened in her hand as she held him close, steadying him, grounding him.

Loving him.

"Mag—"

He cried as if almost in pain, his voice echoing around the shower stall, coming in long, fierce pulses. She moved with him until she was sure he was done, then she held his trembling body in her arms as the water rained down on them.

***

Maggie's head rested on Blackman's chest, his chest hairs tickling her nose, her warm, naked body pressed against him, her leg stretched across his bare thighs. She ran her fingers lazily over his stomach as she listened to him drift off to sleep. After months of sleeping on the edge of her side of the bed, it felt so good to occupy this space with him. He felt so good pressed against her body.

As his breathing deepened, she smiled to herself. She let her mind drift, her fingers tracing delicate designs on his skin, before tapping out a soft, gentle rhythm against his hip, images dancing across her mind.

Fall leaves floating in the wind, caught on cool breezes...

A wooden bench...

Heavy boots on gravel...

The soft sounds of deep throated laughter ...

A heavy tan coat that smelled of cedar...

The soft swish of loose fitting pants...

A pale moon high shining in a too bright blue sky...

Lights shining outside the tall windows...

Brown eyes watching...

Always brown eyes...

Watching...

Maggie drifted off to sleep, a poem unfurling in a mind that was finally at peace.

***

It wasn't quite dawn the first time Blackman woke up on Sunday morning. He was naked and curled around Maggie, who was wearing his old hockey jersey. She must have gotten cold during the night and pulled it on. Since they had been together, it was one of her favorite things to wear.

The first time he saw her in his jersey, standing in his kitchen, which would become their kitchen, he thought he might die of ... Joy? Love? Want? Need? Because he had been waiting his whole life for her to love him. And now they were in bed, their bed, and she was wearing his jersey from his college days, and even though his hockey playing days were over two decades behind him, the sight of her wearing his name and his number stitched across her back still meant the world to him. It always would. He buried his face in her hair and went back to sleep.

The next time he woke up, he was on his side, and she was pressed against his back, her arm around his waist, holding him close. She was so soft, so warm, so exquisite, so perfect. They stayed like that for a long time before he slowly turned over to look at her. Her hair was splashed over the white pillowcase like a spill of vivid red paint. She was breathtaking and brilliant, and he watched her until she opened her eyes and looked at him.

"Good morning, love," she whispered, reaching out and cupping his face as if nothing had changed between them, and he knew nothing had. Not really. She had left but never really left, and she had come back because she wanted to come back. Because she knew what they had together was more important than what she feared they might lose.

"Good morning, sweetheart," he said gently. He leaned forward and kissed her softly.

"Would you like toast with your coffee?" he asked as he wrapped his arms around her and pulled her close to him. She rested her face against his bare chest. He could feel her smile against his skin before she kissed him gently.

"In a little while," she whispered as she closed her eyes again.

Chapter 23

Marquetta Muhammed Abdullahi sat alone at a table in a small coffee shop three blocks from her house and five blocks from her office. She liked this place because it opened early on weekdays. Significantly earlier than the local Starbucks, which she hated on principle. How could a company charge that much money for burnt coffee? How could consumers spend that much money on burnt coffee? And she hated the people who worked in that particular Starbucks on principle because everyone who worked there acted like they would rather be anywhere else, maybe even in court with her, instead of making complex coffee concoctions for boring people. *And* they never got her name right, and they rarely got her order right, either. Further, they seemed to resent the people who ordered only one overpriced coffee, which they nursed for hours while completing more, or sometimes less, meaningful tasks on the free WIFI. Which, in Marquetta's opinion, was the entire point of a Starbucks. If management wanted their customers to buy more than one drink, maybe they should make the drinks more affordable.

Whereas this little hole-in-the-wall coffee shop run by two Mexican immigrants served incredible coffee and affordable pastries and didn't mind that people whiled away too many of their hours sitting around doing whatever they needed or wanted to do on the free WIFI. In fact, the two men were so grateful for the business that some days, they refilled an empty coffee mug for free.

For free!In this part of the city? With this kind of rent?

Incredible.

Marquetta, when she could afford it, left egregiously large tips. When she couldn't afford it, she left a standard five on the table. She had two boys in private high school and an ex-husband who was only good for writing checks when he had the money to cover them, which wasn't often. Goddamn smooth talking musicians with their goddamn sharp as glass cheekbones.

Marquetta was a fucking cliche, and she knew it. Because of their father, whom they never saw – her decision *not* his, and she would never apologize for it – her boys had never been allowed to go near a musical instrument. In fact, she raised them with a healthy disdain for the arts, which she sometimes felt guilty about. She was like the overbearing mother in the James Baldwin play *The Amen Corner* who tries to keep her only son away from jazz music, only to have him become obsessed with jazz music. Then, to add insult to injury, he falls for a white girl musician. Or maybe she had been a singer. Or perhaps she had just been a hanger-on.

Either way, she sure as shit wasn't a white girl with a decent job.

"May I join you?"

Marquetta looked up from her musings and scowled at Blackman Smith, who returned her scowl with an easy, affable smile.

She nodded curtly toward the empty chair on the other side of her table. Blackman set down his coffee cup and a bag of pastries before he settled into a chair that was clearly too small for him. If he minded, he didn't say so. Marquetta imagined that it was a common occurrence for a man his size. The world was no more designed to fit the unusually petite as it was to fit the exceptionally tall.

She glared, and he smiled, smiled as if he didn't have a care in the world, which was strange because last week, he looked like he was about to buckle under the weight of something unimaginable. Marquetta had seen the boss in Blackman's office, and there seemed to be some tension between them. She wasn't sure what was said, but she had the impression that if Nicholson hadn't left when he did, Blackman would have come around his desk and beaten the shit out of the smaller man. And wouldn't Marquetta have just loved every minute of that? Jesus, half the office would have been thrilled. Nicholson was no Jon Pierce, and no one would let him forget it. If

Nicholson and Smith had come to blows, Marquetta would have defended Blackman for free. Well, not for free. Old Main Line money didn't need a pro bono defense attorney, but she would have given him a discount.

"How's your Arabic?" he asked after a few moments.

"Better than yours, I imagine," she answered sharply. She watched Blackman with cold, appraising eyes. She had liked him once, trusted him, at least as much as she trusted any man who looked like him, but those days were behind her. Far behind her.

"Probably," Blackman said as he leaned back in his chair, crossed his legs, and switched languages. "My Egyptian is better than my standard, but my standard is still excellent, so I'm sure we can manage. Peace be upon you, my friend."

"And peace be upon you," Marquetta replied automatically in Arabic, a language she had learned from her parents, Nigerian immigrants. After a moment, she added, "I didn't know you spoke Arabic."

"My mother taught me, *verily we belong to Allah and truly to him we will return*, when I was young. I've kept it up out of respect for her; my son, Jamie, speaks it, but not as well. We're still working on that," Blackman said with that same easy smile.

"Your mother?" Marquetta asked, unable to keep the incredulity out of her voice.

"That's a story for another day, God willing. Now we have other things to discuss."

"Like what?" Marquetta asked warily.

"Like your future." Blackman paused and took a sip of coffee. "I'm leaving the DA's office today." He turned over his wrist and looked at his watch, an expensive Rolex Lennie had given him one Christmas. "I have a meeting with our boss in an hour, at which point, I will explain to him that I feel I was unjustly assigned the Dixon case and that he should reassign the case to you immediately, as you are surely as qualified if not more qualified than I. Plus, I'm leaving, as I said. Early retirement."

He paused.

Marquetta said nothing.

Blackman waited as if he was a man with all the time in the world. Maybe he was.

"And if he doesn't come around to your way of thinking?" she finally asked because that was obviously what he wanted her to ask. Blackman took his time with the answer. He reached for a pastry from the sack, broke off a piece, popped it into his mouth, and chewed thoughtfully.

"He will, but just in case," Blackman said after he swallowed. "I have a lunch meeting with a friend from college, a good friend. We played hockey together. They currently write for the New York Times. They're in town for a couple of days at my behest," Blackman said as he reached for his coffee. He took a sip and returned the cup to the table. He moved fluidly for a man his size; she found it almost unnerving.

"My friend's favorite topic is systemic racism. They're writing a book on it, in fact. And they're particularly interested in how systemic racism manifests itself in the judiciary system, especially in the DA's office. When they get interested in something, they're like a dog with a bone, and they're kind of an asshole. Like me. That's why we're friends," he said with a self-deprecating smile because they both knew he wasn't exaggerating. He could be an asshole when he wanted to be. She'd always liked that about him back when she liked him.

Marquetta narrowed her eyes. "I don't need a man to fight my battles for me, Smith, especially..."

"A white man," Blackman said, finishing her sentence. "I know, but I'm in the mood to be a bastard and maybe burn a few bridges while I'm at it. So why shouldn't you benefit from my – let's call it – a fit *of temper*, shall we?"

Marquetta leaned back in her chair and looked at Blackman with unabashed curiosity.

"Why?" she asked. "Why are you doing this?"

"Because," Blackman said with a smile. "It's the honorable thing to do, and my mother raised me to be an honorable man."

Marquetta wasn't going to let him off that easily.

"Does all of this have something to do with what happened last week?"

Blackman met Marquetta's eyes and studied her. His look was so intense that if she were a lesser woman, he would have made her uncomfortable, or, God forbid, he might have turned her on.

"My wife left me."

"I'm sorry to hear that, Smith," Marquetta said, and she meant it.

"I appreciate that," he said with a small smile. "But she came back home. We're working through some things, but I think it's time for a change of scenery."

"I'm glad you two are working things out. She seems like a nice woman," Marquetta said, and the kind words were more of a surprise to her than they were to him. Blackman finished his coffee and started to get to his feet, but Marquetta held up her hand. He settled back down again on the too small chair.

"Your friend from the *Times*," Marquetta said. "Regardless of what happens with the DA today, they're going to run the story? You're really going to torch the office on your way out the door?"

Blackman held Marquetta's eyes. His were bright in the early morning light, but his face was tight. He didn't look quite angry, but he looked something akin to angry.

"You thought I took the Dixon case from you. You thought I was part of Nicholson's boys' club." It wasn't a question.

"Yes," Marquetta said honestly. She held his gaze.

"I'm not that kind of man," Blackman said evenly.

This time, when Blackman got to his feet, she didn't say anything. He stood tall, looked down at her, and flashed a smile she recognized from court, the one he used when he was about to take someone apart on the stand. "But I *am* the kind of man to ruin a man's career for upsetting my wife."

Switching back to English, he said cheerfully, "See you 'round, counselor."

Then he turned and walked away, leaving Marquetta to wonder what had just happened.

***

As Blackman walked back to the office, his phone buzzed in his pocket. He pulled it out and saw a text from Fitz. It was a link. Blackman clicked on it.

Decorated Police Detective Commits Suicide: Detective Terrance Semple was found in his car in Gray's Ferry last night, dead from a self-inflicted gunshot wound. Semple had recently been charged with possession of child pornography.

Blackman smiled and pocketed his phone.

Sometimes, it wasn't enough to ruin a man's career.

Sometimes, you had to ruin a man's life.

Epilogue

Blackman had never been unemployed, and he found unemployment suited him. As a matter of fact, he enjoyed it. Immensely. He spent the winter and part of the spring making all the arrangements for the move to London. He flew back and forth several times, sometimes with Maggie, other times with Jamie, and a couple of times with Fitz. Rarely, if ever, did he fly alone.

Sherry helped him find a beautiful townhouse in the neighborhood close to the rest of the family, with a large garden Fatimah would have loved. He enrolled Jamie in the same private boys' school the cousins attended, like their fathers before them. It was across the park from the private girls' school the rest of the cousins attended. And Blackman admitted only to himself that he was secretly happy Jamie would finally be abandoning that damned purple and gold for a much more handsome red. And since American football was no longer an option, Jamie finally considered following in Blackman's hockey footsteps.

Although European football didn't seem entirely off the table.

And at his size, Jamie would make a formidable midfielder.

Jamie had taken the decision to move to London in stride. He seemed to understand his parents needed to be closer to the family, and he wanted to be closer to the family, too. He missed them even though he was loathe to admit it. Fitz, of course, flat out refused even to consider going back to London, but as June drew closer, he seemed to rethink his position.

"Perhaps, it's time for me to go home, too," he admitted one night over dinner. Blackman hadn't wanted to push Fitz into a move he didn't want to make, but he also couldn't imagine going from seeing Fitz several times a week to only seeing him a few times a year. The sticking point seemed to be Gabe, who hadn't been excited about relocating, but it also seemed he wasn't wholly resistant to it either. It wasn't like he couldn't continue to work in law enforcement on the other side of the Atlantic.

Maggie's final day at the university was the same day she submitted her final draft of her latest collection of poetry to her London publisher. It was scheduled to be published in the fall, and she was already working on another collection. Having finally overcome her writer's block, she was writing some of the best poetry she'd written in years.

While Maggie finished up with the university, Fitz handled the sale of the Philadelphia house, and the day Jamie finished his last exam, they drove from his school to the airport and caught a late afternoon flight to Heathrow. Blackman met them after they cleared customs with a wide grin on his face and a bouquet of flowers in his hand. He'd been in London for the better part of three weeks, making the final preparations for his family's arrival. It was the longest they'd been apart since the night he watched Maggie walk away from his apartment a lifetime ago.

The last time Maggie had seen the London townhouse, it had been plain and empty, nothing more than a series of rooms waiting to be made into a home. This time, when Maggie and Jamie walked through the front door, they were greeted by walls that were painted in all the soft colors Maggie loved and rooms filled with the soft, overstuffed furniture that best fit Jamie and Blackman's long bodies. Modern art pieces, nature photography, and framed family pictures hung on the walls. Blackman had turned the front room with the floor to ceiling bookshelves into a spacious office for Maggie. Her writing desk sat below a large bay window overlooking their quiet, tree lined street.

As Maggie stood in awe of the beautiful work Blackman had done, Jamie eagerly ran upstairs to investigate his new bedroom. A lovely, airy, renovated attic space that reminded Blackman of Lennie's office, which, of course, was now Nick's office.

"Welcome home, sweetheart," Blackman said, wrapping his arms around Maggie as she stood in the doorway to her new office. Her hands pressed against her chest in shock.

"I can't believe you were able to do all this," Maggie said quietly. It was incredible, considering Blackman had also been preparing for the Solicitor's Qualifying Exam, which he planned on taking in the next couple of weeks.

"Anything for you, my love," Blackman whispered before he kissed the top of Maggie's head.

***

In the fall, Maggie decided to take time away from teaching to work on writing full-time, intending to finish the book she had abandoned after the shooting. Blackman passed the SQE, completed his immigration process, and had British citizenship by the holidays. Having left nothing back in the United States, it wasn't hard for him to give up his citizenship; everything he needed or wanted was in England. Blackman took the job Nick had offered him almost two years before, and he found working for the family enjoyable and infinitely less stressful than the DA's office. Jamie continued to excel in school and successfully balanced classes, football, and a new interest in theater that Maggie suspected had something to do with a romantic interest.

She wasn't wrong.

With Jamie's brilliant smile, six foot eight frame, and stunning hazel eyes, he cut quite the figure on stage.

"At least he's less likely to do permanent physical damage to his body trying to impress a girl this way," Blackman whispered while he and Maggie watched Jamie's first play, a reimagining of *The Crucible* where Jamie played a gloriously tortured John Proctor. Maggie rested her hand softly on Blackman's bad leg. She leaned her head against his shoulder and took in this new version of her son.

Jamie graduated top of his class and decided to pursue architecture. He considered attending Cardiff University because his girlfriend Karla was planning on attending in the fall, and then he considered Queen's University, Belfast because his theater friends were going there. However, after much consideration, he decided to stay closer to the family and follow Joseph's boys and Oliver's twin daughters to University College London. For some reason, he didn't want to tell his parents about his unwillingness to travel too far from home, but he willingly shared it with Fitz over pints at their favorite local.

Yet, a few years later, Jamie took full advantage of an opportunity to study in Venice. He'd been studying Italian in addition to Arabic while at university and had been talking about going to Italy for years. Blackman wondered if he was as interested in Italian architecture as much as he was interested in Italian girls.

While Jamie grew up and pursued his own life, Maggie and Blackman continued living theirs. Maggie returned to academia, taking a teaching position at the University of the Arts in London, where she taught part-time in their MFA program while writing her own poetry and editing a variety of poetry journals. Their lives were considerably less hectic than when they lived in Philadelphia, and Blackman and Maggie were able to spend more time together. Although they rarely spoke about the events that led them to change their lives so dramatically, privately, they were grateful for the decisions they had made in the aftermath of the broken dishes.

Right before Jamie left for university, Blackman and Maggie bought a cottage by the sea, where they spent more and more time. They would never say it to Jamie, but they both looked forward to the weekends by the sea with their future grandchildren.

"But not too soon," Maggie always said to Blackman as they watched Nick's oldest son hold the first born grandchild. "I don't think I'm quite ready for that, yet."

And Jamie was too busy playing the field, so to speak, to worry about settling down. While in Venice, it seemed he had met someone, another architecture student, and something had gone right, and then something had gone wrong, but whatever it was, Jamie wasn't talking about it. Maggie tried to get him to open up about what had happened, but when he resisted, she didn't push. She knew he would talk to her and Blackman when he was ready. He did talk to the cousins about it, though, so Maggie felt better knowing he at least had a support system. Navigating a complex relationship was hard enough, but it was worse when one had to do it alone. So, if Jamie wasn't ready to share with his parents, at least he could share with his cousins.

"I want to concentrate on school," Jamie said one night as he and Maggie sat in the garden drinking wine. It was a beautiful late summer evening, and Jamie had lingered longer after dinner than usual. It seemed to Maggie that he was caught between wanting to discuss what was bothering him and not wanting to discuss it. Maggie understood acutely what that was like. To be caught between a rock and that particular hard place.

"Of course, love, I understand," Maggie said soothingly. She sipped her wine while Jamie watched the soft colors of the sky deepen as the sun crept beneath the horizon.

"You and Dad met when you were both in school?" Jamie asked after a while. He seemed to be mulling something over while drinking his wine.

"Yes, we did," Maggie answered, knowing full well that the answer was a little more complicated than that.

"How did you make it work?" Jamie asked. His voice was low and thoughtful.

Maggie leaned back in her chair and watched the sky thoughtfully. Sunset was her favorite time of day. She set her wine glass down on the ground and looked at Jamie.

"Well, when we met again, for the third time, your father was out of law school and working for the DA's office," she said with a laugh. "I was still in school, but he didn't see that as a problem." She paused and reached for her wine. "I was always reluctant to get into a relationship with your father, so I used school as an excuse to put him off. To put us off, I suppose. But that last time we met, he pointed out that I was going to be an academic, and I'd always be in school. I knew he was right, *and* I knew I was using school as an excuse because I was afraid, but I took the chance anyway."

"Chances are scary," Jamie said. His eyes drifted back to the sky. Maggie watched him as he sipped his wine. He seemed so far away at that moment, and she wondered where he was and with whom.

"Love is always scary, darling," Maggie said gently. "But in the end, it tends to be worth it."

Later that night, while Maggie and Blackman lay together, hot, sweaty, and satiated, she recounted the story.

"I thought that about you once upon a time," Maggie said, her cheek pressed against his chest. She ran her hands absently over his still stomach.

"Well," Blackman said, pulling Maggie close to him as he kissed her hair, "if it's meant to be, they'll figure it out."

"Persistence does run in the family," Maggie said on a sigh. Then she whispered to Blackman, "Maybe *we* should be persistent in the bath."

Blackman chuckled and slipped out of the bed.

***

After graduation, Jamie was recruited by architectural firms as far away as Poland and Czech Republic, but again he chose to stay in London. Remembering what his own father had done for him, Blackman and Maggie insisted they buy Jamie's first flat.

"You don't have to do this," Jamie said the day they signed the papers for a spacious flat in a converted townhouse in a respectable neighborhood a respectable distance from his parents' townhouse.

"Nonsense, Habibi. Your grandfather did this for me, and someday you will do this for your child," Blackman said as he pulled his son into a tight hug. For all his father's faults, the old man had made Blackman a wealthy man by the time he was thirty, and thanks to Fatimah's teachings about financial responsibility, Blackman had remained a wealthy man.

"So, Habibi, you must remember that Jedda," both men paused and recited the words that were appropriate to honor Fatimah. "Would want you to understand how blessed you are, and that you must always seek to help the less fortunate."

Jamie looked down for a moment, ever the serious young man. "Do you think Jedda would be proud of me, Dad?"

"Oh, Habibi. You were the joy of her joy," Blackman said, smiling.

He could still recall the look on Fatimah's face when she first held Jamie—that look of joy and pain, love and loss, and utter adoration.

"I want to make her proud."

"You make all of us proud, son. Never forget that," Blackman said. "And now that you're a homeowner, I imagine I'll now spend all my weekends watching YouTube videos about fixing things in my house and yours."

***

A year later, Jamie called Maggie at school and asked if he could bring a friend around for Friday night dinner. Maggie, who had been about to walk into a faculty meeting, stopped so abruptly in the middle of the hallway that another teacher walked into her. The other teacher muttered something angry in Welsh as she walked around an unapologetic Maggie.

"Of course, darling. That would be wonderful," Maggie said, trying not to sound too excited but failing.

"Okay," Jamie said awkwardly. Maggie couldn't tell if he seemed unsure about bringing someone over for dinner or if he was unsure wanted to say anything more.

"Darling, does your friend have any food allergies?" Maggie asked in an attempt to draw more information out of him.

"No," Jamie said. Maggie waited to see if he might elaborate or say anything remotely helpful about his friend, but he did not. Maggie continued.

"Vegetarian?"

"No."

"Vegan?"

"Christ, no."

"Aversion to alcohol?

"No."

"Okay, your dad's making lamb. Does your friend like lamb?"

James hesitated a moment.

"Yes," he finally answered.

"Wonderful. We'll see you at seven?"

"Seven's fine."

"Okay, darling, I'm heading into a meeting, so I'll see you then. I'll text you later."

"Okay, I love you, mom."

"Love you, too, darling. See you Friday."

Maggie ended the call and immediately texted Blackman.

Maggie Rhymer Smith

OMG! J's bringing a friend *to dinner.*

Blackman Smith

Ok.

Maggie Rhymer Smith

A friend friend. (winky face emoji)

Blackman Smith

Does this friend friend *like lamb?* (Eyebrow raised emoji)

Maggie Rhymer Smith

J thinks so.

Blackman sent a thumbs up emoji, and Maggie pocketed her phone and walked into her meeting.

Maggie sat on the counter and watched Blackman chop herbs. She loved to watch her husband cook. Blackman was dressed casually in loose fitting khaki pants and a blue jumper. His hair, which he wore longer these days, was now salt and pepper gray, but Maggie liked that it was more salt than pepper. It suited him. He had late afternoon stubble because he'd had time to shower but not to shave. Like Blackman, Maggie, too, was dressed casually: blue jeans and a loose-fitting blouse that probably had more buttons undone than was strictly prudent for dinner with Jamie and his friend, but she'd fix that before they arrived.

"Why are you sitting on my counter?" Blackman asked.

"Because this is where the wine is," Maggie said, pouring herself another glass.

"You can move the wine," Blackman observed.

"But then I can't stare at your ass while you're being all domestic."

He looked at her with a raised eyebrow, his brown eyes bright in the late afternoon sunlight. "Get off my counter."

"Make me," Maggie said with a wicked grin.

Blackman put down his knife and stepped between her legs. He looked down her shirt as he slid a finger over the swell of her breast.

"What are the odds Jamie will be running late?" Blackman whispered as he pushed Maggie's hair out of the way and kissed her neck.

"How late?" Maggie asked, wrapping her legs around Blackman's waist.

"Like Saturday night late?" Blackman mumbled into her neck as his hands slid around her waist. She wrapped her arms around him.

"I could text him and tell him we're running late. Maybe give us half an hour?"

"I'm planning on needing more than half an hour," Blackman said against her mouth.

"Mmmm – tell me all about it."

The chirp of the front door alarm stopped them.

"Shit," Maggie said, reaching for the buttons of her blouse as Blackman took a step back and adjusted himself. Honestly, it was like they had the only child who was perpetually early for meals.

"Fix your blouse," Blackman hissed as he turned back to the counter and reached for the wine.

"Mom? Dad? We're here," Jamie called.

"In the kitchen, darling," Maggie called as she buttoned up her blouse so the lace bra was no longer showing. She and Blackman turned and faced the entryway to the kitchen just as Jamie, looking as handsome as always in dark jeans and a black shirt walked in. His hair was freshly cut, his red beard neatly trimmed. Next to him stood a shorter young man with a long, lean runner's body. A marathoner, probably. His dark hair was cut short, and his eyes were a rich brown. Unlike the rest of them, the young man was dressed formally in a dark gray suit with a white shirt and a blue tie. He was holding flowers and a bottle of wine.

Blackman instantly thought of the night he met Lennie Harrington and the brothers.

"Mom, Dad, this is Adam Sayed," Jamie said slowly. "Adam, this is my mother, Dr. Maggie Rhymer, and my father, Blackman Smith."

Maggie blinked. She looked from Adam to Jamie, from the flowers to the wine, from the shy look on Adam's face to the nervous look on Jamie's. It only took Maggie a moment to recover. When she was a teenager, she'd almost beaten a man to death for calling Fitz a homophobic slur, for making her beloved brother feel small because he loved someone who was different from whom he was expected to love. It never once occurred to Maggie that Jamie might be gay, but evidently, he was, and now there he stood with this handsome well dressed man with the shy smile.

For a moment, she wondered why he had never said anything, but then she considered what she'd been saying to him since he was old enough to date: we'll love whomever you bring home as long as they're a good person. So clearly, Jamie expected Maggie and Blackman to be the parents they'd always purported to be.

"Adam," Maggie said, crossing the kitchen with her arms open, "it's such a pleasure to meet you."

Adam seemed a bit surprised by the open arms, possibly because he was holding flowers and wine, possibly because he was meeting his partner's parents for the first time. Perhaps because he wasn't used to such overt acts of affection and acceptance, but regardless, he smiled a bit awkwardly and offered his gifts to Maggie.

Maggie ignored the offerings and wrapped her arms around the young man. When she was done embracing him, she stepped back and embraced her son. Blackman was close behind, and he mercifully took the offerings out of Adam's hands, then extended his hand.

"It's nice to meet you, Dr. Rhymer, Mr. Smith," Adam said, looking from Maggie to Blackman, who smiled at the young man and, again, thought back to the day in the library with Lennie Harrington. How'd he'd been so nervous standing there wearing his best suit and tie.

"Please, darling, it's Maggie and Blackman," Maggie said with a smile. Although Adam Sayed was maybe six foot one, he still looked much shorter than Jamie or Blackman.

"Adam Sayed?" Blackman asked thoughtfully. "Didn't I read about you in the *Financial Times* the other day? You're handling the Afghan Interpreter's case, correct?"

"Yes, I am." Adam stood up straighter and blushed slightly.

"That accent? Lebanon? Beirut?" Blackman asked.

"Beirut," Adam confirmed.

"Of course, my mother was from Beirut. What can I get you? Beer? Wine?"

"Wine, thank you," Adam said, still slightly shy.

"Jamie, get us some wine," Blackman said turning back to the counter. "That's quite the case, Adam." Blackman picked up the knife and went back to cutting vegetables. "Immigration law is quite the challenge right now, but more important than ever. You're doing amazing work, and I don't think the Times gave you enough credit."

Maggie walked over to the kitchen table, taking Adam by the elbow and depositing him in the seat next to her as Blackman steered the young man into a long conversation about the law.

Later that evening, while Adam and Blackman continued to talk law, Jamie came over and sat next to his mother. He put his arm around her. Maggie leaned her head against her son's shoulder and breathed in the scent of his new cologne, and what she suspected was new shampoo.

"So, Adam's who you met in Venice?" she asked.

Jamie nodded.

"So, you two have been trying to sort things out for a while then?"

Jamie nodded again. "The timing was bad, and the whole thing took me – took me by surprise," he admitted. Maggie could only imagine how difficult it must have been for Jamie to find himself in unchartered waters so far away from home, from family.

"You could have talked to me or Dad about it," Maggie said gently.

Jamie looked at his hands, and for a moment he seemed so fragile despite his towering height and his strong body.

"I know. I just --- I just wasn't ready," he said slowly. Then he looked at Adam and Blackman, who had moved from wine to bourbon.

"He's a great guy. Smart. Kind," Jamie said softly as he looked at Adam with unabashed loved. It made Maggie's heart flutter in her chest, knowing that her son had met a man who made him feel the way Blackman made her feel. The way everyone should feel when they've found the right person. Maggie smiled.

"I imagine he is. I hope you'll both be spending more time with us, and you'll have to start bringing him to the Sunday dinners."

"We're moving in together," Jamie blurted. "Into the flat."

"Well, then," Maggie said easily, "he's definitely going to have to start going to Sunday dinners." She paused and looked at Adam and Blackman, who were deep in conversation.

"Have you met his parents?" Maggie asked.

"No, they disowned him when he was at school," Jamie said as sadness and anger flashed on his face. "After he told them he was gay. He's been on his own for a long time."

"Well, it's a good thing you're bringing him into *this* family. The poor man will never be alone again," Maggie said with a laugh, and she couldn't help but think of Blackman, and the way her family had embraced him and Fatimah all those years ago.

Jamie chuckled quietly.

"I love him," Jamie said as if he was unaccustomed to saying such things, and Maggie wondered if Jamie had been the resistant one and if maybe Adam had been the one more comfortable with being in love.

"I'm glad, darling. I'm glad you're happy," Maggie said. She reached for Jamie's hand and threaded her fingers through his. They sat in silence for a few minutes.

"When you first met Dad, did you know you were in love with him?" Jamie asked as if he'd been trying to find a way to ask it all night or maybe since he'd met Adam.

"The first time I met him, I suppose. We met in a dive bar of all places. I was underaged, and he was all moody good looks." She huffed a laugh. "But," she paused thoughtfully. "I resisted it, resisted loving him. But when I finally gave in to the inevitable, there was no one else I ever wanted to be with. It was always your father who made me happy."

"Even when you left us?" Jamie asked. There was no edge or judgment to his voice. Only sincere curiosity.

"*Especially* when I left you," Maggie answered gently. "Love," she continued, "isn't easy. It's messy and hard and frightening, but I'm sure I'm not telling you anything that you don't know."

"I hope... I hope I'm good enough... for him," Jamie said slowly, and Maggie's heart ached for him because she knew that fear all too intimately. Maggie looked at her son for a long time before she lifted their intertwined hands and kissed his big knuckles softly.

"I think every person who has ever been in love has had that same concern, but all we can do is be the best people we know how to be, and that will have to be enough."

"And when it's not?"

"Then be good in bed," Maggie said with a grin.

"Jesus, mom," Jamie said, shaking his head and pulling his face back. Maggie laughed because she knew he knew she was right.

That night as Maggie and Blackman lay together in bed, Blackman pulled Maggie close and whispered, "I love you, sweetheart."

"I love you, too, my love," Maggie said on a sigh.

She closed her eyes as she and Blackman entered a new stage of their lives together. Their family had grown that night in an unexpected but wonderful way, but their lives had always been filled with the unexpected.

And they were grateful for it.

They were grateful for all of it.

Acknowledgements

First, I would like to thank Morgan Waddle, my incredible editor. Honestly, you're amazing. Your kindness, your faith, your insight. Without you, this book would still be hidden away on my computer. I'm incredibly lucky to have you in my corner.

Thank you, Debbi, for reading this book **three** times!!! And for telling me I had to do something with it. Thank you for making me believe someone else would want to read it.

Thank you, Janine, for being you. For making me laugh, helping me put my life/ career into perspective, and texting me fifty times a day. Whenever someone drinks a bourbon, it's for you!

Thank you, Chris, for being *the one* and for having the patience of Job. I love you, baby.

Thank you, Matthew, for making me laugh and caring about this book just because I wrote it. You're the best.

Thank you, Carol and Beth for always being so excited for me!

Thank you, Elizabeth, for encouraging me, making me laugh, and telling me I'm not the problem!

Thank you, Eliot, for getting so incredibly excited the minute I told you I wrote a book!

Finally, thank you, Mom. I know you always believed I could do this, and Dad, I'm just sorry you didn't get to see me publish my first book. I know you would have been proud.

About the Author

Hayden Evans grew up in Philadelphia where she started her career teaching the boys who wear purple and gold. She married a soldier and moved to the DC metro area where she continues to teach high school and roots exclusively for Philadelphia sports teams. She has an amazing husband, a wonderfully sarcastic son, and too many cats. She is happiest when she's in the mountains with her friends and family or when she's curled up with a good book and a glass of red wine.

Find me at:
www.haydenevanswriting.com
Instagram: @hayd_enevans
Facebook: @hayden.evans.writer

Made in the USA
Middletown, DE
01 February 2025